Born in Somerset and raised in the W~ ², ʔ
Nikki Copleston worked in loca
years. Her grandfather and great-₁
may explain why she's always enj₁
television and reading crime novels.

She is an active member of Fr _₁ve, which
supports and promotes writers in tl ₁ea. When she isn't
writing, she enjoys exploring the West Country with her camera. She
is already working on the next DI Jeff Lincoln novel. She and her
husband now live in Wells, Somerset, with their cat.

*To Mum and Dad, and John*

# CHAPTER 1

## SUNDAY 7TH SEPTEMBER

'No, no, wait!'

Maisie was halfway out of her knickers when she saw a bundle of blue tarpaulin in the tall grass, only inches from where she'd spread the picnic rug. She wasn't going to let Joe make love to her with a heap of tarpaulin in the way. It was bad enough that they were on the edge of the golf course, with old men dragging their stupid trolleys past them every five minutes. She didn't need any more distractions.

Joe wasn't bothered. 'It's just a sheet of plastic someone's chucked away, Maize. If it's putting you off, look the other way.'

'I can't. It's probably full of creepy-crawlies.' She tugged her knickers up and scrambled on her hands and knees across the picnic blanket and into the unmown grass. She took hold of the edge of the tarpaulin and tried to fold it away out of sight – but instead, it fell open and she saw what was inside. A girl, and she was dead.

Worst of all, Maisie knew who she was.

It was nearly three when DI Jeff Lincoln swung his car into Southlawns Golf Club and parked beside the Nineteenth Hole clubhouse. Blue lights swirled on patrol cars and ambulances, but an eerie quiet muffled the place. He nerved himself before stepping out of the car, a headache thudding behind his eyes. Too much sun, not enough to drink, nothing to eat since a breakfast of cold mushroom pizza and a packet of salted peanuts swilled down with a mug of black coffee.

No wonder he felt like crap. He'd planned to shower, have something to eat after a couple of hours' gardening, but the call from Mike Woods, his detective sergeant, had put paid to that.

'Emma Sherman, boss. Couple of kids messing about on the edge of the golf course found a body in the undergrowth about an hour ago. Pretty sure it's her.'

Fifteen-year-old Emma had been missing since Thursday night. Lincoln had wanted to believe she'd run away from home after a row, but he'd had a hard time convincing himself. He was thinking murder even before they'd hit the weekend.

'Okay, Woody, give me twenty minutes.'

'No hurry, boss. She's not going anywhere.'

So here he was now, that leaden feeling in his stomach as he walked towards the scene of a suspicious death, acting calmer than he felt, pushing through the growing crowd of responders: officers in high-vis jackets, some in uniform shirtsleeves, some casually dressed like himself, summoned on their day off, grabbing the first clothes that came to hand. Lincoln was wearing his gardening jeans, the ones with the dodgy zip, and – beneath a dark green fleece – an orange souvenir T-shirt his big sister Ruth had sent him from Chicago several years ago, when he was a few pounds lighter and they were still speaking to each other.

There was an atmosphere of anticipation while everyone waited for the right people to arrive, like the buzz before a big match when you don't know who'll be on the team. He felt sick.

Woody came to meet him. 'Sorry to drag you in on your day off, boss. Sunning yourself in the garden?'

'Hacking my way through it, more like. Who was it said gardening was relaxing?'

'Me, probably. Or someone from HR. One of their welfare pep talks.'

They walked in step towards the clubhouse.

'Supposed to help you unwind, gardening,' Woody said.

Lincoln snorted. 'Unwind or unravel?' He'd had such high hopes when he moved into the Old Vicarage six months ago: a vegetable plot, some soft fruit bushes, a lawn bordered by a nursery catalogue of flowering plants. Instead, the overgrown wilderness had proved a bit more of a challenge. If gardening was the answer, he must have got the wrong question. Or the wrong bloody garden. 'So, the Sherman girl – what do we know?'

He sprang out of the path of a shiny black Land Rover Discovery that rushed past, heading for the exit gates. A girl of about Emma's age stared out of the back window, her eyes locking onto his as she sped past.

'That was one of the kids that found the body. And there's the lad she was with, over in the doorway. Joe Day. They've given prelim statements but you might want a word before the SIO arrives.'

Lincoln sighed. Until a few months ago, he'd have been senior investigating officer himself, no question, but an ongoing reorganisation of the force had brought some policy changes. As a mere detective inspector, he was no longer deemed senior enough to run a homicide case. Within the next year or so, Barbury's Barley Lane police station would close down, and he and his team would move to the larger Park

8

Street nick four or five miles away in Presford.

Until then, he had to defer to a higher-ranking officer from Park Street. For Emma's sake, he put his resentment aside and headed towards the youth who stood hunched in the back porch of the clubhouse. Before he could reach Joe Day, though, Lincoln was ambushed by a middle-aged man with pepper-and-salt hair and a ruddy complexion, who was clearly furious.

'This is all very well,' the man snapped, 'but you've closed the whole bloody course off! Where are we supposed to play?'

'That's *your* problem.' Lincoln shook his arm free of the man's grasp. 'A girl's been found dead on your golf course. As far as I'm concerned, you should be over in the clubhouse, well away from the crime scene.'

'But I'm president of Southlawns!'

'You could be President of the United States, you still need to be outside our cordon.' Lincoln pointed towards the perimeter tape. 'Mr...?'

'McTimothy. Nigel McTimothy.'

'Mr McTimothy. I won't ask you again. Please move back beyond the cordon.'

'I'm taking your name.' He fumbled in his blazer pockets for a pen and paper.

'You're getting back behind the tape first.' Lincoln pointed like a referee sending a player off the field, and McTimothy marched away in a huff.

'That's you off his Christmas card list,' Woody chuckled.

'I'll survive.' Lincoln turned his attention to the ashen-faced lad in the doorway. 'Mr Day? I'm Detective Inspector Lincoln and this is Detective Sergeant Woods. We need to ask you—'

'Wouldn't have a fag, would you, mate?' Joe was shivering, shock kicking in.

'No, but they'll have some behind the bar in the clubhouse. You found the body?'

'My girlfriend did. Maisie. Thought it was just a bit of rubbish.' He slouched lower into his hooded sweatshirt.

Lincoln spotted Shauna Hartlake. He knew she liked a smoke, and called her across. The young detective constable handed over a cigarette and a throwaway lighter, and waited while Joe lit up before continuing on her way to the clubhouse.

Lincoln breathed in the sharp tang of nicotine as the lad took

9

a long drag. He hadn't smoked in twenty years but still savoured the smell of other people's cigarettes. 'Your girlfriend's gone home without you?'

'Don't live together. Her dad don't want her to leave home.'

'That's dads for you,' said Woody. 'How old are you?'

'Twenty-one.'

'And Maisie's how old?'

'Sixteen. Nearly.'

'Big gap, your age. You can understand her dad.'

'You often come here with Maisie?' Lincoln asked.

'Few times. Kind of private but you can park in the layby, take a short cut through that gap in the hedge. Southlawns people don't like it but fuck 'em, they don't own the fucking countryside!'

'Actually, they own this particular part of it.'

Joe shrugged. 'That's all right then. Maisie's dad's on the committee.' He tried a smile.

'The gap in the hedge,' Lincoln went on. 'You think many people know you can get in through there?'

'Everybody knows.' Joe swept his arm out wide, then started to sob, head down, a trembling hand shielding his eyes. They gave him a minute or two, no point rushing him. 'I'm okay,' he sniffed. 'It's the shock, y' know?'

'I know.' Lincoln patted his shoulder. 'You need to get home.'

The girl's body lay under a hedge, hidden by tall grass and weeds, close to the perimeter of the course.

The pathologist, Ken Burges, was still documenting the scene, so Lincoln had to make do with watching from several feet away. Even at that distance, the pungent stench of decay made his nostrils flare. She lay on a blue tarpaulin sheet, ragged along one edge. Her head was pillowed by the sodden mass of her hair, and her hands were crossed over her breastbone. Apart from a bra, she was naked.

Ken looked up, raised an eyebrow at Lincoln's T-shirt. 'Chicago? The city or the musical?'

'The city. It's on my bucket list. What've we got?'

'Young girl, partly wrapped in this sheet, woven plastic – the sort of thing decorators use, builders, gardeners. Nothing to identify it without a closer look.'

'Time of death?'

'I'd guess no later than the middle of Friday.'

So, not long after she went missing. Lincoln stepped as close as he dared, knowing this was the only chance he'd get before the senior investigating officer arrived and took over.

Her tarpaulin shroud had preserved Emma well. Another night in the open, and marauding foxes would have ripped away her covering, exposed her to the elements and anything that feeds on dead flesh.

He could see dried blood on her face, and smears of dirt or dried blood on her knees, and on the insides of her thighs. On her throat and neck, bruises the colour of thunderclouds betrayed the most likely cause of death: strangulation by hand, the shapes of fingers, a thumb, still faintly visible, although the mottling effect of decay could be confusing him.

However she'd died, Emma's killing had been brutal.

He squatted down, looked around him. Why dump her here? A patch of weeds under a hedge, the only outlook a narrow view of grass and bushes stretching towards the phoney landscape of the golf course, the dove-grey pinnacles of Barbury Abbey in the distance.

He stood up, his knees creaking. Getting too old for this game.

He left Ken to get on with his work and went in search of Woody, who was already out in the lane beyond the hedge.

'Killer could've parked down there in the layby,' he said, pointing. 'Not far to carry her. No houses close by, not a lot of traffic after the evening rush.'

'And not a camera in sight.' Lincoln sighed. The council had put up experimental CCTV cameras in a few laybys to discourage fly-tipping, only to find them vandalised within days. The experiment had been abandoned.

They pushed their way back through the hedge.

For a minute or two, they watched the drama unfolding around them, as barriers went up to create a wider exclusion zone, keeping all but essential personnel at bay.

'Pam offered to go to the house when we heard a body had been found,' Woody said, 'so her mum wouldn't have to hear it from the press first.'

DC Pam Smyth was someone Lincoln could rely on to be discreet and sympathetic. She'd know what to say and what to withhold.

'Bryn Marshall coming in as SIO?' Lincoln looked around, searching the faces of officers gathering near the clubhouse. He'd known Bryn for years, a DCI at Park Street nick.

'I heard they're putting DCI Bax in charge. She'll be here any minute.' As if on cue, a tall, broad-shouldered woman came striding past the clubhouse and through the shifting shadows under the trees, making her way towards the spot where Emma's body lay. Her hair a frizzy mop of tight, dark curls, Bax made few concessions to femininity or fashion.

Arabella Bax had transferred down to the county force from the Metropolitan Police less than twelve months ago. She and Lincoln went way back, but so far she'd shown no sign of recognising him.

'So what have we got?' She stopped short of the body and stood with her hands stuffed into the pockets of her sleeveless Puffa jacket. He filled her in on the background: fifteen-year-old girl goes missing, turns up dead three days later. No suspects, no witnesses.

All the time he was talking, he noticed she didn't look at him once. Instead, her dark blue eyes were absorbing the scene before her, scanning the horizon, watching the growing crowd of press and onlookers gathering beyond the main gates fifty yards away.

'The mother should have been informed by now, ma'am,' he said, checking his watch. 'And Ken Burges has done the initial examination and—'

'Get a tent over her.' She turned away and headed towards the clubhouse. 'Stop these gawpers getting even a glimpse. What a fucking shambles! This is a crime scene, not a bloody circus. I'll see you back at the station.'

The Nineteenth Hole clubhouse was buzzing with complaints and speculation. Little more than a tarted-up sports pavilion with a bar at one end, its jolly colour scheme of red and gold failed to make the room feel welcoming now. About twenty golfers, mostly male and over fifty, hovered around, impatient to get out on the green, even though they'd been told there'd be no play today.

Nigel McTimothy lunged at Lincoln again. 'You can't close the whole club down! You're only interested in a bit of the course, so why can't we carry on as usual? We won't be in your way.'

'You'll impede our investigation simply by being here. Until we understand better how this crime's been committed—'

'Are you suggesting one of us had something to do with it?' The mauve veins on the club president's nose seemed to swell along with his temper.

'We need to control who comes in, who goes out. As soon as

you've given your statements, you'll need to leave the site so we can get on with our work.'

Another man joined them, pleasant-faced, early forties, more relaxed in denim jeans and a jacket of soft brown leather. 'Let them get on with their job, Nige. The sooner we can get out of their hair, the sooner we'll get the greens back. I'm Steven Short,' he added, turning to Lincoln. 'That part of the course isn't used much these days, not since we had our redesign last year.'

'Were you aware that courting couples were sneaking in through the hedge there?'

'The greenkeeper found a few used condoms over there the other day but we thought it was an isolated incident. So the body – what was it, a lovers' tiff?'

'We don't believe the victim was killed here.' Lincoln didn't want to give too much away, although the relief that flooded the faces of both golfers was obvious: at least no one had actually been killed on club property. 'You've got surveillance cameras?'

'Round the clubhouse,' McTimothy said. 'Some valuable stuff here in the shop and the bar.'

'I'll need those security tapes.'

'Ah, you'll have to speak to our facilities chappie tomorrow. He doesn't work on Sundays.'

Lincoln's fists clenched with impatience. 'This can't wait till tomorrow, Mr McTimothy. We need to get this sorted now.'

While McTimothy hesitated, Steven Short whipped his mobile out of his jacket pocket and dialled the man's number. He turned away when he got through. 'Hi Clive, it's Steven. No problem, not exactly, but could you get over here ASAP?'

He pocketed his phone and smiled at McTimothy as if to say, Wasn't so hard, was it?

'Thanks.'

Short nodded towards the far end of the room, where a triangle of tables stood partly draped in the green-and-yellow livery of some venture called Revyve – *Bringing YOUR Buildings Back To Life.* 'I'll have a word with the girls,' he said. 'There's a big corporate do in here tomorrow, but you'll want them to clear out, I expect?'

'Please,' Lincoln said, watching as Short went over to one of the young women setting the tables up. She broke off trying to string a garland of paper bunting across the window frame and listened while Short, his hand squeezing her shoulder, broke the news that she and her colleague would have to abandon their plans.

She cast a reproachful look in Lincoln's direction, then started to help the other girl clear the tables of Revyve-branded mugs, ballpoint pens and goody bags.

Lincoln went back outside, surveying the scene once more. Why had Emma been dumped here, instead of in a field gateway, in one of Barbury's many rivers and streams, or somewhere up in Greywood Forest?

Opportunity, he guessed: a bit of light from streetlamps, but not too much. A road surface that wouldn't retain tyre impressions the way a muddy track would.

And maybe whoever dumped her here was making a bit of mischief, putting the wind up those staid, stuck-up members of Barbury society who belonged to Southlawns Golf Club – though what kind of bastard would murder a teenager simply to put two fingers up to the likes of Nigel McTimothy?

Beneath the trees, a tent was being set up to shield Emma's body, and extension cables were being unrolled so Ken could have enough light to complete his unenviable task. Satisfied there was nothing more he could do, Lincoln headed back to Barley Lane police station, his heart heavy with disappointment that the lost girl had been found too late.

DC Pam Smyth arrived at the Shermans' house in Folly Hill Crescent to find a black Land Rover Discovery parked on the drive. The front door of the house opened and a man strode out onto the wide step. Mid-fifties, in expensively casual shirt and slacks, he was tall and muscular, his thick, wavy hair streaked with silver.

'Donal Finnegan.' He held his hand out to her but quickly let it drop. 'I know you can't say for sure that it's Emma but I'm here anyway. Old family friend.'

Pam was relieved to see that Emma's mother, Crystal, had someone so capable to help her through the next few hours. Finnegan had his own property business and was often in the local press supporting good causes with generous donations and a ready smile for the cameras. He was also one of the town's biggest employers. A good man to have on your side in times of trouble.

Crystal peeped round the door. When she recognised Pam, she put her fist to her mouth and started to cry.

# CHAPTER 2

'You'd better come out, love. I'm not coming in after you.' DC Graham Dilke waited outside the locked bathroom door of Flat 3, Michaelmas House. 'Jackie? Come on out. Please.'

Down in the street, Jackie's boyfriend Liam Coe was speeding off by ambulance to A&E at Presford General, five miles away. He was lucky to be going by ambulance and not by mortuary van, since the broken bottle Jackie thrust into his neck only missed his jugular by millimetres.

'You won't get her to come out. She stays in there all day some days.'

Dilke turned to see a skinny girl in the doorway of the other bedroom, the one that wasn't decorated with Liam's blood.

'What's your name, love?' This must be Jackie's daughter, who was about fourteen and spent more time in care than with her mother.

'Lorren.' She pulled her sleeves down, but not before he glimpsed the marks of self-harm. Her auburn hair looked as if she'd trimmed it herself without a mirror. Huge eyes, wide mouth. Freckles.

'Okay, Lorren. Someone's going to call your social worker. You won't be able to stay here.'

'Wouldn't want to. Not now.' She chewed her thumbnail. 'Liam gonna be okay?'

'Too soon to tell. Let's hope so for everyone's sake.'

'He was after me. He's always after me.' She shrank back into her bedroom. 'He deserved it.'

'Maybe, but—'

The bolt slid back, the bathroom door opened a crack and Jackie came tumbling out into Dilke's arms. She threw up all over him – mostly booze, although there were bits in it. It was all he could do to stop himself throwing up in sympathy.

A thickset woman in a football shirt who announced herself as 'Micky from Family Services' arrived a minute or two later to ferry Lorren back to her foster carers, while Dilke and two uniforms, with Jackie moaning in the back seat, sped off to Barley Lane nick with the windows wound right down.

15

# CHAPTER 3

The deserted CID room at Barley Lane smelled hot and stuffy as afternoon became evening; no windows open, and nothing much anyone could do till morning.

DCI Bella Bax stationed herself on the dais in front of the whiteboard. Just her and Lincoln.

'Okay, Jeff, I'm in charge of this investigation, but I'll value your input – as long as you don't go off-piste and frighten the horses.'

'Off-piste?'

'Your last big case. You ignored your super's advice and went after the assistant chief constable.'

'Who was guilty as hell. Ma'am.'

'Lucky for you.'

Not so lucky for ACC Pobjoy. The *late* ACC Pobjoy. Lincoln said nothing.

Her gaze travelled down to his orange Chicago belly, then back up to his face. 'And let's drop the "ma'am".' She strolled across the dais, strolled back. 'So what do we know about this Sherman kid?'

'Her mother thinks she was pure as the proverbial, but she could've been seeing someone. We'll know more when we get her phone records. Mrs Sherman strikes me as a bit overprotective.' A bit neurotic was how she came across, but he kept that to himself. Any mother would be a bag of nerves if her only daughter was missing. He only wished he'd taken her more seriously instead of trying to reassure her the girl was okay.

'Thursday night, the kid was supposed to be at a dance class, yes?' Bella looked round at him, checking her facts.

'Never turned up. We're thinking she skipped the class to meet a boyfriend behind her mother's back.'

'Any names?'

'Not so far.'

'How come this super-protective mother let her kid walk to and from town after dark? Don't parents chauffeur their kids everywhere these days?'

'Crystal Sherman doesn't drive, and the father's been dead for years. Anyway, Emma was fifteen. It's a route she took several times a week, ten minutes, fifteen tops, well lit all the way. She had her phone with her. Her mother thought she'd be safe.'

Bella snorted. 'More fool her. Get her to do the ID first thing, then Ken can get on with the autopsy. He thinks cause of death was manual strangulation. No sign of a ligature.' She glanced at her watch, a classy-looking affair with lots of dials and buttons. 'Not much more we can do tonight.'

'At least we've found her—' he began to say, but she cut across him as she strode out of the room.

'Team briefing at eleven, Jeff, okay?'

By the time Lincoln got home to the Old Vicarage, the sun had long since set. Before it was too dark to see, he retrieved the sickle he'd left in the grass when Woody phoned him earlier. So much for knocking the garden into shape!

He'd found the house by chance last year, a dilapidated wreck that begged him to buy it and bring it back to life. He'd been trying to restore it ever since, but there was still a long way to go, and it looked as if he was on his own again.

If only Trish was here to tell him everything would sort itself out. They'd met last year, a big murder case he was working on, the victim someone she knew, the prime suspect someone she knew even better. A messy start to a relationship.

Still, he'd fallen for her when he thought he'd never fall for anyone again, and because of her, he bought the Old Vicarage last Christmas. Soon after New Year, he moved out of the shabby bedsit where grief and inertia had held him hostage for two years, and moved in with Trish and her daughter until the Old Vicarage was fit to live in. He'd always been a bit of a loner, and the breakup of his marriage had cut him off from the few friends and family members to whom he'd ever been close. Trish Whittington had given him a second chance at love, even though he didn't deserve it.

Except he'd thrown it away again. As soon as he moved into the Old Vicarage and stopped seeing her every day, they drifted apart. His fault? Hers? Unspoken mutual consent? He knew from Woody – whose wife, Suki, was her older sister – that Trish had taken on some new responsibilities at the library where she worked. All her spare time was devoted to taking her daughter Kate to this music class or that sleepover. Yet it sounded more like an excuse than a reason, and which of them was going to make the first move to put things right?

As he went indoors, he glanced across at Fountains, the modern house backing onto his. It'd been empty all the time he'd lived here, but it looked as if someone was moving in. Lights beamed out onto its patio and he could see stacks of boxes inside, a ladder, decorating stuff. Bugger.

He shoved open his own back door, switched the kitchen light on. The Old Vicarage was chilly, but he couldn't face the usual pantomime with the boiler so he turned the immersion heater on. At least he could have a shower later.

Still so much to get fixed! No hot water supply to the trough-like kitchen sink. A big old gas cooker that had somehow blagged its way through the safety tests. Clumsily painted wooden shelves where kitchen cabinets should be.

He'd had the washing machine and dryer installed as soon as he moved in, so at least his rest days weren't spent at the laundrette anymore, falling asleep over tattered back numbers of *Closer* or *Practical Carp*.

On the windowsill lay a list of local workmen, but he'd so often picked it up and put it down again, undecided, that it was dog-eared and creased. He'd been so sure he'd get the Old Vicarage fixed up by Christmas.

'Yes, Jeff, but *which* Christmas?' he could hear Trish asking, exasperated. Now Emma Sherman's disappearance had become a murder case, and everything else would have to be put on hold.

Too late to cook a meal. He found two slices of bread, a bit past their sell-by date, and dropped them into the toaster. A pleasing glow suffused the element.

He'd wished so hard that Emma would turn up alive, holed up with a boyfriend in Bournemouth or Swindon or Bath. Thank God Pam had offered to go and break the news to the girl's mother!

The first time he'd had to call on parents waiting hopefully for a child who hadn't come home, he'd been in uniform, a couple of months into his first posting with the Met in North London. The boy, a youth of sixteen, had come off his motorbike on the North Circular and gone under the wheels of a lorry. Lincoln had to go and tell his parents. He could hear it now, the shriek the mother let out – Deirdre, her name was. The boy was Anthony. The suddenness of the father's bellow, and above Lincoln's head, scuffling sounds and sobbing, Anthony's little brother and sister eavesdropping on the stairs.

He hadn't known what to do, what else to say. Deirdre was so distraught, he was scared she'd have a seizure or something. And the anger in the father's eyes, as if it was all Lincoln's fault...

He'd never forget that first time and how feebly he'd handled it.

In the morning, Pam Smyth would bring Emma's mother in for the formal ID. Crystal would no longer be able to cherish a last hope that they'd got it wrong, a case of mistaken identity, a police screw-up.

His toaster fizzled and died. Smoke spiralled from the top of it. The bread was burnt black, inedible.

He leaned against the door frame and surrendered to fatigue. Oh, to be back in the garden seven hours ago, with nothing more to trouble him than an ongoing battle against stinging nettles and a blackberry thicket!

He gave up on food, instead pouring himself a long measure of American dry ginger in a tall glass. He left enough room to top it up with Jameson's and took it up to bed with him.

It might help him sleep.

# CHAPTER 4

## MONDAY 8TH SEPTEMBER

Folly Hill Crescent was a sedate cul-de-sac of half-timbered houses built between the wars. The windows were leaded, the front doors solid wood, the doorsteps the colour of ox blood. Stained-glass panels in the tops of the garage doors depicted 1930s Bentleys driving towards each other along lanes of lollipop trees and candyfloss clouds.

So English, so unspoilt, Pam thought – until yesterday evening, when she'd called at Number 4 to tell Emma's mother a body had been found, and that it was almost certainly her daughter's.

Little more than twelve hours later, with DC Shauna Hartlake, she was back to take Crystal to the mortuary at Presford General Hospital. Donal Finnegan's Land Rover had been supplanted by a shabby maroon Peugeot estate that looked as if it had a lot of miles on the clock.

Crystal let them in. The house smelt of polish and one of those expensive room fragrances that come in cut-glass bottles. 'Will this take long?' She was so tense she was trembling.

Naturally pretty, with high cheekbones and a smooth complexion, she wore only a trace of make-up, her hair short and simple, with little attempt to style it. The navy skirt and jacket she wore over a cream blouse were more like a uniform than a fashion choice.

'I shouldn't think so,' Pam said. 'Soon as you're ready.'

A woman's face peeped round the kitchen door: middle-aged and plump with a brassy perm. 'You want me to come with you?'

'No, I'd rather you didn't.' Crystal turned back to Pam and Shauna. 'My sister.' She headed for the door. 'Can we go now, please?'

An hour later, she'd identified her daughter's body and they were back outside the mortuary. Cruel bright sunlight ricocheted off the bonnets of parked cars.

'How long can your sister stay with you?' Pam asked. For all her apparent self-control, Crystal would need someone to be with her when the shock wore off and grief took over.

'As long as I need her to.' She walked stiffly down the concrete path, leaning against the handrail for support. 'What about Emma's clothes? Will you have to keep them?'

'She wasn't wearing any,' Shauna said.

Pam shot her a filthy look. 'Emma had her underwear on.' A white lie. 'And she was wrapped in a sort of canvas sheet.' As if that might have preserved the girl's dignity. 'If there's anything more you can tell us...'

'All I know is, my little girl's dead. I told you she'd come to harm and nobody took me seriously. You were wrong, and nothing you can do will make it right. I need to go home.'

'Right, so what have we got?'

Bella Bax stepped away from the whiteboard and paced round the edges of the room, a panther sizing up her prey.

Lincoln's mouth went dry. He hated working under someone younger and less experienced.

'Jeff?' She was giving him the floor, so he rose and began to set out what they knew.

'Emma Sherman, fifteen, living with her widowed mother in Folly Hill Crescent.' He pointed to a photo of the girl in her Barbury Fields school uniform. 'Never been in any trouble. Told her mother she was going to Bods Gym last Thursday evening for a dance class. Set off at quarter to seven to walk into town, should've been home by half past nine. She didn't turn up for her class. Mrs Sherman phoned us at eleven when Emma didn't come home.'

He tapped the sequence of monochrome CCTV images. A young girl, slightly built, pale hair pulled up into a ponytail. Striped jersey, dark pants, dark top with the hood down. White trainers, a gym bag slung over one shoulder. She was straight-backed, graceful, a few minutes away from the gym on the last night of her life.

He moved across to a row of photos of the dump site, jabbed them with the end of his marker pen.

'Yesterday afternoon, Emma's body was found in undergrowth on the perimeter of Southlawns Golf Course. She'd been killed elsewhere, probably soon after she went missing. We'll know more after the autopsy, but it looks as if she was beaten and strangled, probably sexually assaulted. When she was found, she was wearing only her bra. The rest of her clothes and her bag are still missing.' All eyes were on the photos of the dead girl.

'And the gym is where?' Bella asked.

'Inside the Half Moon Centre, the shopping mall off the High Street. Apart from a couple of shops – Specsavers, Smith's – Bods is the first place you come to. We know she got that far because traffic cams outside the High Street entrance picked her up at 19.02, heading into the centre.' He jabbed the first set of photos again.

Bella moved towards the front of the room. 'So we don't even know for sure she went into the gym?'

Woody spoke up. 'That time of night, the rest of the Half Moon's locked, so there was nowhere else she could go once she was inside.'

'Are we thinking she was abducted inside the gym?'

'No one was caught on camera coming out with her.'

Pam put her hand up. 'She could've used the gym as a cover for meeting someone. She was a member so she had her own locker, could've kept a change of clothes there. The bra she was wearing – from the photos, it looks a bit fancy to wear for a dance class, but you might wear it to impress your date.'

Bella nodded. 'Okay, so she turns up in trackies and trainers, changes into the glam outfit she's got hanging in her locker... Any CCTV footage inside Bods?'

'They turned their cameras off in July after someone complained about privacy issues,' Woody said. 'The only camera inside is in the foyer. Except it was switched off that night.'

'We know why?'

He shrugged. 'Reckon someone forgot to turn it on.'

'You didn't *ask*?' Bella sounded as displeased as a schoolteacher sold short by a pupil who hasn't done his homework properly. 'Was it merely a *coincidence* that the camera was off the very night one of its customers disappeared?'

'I don't know about that,' Woody said, 'but when Breezy – er, DC Breeze – checked her locker on Friday, there was hardly anything in it.'

Bella looked round the room. 'And where is DC Breeze this morning?'

'On holiday. Flew out Saturday.'

She pursed her lips, unimpressed.

'Emma could've changed in the locker room and stuffed her gym clothes into her bag,' Pam suggested.

Dilke put his hand up. 'We could go over the CCTV footage from the High Street cameras again. We've been looking for a girl in a tracksuit but if she'd changed into something else...'

Bella nodded. 'Okay, but let's not get sidetracked. This all depends on you being right about the fancy bra, Pam.' She made a face. 'Not a phrase I was expecting to come out with this morning.'

'The mother's refusing to accept that Emma might have skipped class to meet someone,' Lincoln went on. 'It hasn't helped that the media found out her father left quite a bit of money in his will, dubbed her "the teenage heiress" and started speculating about her being kidnapped. But there's been no demand, no ransom note, so we've discounted that one.'

'Bloody tabloids. No other way out of the shopping centre? A back door?'

Lincoln waved towards the whiteboard, where an enlarged ground plan of the Half Moon Centre covered most of the lower half. 'Not for the public, no. And no one saw her once she was inside.'

'She can't have just vanished!'

'She might as well have done,' Woody said.

Bella gave him a cold stare. 'Okay, so let's assume she left the gym willingly, possibly in a different outfit to the one she arrived in. What kind of social life's she got?'

Pam took her notebook out. 'She certainly wasn't the most popular girl in the school. I managed to track a few classmates down, but they weren't exactly positive. To quote the girls I spoke to: Bit of a snob, didn't really mix. Kind of up herself. Kept on about being a big star one day. Ballet classes, singing lessons. Got her picture in the local paper a few times for various things. Always on about "when I'm famous", as if she was going to be discovered any minute. She got the star part in the Board Treaders' end-of-term play, and it sounds as if she let it go to her head.'

'Board Treaders? What's that?'

'A youth drama group run by Barbury Theatre.'

'What about the family? Mother got a boyfriend, man friend? That's often where the tensions start.'

As if they didn't know.

'We've been to the house several times now,' Pam said, 'and there's been no sign of anyone else living there. A family friend was there yesterday, Donal Finnegan.'

'Finnegan, as in Maisie?' Lincoln made the connection, annoyed that he hadn't made it when he read the girl's statement yesterday. 'So it was Finnegan's daughter who found the body?'

Pam nodded.

'You searched the house?' Bella went on, without hesitation

23

discounting Donal Finnegan as a likely suspect – probably quite rightly, but the assumption, that if you've got money and give lots of it away, you can do no wrong, niggled at Lincoln.

'We did a routine search when Emma went missing,' Woody said. 'Everything looked normal.'

'It usually does. Talk to the neighbours?'

'We asked around. Nothing out of the ordinary except one of them heard Emma and her mum having a row that morning.'

'So you thought the kid had flounced off in a sulk, to teach her mother a lesson?'

'That was one theory, yes.'

Bella put her hands on her hips. 'Get back to the house, go through it again – properly. And get a thorough house-to-house organised.' She turned back to Lincoln. 'And we need a hurry-up on those phone records. Did they say when they'd have them?'

'Just waiting to hear from the service provider so—'

'Be proactive, Jeff. It's the only way to keep on top of things. Don't wait for some dozy clerical assistant to work through her to-do list.'

The sound of her mobile startled Maisie out of sleep. It was Joe.

'How you feeling, babe?'

'I'm fine,' she said, even though she wasn't. She pulled the duvet up round her shoulders, slid down the bed, unable to get warm. 'You at work?'

'Fag break. Your dad say anything?'

'Only that I should stop seeing you.'

'No change there, then.' Joe's laugh was bitter.

'He worries, that's all.'

'Doesn't wanna lose his little girl. Listen, Maize, I gotta go. Call you later, okay? Love ya.'

'Love ya.' She shoved her phone under the pillow and turned her television on, watching without taking anything in, her thoughts churning.

# CHAPTER 5

'I can't bear all this.' Crystal Sherman watched as a team of officers, led by Pam and Dilke, began a thorough search of her house. 'It's bad enough having reporters camped outside the house all hours without you people going through everything.'

Pam tried to reassure her. 'The family liaison officer will take some of the pressure off you, act as a buffer.'

'I don't want a family liaison officer! I don't want anybody!'

'We can't insist, but it's normal practice to—'

'What the hell does that mean?' Crystal's voice became shrill. 'This isn't normal practice for me!'

'Listen, we've got a job to do. For Emma's sake, let us get on with it.' Pam guessed Crystal's angry obstructiveness was her way of coping until grief took over. People reacted in such different ways to the loss of a loved one, but she couldn't begin to imagine what it must be like to lose your only daughter, and in such a violent way.

Desperate to smooth things over as best she could, she scanned the array of photos in the Shermans' hallway: Emma from babyhood to teens. Even at twelve or thirteen, Crystal's daughter planned on going places – you could see it in her eyes, a kind of glamour, a knowing look beyond her years. 'So she was at the Abbey School?' A photo of her at nine or ten, in the distinctive blue uniform.

Crystal relaxed a little. 'For a while, yes, and then Barbury Fields.'

The last photo in the sequence showed a group of teenagers, all in black, only their faces lit. 'Friends from school?'

'No, that's her drama group, the Board Treaders. They did *Our Town* at the Barbury Theatre in July. Emma had the star part.'

Except for a chubby lad in glasses, the group was all girls, mid-teens like Emma. They all smiled for the cameraman – except for Emma, who gazed up, lips in a pout, cheeks sucked in, eyebrows lifted, head turned a fraction so her cheekbones stood out against the dark background. Her soft fair hair was piled up on top of her head, a few strands falling loose.

Pam recognised that look: a girl who fancies herself, who's prac-tised her poses in front of a mirror and knows how to photograph well, as if she's trying to seduce the lens – or the person behind it. No wonder the other girls didn't like her much.

'Could we make a copy of this photo?' she asked.

'I can't let you take it away!'

Dilke pulled his phone out. 'It's okay, Mrs Sherman. I can take a picture of it.' He took a couple of shots. 'You haven't got their names?'

'The only one I remember her talking about was the boy, Simon Lovelock, on the end there.'

As Crystal restored the treasured photo to its shelf, her sister bustled out of the kitchen, drying her hands on a tea towel. 'I'll put the kettle on, shall I?'

'Tania, they're not here to socialise.' Crystal hurried into the kitchen, pulled her sister after her and slammed the door, leaving Pam and Dilke in the empty hallway.

Pam sighed. 'I could've done with a cuppa, too. Ah well, let's you and me start upstairs.'

Emma's bedroom was candyfloss pink and white, the furniture and picture frames solid but dated. It didn't feel like a teenager's room, or even that of a child – far too neat. Had her mother tidied up?

Pam rolled her latex gloves on, something she'd hated doing ever since Breezy had remarked with a leer that it was like putting on a pair of condoms. 'So what are we looking for?'

'You were a girl once. Anything that doesn't look right.'

'Was I really a girl once?' She caught sight of herself in the triptych of gilded mirrors on the dressing table. They gave back reflections of each other until she disappeared towards infinity. 'Not sure I remember.'

'Might have better luck talking to the Board Treaders – a small group like that, she must've been close to one or two of them.'

'Don't count on it, Gray. Her expression in that photo, it was like she was doing them a favour being in the same room with them!'

Flipping open a velvet-covered jewellery box, Pam found a plastic ballerina who began to pirouette slowly to the tinny strains of "The Dance of the Sugar Plum Fairy". Maybe it had been her mother's. These days it would probably count as vintage.

The jewellery box had a few hair clips in it, bracelets, beads. She snapped the lid down, cutting Sugar Plum off mid-twirl. 'I wonder why she left the Abbey School? Must have been a bit of a comedown, going to the local comprehensive.'

'Failed the entrance exam for the senior school, maybe?' He leafed through some magazines on the windowsill.

Pam shook her head. 'That doesn't matter if you've got enough money.' She hunted through a neat drawer of underwear: smart rather than sexy, and nowhere near as glamorous as the lace-trimmed bra Emma was wearing when she was found.

She sighed, frustrated. 'Maybe we're wrong about a mystery boyfriend. She could've skipped her class for some other reason.'

'But the bra – you said it was a bit too fancy for a dance class.'

'Yeah, like I'd know! Horses and bikes, that's my idea of fun.' She flicked through the pages of some paperbacks and found a birthday card tucked inside one of them: *10 today! Now you're into double figures, poppet! Lots of love and kisses from Uncle Todd.* She stuffed the card back into Roald Dahl's *Matilda*.

Propped on the bookcase was a photo of Emma arm-in-arm with another girl the same age. Pam looked on the back: *Em and M. Darricott School of Dancing.* According to the date, they must have been about six or seven. M was plump, with almond-shaped eyes and thick, straight hair, in contrast to skinny, round-eyed Emma and her froth of soft curls.

Dilke looked round the room. 'No computer. Not even a desk.'

'Must be downstairs. Perhaps her mum doesn't like her going on the internet unsupervised.'

'What? She's fifteen! What fifteen-year-old has to get her mum's permission to go on the internet?'

'You'd be surprised.' She flung the wardrobe open on a mass of dresses, jeans, tops, jackets – their diaphanous polythene shrouds shifting in the draught. When did the kid ever get a chance to wear all of these?

Dilke shoved another drawer shut. 'There's nothing here. No diary, no address book – though I s'pose most of that'd be in her phone.'

Hands on hips, Pam surveyed the room one last time. 'There's something so *virginal* about this room, like it belongs to a little girl, not a teenager. No posters of boy bands, no family photos – nothing.' She went over to the window and looked down the long, tree-lined back garden. An emerald lawn stretched away towards a hedge of copper beech, beyond which the roof of a summer house was just visible. What a wonderful world for a little girl! Plenty of hidey-holes and places to make a den.

Dilke flipped open the jewellery box, starting Sugar Plum off again. 'Cool.' He watched the plastic ballerina's jerky gyrations for a moment, then picked the box up, tipping Sugar Plum backwards. 'Hey, look.'

Another cache of costume jewellery lay in a compartment underneath the mechanism. And with it, a photo, the size you need for a passport: Emma and an unknown boy, cheek-to-cheek, pulling silly faces for the camera.

They found Crystal in the kitchen, staring into a cup of tea while the search team worked around her. Her shoulders were hunched, braced against the intrusion, as if the opening of cupboards and the inspection of their contents were assaults on her own body.

Tania stood close behind her. They looked more like old friends than sisters: similar ages, very different life stories.

'Can you tell me who this is?' Pam thrust the photo out.

'Who on earth...?' Crystal laid the evidence bag on the table, smoothed it flat so she could see the photo better. Her face softened as she gazed at a picture she'd clearly never seen before.

'You don't recognise him?'

'No. This must be quite recent. She bought that top in May. And she had those silly highlights put in her hair at the end of July, after the play finished.'

'Let's have a look.' Her sister leaned round her to see, but Crystal tilted away from her as if she had body odour.

'Do you recognise him?' Dilke asked Tania.

She shook her head sadly. 'Didn't know any of her friends. No use asking me.'

'Where's her computer? Emma did have a computer, didn't she?'

'She always worked in the sitting room.'

'You stay there, Crystal.' Tania spoke to her sister as if she was an invalid. 'I'll show them.'

She led them into the sitting room, which was furnished in neutral tones of coffee and beige, as if someone had turned the contrast down on an old television, muting everything. The colours, the sounds, the very textures of the room were bland and smooth.

DC Charlie Trufitt had already begun in here. Pam didn't like him much. He was cut from the same dilatory cloth as Dennis Breeze, though marginally more reliable.

'Computer,' Trufitt announced, pointing a gloved finger at an old-fashioned desk in the corner. 'I was about to come and tell you.'

The mahogany desk wouldn't have looked out of place in a Victorian office – except that in the exact middle of it sat a Sony laptop, a bundle of pens and pencils next to it.

Pam sat herself down at the desk, imagining Emma sitting here to do her homework. No privacy. A workspace as impersonal as a study carrel in a college library – except for one thing: sitting on the corner of the desk was a little plush teddy bear wearing a jumper with an E on it. His jumper was matted, the embroidered 'E' beginning to unravel.

On the velvety sole of his right foot, Emma had printed Eddy Gumpa in biro. She may have behaved like a teenager, but she wasn't really much more than a child. This little teddy must have given her some kind of solace.

Pam realised then what was missing from Emma's bedroom: no dolls, no old toys, none of the usual parade of stuffed animals that young girls accumulate, the much-loved mementoes of childhood.

She stared into the teddy's sombre glass eyes and her heart softened.

'Did you find anything?' Crystal's sister was there behind her.

'We'll need to take the laptop away. And any disks or memory sticks.'

'The what?' Tania frowned doubtfully.

'Things like these.' Dilke held up a couple of USB drives he'd found in the drawer.

She smiled in benevolent mystification. 'Well, you seem to know what you're looking for. I'll let you get on with it.'

When they got back to the kitchen, Crystal was standing at the sink, staring down the garden.

'Have you taken anything out of Emma's bedroom since she went missing?' Pam asked. 'Her room looks unusually tidy.'

'That's how I brought her up. Everything in its place and a place for everything. That way, you never lose anything.' She pressed herself against the sink, her shoulders rigid, but Pam saw again the tremor she'd first noticed at the mortuary.

'The boy in the photo – you're quite sure you don't know who he is?'

'She wouldn't get involved with anyone without telling me. She knew I worried.'

'Did she spend much time on the internet?' Dilke asked. 'There's no chance she met someone that way?'

'She wasn't that sort of girl.'

Pam glanced across at him, exchanged a helpless look. Few of the underage girls seduced on the internet were "that sort of girl".

'Anyway,' Crystal went on, 'she only used her laptop for her homework, as far as I know. Why do you need to take it away? You won't find anything on it.'

'We need to look, just to be sure.'

'Listen, my daughter wouldn't have met someone without telling me. You're wasting time raking things over like this.'

'Mrs Sherman, Crystal...we'll deal with this as delicately as we can. But if we're going to find who did this to Emma, and stop them doing it to somebody else, we've got to follow every lead. Look,' Pam added, more gently, 'the search shouldn't take much longer. DC Dilke and I are going back to the station now. Is there anything else you can tell us?'

'I've told you all I can.'

'Which evening did Emma go to Board Treaders?' Dilke asked.

'Mondays. She should have been going there tonight.' She bit her lip, her chin puckering.

'A neighbour heard you and Emma having a bit of an argument the day she disappeared. Can you tell us about that?'

'Argument? No, I was just fed up with her checking her phone the whole time when I was trying to talk to her, that's all.'

'He thought it sounded quite heated.'

'He had no business eavesdropping. Emma went out into the garden and had to shout to make me hear. My neighbour was mistaken,' she concluded icily.

Tania showed them out, peering warily towards the hedge where a couple of press photographers had sprung into action at the sound of the door being opened. 'I'm sorry she was so short with you about a family liaison officer. She's a very private person.'

'See if you can talk her round. We'll need to speak to you again, Tania. I didn't catch your surname.'

'Tania Tremlow. Mrs.'

'Were you and Emma close?'

'You know what teenagers are like. And it hasn't been easy for Crystal, bringing a kiddie up on her own.'

'Anything else you can tell us about your niece?'

'Haven't seen much of her these last few months. Bit of a trek from where we live so I don't visit often. I've got a teenage daughter of my own, you see. Stephanie. She's nearly seventeen. Special needs.

Not easy to get away.' Tania glanced at her watch. 'In fact, I need to phone home, see how things are.'

'Who's looking after her while you're here?'

'Her dad, Todd.' She took a deep breath before blurting out in a harsh whisper, 'Do you know, my sister didn't even tell us Emma was missing? Not a word. We were so cut up. If you don't want your own family round you when things go wrong, well...we had to read about it in the paper. It's been hard for her, I know, but wouldn't you think...?'

'Maybe she didn't want to worry you. It must be hard, having to be there for Stephanie all the time.'

'Yes, and there's no end to it.' She sighed heavily. 'Todd'd be here himself but I thought, well, she's *my* sister. They're very close, Crystal and Todd, but at a time like this, you want family round you, don't you?'

'We'll need to speak to your husband,' Dilke said, 'in case he can add anything.'

'I doubt if he can. Will he have to come all the way over here to the police station?'

'We can come to your house,' Pam said. 'What's the address?'

They lived in a village thirty minutes away – not what Pam would have called "a bit of a trek", but then she didn't have a disabled daughter to look after, and a sister who'd rather be left on her own.

'Look, I really must phone home.' And with that, Tania shut her sister's front door.

On the pavement, against the hedge, unseen hands had propped bouquets of chrysanthemums, lilies, gypsophila. Teddy bears, stuffed toys from card shops, a Barbury Fields school scarf, a growing heap of messages. A tea light in a tiny lantern had either blown out or never been lit.

Emma would have hoped for a different sort of fame.

When Lincoln knocked on the door of Bella's office – or rather, of the stationery store she'd commandeered – he found it empty, a mug of aromatic Earl Grey tea cooling on a Barbury Ales beer mat.

The missing persons file on Emma Suzanne Sherman was next to the mug, open at the report DC Dennis Breeze completed after visiting Bods Gym.

It was scrappy. Even when he looked at it upside down, Lincoln could see that Breeze had been in such a rush to get away for his holiday, he'd submitted a half-arsed report. Someone – presumably Bella – had ringed in red ink his brief description of the contents of Emma's locker: Towel, hairbrush, bag.

Too late, he heard Bella behind him.

'No need to sneak a peek, Jeff. You should know this file inside out. Not that there's much to memorise. Any idea what sort of bag Breeze saw in her locker? Did he have the temerity to open it or stick it in an evidence bag and bring it back here? Like fuck he did. 'Scuse my French but that man's a bloody liability. Where's he gone, anyway?'

'Spain somewhere.'

Breezy's idea of a good holiday was anathema to Lincoln, but right now, twenty-one days in the sun on a crowded Spanish beach seemed infinitely preferable to a dressing-down from Bella.

'No loss.' She squeezed past him and dropped into her chair. 'What about the staff at Bods? You ran the usual checks?'

'Of course, and we even managed to track down most of the customers who were there that evening. Nothing untoward.'

'So if she got as far as the locker room, do we think something happened there?'

'No sign of a scuffle or assault.'

'Huh, if it was Breeze who checked, how can you be sure? Get someone to go back and check again. I don't want the idiots at the gym tidying things up now they know the girl won't be needing her locker anymore.'

'I'll get DS Woods onto it straightaway.'

'And the phone records?'

'Should be with us by five.'

'Christ, why does everything have to take so long?' She shoved her hands through her hair. 'I'm off to Presford in a few minutes to sit in on the autopsy. We should know a bit more by the end of the day.'

Lincoln found Woody about to tuck into a sandwich. 'I need you to go over to Bods.'

Woody crammed the lid back on his lunch box. 'Reckoned I was being a bit optimistic.'

'Get the Sherman girl's locker searched and sealed, and follow up on Breezy's report. And check out the camera in the gym foyer, find out why it was turned off that night. Probably a coincidence but we need to be sure.'

Woody hurried away, chomping on his sandwich as he went.

When Lincoln turned round, Bella was close behind him, putting her jacket on, readying to leave.

'Wishing you were SIO yourself, Jeff?'

'Not senior enough to run a homicide, am I? Not now Barley Lane's being run down and they've moved the goalposts.'

'And you expected Bryn Marshall to be assigned instead of me?'

Bryn Marshall – a DCI a year or so older than himself. A bear of a man, hearty, good at his job. A man you could have a drink with. 'He seemed the most likely candidate, yes.'

'Problems at home? Might explain why you're not on top of things.' She cast a scornful look over the muddled contours of his cluttered desk. He knew it looked a mess but he knew where everything was. More or less.

'Who says I'm not on top of things?' And her question implied he'd got marriage problems, relationship problems, and, well, his marriage had ended years ago and he wasn't sure he and Trish were ever really in a relationship, not the way Bella meant.

'You were slow to act on this one, Jeff. The Sherman girl's disappearance was out of character. You lost vital hours.'

'Hindsight's always twenty-twenty,' he said. 'Emma and her mother had a row that morning, loud enough for the neighbours to hear. That made us think she'd stayed out to wind her mother up. I assumed—'

'Never assume.' She parked herself on the edge of his desk. 'Tell me about Breeze.'

'What about him?'

'Why's he still here? Based on what I've seen today, I'd say he's incompetent. You'll need to take steps when he's back from leave.'

'Take steps?'

'Reassessment. Retraining if necessary. Either that or he needs to think about an alternative career.' She drew herself up. 'He may not be the only one, Jeff. There really is life after police work, you know.' And patting him on the arm as if he were already a pensioner, Bella Bax turned on her heel. 'I'm off to Presford General.'

Fuming, he watched her swerving through the obstacle course of desks and chairs and filing cabinets as she returned to her office in the stationery cupboard. He felt like throwing something after her – a stapler, a paperweight, a telephone – but thought better of it.

# CHAPTER 6

She'd loved her the moment she set eyes on her. Her heart was Emma's from that very second, like a current passing between them. She'd wanted nothing else, no one else.

Fifteen years later, Crystal's heart had been taken from her. That's how it felt, as if someone had reached in and hauled the very soul from out of her body.

She gazed down the garden, seeing Emma playing there, and a slideshow of memories stuttered through her mind's eye: Emma in the paddling pool. Aged four, twirling on the lawn in her first tutu and little ballet shoes, fluffy fair hair pulled back in a ponytail.

By the time she was eleven, she was acting out stories she'd seen on television, singing her heart out on the lawn, with a vocal range that astonished her music teacher. A year later, suddenly a gawky teenager, she was leaping over flower beds, showing off the moves she'd learnt at jazz dance classes, entertaining an audience of one: her mother, watching from the kitchen window.

All gone.

Crystal turned away. She didn't want to remember more recent times, when Emma hadn't been as lovable. That didn't matter now; it was past and gone. The boy in the photo didn't matter either, not anymore.

The ice-blue china vase on the windowsill sparked a memory of little Emma charging in from the garden, her chubby hands full of flowers. 'Look what I picked for you, Mummy! I'll put them here where you can see them.' Stuffing them into the vase, leaves, pollen, petals tumbling everywhere.

'No, darling, you know I don't like flowers in the house.'

The crushed look on Emma's face...

Tania bustled in. 'They seem to know what they're doing, the police. They're being very thorough.'

'They're being very intrusive. They're trying to make out it was all Emma's fault.'

'Don't be silly. They're going now, anyway.'

'I need to lie down. Go home, Tania. Stephie needs you more than I do.'

'She'll be fine with Todd. She's such a daddy's girl.'

Good old Todd. The perfect husband and father. Perfect brother-in-law. Perfect uncle.

'I'll be fine, Tania, really. I'd rather be on my own right now.'

'Well, if you're sure...'

'Thank you for everything.'

Leaving her sister to clear up in the kitchen, Crystal slowly climbed the stairs. She lay down on the bed and shut her eyes, only to find the photo booth picture of Emma dancing behind her eyelids.

How could she do that to her?

She heard the slam of the front door as Tania left. Only when she heard the Tremlows' elderly Peugeot rattling away down Folly Hill did Crystal give way to tears and – eventually, unexpectedly – sleep.

# CHAPTER 7

Woody took DC Shauna Hartlake with him to check Bods Gym again. Breezy probably hadn't been as diligent as he should have been. He rarely was.

Monday afternoon and Bods was busy, full of older men keen to keep active in retirement, and 'yummy mummies' from the surrounding villages cramming in a couple of hours in the gym or the pool between school runs.

Woody pressed the buzzer on the front desk. He looked round, his eyes bombarded by slogans encouraging him to get fit, lose weight, slim those thighs, firm that butt. For a man in his early forties, a keen cricketer and five-a-side footballer, he knew he was in pretty good shape, but he reckoned Shauna could lose a few pounds. Especially round her middle.

'Cameras seems to be working now.' He nodded towards the pinpoints of red light blinking on the CCTV cameras over their heads. 'Wonder why they weren't switched on the night she disappeared?'

'A lot of cameras are just for show. Where is everyone?' Shauna jammed her thumb on the buzzer and kept it there until a dumpy woman of fifty-something emerged from the office behind the counter.

Black leggings and a purple polo shirt with *BODS* embroidered on it in golden italics couldn't disguise a figure unused to exercise. The badge on her chest said this was Carol.

'Remember her?' Woody held up the school photo of Emma. 'We came round on Friday after she went missing but we need to look at her locker again.'

'You found her, didn't you?'

Shauna leaned across the counter. 'We are investigating a *murder*. We need to revisit the place where the victim was last seen alive, and we need to look in her locker.'

Carol made a tight line of her mouth, sized up the heavily built tower that was DC Hartlake and clomped back towards her office.

'You'll want the key. Number twelve, wasn't it?' She opened the key safe, clanged it shut, then bellowed to someone else in the office:

'I'll need you to cover for me. On the desk. I've got to go down the locker room with these two.'

As she came round the counter, a young man came bounding out, stationing himself in her place. Tall and athletic in his purple polo shirt and tracksuit bottoms, he could have leapt straight out of a Bods Gym poster.

'Get me on the walkie-talkie if you need to,' she told him, clipping her own handset to the waistband of her leggings.

'I'll be fine.' He gave her a big grin. 'Safe pair of hands.' And he held his hands up to show her.

'My arse.' She led Woody and Shauna across the lobby and barged open a swing door labelled *TOILETS & CHANGE*.

'Bit of a live wire, that one!' said Woody.

'You can say that again. But then, live wires can give you a shock.' Carol chuckled at her joke. 'Give *himself* a shock, that one will. Too clever by half.'

She led them down a dim corridor to the locker rooms, a row of uplighters illuminating little more than the passageway's water-stained ceiling tiles.

'Is it usually this dark?' Woody asked.

'Supposed to be sensors that turn the light on when someone comes along, but they haven't been working for weeks. I keep reporting it.'

Shauna tutted. 'Don't your customers complain? It's like walking into the Black Hole of Calcutta.'

Carol stopped, turned round and gave them both an old-fashioned look. 'I'm not management. That's who you should be lecturing.' She set off again, her rubber mules making farting noises as they slapped against the soles of her feet.

At last she shoved open a door marked *LADIES' CHANGE*. Woody felt there was a joke in there somewhere but let it pass. Overhead lights buzzed on as they entered: at least these sensors worked even if the ones in the corridor didn't.

She opened locker number twelve for them, standing back so they could inspect its meagre contents.

Woody slid gloves on. Just as Breeze had recorded: hairbrush, towel, bag. Inside the zippered bag were a packet of tissues, a stick of lip gloss and two cellophane-wrapped tampons. 'Right,' he said, doing the bag up again and dropping it into the evidence sack.

'What about the shelf?' A couple of inches taller than Woody, Shauna reached up and ran her hands over the shallow ledge at the top of the locker. 'It's filthy,' she said, inspecting her gloved fingertips. She turned her hand towards Carol so she could see for herself. 'Look. Filthy.'

Carol made a face and shrugged.

'Hold on.' Shauna's groping fingers had found an envelope, addressed to Emma in untidy capitals, posted the last week of July. She passed it across to Woody while she checked there was nothing else.

He opened it to find a good luck card inside: a black cat on the front, surrounded by horseshoes and shamrock, although the words scrawled inside were anything but well-meaning: *Bad memory, Emma? Your gonna be shit on stage.*

It wasn't signed.

A newspaper cutting slid out of the envelope too. 'This is from *The Messenger*,' he said. 'That Vox Pop column, you know, when they stop people in the street and ask them what they think about something in the local news.'

*Vox Pop Princess*, it said above a photo of Emma, caught outside the Half Moon Centre. She'd been asked for her views on the upcoming launch of the Paragon, Barbury's new arts centre. The foundation stone was due to be laid at the end of September. *"Aspiring actress Emma, 15, who loves to dance, hopes the Paragon will provide a generous performance space."*

In a long T-shirt over skinny jeans, and wearing thick-soled baseball boots, she looked to Woody like all the other teenagers who clogged up the pavements and got in his way when Suki insisted on taking him shopping. Except that her eyes were missing, poked out of the photo by the same person who'd scrawled *BITCH BITCH BITCH* across her body.

Shauna took the envelope from him. 'We shouldn't have opened it,' she said, handing it back with a grin. 'Look, it's marked *"Private and confidential"*.'

'"Confidential"? We've got a brainy one here, then.'

Carol craned forward for a better look, but Woody slipped the card and cutting back into the envelope, and then into the evidence sack along with everything else.

'Any surveillance cameras in this part of the building?'

Carol shook her head. 'No, and if there were, chances are they wouldn't be working. We keep telling Gavin, but nothing gets done.'

'Gavin?'

'Gavin Lyons. He's management.'

That must have been who Breeze spoke to last week. 'We understand the foyer cameras were out of action the night Emma was last here.'

Carol thought for a moment. 'That was Thursday, wasn't it? Yes, something in the system went a bit peculiar and whoever was on the front desk didn't know how to reset it.'

'Who was on the front desk that night?'

'Ashley and Gina.' She rolled her eyes. 'Both as useless as each other when anything technical needs doing.'

'Emma and a mystery boy in a photo booth.' Triumphant, Pam slapped a passport photo down on Lincoln's desk. 'Not looking especially romantic, but it's a start. Graham found it hidden in Emma's bedroom.'

'Any idea who he is?'

'Her mother knew nothing about him,' Dilke said. 'You could tell by the look on her face.'

Lincoln studied the picture more closely. The lad looked a bit older than Emma, thick, fair hair, clear skin, handsome. 'We need to put a name to him ASAP. Strange no one mentioned him when she went missing.'

'Maybe they only went out together once or twice,' Pam said. 'Could all have been over in a couple of weeks.'

'And we brought her laptop back,' Dilke added, 'and some memory sticks. She had to use the laptop in the sitting room, like her mum wanted to keep an eye on her. That was seriously weird.'

'Her mother's probably read about all these internet perverts who pose as teenage boys to seduce girls. She was trying to protect her.'

Pam snorted. 'It's the real boyfriends she should've worried about, not the virtual ones.'

Lincoln felt in need of caffeine. 'What's on the memory sticks?' He levered himself out of his chair, stretched, rolled his shoulders, heard little creaks and crunches, stiff muscles grumbling as he ambled across to the kettle with his mug. He wondered which was doing his health more damage: gardening or sitting at a computer for most of the day. He needed to get himself fit again, somehow.

'Haven't had a chance to look.' Dilke waited while his computer booted up. 'I've left her laptop with Raj, see what he can get off the hard drive.'

Lincoln tipped coffee granules into his mug. He never bothered with milk, but a jam jar of sugar sat beside the kettle, its contents clumpy where he always dropped his damp spoon back into it. He knew he was the culprit: no one else took sugar these days.

Pam joined him at the kettle, her bone china cup and saucer prepped with a peppermint teabag on a string. 'There's something odd about that house, though,' she said. 'As if time stood still.'

Dilke agreed. 'More like a B&B than a home.'

Lincoln had only met Crystal once, last Friday, when he'd gone to the house with Pam. She'd seemed tense, almost hostile, but who could blame her? Her daughter was missing and she was alone, desperate for news.

'Emma will be back soon enough, Mrs Sherman,' he'd assured her. 'We're doing all we can to find her.'

Now he regretted last week's confidence.

'Still, it's nice that Mr Finnegan's there for her,' Pam went on, 'and her sister seems a good sort. Bit of friction between them, though – Tania and her husband didn't know Emma was missing until they saw it in the papers, so she's obviously not the first person Crystal turns to for help.'

'Yeah, but Tania was fussing round her all the time,' Dilke said. 'That'd drive anyone up the wall. Knows nothing about computers, either – when I asked her about disks and memory sticks, she looked at me like I was talking Vulcan.'

Lincoln grinned. 'Not everyone shares your enthusiasm for all things digital, Graham. So – Donal Finnegan. You think he and Crystal are an item?'

Pam shook her head. 'I don't see her as the type. Much too uptight. And he's married, anyway.'

'According to the tabloids, Derek Sherman was still married when Crystal moved in with him.'

'Yes, but that was years ago. Hardly likely now, is it? She's in her fifties.'

Lincoln didn't like to point out that the over-fifties were more likely to play away than younger couples. 'So this Tania and her husband – were they close to Emma?'

'Used to be, but they hadn't seen much of her the last few months. That's understandable, though – Emma out at her classes all the time and the Tremlows with their daughter to look after. She's got special needs. Can't have been easy.'

'Did you get any feel for how close Emma and Finnegan were? He'd have been a bit like a stepfather if he was round there a lot.'

Pam made a face, uncertain. 'I get the impression it's only since Emma disappeared that he's been back to the house. He said he was an old family friend, but maybe that was through Emma's dad.'

Back at his desk, coffee in hand, Lincoln scanned his notes again. Could his team have done more when Emma was first reported missing last Thursday night? Could *he* have done more? They'd checked at Bods first thing Friday morning, scanned the High Street CCTV footage, seen her going into the Half Moon Centre but not coming out again. They'd searched the shopping mall in vain.

Breeze had spoken to the Shermans' gardener, Gordon Judd, but he said he never went into the house and rarely saw Emma because she was at school when he was there. He didn't mention Finnegan and neither did Crystal, so maybe Pam was right, and the property developer hadn't been in the picture much until the girl went missing.

And over and over again, Crystal, intransigent, insisted there was no boyfriend, girlfriend, no place Emma might have run off to.

'The stuff on these flash drives is all school stuff,' Dilke groaned. 'GCSE revision, coursework.'

'Let's hope Raj finds something more exciting on the hard drive.'

The door barged open and Woody and Shauna came in looking pleased with themselves.

Lincoln put his mug down. 'Tell me you found all the answers at the gym.'

Woody slung an evidence sack onto the desk. 'In your dreams. Looks like we've brought back more questions. We found this in her locker.'

He passed a greetings card across: Good Luck, except the message inside wished Emma quite the opposite. Lincoln held the newspaper cutting up to the light. Her newsprint eyes had been gouged out completely. Not the work of a well-wisher. He peered at the envelope. '"Confidential"? That's a new one!'

He imagined Emma picking up the post from the doormat, intrigued at the sight of the big envelope. Opening it in her room or saving it until she was away from the house so her mother wouldn't ask awkward questions. How must she have felt when she read that ugly message and saw the way her photo'd been defaced?

'Someone from school or drama group?' he wondered. 'The handwriting looks young.'

'And they can't spell for shit,' Shauna added. 'Maybe someone who lost her boyfriend to Emma? Doesn't take a lot to upset someone when you're that age. Kids fall out all the time, even when they've been best mates.'

Woody shrugged. 'Like I said, reckon we've brought back more questions. Still, a bloke called Ashley Tyler's dropping in when he knocks off work. He was on the front desk last Thursday night. Let's hope he can tell us all we need to know, because the other one on the desk, Gina Gulliver, flew out to Rhodes on Saturday for two weeks.'

Shauna tutted. 'Lucky cow.'

Lincoln crossed to the whiteboard and tapped a blow-up of the photo booth picture. 'The house search came up trumps. So much for Emma not having a boyfriend! Now all we've got to do is find out who he is.'

He turned round to see Woody beaming at him.

'That lad works at the gym, boss. He was there this afternoon. Reckon that's how Emma left Bods without being seen – he let her out the staff exit.'

'Could be one mystery solved, then.' For the first time in days, Lincoln felt they were getting somewhere. 'And with any luck, the phone records should be here soon. What's the betting this lad's number comes up?'

While Woody was finding out the name of Mr Live Wire at Bods, Dilke was going through Emma's phone records.

'Not many calls,' he told Lincoln. 'Not many contacts, for a teenager. She was texting, mostly.'

'Can we find out what was in the texts?'

'Not if they were sent more than a week ago. The service provider only holds stuff on the server for seven days, and then the content's trashed. If her phone turns up – unless she deleted everything – we'll be able to see the messages, but not otherwise.'

'And the night she disappeared – just this one short call, forty-three seconds at seven o'clock when she was walking into town?'

Dilke nodded. 'Unregistered, a burner. I've called it but it's already been dumped.'

Lincoln could see a barrage of missed calls from the Shermans' landline number from 9.30 onwards as Emma's mother tried to reach her. She didn't give up until Sunday afternoon.

'We'll just have to hope her phone turns up. Meanwhile, if you can put names to these numbers...' Lincoln paused as his mobile rang. It was Woody telling him the boy in the photo was Thomas Crane, and an address in Amberstone.

'Thanks, Woody, come back and pick me up. We'll go together.'

# CHAPTER 8

Barbury's community centre, converted from an old school, stood in the run-down part of the town near the station. As rain clouds thickened, its Victorian Gothic exterior looked as inviting as a prison. When Dilke pushed open the heavy iron-bound door, he found the Board Treaders rehearsing in a draughty, poorly lit space, two old classrooms knocked together with a shabby platform at one end. Patches of damp darkened the walls and ceiling, and strips of duct tape showed where the floorboards had been repeatedly repaired.

Two teenagers faced each other across the bare stage, shouting at each other in terrible American accents. Both were heavily built, the girl pallid, the boy red-faced. Dilke remembered his name from the photo Mrs Sherman showed him: Simon something. Half a dozen other young players – all girls – stood around with scripts folded to the relevant page. Most of them found their phones more engaging than the performance.

Dilke and Trufitt were intercepted by a small, thin woman in her thirties with very short hair and lots of piercings. She was dressed all in black – polo neck, leggings, ballet pumps – her fingers weighed down by chunky silver rings which drew attention to nails she'd bitten to the quick.

'This is a private session,' she shrieked. 'You can't come in. What do you want?'

Dilke had his warrant card ready. 'I'm DC Dilke and this is DC Trufitt. Are you the lady in charge?'

'Rachel Darricott. I'm the drama tutor.'

'We need to talk to your group about Emma Sherman.'

Dilke heard the fake American slanging match onstage cease abruptly. Everyone closed in round him and Charlie, while the pasty-faced girl clambered down and lumbered over to join them, leaving only Simon onstage, his eyes wide with shock.

Up on the stage, Simon felt his insides tremble, like he was about to get the shits. He breathed slow, deep, like Em had taught him, to calm his nerves.

44

So it was definitely her. So now he knew. It was a relief in a way, but it left him empty. Every day, he'd wanted them to find her and bring her home, but every day it'd seemed less likely they would.

These cops didn't look like cops. One of them looked like he wasn't long out of sixth form. After Rachel stepped back and let him take over, he introduced himself as Graham Something.

The other one – Charlie, did he call him? – was older, rat-faced, going bald. He hovered behind Graham like he needed protection. Waste of space, really.

Rachel clapped her hands and made them all stand round with the cops in the middle. Una had already shifted her fat arse down off the stage, but Simon stayed where he was, not sure what to do, not wanting to move.

Until he heard them say it, he could pretend everything was still okay: Em was only missing, she wasn't dead. On the news, they kept saying, 'The identity of the body is unconfirmed', but he'd known. He'd known as soon as they said it.

He climbed down at last, his legs rubbery, afraid his knees would give out and he'd fall over.

'Simon? Is that right?' Now Graham Thing was talking to him, like he'd singled him out. How did he know his name? 'Did you know Emma well?'

'Not especially.' Simon didn't dare look at Fat Una because she'd make a face at him like "*Who are you kidding?*"

'She ever mention boyfriends, seeing someone?'

His face got hotter. His neck was on fire. Everyone was looking at him, seeing his neck burning and his face glowing like a red balloon.

'Don't think so. Her mum didn't like her going out at night except to her dance classes. And here, of course.'

'When was the last time any of you saw Emma?'

The detective flipped open a folder, and for a moment Simon was scared he was going to show them a picture of the body. But no, it was just a head-and-shoulders shot like they all got in Year 10. She looked so young!

'Simon?' They were picking on him because he was the only boy. His mouth was too dry to make words. He felt the flare of red in his cheeks ebbing away, running down his throat, his chest getting hot now instead, his crotch, the backs of his knees.

'I saw her here last week,' he managed to say. 'She was always here.'

Graham Thing asked for a list of people in the group, and Rachel shot over to fetch the register and then Graham started calling everyone's name out.

'Alexandra?'

Loopy Lexie stepped forward, like he wanted to ask her something, but he was only doing a roll call, looking round to see who was who.

'Thomas?' He must have seen that Simon was the only boy there, but he kept saying it: 'Thomas? Thomas Crane?'

'Thomas hasn't been here for a few weeks,' Rachel said, as if she didn't know why, and then the cops shuffled round a bit and Graham Thing thanked everyone and got them to promise to let him know if they thought of anything, anything at all.

Then he held out his card for Rachel to take, but she was looking the other way, or else she didn't want to dirty her dainty little fingers taking it off him. Either way, he was left holding it out like a twat, like those guys in the marketplace on Saturdays trying to get rid of flyers for stupid discos and raves and money off at Subway.

Simon took the card from him. 'In case I think of something,' he mumbled. Their eyes met. The Graham guy seemed a bit vulnerable himself, like he might understand.

'Might not seem important, Simon, but any little detail...'

Then Graham did a Columbo, turning to go and then at the last minute, turning back. 'Oh,' he said, and he scrabbled in his folder for something. 'Do any of you recognise the boy in this picture?'

And he pulled out a blurry blow-up of a passport photo: Em and Tom, Tom being an arse and Em clowning it up, sucking her cheeks in hard. She'd just had the streaks put in her hair. She looked like a model, only she was crossing her eyes. Simon's heart squeezed tight, like a stomach cramp, only higher.

'That's Emma,' said Loopy Lexie in that stupid drawl of hers, and Rat Face tutted and said yeah, they knew that, but who was she *with*?

'Oh, that's Tom.' Lexie laughed.

'Tom? What's his last name?'

'Crane,' said Rachel. 'That's Thomas Crane. You called his name out five minutes ago.'

And then Graham and his weird sidekick were gone, armed with Tom's address, and everyone was snivelling like they were upset about Emma, and Rachel clapped her hands and said maybe they'd better take a break, and Loopy Lexie said maybe they should pack up and go home, what with Emma being dead and that.

There was general agreement that Lexie had spoken for all of them, so Rachel called it a day.

A lot earlier than usual, Simon helped her clear up. Any other Monday, it was him and Em clearing up together. The goody-goodies.

Rachel turned off the lights and set the alarm while he waited in the porch. 'Thanks, Simon,' she said. 'You didn't have to stay behind. I know you two were close.'

'Not especially.'

She zipped up her high-vis jacket. 'You ever see Maisie Finnegan these days?'

'Maisie? Why would I see Maisie?' He hadn't seen her in ages. Before Em came along and stole the show, it was Posh Maisie who was teacher's pet – until Rachel pulled her up on something and Maisie called her a cunt and walked out. That was months ago, before Christmas. Why did Rachel think Maisie would have anything to do with *him*? It was Tom she'd had a thing about.

Together they picked their way along the puddled alleyway towards the street. Rachel pulled her hood up and headed for her moped. She squinted up at him. 'You okay to get home?'

'Yeah, I'm good.'

That sounded cool but it wasn't true. No one was coming to pick him up, and he couldn't face waiting for the bus. The walk would do him good, give him a chance to think about Em some more before he got home, get his head straight. It wasn't his fault, what had happened.

Was it?

No, course not. He'd wanted it not to be true, but it was. She was dead. His nan would see it on the news. She probably wouldn't remember who Em was, but he needed to work out what to say in case she did.

# CHAPTER 9

Thomas Crane lived in Amberstone, a couple of miles outside Barbury, fast becoming a dormitory for commuters who could afford one of its growing number of 'executive-style' new-builds – especially since the notoriously smelly Bonzo Bix dog food factory had moved away to an industrial estate on the London Road.

Lincoln and Woody drove into Rackham Close, where the Cranes' house was one of six built to look a century older than they really were. A mud-spattered Range Rover was parked outside. In the storm porch, two pairs of green gumboots and a pink pair with polka dots stood in line beside a pair of leather ankle boots that were still muddy, recently discarded. A big pottery bowl warned them the Cranes had a dog, probably a large one. On cue, a low barking began in the depths of the house.

Before Woody could lift the brass knocker, the door flew open and a woman burst out onto the step.

'Oh God, I thought you were Tom!' She was hanging onto two massive golden-coated dogs – Labradors, Lincoln guessed, crossed with something else. Ponies, perhaps? 'Can I help you?'

'Mrs Crane?' He flashed his warrant card.

'Oh God, what's happened?'

'We need to speak to Thomas. Is he here?'

'He's not home yet. What's this about?'

'Can we come in? If you could get those dogs under control…?'

'Oh God!' She hauled the pony-dogs back and steered them through a door and into the garage. Claws scrabbled a few times in protest but then gave up.

Lincoln and Woody followed her indoors. In her late thirties, with untidy ash-blonde hair and a tan that probably owed more to an outdoor life than to sunbathing, she wore white slacks, a black sweatshirt and scarlet socks. She smelt of stables.

'I've only just got back myself. Tom should be home by now.' She snatched her phone from her hip pocket and speed-dialled. 'No answer. He left work at 3.30. He's always back by 4.15 if he's on the early shift. What is it now, six o'clock?' She pushed her sleeve up to reveal a narrow, sinewy wrist: no watch.

'Quarter past,' Woody said. 'He drives? Or does he get the bus?'

'He cycles.'

'Along the main road?'

'Mostly.'

'We know he left the gym on time,' Lincoln told her, 'because we went there looking for him. He must have gone somewhere else on the way home.'

'He doesn't usually.' Anxious, she led them into a small sitting room lined on three sides with spotless leather sofas. The shin-high coffee table was heaped with piles of thick glossy magazines, like an upmarket dentist's waiting room. The giant dogs wouldn't be welcome in here. 'Is he in some sort of trouble?'

'Just got a couple of questions for him.'

'Is this about that Sherman girl?' She swept her unruly fringe back from her face. 'He didn't know her well, although they both went to Board Treaders. He hasn't been going lately, not since he's been working.'

'Did he know her before that?' Woody asked.

'How could he?'

'They might have met at school.'

'Hardly! He was at Forrester's in Presford. All boys.'

And fee-paying, Lincoln thought. Emma had to make do with a mixed comprehensive.

'So what's this about?' Her voice was harder now.

Woody fished a copy of the photo booth picture out of his folder. 'We found this at Emma's house.'

Mrs Crane took the photo from him, a frown creasing her forehead while she studied it. 'They don't look exactly lovey-dovey, do they? They're pulling stupid faces.' She thrust the photo back. 'As I said, they both went to Board Treaders but that's all.'

A phone rang in the kitchen and when she hurried away to answer it, Lincoln inspected the proud array of framed family photos on the wall. The Cranes were a good-looking couple, with two handsome sons.

'Thomas must have a brother,' he said, 'a bit older.'

'Probably away at uni.'

The older boy was dark-haired, strong-boned, taking after his father, while Thomas favoured his mother's fairer colouring and softer features.

Mrs Crane came back into the room. 'That was my husband. He's on his way home.'

'He works locally?'

'He's a college lecturer in Southampton. Visual arts.'

'Bit of a commute.'

'It's worth it. He's got a good position. I'm Moya Crane, by the way,' she said as an afterthought.

'We're hoping Thomas can help us find out what happened to Emma,' Lincoln said.

'Tom. We call him Tom. He doesn't like being called Thomas. He was working at the gym that night. He was home by half past nine and didn't go out again. We were here together. He certainly wasn't going out with the Sherman girl, if that's what you're trying to say.' She shoved her hand through her hair. 'I'll try him again.'

'Maybe he's had a puncture or stopped off at a friend's house.'

'He'd have phoned.' She rang her son once more, got voicemail, left a message: 'Tom, it's Ma, wondering where you've got to. Can you call me as soon as you get this?'

At the sound of a car, she flung open the front door and rushed out, hardly giving her husband time to get out before she was grabbing him by the arm. 'Duncan, Duncan! Tom isn't home and the police are here.'

Crane looked horrified, naturally assuming the worst. 'He's had an accident?'

'Mr Crane,' Lincoln began, but then a fair-haired boy came freewheeling into the driveway, swerving to a stop at the door.

He grinned at Woody. 'Hello again. We met at the gym earlier, didn't we?'

Clearly confused, his father stepped between them. 'What's this about?'

'That girl who went missing,' Moya said.

'Can we talk about this inside?' Tom calmly parked his bike against the house wall, tugged his rucksack off and dumped it inside the front door. 'If you don't mind?'

She clutched at his sleeve. 'What held you up? Couldn't you have phoned?'

'Stopped off for a coffee, got sidetracked. Didn't notice the time.' Lean and sinewy, with a sprinter's physique, he shrugged her off and led the way into the kitchen.

Lincoln laid the photo down on the island counter. 'Were you and Emma Sherman close, Tom? This picture makes me think you were.'

He gave it no more than a cursory glance. 'Mates, that's all, through Board Treaders. Nothing serious.'

'Where were you the night she disappeared, last Thursday?'

'He was working,' Moya said before her son could answer. 'Listen, why don't we all sit down? I'll put the kettle on.'

Lincoln ignored her. 'Tom? Where were you last Thursday night?'

'I was at Bods from half three. Finished at nine-fifteen. I was back here by ten to ten.'

'That's right,' she said. 'I was here. Duncan, would you like to take these guys into the other room?'

Once more, Lincoln didn't even look her way. 'Mr Crane?'

Duncan Crane cleared his throat. Tall, with dark hair slicked back, he wore horn-rimmed spectacles that gave him a severe, academic look. 'I'm out on Thursdays now the term's started again. I take an evening class at Presford College. I'm never home before ten.'

'Was Tom here when you got back?'

'Of course. I'd have been concerned if he hadn't been.' He held up a hand. 'Let's go through.'

They trooped into the living room, its furniture glossier and more expensive than any shop in Barbury or even Presford could supply. They took their places at the polished oak dining table while Moya went to make tea and coffee.

Woody took up the questioning. 'Did you see Emma that evening, Tom? She went to the gym, so chances are, your paths crossed.'

Tom shook his head, scratched the back of his neck, fussed with the collar of his polo shirt. 'No, sorry.'

'Tell us about the photo.' Lincoln had rescued it from the kitchen, and pushed it across the table now where it was harder to ignore.

'Some of the girls at Board Treaders were giving her a hard time, okay? She wanted them to think we were going round together. One day, we were walking past the booth at the bus station and she had this idea about having our picture taken, to wind the others up. And I thought, Why not? What's the harm?'

'It was nothing more serious than that?'

'He's told you.' Crane Senior leaned forward to push the photo away.

'She never told you about a boyfriend, anyone she was meeting? You know she skipped her dance class that night?'

'Really?' Tom's gaze stayed fixed on the photo.

'Nothing else you can tell us?' Woody cartwheeled his pencil on his notebook. 'Can you tell us where you were the rest of last week, between Thursday night and Sunday afternoon?'

'This is absurd!' Duncan Crane shot up.

'No, it isn't.' Lincoln didn't take his eyes off Tom. 'If your son hasn't anything to hide, he won't object to telling us where he was between the night of Emma's disappearance and Sunday afternoon, when her body was found.'

For the first time, Tom looked unsettled, his earlier bravado gone. 'It's okay.' He spread his hands on the table, counting off the days. 'Friday, I was at the gym from nine to three-thirty. Came home, had something to eat. Badminton practice at six. You can check all this. I go to the country club.'

'Press Vale?'

'Yeah.'

Woody scribbled it down.

'Saturday, Dad and I went to Yeovil, to the football. Yeovil Town against Bournemouth.'

'They lost one-nil,' Crane threw in crossly. 'You can check *that* too.'

'Sunday, I had a lie-in and then we all had a late lunch.'

'Shame you didn't come forward sooner.' Lincoln pushed the blow-up of the photo booth picture towards him again. 'You must've known we'd find this eventually.'

A shrug. 'Didn't know she'd kept it. It wasn't as if we were *involved*.'

Duncan Crane folded his hands on the table. 'And it's not as if Tom's told you anything you don't already know.'

Lincoln treated father and son to a frown of disapproval. 'I'll be the judge of that. An investigation like this, any scrap of information could make a difference.'

Moya returned with a tray of cups and saucers. 'I'm never going to remember who wanted tea and who wanted coffee...' She handed the drinks out, swapped Lincoln's for Woody's, and slopped Duncan's tea into the saucer in her haste.

'When did you first meet Emma?' Lincoln took a sip of his coffee and sat back, keen to ease the tension round the table.

'Must have been January, when she joined Board Treaders.'

'Not long, then.'

'Long enough to get to know her as, you know, a friend. Nothing more than that, though.'

'And he doesn't go to drama group anymore,' Moya put in, 'because it clashes with work.'

'So – when did you last see her?'

'A couple of weeks ago? Round town, maybe?' Tom lifted his coffee mug with both hands, almost hiding his face, but not before Lincoln saw a rush of colour spread along his cheekbones.

'Can you think of anyone she'd fallen out with recently? Another girl, perhaps, over a boyfriend?'

'Not sure she was friends with anyone in particular. Kind of... aloof, Emma was. Or that's how she came across. Although—'

'Tom's told you all he knows,' his father snapped.

Lincoln pushed his cup aside, stood up. 'I expect when you've had a chance to think about it, Tom, you'll remember one or two things you can't bring to mind right now.' He caught the lad's eye. 'If anything occurs to you, you've only got to pick up the phone, text me, or drop in at the station and ask for me or DS Woods.' He handed him his card. 'Okay?'

Tom nodded, staring at the card. 'Okay.'

'Oh, and we need your mobile number and landline. Elimination purposes,' Woody said, pushing his notebook and pencil across the table.

'Sure.' Tom wrote both numbers down, underlined them with a flourish and pushed the notebook back.

'Not exactly a bundle of laughs, are they?' Woody remarked as they drove back.

'Wouldn't want to have dinner with them, if that's what you mean.'

'Doubt they'd invite you, boss.'

'That boy's not telling us the whole truth and the parents know it.'

'How come Breezy didn't speak to him last week?' They reached the dual carriageway and Woody put his foot down.

'Breezy must've thought he'd spoken to everyone who worked at the gym. Tom's only a temp, probably wasn't even on the staff list. If it hadn't been for that photo...'

'Reckon he and Emma were going out together?'

'We'll soon find out when we look at her phone records, see how often his numbers come up. I'd say it's likely.'

'His alibis sound solid.'

'Almost *too* solid. His mother was very quick to tell us where he was at the relevant times.'

Woody negotiated the Green Dragon roundabout and they headed into town. 'He seems an ordinary enough lad – a bit cocky, but then, he's eighteen. Most lads are cocky at eighteen.'

'What did you make of Crane Senior? Bet he could be a tricky bugger if we put a foot wrong.'

They drew up outside the police station, and Woody nodded towards a burly figure in a purple polo shirt, no jacket, tight tracksuit pants. He was swinging the heavy front door open as if it were weightless. 'That must be our Mr Tyler from Bods.'

Lincoln opened the car door, stepped out. 'I'll get Pam to sit in on this one, Woody. See you in the morning.'

# CHAPTER 10

Tania Tremlow dumped her bags down on the kitchen table. She was exhausted, worn out by the strain of spending time with Crystal.

She'd shopped at the supermarket on the way back from Barbury, deliberately delaying her return. She'd even had a cup of tea in the café there and sat with it a good half-hour before driving the rest of the way home.

Todd had been on his own since yesterday evening – apart from Stephanie and she didn't really count. He'd gone quiet when she told him Emma'd been found. He'd known better than to offer to take her over to Crystal's – someone had to stay with Stephanie anyway – and he'd said very little when she'd phoned him.

She found him sitting in the half-dark in the living room, the curtains drawn.

'You're back early.' He sounded as tired as she felt.

'Crystal didn't want me to stay. I offered but you know how she is.'

'How's she coping?' He rubbed his cheeks.

'You know Crystal – always good at putting on a brave face, like when Derek died. Always shows a lot of dignity, does my sister.'

Todd stood up, staggered a bit. Must've been drinking. Tania cast a look round the room but couldn't see any evidence. 'They caught him yet?' he asked. 'That boy?'

'Boy?'

'You said on the phone…' He steadied himself against the back of the chair. 'They found a photo, you said, Emma and some boy.'

'Oh, I don't think it was serious.' She watched him lurch slowly across to the door. 'Shall I run you a bath?' That usually cheered him up, having a good soak, especially when he'd been drinking.

'No. I'm going up to bed.'

She sighed. Quarter to seven and he's already trudging up the stairs. He'll have been up all night. If he goes to bed now, he won't sleep.

Not that his sleeplessness would disturb her: they hadn't shared a bed for years, ever since they knew Stephanie would always have the mind of a five-year-old, and the ungainly body of an outsize toddler.

In the kitchen, Tania found an empty Scotch bottle in the pedal bin. She retrieved it, rinsed it out, dropped it into the recycling sack. Todd hadn't eaten the ready meal she'd left in the fridge for him; didn't even seem to have made himself a cup of tea or coffee. All she had to wash up were Stephanie's mug and bowl, her beaker and spoon.

Poor Crystal, alone in that house! Tania thought about phoning her but something stopped her: she'd probably gone to bed, taken a pill to help her sleep. It'd be a shame to wake her now. And if she needed anything, she knew she could call anytime.

Not that she ever did. Crystal never seemed to need anyone, not even her own sister.

Tania folded the tea towel, hung it over the rail of the Aga, smoothed it down. She'd go and look in on Stephanie, see if she needed changing.

# CHAPTER 11

Ashley Tyler was waiting in reception, leafing through an old copy of *Which?* magazine. When Lincoln introduced himself, he cast it aside and stood up.

He had the physique of a bodybuilder: bulky thighs, torso widening sharply from narrow hips and waist, sloping shoulders almost seamlessly tapering up into a hefty neck and a head like a bullet. The bullet was covered in oiled spikes of dark brown hair, pale scalp shining through and catching the light from the fluorescent tubes that ran the length of the corridor leading to the CID room.

'Thanks for coming in, Mr Tyler.' Lincoln directed him to a seat beside his desk as Pam came in, pulled a chair up and got her notebook out.

'Anything I can do to help,' he said. 'Y' know...'

'You knew Emma Sherman? A regular at Bods, wasn't she?'

'That's right.' The sweet aroma of coconut rose from him, probably from the gloop he'd spread through his hair. He propped one elbow on the edge of the desk, clasped his hands together.

'Do you remember her coming in last Thursday evening, about seven?' Pam asked.

'No, but we only speak to the ones who need to pay. Members go straight through.'

'You've no way of controlling access to the areas beyond reception?'

'We've never had any trouble.'

'Until now.'

He sat up straighter in his seat. 'Not my fault the bosses don't put a better system in. And she wasn't attacked at the gym, was she?'

'We don't think so, but it's too soon to say.' Lincoln paused. 'We understand the cameras in the foyer weren't working that night. Does that often happen?'

'Depends who's on duty. Gotta remember to turn them on in the security box.' Tyler shifted his weight, crossed his ankles, left over right, right over left.

'The security box?'

'Yeah, it's a little room up top where all the systems are controlled –

the PA system and everything, but it's like a broom cupboard.'

'Who checked the cameras the night Emma disappeared?' Pam persisted.

'Me or Gina shoulda checked they were on. Gina probably thought I'd done it and I probably thought she had.' He twitched his head round as if ridding himself of a knot in his neck. The smell of coconut intensified.

Lincoln turned to Pam. 'Better look at this security box if it hasn't been done already.' Breezy had probably stuck his head round the door, not liked the look of the place and backed out again.

'You'll need to speak to Gavin, the manager,' said Tyler.

Lincoln checked Breezy's notes. 'That'd be Gavin Lyons?'

'That's right.'

'How well do you know Tom Crane?'

'Tom? Not that well. Different shifts, or else he's in the back office when I'm out front. He hasn't been working at Bods long, only since he left school. Six weeks?'

'Ever see Tom and Emma together?'

Ashley looked surprised by the question. 'Never.'

'Did Emma get talking to anyone else at the gym?'

'Wouldn't know. When you're on reception, you don't go in the gym. And after they shut down the inside cameras...'

'Why was that?' Pam asked. 'Had customers complained about being watched?'

'No one was ogling!' Tyler retorted. 'The screens were on the front desk so we could keep an eye on things, not spy on people!' His upper lip glistened.

Lincoln leaned forward, changing tack. 'The night Emma Sherman disappeared, you or Gina were on reception the whole time?'

'Yeah, half three till nine. Someone's always gotta stay on the desk.'

'You didn't notice anything out of the ordinary that evening?'

'Nope.' Tyler unclasped his hands so he could run a finger over his damp top lip.

Pam leaned towards him confidentially. 'What we think happened, Ash, is that Emma came into Bods to change her clothes before going to meet someone. Except we're pretty sure she didn't go out the main exit. How else could someone get out of Bods if they didn't want to use the main doors?'

Another quick wipe of the upper lip. Another uncrossing and re-crossing of the thick ankles in their white sports socks.

Tyler rolled his shoulders. 'There's the emergency exit, the fire door. Goes out into the service area, past the bins. But she wouldn't have gone out that way. She'd have to push the crash bar down and that sets the alarms off.'

'So how do any of the staff get outside – for a smoke or a breath of fresh air?'

'Oh yeah, right. There's the service door, through the back of the office. Opens into the delivery yard. Out by the bins. We've all got our own swipe card so Gav can keep track of who goes in and out that way. You can't open it without a swipe card except in an emergency.'

'You say Gavin keeps track of the swipe cards – does he keep a log of some sort?'

'Must do. Probably on one of the computers in the security box. But that's Gav's empire, that is. He's the only one who knows.'

A few minutes more, and he was gone.

'Like pulling teeth!' Lincoln stood up, yawned and stretched.

Pam flipped through her notes. 'If Breezy'd done his job properly last week, we'd already know about the service door and the security box and the swipe cards.'

Lincoln picked up the phone and called Gavin Lyons, the gym manager.

'I'm off duty for the next few days actually,' said Lyons, 'but give me half an hour and I'll meet you at the gym. Anything I can do to help...'

Bella came in while Lincoln was on the phone. She headed straight for her cubbyhole, but by the time he'd hung up, she'd come out to make herself a cup of tea. She looked tired.

'Autopsy, edited highlights,' she said as she and Lincoln stood beside the kettle. 'Manual strangulation after she'd been raped.'

It seemed ludicrous to be making themselves hot drinks as they talked about this, but it gave them something to focus on while they tried to avoid each other's eyes.

'Time of death?'

'Estimated at Thursday night, between seven and midnight. No alcohol, no drugs in the stomach contents, though the full tox will take a bit longer.' She poured water into her mug, dunked the teabag a few times while Lincoln made his coffee. 'She was probably killed in the woods somewhere. Pine needles in her hair, dirt under her fingernails and in abrasions on her knees, consistent with woodland soil.'

Lincoln visualised the vast, shadowy reaches of Greywood, the forest that spread over the downland to the south-west of the town. 'What are the chances of recovering DNA?'

'So-so. Wrapping her in that tarpaulin preserved a lot of the evidence but there's been some degradation, inevitably.' She sighed. 'Still, if and when we have a suspect, he's likely to have blood on his clothes, a hair, fibres, something... Be great if he was in the database already.'

He told her they'd identified the boy in the photo as Tom Crane, his parents providing him with all the alibis he could ever want.

'Viable suspect?'

'Depends how his alibis check out. I'm betting his number's one of the few that Emma was calling.'

'So they could've been involved. Mind you, there's nothing from the autopsy to suggest she was sexually active.' She hunted for a teaspoon to hoick her teabag out. 'You look like you're off home already.'

'Pam and I are off to the gym.'

She raised an eyebrow. 'The gym?'

'To check out their security. The manager's coming in specially. Seems a bit of a coincidence that Emma disappeared from the place where Tom works.'

'Don't let me keep you, then.' She chucked her exhausted teabag into the bin with a thunk. 'Did we know she had a tramp stamp on her arse?'

'No, we didn't.'

'Tattoo of a butterfly. Very pretty. Professionally done. And do you know what a Brazilian is? Apart from very painful.'

'Enlighten me.'

She grinned. 'Removal of the pubic hair with hot wax. A turn-on for some, no doubt, but you've got to wonder why a fifteen-year-old wants to rid herself of something as womanly as her bush.'

He hoped he didn't look as embarrassed as she made him feel. It was the sort of thing you could joke about with another bloke – should the topic arise – but it was weird discussing it with Bella.

'Wanting to please a boyfriend?' he ventured. 'Even if Tom's in the clear, everything points to her being involved with *someone*.'

'Someone who, presumably, likes them naked as the day they were born.'

'Get anything off the tarpaulin?'

'Still being tested. The only other thing of note – Ken found some friction burns on her shoulder blades, base of her spine, as if she was shoved around on a rough surface – sacking, coconut matting, sisal carpeting, maybe? Won't help much until we find a likely murder scene, but if there happened to be a rush mat on the floor...' She glanced at her watch. 'Don't miss your session at the gym.'

# CHAPTER 12

'Not going out again, are you? You heard what happened to that girl that went missing.'

Lady flounced past her mother, close enough to brush against her bulging belly. 'I can't stay indoors till they catch the creep who did it.'

'You going with Tara?' Polly rubbed her aching back, the muscles roaring, her spine on fire. She wanted this over, this baby out, her body her own once more. Last thing she needed, her bloody daughter racketing round the flat, acting the prima donna.

'Tara? Why would I go anywhere with Tara?'

'Thought you were friends?'

'Fuck I want with that cunt? Bloody mental.'

'Who then?' Polly lowered herself gingerly onto the kitchen chair. It was weeks since she'd been able to get down as low as the sofa.

'None of your business. Whoever I said, you'd pick holes, so best not say anything.' Lady helped herself to loose change out of the old money box. Polly was too exhausted to stop her, even though she'd been saving the coins for the laundrette – though Christ knew when she'd feel strong enough to get there.

'What time you back?'

Big shrug. 'Be back when I'm back. I got keys.'

'Who's driving?'

'Didn't say anyone was.'

'Oh yeah, you're going on the bus. I *don't* think.'

'Get off my back, Mother.'

Polly's heart flipped. Once upon a time, Lady called her 'Mother' to send her up, affectionate, teasing. Now when she said it, it was like an insult. 'Call me if you need to.' She reached out to pat Lady's arm but her daughter ducked out of reach, grabbed her jacket off the chair and was gone.

Lady jogged to the bus stop – not the one near the flat but two stops farther on, so her mother wouldn't see her.

She checked her phone. Nearly 7.30. Her stomach was fluttering. She'd been too nervous to eat so she was hungry too, aching and taut inside. She had no idea when the next bus was due. She wanted to get away from here before she changed her mind. Except she wouldn't, not now. She'd been hoping and praying for this, going to one of Arlo's parties. Only he didn't call them parties, the pretentious wanker!

'It's a *happening*,' he said when he invited her. 'You must come to my happening.'

She and Jess had been lying on the grass in the Abbey grounds a few days ago, Friday, passing a joint between them, sharing a can of Special Brew although Lady hated it – it tasted like men's piss would. She took the can and tilted it, taking the smallest sip, passing it back.

'There's Arlo,' Jess said, leaning back on her elbows so her T-shirt pulled tight across her nipples. Her tits were so small, she had to make the most of them.

Lady looked up, across the dry, scuffed grass, and there he was, the famous Arlo James, tall, rangy, dirty as a pirate, his long dark hair caught back, his jacket slung like a cloak across his shoulders. He was wearing make-up, she was sure: eyeliner, smudgy shadow on his eyelids.

'Looks like a girl!' She flopped down on the grass again.

'Does he fuck!' Jess sat up, waved him over.

Arlo loped across, slowly approaching on long, thin legs, taking the cigarette out of his mouth, chucking it down, walking over it, leaving it smouldering.

'Who's this?' He was asking Jess but looking at Lady as if she'd been served him on a plate. He sounded interested. He was older than she expected, thirties, weather-beaten.

His gaze slid down her body like a caress. Her heart fluttered in her chest and her mouth went dry.

'This is Lady,' Jess said.

'Your ladyship.' He doffed a phantom hat, bowed low and held out his hands to help Lady to her feet.

She stood looking up at him, into eyes that had already stripped her naked. 'I'm not really a lady,' she said, going red. 'It's a nickname from when I was little and I couldn't say Lainey.' Or even Elaine, her real name, her hateful name. She'd never be Elaine again. Who, her age, was called Elaine? 'And you're Arlo?'

'That's me.' Another daft bow. 'You coming to my happening next Monday?'

'Happening?' She threw her head back, laughing. 'Isn't that a bit 60s?'

'You're not into the 60s?' He made a hurt face.

'Well, yes, but... What, is it like a band? Is it open air? Is it music?'

'All of the above.' He tugged his jacket more securely onto his shoulders. It was a velvet coat with gold frogging, like a bandsman's jacket. 'You a singer? Play anything?'

'I love singing. I drive my mum up the wall!'

'Can't wait to hear you. Jess'll tell you all about it.' And he whirled round and ambled off the way he'd come, giving a farewell wave without looking back.

So here she was, heading for Arlo's happening, her stomach trembling and empty, her brain buzzing. Why the fuck had she told him she could sing? "Corncrake", her mum called her.

'He likes you,' Jess had said on the Abbey lawns. 'He really likes you.'

And I really like him, Lady thought as the bus pulled up and she climbed in, already imagining his eyes on her legs, her hair, her mouth. She sat in a window seat, resting her head against the glass, dreaming of what was to come.

# CHAPTER 13

It was after eight and getting dark by the time Lincoln and Pam arrived at Bods to meet the manager, Gavin Lyons. A wiry man in his forties, he was dressed down in a Man City sweatshirt and denim jeans. The smell of cigarettes hung about him.

'I've had to bring the littl'un along,' he said, pushing a young boy ahead of him as they climbed to the first floor. The child had a frizzy halo of ginger hair, a smattering of freckles, and glasses that made him look earnest. 'His mum's out for the evening and he's only ten. Bit young to be left on your own, eh, kiddo?'

Lyons unlocked a narrow door and led them into a windowless cabin. Overhead lights sputtered on, buzzing fitfully. The cabin smelt of sawdust and hot circuit boards, but it smelt musty too, as if rainwater had got in somewhere. The dull thud of several different streams of rock music clashed under their feet. It was like being suspended in a mildewed tree house above a fairground.

A workbench ran along one side, packed with laptop computers, two big printer-scanners, and all the usual electronic gear essential for any business.

'The security box.' Lyons swept his hand out like a tour guide. 'This is where it all happens. Computers control the CCTV cameras, the tills, everything downstairs. All done from here.'

'You keep a log of when the service door's opened with a swipe card – is that right?' Lincoln had a fair idea Tom Crane knew more than he'd admit, but he wanted to keep an open mind.

Lyons nodded, ruffling his son's curly hair. 'That's right. What do you need to know?'

'We think Emma Sherman left through the service door,' Pam said, 'so we need to know who came in and out that way last Thursday night.'

'You're welcome to check the log, but it's not going to tell you much. The girl didn't have a card, did she?'

'No, but maybe one of your staff opened the service door so she could slip out without being seen.'

'You think a member of my staff *colluded* with her?'

'They may have thought they were doing her a favour,' Pam said. 'Wouldn't have seemed like a big deal at the time.'

'But even so...'

It took only a few minutes to discover that card 933 had opened the door at 7.12 the night Emma disappeared – a time that didn't match the start or end of anyone's shift.

And whose card was 933?

'Let's see...' Lyons checked while his son stood mute and bored across the other side of the stuffy cabin. 'Card 933 is Tom Crane.'

Lincoln nodded. Just as he expected.

'Thanks for coming in on your day off,' he said as they got ready to leave. He jerked his thumb at the array of equipment. 'You've certainly got some impressive kit in here.'

'Better printer-scanners than anything we've got at Barley Lane,' Pam agreed.

Lyons shrugged. 'We always need to take copies of stuff – for interviews and that. And we do most of our own publicity. Anything happens out of the ordinary, we need to do notices, posters. False economy, buying crap printers that are gonna let you down.' He propelled his son ahead of him out of the cabin. 'You don't know who did it, then?'

'We're trying to put it all together.'

'Don't suppose you can say much.' Lyons locked the door and led them back down to reception. 'He's a good kid, Tom. Bit of a show-off but we're all like that at his age, eh? He'll get his corners knocked off at uni!'

'You might want to think about tightening your security,' Pam put in. 'Doesn't seem right that anyone can walk through to the locker rooms without being stopped.'

'Reception staff are supposed to ask members to show their cards. It's not meant to be open house, but if I've got morons on the front desk...' Lyons shrugged. 'Let me know if there's anything else, okay?' He pushed his son ahead of him towards the car park. 'Come on, matey, you should be in bed.'

# CHAPTER 14

## TUESDAY 10TH SEPTEMBER

Tuesday morning, and Lincoln was sitting at his computer, scarcely awake enough to read what was on his screen. After a restless night, he'd got up at five, showered, had coffee. Couldn't think of anywhere better to be than at the station trying to find out who killed Emma Sherman.

The CID room was quiet, dim. Pam, the only other early bird, swept in soon after eight, chirpy as ever.

'Breakfast meeting with Bella?' She switched her computer on even before she'd pulled her chair out.

'You trying to be funny?'

She grinned. 'Couldn't think why else you'd be in so early.'

'Couldn't sleep.' Now, though, he could think of nothing better than to be in bed, BBC 6 Music droning quietly beside him, lulling him back into a doze.

'It's all that coffee.' She smiled at her screen. 'Did I hear you telling the sarge you knew Bella years ago?'

When the dark, statuesque new detective chief inspector had been introduced at a Park Street briefing about six months ago, Lincoln had done a double take. As a young trainee at Hendon, his best friend had been Edmund Bax, whose family home was only a couple of Tube stops away from the police college. Ed's mother had felt sorry for the shy Lincoln, who rarely managed to get home to his parents in Worcestershire, and she often prevailed upon Ed to bring him back to the house for a "proper" meal.

The first time he visited, Lincoln saw a young boy of about twelve hanging around at the top of the stairs: all angular arms and legs, a mop of unruly dark curls, a scowl.

'I didn't know you had a brother,' he said as Ed took him through to the big kitchen, where Mrs Bax was making pastry.

'Brother?' said Ed. 'That's my kid sister, Bella.'

She'd refused to be introduced to him that first evening, taking refuge in her room, but after Lincoln had come over for supper a few more times and even stayed the night, she'd shyly trailed round after him until Ed told her to bugger off and leave them alone.

That scrawny tomboy had grown up to become DCI Bella Bax.

'You were probably her first love,' Pam grinned when he'd finished explaining how he and Bella had met. 'You think she remembers *you*?'

'I've put on a bit of weight since then.' Lincoln patted his stomach. 'And gone a bit grey. We're talking twenty-five years – no, twenty-six. She won't remember, and I'm not going to remind her.'

How quickly those years had evaporated! And what had he got to show for them? He forced himself to concentrate on the case, going over to the Barbury street map on the wall and jabbing the black rhomboid shape of the Half Moon Centre.

'If Tom let Emma out through Bods' service door, where would she end up?'

Pam stood alongside him to trace Emma's hypothetical route, and he was conscious of her petite shape, the spikiness of her short blonde hair. 'She'd come out through the delivery yard and into Spicer Street,' she said, 'which is one-way traffic.'

'So if she was being picked up by someone, he'd have to drive her up Spicer Street, left turn into High Street, left turn into Abbey Street. And a good chance a camera would've caught them.'

'With any luck. There are cameras at every set of traffic lights along there. I'll get on to John Spooner at the control centre, see if his team can spot anything.'

Lincoln went back to his desk. 'I checked her phone records first thing. The Crane boy's number crops up a lot – they were sending each other texts most days. They must've been closer than he made out last night in front of his parents.'

'But it wasn't Tom she was meeting outside the back of Bods, was it? We know he was working.'

'She may have told him who she was meeting, though.'

They were interrupted by Sergeant Bob phoning through from the front desk. 'Young gentleman to see you,' he said. 'You coming to collect him?'

In the cluttered confines of the CID room, Tom Crane looked even taller and blonder than he had yesterday. He and Emma would have looked good together.

'You said to drop in,' he said. 'So here I am.'

Lincoln pulled a chair out for him, got straight to the point. 'Tell us about the service door behind Bods. And don't look so surprised – you must've known we'd check the swipe card log.'

'Yeah, I should've thought of that.' Tom gave a sheepish grin. 'That's what I came to tell you. Thursday afternoon, Em called me to say she was meeting someone on Spicer Street instead of going to class, and was there a way out the back so no one would see her? I told her to come through to the office and I'd open the door for her. He was picking her up at 7.15.'

'Who was? Who was picking her up?'

'Big secret. She wouldn't say.' He ran both hands through his hair, tucked it behind his ears and tried to smooth it down at the back, but it was too thick, too wayward to be tamed. 'Not that I was interested.'

'Why did she come into Bods if she was meeting someone in Spicer Street?' Pam asked.

'Some old lady in her road told her mum she'd seen her hanging about in town, and Em got a bit paranoid, started to see spies everywhere! So she came into Bods as if she was going to her class, got changed and went out again.'

'You remember what she changed into?'

'Jeans, T-shirt, red shoes.'

Pam jotted it down. 'So when she was back from her date, you were supposed to let her in again?'

'We'd got it all worked out. I told her to be at the back door by nine, no later, and to text me when she was outside. Then she'd still have fifteen minutes to change and go out the main doors before everything shut.'

'And you didn't see who picked her up?' Lincoln said.

'No windows out the back – that's why she'd have to text me. Only she didn't.' Tom stared at his hands, clasped loosely on his knees.

'So, Tom...' Lincoln paused, waiting for the boy to look up at him, allowing silence to build up for a few moments. 'What did you think when she didn't text you?'

'Thought she'd decided to stay the night with him.'

'On the first date?'

'Some girls, you know...' His shrug was so careless, Lincoln wanted to shake him. If only he'd said something at the time! Emma was probably still alive when her mother reported her missing that night. If Tom had gone to the police when she didn't come back, they might have been able to find her, to save her...

'So when she didn't come back to the gym, what did you do?'

'Hung about till 9.15 in case she'd got held up. Kept checking my phone but she didn't call or text. I didn't like to phone in case

I interrupted something.' He tried for a smile, but quickly gave up. 'I was home by ten to ten, had something to eat, went to bed about quarter past.'

'Hope you slept well.'

'I usually do.'

Lincoln raised an eyebrow. 'Your parents there when you got back?'

'Mum was but Dad teaches Thursday evenings, doesn't get back till late.'

'How did you get home from the gym that night?'

'Biked it as usual.'

'Got decent lights?'

'And a high-vis jacket. And armbands.' Tom gave another sheepish grin. 'Mum worries.'

'You don't drive?'

'Er – no.' He looked away. 'My brother died in a crash last year.'

'I'm sorry.' Lincoln recalled the older, darker boy in the Crane family photo. No wonder Moya was so anxious yesterday when Tom was late coming home.

Pam leaned in. 'Did Emma confide in you? You must've been one of her closest friends.'

Tom shook his head emphatically. 'That photo of us together, that was just to wind up the girls at Board Treaders. We weren't sleeping together.'

'I should hope not,' Lincoln said. 'She was only fifteen.' He noted the consternation that briefly clouded the boy's face. 'So, you say you didn't know her that well? You weren't phoning and texting each other nearly every day? We've been through her phone records, Tom. Your number shows up a lot, your mobile and your landline.'

'My landline?'

'Remember? You gave us your numbers yesterday when we came to your house.'

'Yes, but she wouldn't have called my landline...' Why was he acting so puzzled? He could hardly argue with the phone records.

'So the two of you were, what, "just good friends"?'

'That's all. Honestly. Since she joined Board Treaders. The girls there were kind of hostile, so she stuck with me and Simon.'

'That'd be Simon Lovelock?' said Pam.

'Yeah.' He watched her write it down. Lincoln sensed tension beneath the boy's bravado.

'You're absolutely sure you don't know who she was seeing or how long it'd been going on for?'

'Honestly, I have no idea.' Tom put his hands on the tabletop: long fingers, spatulate, soft, with the light tan of a young man who enjoys the open air but doesn't need to work outdoors in all weathers. 'Listen, Inspector, I'm truly, truly sorry about what happened to Em but she wasn't stupid. She knew who she was mixing with. She knew what she was getting into.'

'Sounds as if you knew too.' Lincoln's turn to lean in close.

'I didn't know. Not for certain.'

'Wild guess.'

A long pause. Tom bit his lip, uncertain, as if he was weighing up the risks. 'Arlo,' he said at last. 'She was seeing Arlo James.'

'Who the fuck is Arlo James?' Bella chucked Tom's statement down on her desk.

Lincoln had gone back through criminal records, found very little.

According to Tom, Arlo held musical get-togethers he called "happenings" – stupid 60s word – that were advertised by word of mouth amongst the local kids. Music, drink and a bit of weed were freely available, the kids taking along their instruments for a jam session, all very laid-back.

'Emma went up there a couple of times,' Tom had said, 'sang a few songs. It's like an open mic session without a mic.'

'Right.' Lincoln had been to a few open mic sessions in some of Barbury's less salubrious pubs like the Globe and the Moonraker, just to pass the time. Poetry, stand-up, folk songs, old rock favourites. Arlo was probably doing the town a favour inviting would-be stars up into the woods to show off.

'And Emma had a great voice,' Tom had added. 'She sounded like Kate Bush.'

From a couple of articles he found on the internet, Lincoln had also found out that Arlo – who didn't seem to use his surname much – was the younger son of Hugo James. He'd dropped out of university and kicked around the world for a few years before settling back in Wessex. Now styling himself an artist and musician, he was restoring a cottage at Mayday Farm in the middle of Greywood Forest. When the cottage was finished, he said, he planned to cultivate the surrounding land and become totally self-sufficient. He might even establish a community there, where like-minded people

71

could live and work together in peace and harmony.

It sounded like New Age bollocks.

'He's thirty-eight,' he told Bella now, passing her his notes. 'Single, no fixed abode. If his family's got money, he's probably thrown it away or been disinherited. He's a folk singer with a guitar and not a lot else.'

'Sounds fun.' Her lips puckered sourly as she skimmed through the details. 'He lives in the *woods*?' She studied a photo of him playing at a minor folk festival three years ago, battered top hat set at a rakish angle while he strummed his guitar to a small but devoted-looking crowd.

'According to Tom Crane, he's got quite a following among the local youngsters.'

'Drugs?'

'And the rest of it. Parties, music, booze, free love.'

'So, this hippy was Emma's boyfriend? He's more than twice her age! Any history of violence?'

'He's got involved in some protests, scuffles with the police – presumably nothing serious enough to get him noticed by Special Branch. He's against blood sports and the Countryside Alliance, fell out with Taylor Wimpey—'

'Taylor Wimpey?'

'They wanted to build on a wildflower meadow over Steepleton way and he organised a sit-in. Probably didn't do the flowers much good.'

Bella shot him a chilly look. 'So he attaches himself to causes, lives off the land, et cetera, et cetera. But nothing to suggest he's a killer?'

'No, nothing.' Lincoln paused. 'Unless her death was an accident, something going wrong when they were having sex. He could've been under the influence of drugs – who knows?'

She allowed the possibility, if grudgingly. 'So we think she fell for his ageing rock star looks?'

'I know it sounds unlikely, but the Crane boy seemed sure that's who she was going to meet. And there's the forensic evidence – Emma was killed in woodland, and that's where he lives.'

She heaved a sigh. 'Better bring Arlo in, then. If you can find him.'

# CHAPTER 15

'They came to Board Treaders Monday night,' Simon said. He dropped his voice even though Shakin' Stevie's milkshake bar was almost empty. 'Two cops. They had a photo of you and Em. Rachel gave them your address.'

Tom sniggered. 'Rachel? Bet that bitch was wetting herself with excitement. Couldn't wait to stitch me up.'

'You were pretty rude to her.'

'That fucking dyke deserved it, screaming at me for changing some of my lines in that shitty play! She's lucky I didn't punch her ugly little troll face in. I should've stopped going months ago. Don't know why you're still going.'

What would Simon do without Board Treaders? Every session was a chance to step outside his own manky life for a couple of hours, and his nan would want to know what he'd done wrong if he stopped going. Unlike Tom, he couldn't afford to walk out on the £50 subscription he'd so carefully saved up.

'I'll maybe finish at Christmas,' he said. 'I'm signed up for the term now.'

They sipped their shakes in silence. Simon meant to cut back on milk, but this was Tom and it was the first time in ages, and he needed to talk. And if Tom wanted to go to Shakin' Stevie's for breakfast, then fuck the diet.

'They came to see me too.' Tom swung round on his stool so his knees were pressing into the outside of Simon's thigh. It would have hurt if it hadn't felt good too. 'You don't think I had anything to do with it, do you, Si? All I did was let her out the back door so nobody'd see her. How was I to know...?' He swung his legs away again. 'You gonna tell the cops anything? She used to tell you stuff she didn't tell anyone else.'

'Not about that, though.' Simon's chest felt full of putty, something soft that was hardening, expanding, its sharp corners hurting him from the inside. This feeling of losing her was never going to end. She hadn't simply left the room or gone on holiday or away to uni. She was *gone* gone. Forever.

'You'd tell me if you knew, right?' Tom stood up, barging his stool aside.

'You know I would.'

Tom looked at him as if he wasn't sure of him anymore, before striding through the door and out into the Half Moon Centre, heading for the gym, running late for work. They'd been friends for too long to let this drive them apart. Unlikely friends, okay, but friends nonetheless. Through thick and thin. Fat and skinny. Dark and fair. Gay and straight. Ba-boom.

Simon pushed his carton aside, missing Em more than he thought he could ever miss anyone. Too late to tell her now.

# CHAPTER 16

'You recognise this tat?' Shauna Hartlake slapped a photo of Emma's butterfly design onto the desk at Inky Fingers in Anchor Lane.

The tattoo parlour stank of chemicals and – if she wasn't much mistaken – weed, along with sweat and TCP. She loathed these places, daylight obscured by designs plastered on the windows, lamps dimmed except in the cubicles. Tinkling ambient muzak or muted heavy metal.

Inky Fingers was the fourth tattoo studio she'd visited and she was running out of legitimate places to try. She prayed she wouldn't have to start on the dodgy ones.

Kammerun picked up the photo, his stubby fingers covered with a filigree of purple, red and blue, as if he'd stuck his hands in ink-soaked cobwebs. He smacked his lips, taking his time, winding her up and enjoying it. They all did, she knew that. She was tall and broad and built like a brick shithouse but she couldn't use any of that potential power because of what she was: a police officer.

'Butterfly, is it?' Kammerun pushed back his felted Rasta locks. Dreads always looked dirty on white guys, like they couldn't be arsed to wash their hair. Stubble. Bad teeth. More rings along the rim of each ear than she could count, plus a plug the size of a two-pound coin in each lobe.

'Not one of yours, then?' She made to pick the photo up, but he snatched it back again.

'Might be.' He peered at it, held it up to the light.

'C'mon, you're wasting my time. I expected you to recognise the design but if you're not that well-up on who's doing what...'

'Okay, yeah, yeah, it's one of mine.'

A kid came to the door, peeked through the window, face pressed against the glass, a kid of twelve, thirteen. Too young to come in here legally. Kammerun waved him away, shook his head in silent remonstration.

'I've done quite a few of these,' he went on, probably hoping to distract her. The kid went away. Shauna gave him her full attention again. 'Only since Christmas. It was a new design I worked out.

The butterfly's body's like a rose. Some people see the rose first, some people see the butterfly.'

'Who wanted this one?' She leaned over the desk. 'If you want some help remembering, I'll give you a clue. Fifteen-year-old girl. Not a kid who looked old for her age either, so you can't play that one.' She laid a photo of Emma next to the photo of the butterfly tattoo. Emma in her school uniform, butter wouldn't melt...'Okay, Kammerun, what's the fine for underage tattooing – £5,000, plus a record for child abuse?'

'Either way I'm fucked.' He slid off his stool, shoved his bare feet into a pair of wooden sandals and clomped across the shop to a cupboard where he kept paperwork in a carrier bag. 'I'll have to check,' he said over his shoulder. 'You okay to wait?'

A few minutes later he presented her with a dog-eared record book, open at the smeary page for the second week of August. *Butterfly/flower Emma Smith.*

'Chatty little thing, now I think about it,' he said. 'Told me she wanted this done because she was having her picture taken.'

'What, a picture of her arse?' Shauna shoved the record book back to him.

'Only telling you what she said.'

# CHAPTER 17

A blanket of quiet lay over the reference room of Barbury Library, disturbed only when someone shoved a heavy volume along a shelf or spun a creaky display stand in search of a leaflet to scribble on. Every now and again, despite the polite prohibition notices Blu-tacked to every flat surface, a mobile phone pinged into life or played the opening bars of some irritating signature tune.

Trish Whittington slipped into her office, hoping for a few minutes' privacy. Sixteen new emails in her inbox while she'd been on the enquiry desk, only one of which interested her: confirmation from the Charles Lundy Library that she'd been shortlisted for the post of archivist.

'Trish, have you got a minute?'

Her excitement on hold, she looked up to see Selina, one of her library assistants, hovering in the doorway.

'Come in, have a seat.' Trish cleared some old maps off the only other chair in the office and stacked them next to a pile of even older ones.

Oh God, she thought. It's like this at home, a continual chess game, moving one pile of clutter to somewhere else just as cluttered.

'What's up?'

Selina tossed back her heavy black plait. She was twenty but looked younger, her Anglo-Indian heritage evident in her dark colouring. 'I need to take some time off. I know I've got leave left, but I'm saving that for my trip in December.'

My trip. This was the long-awaited, meticulously planned journey Selina was undertaking with her younger sister, Anita: a pilgrimage to India, the country of their father's birth. He'd made all the arrangements himself – before dropping dead in the storeroom behind his paper shop in May. Trish had wept with Selina when she'd heard what happened.

Now instead of Mr Rani taking his daughters to India, the girls would be taking his ashes. They'd be taking him home.

'Is it your mum?' Trish knew Mrs Rani hadn't coped well with her husband's death.

'No, it's Anita, my sister. Term's only just started and she's already bunked off school three times. I need to make sure she goes through those gates every morning and I need to be there to pick her up at the end of the day.'

Trish stared glumly at the diary. 'I was counting on you to do a couple of displays next week. You're so good at that sort of thing.'

Selina resisted the emotional blackmail. 'I know it's difficult, but suppose I broke a leg?'

'And that would help how?'

'If I broke a leg, you'd have to manage, wouldn't you? You must have to allow for contingencies.'

'If you broke a leg – heaven forbid, and please, Selina, don't do it just to prove a point – I'd have to get someone in, but that's different.'

'Why's it different? I'd still not be here. The effect would be the same.'

'Stop, Selina, please!' Trish held both hands up. It was like arguing with Kate. She dreaded her daughter becoming a fully-fledged teenager, bursting with indignation, as argumentative as Selina was now. 'How can you stop Anita going out? You can't lock her up, can you?'

'No, but if I can just get her through the school gates... She's made friends with a girl she met in the Half Moon who introduced her to this boy, and now she's fallen for him big time.'

'Young love!' Trish grinned.

'Yes, but this boy's much older than her. She's only fourteen and he's at least twenty.'

'Ooh.' Not Romeo and Juliet then. No wonder Selina was worried. Trish flipped through the pages of the diary. 'Okay, look – take a couple of days off to see if you can sort things out and then we'll take it from there.'

With a sigh of relief, Selina rushed out of the office.

At lunchtime, Trish was desperate to get out of the building. An almond croissant and a large latte at Caffè Nero were more tempting, and more calming, than the salad sandwich she'd brought from home. A little self-indulgence would hit the spot nicely.

So she'd been shortlisted after all! The Charles Lundy Library had secured funding to employ its first full-time archivist, a three-year contract, accommodation on site. The pay was similar to what she was earning now, but she'd be the first person to take charge of the antiquarian's scholarly papers and books.

The downside? The library was over 150 miles away on the Essex coast.

If she was going to make a move from Barbury, now was an ideal time, before Kate got stuck into her GCSEs. Changing schools would be a wrench but she'd be settled again before she had to start her exams.

Trish's father Ted was still fit and well, a widower now for ten years, his allotment and his voluntary work keeping him busy. Her sister Suki lived a stone's throw away from him so he'd be fine – and Essex wasn't the other side of the world.

She pushed crumbs round her plate, glanced at her watch, drank the last of her latte and hurried out into the bustle of the Half Moon Centre.

Something nagged at her, and not just self-doubt. What about her and Jeff? He'd moved into her life, and her house, for the first half of the year. They'd had some great times together but somehow...

She stopped to gaze into the window of Next. Why did nothing seem relevant to her any longer? Why did it feel as if the world had moved away, moved along, when she hadn't been looking?

Jeff wouldn't commit himself. Couldn't. He and Cathy were married for years until she upped and left him for some guy she met at a political rally. They'd been living apart for a year or more before she died but Jeff still blamed himself for how things turned out, even though he said he didn't. Trish was tired of trying to compete with Cathy's memory, but unless Jeff could let go of his guilt, could forgive himself, he'd never be happy with anyone else.

Anyway, wouldn't he have called, if he still wanted them to be together? She hadn't heard a word since she and Kate got back from their stay in France.

And now this job had come up – on the other side of the country.

She was heading back to the library when she heard a commotion outside Carphone Warehouse.

'Let me have it!' a girl was shouting. 'Fucking let me have it!'

The sight of two girls tussling over a carrier bag made her look more closely. It was a pale pink bag, stiff paper with braid handles, from Tarara, the fancy new boutique next to M & Co.

Her eyes shifted from the bag to the two girls fighting over it.

Selina! And that must be Anita, smaller, chunkier, but seemingly stronger because she yanked the carrier bag right out of Selina's grasp – only to be rewarded with a slap that resounded across the mall.

A moment's pause, and Anita was charging away into the crowd, her Tarara carrier bag clutched to her chest.

# CHAPTER 18

'Reckon this is the right place?' Woody followed Lincoln round the car, treading carefully. A second car pulled up behind them, spilling three uniforms keen to make an arrest.

'This is where the Crane boy said Arlo James has his happenings.' Lincoln held up the battered sign lying on top of a gate pillar: "Mayday Farm".

The farm was little more than a cobbled yard littered with straw. Whiskery rosebay willow herb, gone to seed, wavered against broken walls. Swifts zipped in and out of the roofless ruins of stables that stood on three sides. Underfoot lay a mass of smashed roof tiles, shattered glass and splintered woodwork. Weeds sprouted from crumbling mortar. Gutters dangled, doors hung askew, electric wires trailed dead across empty window frames.

No sign of life. No sign of a car.

Woody stopped, hands on hips, looking round. 'Doesn't seem to be much *happening* here today.'

'Ha ha.'

Tom had told them a dozen or so youngsters attended Arlo's happenings. He was particular about who kept him company and shared his booze, so you got invited through someone who already belonged to that circle. Yes, Tom said, some people had sex there but it wasn't like an orgy and it was always discreet.

And presumably safe, Lincoln thought, noting the number of discarded condoms lurking in the grass. His own teenage years had been a lot less fun. He crunched over cola cans, takeaway trays, plastic drinks bottles. Cigarette butts dotted the ground.

'So where's the great man himself?'

They picked their way into another yard, overlooked by three dilapidated red brick cottages. The only one with a door also had a blue tarpaulin stretched over its open rafters, as if someone was in the process of doing the place up – though in an amateur, improvised way, renovation in instalments. No one could be living here.

Beyond the dented water butt and the outdoor privy, an old greenhouse stood smashed and derelict. Once upon a time, the tenants of these farm cottages would have tended vegetable plots, grown soft fruit and apples, kept a few chickens or geese. But now, the beds lay barren except for weeds.

'Hello?' Lincoln yelled, his hands cupped round his mouth. His voice echoed back to him. *Lo lo lo.* 'Arlo James?' *James James James.* 'Anybody home?' *Home home home.* They waited a minute or two. Silence.

'I think that's a "no",' said Woody.

'How long have you worked with Inspector Lincoln?'

At the sound of Bella's disembodied voice, Pam looked round the CID room, unsure if it was she who was being addressed. Then she heard the DCI's heavy footfall. She must have strolled out of the cupboard to stretch her legs and top up her oxygen levels.

'Since August last year.' Pam sat back from her computer. 'The first case we worked together was—'

'The Holly Macleod murder. October.'

'That's right.'

'Think he handled it well?'

Pam felt the colour rising in her cheeks. 'He always had his suspicions about the husband, even though everyone kept telling him he was barking up the wrong tree. And he was right, wasn't he?'

'This case, though – no obvious suspect, is there?'

'Not yet. I can't get a measure of the home set-up, Emma and her mother.'

'How d' you mean?' Bella parked herself on the next desk, interested.

'Not sure Crystal's telling us everything. I went back to ask her about Arlo and to see if she thought Emma was being bullied, but she just seemed shocked at the very idea of her daughter doing anything without telling her. We should talk to Crystal's sister, see if she can tell us anything more.'

'Then what are you waiting for?' Bella headed back to her desk. 'While Lincoln's up in the woods playing cowboys and Indians, you might as well go over to Whitpenny and talk to her. Take Dilke. A bit of fresh air should put a bit of colour in his cheeks.'

Less than an hour later, Pam and Dilke pulled up outside Riverside in Brook Lane, Whitpenny, next to a van with *"Penn Property Services, T. Tremlow"* on the side. A steep flight of steps led up to a shabby front door.

'You found us all right, then?' Tania ushered them indoors. 'Like I said on the phone, this village is a bit of a maze.'

Her husband was on the phone in the study, she said, but he'd be with them as soon as he'd finished.

As Tania led the way into the sitting room, they passed the kitchen, and Pam caught a glimpse of the daughter, Stephanie, sitting in a high-backed chair, kicking feebly against the table leg. A bib covered the expanse of her chest and stomach. Hearing her mother and the visitors go by, she turned her face towards the door, her expression blank, her eyes dark and still. Mouth messy with food, she looked like an enormous baby in an oversized high chair.

Pam hurried to catch up with Dilke, and they were soon settled into armchairs either side of the fireplace.

Tania sank onto the sofa. 'Now then, how can we help?'

'We're trying to trace Emma's friends, especially any recent ones.'

She frowned. 'I'm not sure I'd know. Something was said about a boyfriend but I think my sister put a stop to it.'

'You remember any of the details – his name, when this was?'

'I only know he sent her some dirty photos, with his phone. What do they call it? Taking pictures of their you-know-whats and sending the photos to each other?'

'Sexting?' Pam made a note. Odd that Crystal hadn't said anything. 'Are you sure?'

'I'm only telling you what Crystal told me, but perhaps she got it wrong. She doesn't get out much.'

A phone was slammed down in another room, and Todd Tremlow appeared in the doorway, pausing on the threshold as if bracing himself to walk onstage.

'Good afternoon.' He crossed to the window, stood looking down towards the road. 'You've probably got lots of questions about Emma and what she got up to, but I'm not sure we can tell you much.'

He turned round, a tubby man not quite as tall as Dilke, dapper in a navy suit, pink shirt, red tie. He'd have looked smart, Pam thought, except his clothes weren't quite expensive enough, the jacket too tight across the shoulders, the trouser legs half an inch too short. He'd undone the top button of his shirt and loosened his tie. He looked like a commercial traveller at the end of a long journey, a salesman who'd failed to meet his target.

'When did you last see Emma?' she asked.

Tremlow pulled a wooden chair out and sat down at the table in the window bay, steepling his fingers. 'Sadly, not for some little while. Crystal, Tania's sister, lost her husband even before Emma was born and we always felt, didn't we...?' He broke off to look to his wife for corroboration. 'We always felt that Crystal was overly protective, that they were unnaturally close.'

'You think that has something to do with Emma's disappearance?'

'I think it explains why our niece became...secretive, shall we say?' Another glance at his wife as if to check he wasn't overstepping the mark. 'Behaved perhaps in an underhand way.'

'Underhand? You mean not telling her mum she was seeing someone?'

'Exactly. That boy in the photo. That boy she was seeing. I expect it was him. I mean, who else would it be?'

'You think the relationship was serious?' Dilke asked. 'If Emma confided in either of you, then you need to tell us.'

'No, no.' Tremlow shook his head. 'Mind, she could be a little minx if she was crossed.'

His wife agreed. 'Can't all teenagers! That's one good thing with Stephanie – she's never going to be bringing boys home!' Sadness fluttered across her face. 'She'll always be our little girl, Stephie will. Crystal couldn't accept that Emma was growing up, wanting to spread her wings. She couldn't keep her under lock and key forever.'

'That's a figure of speech,' her husband hurried to point out. 'I don't think my sister-in-law actually...' He loosened his tie a little more. 'I wish we could do something to help. As my wife's no doubt told you, we haven't seen a lot of Crystal and Emma in the last few months.'

'Did you fall out?' Dilke wondered.

'No, not exactly but...people go their separate ways, don't they?' said Tania. 'Even families. And it's been hard for us to go over there, what with Stephanie.'

'Shame, but there it is.' Todd Tremlow's gaze drifted towards a photo on the top shelf of the dresser beside the fireplace. 'We used to be such a tight little set.'

Pam held her hand out. 'May I see that photo?'

Tania got up and fetched it down, rubbing her palm over the dusty glass. 'That was taken, what, a year ago?' She looked to her husband before passing it across to Pam.

Emma looked much as she had done in her school photo: wide-eyed, innocent. Behind her, their arms linked across her shoulders, stood her aunt and uncle, beaming heartily. For once, she looked natural, unposed.

'Summer before last,' Tremlow said. 'Took her to Weymouth for the day. She loved that. Ice creams on the beach.'

'We stopped on the way back and put the rug down, didn't we? I'd made a flask, done some sandwiches. More than my sister ever did.'

There was a moment's quiet, then Dilke said, 'Can we borrow that picture?'

'We'd get it back to you as soon as we could,' Pam promised, seeing Tania hesitate.

'All right.' The Tremlows watched Pam tuck it carefully into her bag. 'Yes, such a tight little set,' Tania echoed. 'We still send cards the way we've always done, phone every now and again. But let's just say we no longer feel welcome at the house.'

Pam recalled the way Crystal had shied away from Tania in the kitchen. Was she a little ashamed of her overweight, unpretentious sister and her husband?

'Todd planned this smashing birthday surprise in January,' Tania went on, 'when Emma turned fifteen. He got tickets for *The Nutcracker*, she always liked that, and it was one of the big dance companies, at Presford Palais. He even booked a table at Pizza Express for afterwards, because she was always on about going somewhere grown-up to eat. He knew she'd be thrilled.'

She looked across at her husband, who was staring to one side, out of the window.

'But when he drove up to collect her,' she continued, her voice rising, 'Crystal came to the door and said Emma couldn't go, didn't *want* to go, was going out with some friends from school. And do you know, she didn't even let the kid come to the door so Todd could wish her happy birthday. In my book, that's cruel, that is. Downright cruel.'

'Can we get you people some tea?' Tremlow offered, his hands spread beseechingly, as if to shift the subject away from his humiliation. 'We're not being very hospitable, are we?'

Five minutes later, they were chatting over tea and a plate of digestives.

'Emma never knew her father,' Tania said. 'Derek died some months before she was born.'

'Tragic.' Todd Tremlow bit into a biscuit. Half of it plopped into his cup, splashing him with tea. 'They'd been together all that time and then just as everything's working out for them...' He dabbed at his shirt and tie, making things worse.

'What was Derek's job?' Dilke reached for a second digestive.

'Building trade to start with.' Tremlow peered sadly at his ruined tie. 'Like me. Except I moved into the rental market, better hours and no need for a hard hat!' He chuckled. 'We talked about going into business together but I couldn't get him interested in the sort of schemes I fancied. He teamed up with another fella in the end, got more into the planning side. Made a packet.'

'Donal Finnegan?' Pam asked.

'That's right. He hasn't done badly for himself, either, has Donal!' An envious grimace.

'What happened to the business when Derek died?'

'He let Donal buy him out before he got too ill to know what he was doing. Always liked to do things properly, Derek.' He went on rubbing at his tie, his tea slopping into his saucer.

'Made sure he left it in safe hands.' Tania watched her husband with – what? Disapproval? Pity? Pam couldn't tell.

'So your sister's been well provided for?'

'Oho, yes!' Tania hooted. 'She'll never have to worry where the next penny's coming from!' As if the Tremlows did.

'You said about Crystal being overprotective,' Dilke said. 'Was that why she made Emma keep her computer downstairs?'

Another furtive exchange of looks between husband and wife. 'Crystal didn't want her *spoiled*,' Tania said. 'These rude pictures someone sent her...they really shocked her.'

'Shocked who? Crystal or Emma?'

'Take a lot to shock young Emma!' Tremlow began to laugh, but then he stopped. 'Er, no – it was Tania's sister that was shocked. She's led a very sheltered life.'

'Lives on her nerves, my sister. Always has done, even when we were kids. Highly strung, I suppose you'd say.'

'Does she have a job?'

'Used to work for me,' Tremlow said. 'When Emma was small. Accounts. She could do it from home. But I've got a company looks after the financial side of things these days. Maybe she's doing figure work for somebody else...?'

Tania pursed her lips. 'She keeps the house very clean. Doesn't like anything out of place.'

'But she and Emma always got on well?' Pam persisted. 'You know what teenage girls can be like!' Except the Tremlows didn't, not really.

'She doted on Emma,' Tania said. 'Worshipped the ground she walked on. But you can have too much of a good thing, can't you? She wanted to wrap her up in cotton wool in case anything happened to her, but what kind of life is that for either of them?' She plonked her cup in its saucer. 'A good mother knows when to let go. Though as we told you, we haven't had a lot to do with either of them for a while.'

'And Mr Finnegan – he's always been close to them?'

Tania's tone turned suddenly chilly. 'They were all very close at one time. Maisie Finnegan and Emma are the same age, you see, and they were best friends when they were small. But they fell out, as girls do, and Emma changed schools and that was that. I'm not surprised he's been round there since Emma went missing. Donal Finnegan likes you to see him coming to the rescue. I'm sure we all know men like that.'

# CHAPTER 19

'Shouldn't you be in school?' Arlo lifted the spliff away, passed it to Lady, tipped his head back.

'Told you, I'm starting college. Term don't start yet.' She didn't care if she never saw another classroom, another textbook, for as long as she lived. This was what she wanted: days with Arlo, lazing on cushions in his caravan, sunshine trickling over her body, a breeze lifting tendrils of hair from her face...

'Your mum know what you get up to?'

'Sure she can guess. Not exactly a model student herself.'

'Skiver?' He took the spliff back.

'Probably. Got pregnant when she was fifteen. Had me.'

'Younger than me, then.' He smiled round his smoke.

'I've always liked older men.' She lay beside him on the narrow bed. 'They're so much more experienced.'

Arlo shut his eyes. Such long lashes, curly at the outer corners. He was beautiful. 'I've certainly got experience.' He held the spliff up in the air, beyond her reach. Stretching for it, giggling, she rolled on top of him.

'We could do it now. I like being on top.' Her hair hung down over his face. Her blouse gaped open, her breasts falling forward towards his chest, the gap in his shirt. Between her legs, she felt him harden against his fly, the heat of him setting her on fire. She reached down to his belt, tugged at the buckle, trying to wrench the leather tongue through it, to get him undone, free him—

'No,' he said softly, a gasp, 'not yet.' He threw his head back, moved rhythmically against her, exciting her so much she came without him even touching her with his fingers.

'Oh!' She shut her eyes, spread herself against him.

He held her, the spliff abandoned, strong arms hugging her until she was still again, her breathing slow, her heartbeat quiet once more. Her cheeks burned. She pressed her face into the soft crevice at the base of his throat. She wanted to lick his skin, to suck on him, to eat him. He smelt of salt and earth and caramel and wood smoke and musk and the end of summer.

'I love you.' She was scared he'd let her go if she didn't declare herself immediately.

'I know,' he said, holding her tighter. 'I know.'

# CHAPTER 20

'Where've Pam and Dilke got to?' Lincoln looked round the deserted CID room, reminded once more that he was no longer in charge.

'They're talking to the Sherman girl's aunt and uncle.' Bella came out of her cupboard. Even above the clacking of her keyboard, she could hear all that was going on beyond her half-open door. 'You found Arlo James?'

'We found where he has his get-togethers but there was nobody home.' He dropped his phone and keys onto his desk, slipped his coat off and hung it up. 'I don't rate him as a serious suspect, though. Sounds too disorganised.'

She raised an eyebrow. 'The Crane boy seemed certain enough.'

'Not sure how reliable Tom is. He didn't come forward when she went missing but then he waltzes in here this morning, telling us what he should have told us days ago. He's probably given us a name, *any* name, to make up for it.'

'Anything better to go on? We need to be seen to be doing something. We'll follow this Arlo James lead until we've exhausted it. Okay?' She turned on her heel and strode back to her lair.

It was ridiculous, pursuing Arlo simply to keep the press office and the bosses happy. Lincoln had a good mind to ignore her, concentrating on the phone records and the family background instead – but then Woody put a mug of coffee on his desk, raised his own cup to his lips and said, 'How about asking Trish about Arlo? There's not much she doesn't know about local heroes and villains.'

And if local history librarian Trish didn't know the answer herself, she usually knew someone who did.

This time, though, Lincoln hesitated before picking up the phone. His last exchange with Trish, in the middle of July, had not gone well.

A dull, sultry day at the start of the school holidays, and he'd let himself into her house to find her packing suitcases.

'Going somewhere?'

'We've been invited to Vanda's for the summer.' She hadn't looked up from sorting clothes. 'Me and Kate. You'll be okay, won't you?'

'Bit out of the blue, isn't it?'

'Not really.' She folded a T-shirt he'd never seen before: emerald green, a brighter colour than she usually wore. 'We've been talking about going over there for ages.'

'Over where?'

'South of France. I need some sunshine. We both do, me and Kate.'

No suggestion that he too might need some sunshine, might like to come with them, might like to get away.

As if.

'How long for?' He'd fiddled with the spare set of keys she let him keep even after he'd moved out.

'Don't be a drag, Jeff.'

'I'm asking, that's all.'

'It's the *way* you ask, as if I'm not entitled to my own life.'

'What? When have I ever said—'

'Can you let me have those keys back? I need to leave them with Rula next door while we're away.'

He'd flung the keys onto the kitchen table and they'd skimmed across the polished surface and onto the floor. He hadn't stayed to pick them up.

'Boss?' Woody's voice dragged him back to the present. 'I said, shall I give Trish a ring, see if she can help us pin Arlo down?'

'I'll do it.'

Part of him hoped she wouldn't answer, but after a couple of rings, Trish picked up.

'Lucky you phoned,' she said warmly, as if their unpleasant parting in July had never happened. 'I need your advice on something. Everything okay?'

'Fine, fine... We're trying to locate a bloke called Arlo James. Know anything about him?'

'Arlo? Why do you need to find Arlo?'

'You've heard of him?'

'Of course I've heard of him! I grew up in Barbury, remember? Come round to the library, but don't be late because I'm off at five.'

He put the phone down as Shauna Hartlake came in.

'I've traced that tattoo of Emma's. Inky Fingers. She had it done at the beginning of August, paid cash. Tramp stamps, that's what they call them when they're below your knicker line. She told the guy she was having her picture taken.'

Lincoln grinned wryly. 'Presumably not just head and shoulders.'

'That's what I thought. She was with two boys – from the

descriptions, the Crane boy and that fat lad from Board Treaders – Simon, was it?'

Simon Lovelock lived in the unlovely Crowley Close (a "scheme", the street sign called it) on the edge of the Barbury Down estate. The houses, with their quaint concrete scallop-shell porches and big coal sheds, were among the oldest local authority properties in the town, but they'd always bear the stigma of being 'council', even those that had been bought through Right To Buy and done up.

Dilke and Shauna cruised slowly past a whole row of run-down houses and maisonettes, with churned-up gardens and souped-up cars, satellite dishes and decaying masonry, until they found Simon's house, Number 37.

An England flag, yellowing, torn, hung down from the bedroom windowsill of Number 35. The front garden had been dug over and left, a quilt of dried mud. The front garden of Number 39 was a jungle of overgrown pampas grass, bamboo and fir trees, a slaughtered armchair upside down on the doorstep.

In between them, Simon's garden had a neat lawn and a row of Michaelmas daisies beneath the front room windowsill.

They got out of the car and headed down the concrete path. Canned laughter and applause blared from a television, and cooking smells hung in the air: baked beans, chips, fried bread. After a minute or two, a woman in her late sixties came to the door, waddling back down the hall to the kitchen when they asked for Simon.

'He's out back.' She nodded towards the long garden with a shed at the end of it, then puffed and panted back to her show.

Simon was crouching over a flower bed, weeding, his clothes straining to contain him.

'Hello,' said Dilke. 'Remember me?'

The boy stood up clumsily, brushing his hands down the thighs of his tracksuit pants. 'Oh, yeah, you came to drama group.' His face was red and shiny, and he was out of breath.

'Got your nan living with you?' Shauna glanced back at the house.

'I live with her. My mum died. Nan's brung me up. It's just the two of us. She put in for a bungalow because she can't manage the stairs any longer, but she hasn't got enough points.'

'You got a bathroom downstairs?'

He made a face. 'Outside toilet hasn't worked in years but she's got a commode in there for now. Been waiting ages for them to fix the cistern. They won't let you fix it yourself. Thought going over to a housing association'd make things better but it's ten times worse.' He sounded like a grumpy old man.

'Bloody unfair,' Shauna agreed. 'You rent, you're expected to put up with anything, eh?'

Dilke noted the compost bin, the water butt, the shed with a newish-looking padlock securing it. Probably a fair bit of petty theft round here, so you'd need to keep things locked up. These little estates, if it's not nailed down, someone'll have off with it, flog it down the pub, out the back of a car boot: tools, stone frogs, benches, barbeque kits. 'So who's the gardener?'

'That's me. I like growing things.' He paused. 'You here about Emma?'

'We heard you two were good friends, through Board Treaders – is that right?' Shauna pulled a few leaves off a blackcurrant bush, shredded them casually. 'She didn't have many friends, did she?'

'No, but that wasn't her fault. She came across as full of it, but she was shy, really. People just got her wrong.'

'Not popular though, was she?'

'The other girls were jealous, that's all. The first time she came to Board Treaders, she wore a leotard and leggings, and proper dance shoes, and all the other girls were in jeans. Nobody'd told her it was kind of casual. And then Miss Darricott, the drama teacher, was all over her and the other girls didn't like that. I used to tell Em it wasn't personal, but she took it to heart, and then she'd sulk a bit and everyone thought she was a moody cow. She couldn't win.'

Shauna raised her eyebrows. 'So how come you and Tom got on with her so well?'

He shrugged. 'She didn't show off when she was with us. She was just herself. Me and Tom, we were teaching her to be normal.'

'Normal?'

'Ordinary.' He rubbed a pudgy hand over his forehead. 'It was good fun, doing things together, showing her what she'd been missing out on.'

'Like getting her bum tattooed?'

'It was only a little tattoo.'

'It was illegal.'

Simon flushed so deep a puce Dilke thought his face was going to burst. 'She wanted to be her own person, that's all. Her mum treated her like a kid. Like, with her hair, she wanted her to keep it long, but Em hated it so she had it cut, had streaks put in. Her mum went ballistic.'

Dilke could imagine.

'She told the tattoo guy she was having her picture taken,' Shauna said. 'What was that about?'

'All the big stars get tats, don't they?'

'Did she tell you she had a photo shoot lined up?'

Simon shook his head, his blush dying down. 'Suppose she wanted to be ready in case things took off.'

'Someone told us she was involved with Arlo James. Is that what you'd heard?'

'Arlo?'

Shauna took her chewing gum out, inspected it, shoved it back in again. 'Your friend Tom told us that's who she was meeting Thursday night.'

Simon seemed genuinely bemused. 'Think he's got that wrong. She went to Arlo's farm, to one of his happenings, but that's all. She liked his music, thought he was cool. He sings this really morbid folk stuff, like kind of Bob Dylan, only worse?'

Shauna sniffed. 'I like Dylan.'

'Yeah, but he's old.'

'You think she was having sex with Arlo?'

'Never talked about it.' He looked down at the grassy path, dabbed at a loose clod of earth with his toe.

'You weren't curious?' Dilke wondered.

Another rush of blood. 'That's not how we were. We respected each other's privacy.' Simon looked back towards the house. 'You don't even know if it was Arlo she was seeing, do you?'

'Not for sure, no. We heard someone was sexting her.'

'Dirty pictures, you mean? She never said.'

The back door opened, and his gran peered down the garden towards them. 'Everything all right?'

'Fine, Nan. Be in soon.'

The door banged shut.

'Simon, if someone sent Emma rude photos—'

'No, no, nobody did. Honest.'

'When you heard she'd gone missing, what did you think?' Shauna asked. 'That she'd run off with Arlo?'

'Fuck, no! He's twice her age.'

'What, then?'

'That she was staying with someone, to wind her mum up.'

Dilke didn't believe him. 'You thought she'd stay away for three whole nights? Knowing how her mum was? Did that sound like the Emma you knew?'

Simon shrugged. 'She was private about lots of things. There must've been lots about her I didn't know.' He bent down to retrieve his trowel from the flower bed. What had neat and pretty Emma seen in this lard-arse of a boy?

'She tell you what was wrong with her mum?'

'Nerves, she said. She had to stick to all these rules or everything would fall apart.' He picked damp soil off the scoop of the trowel. 'I understood, see, living with Nan. But Em never let it get to her. Other girls were jealous of her, but if they only knew what it was like for her...'

'Someone sent her a photo that was in *The Messenger*. They'd written something nasty on it, marked her face. Did she tell you about that?'

He bit his lip. 'Was that a photo of when she was little?'

Dilke and Shauna exchanged a look. 'It was the Vox Pop feature in July. Didn't you see it?'

'Oh, that.'

'You know who sent it?'

'No. She never said. But then she wouldn't. Must've upset her.'

'That's what we thought.' Dilke watched the boy's face. 'You can't think who she might've fallen out with – someone at Board Treaders, maybe?'

Simon shook his head. 'She wasn't one of the gang, but I don't think any of the girls would do anything like that.'

'Before we go – where were you Thursday night?'

'Me? Here, with Nan, same as every night. She needs me around if she needs the toilet – I can't even get a job until she gets a bungalow or a ground-floor flat. And you can ask her if I was here but she won't be able to tell you for certain because she loses track. You'll have to take my word for it.'

He held Dilke's gaze, defiant. Then he pushed between them, lumbering knock-kneed up the path towards the house.

# CHAPTER 21

The very air inside Barbury Library was stultifying. Even the rows of laptops with their jolly screensavers did little to liven things up. No wonder all the customers looked like zombies.

Lincoln let himself into Trish's office. He could smell Chanel No. 5. He'd given her the body lotion at Christmas, loved the way the heat of her body warmed the perfume, brought out all the notes... His pulse quickened, though he tried to ignore it.

She looked up from her cluttered desk. 'So...what do you want to know about Arlo?'

He hadn't expected to be smothered in kisses, but a welcoming smile would've been nice, or even a hug. He was more convinced than ever that something had happened in France – she'd met someone, or she'd stayed with someone other than her old friend Vanda.

'I need to track him down. We were told he lived up at Mayday Farm but all it's fit for is his boozy parties. The buildings are in ruins.'

'Boozy parties?' She grinned, resting her chin in her hand. 'That sounds like the Arlo I used to know.'

'Exactly how well did you know this bloke?'

'Arlo James was the nearest thing this town had to a rock star when I was at school. He was only a couple of years older than me and my friends.' Her eyes sparkled. 'We used to hang around on the swings in the park near his school, hoping to cadge a smile from him on his way home. Nothing's happened to him, has it?'

'And did you?'

'Did I what?'

'Cadge a smile?'

'I was fourteen and at the grammar school. Arlo was in the sixth form at Devlin Hall. Always had some girl or other from St Anthony's hanging off him – and you know what they say about convent girls.' She sighed. 'So is he in some sort of trouble?'

'His name's come up, that's all. The local kids hang out with him up at the farm – sex and drugs and...folk songs.'

'That sounds like Arlo. The parties I went to when I was at school, he was always there in the shadows, guitar close at hand, smoking dope with all his fans round him.'

'Fans?'

'Followers. Some people have a certain charisma, don't they? They walk into a room and instantly it's the best place to be. They walk out and everything goes flat.'

'Was he into drugs in those days?'

'He smoked weed. All those Devlin House boys did – probably easier to get hold of than booze back then! Arlo used to act stoned even when he wasn't, just so people would leave him alone.' She paused. 'What more can I tell you? He went away to uni, dropped out, came home to the family pile.'

'Which is?'

'Was. Beechcombe Manor, on the road to Devizes. Some corporate HQ now. His father probably sold it to pay off his debts. Not sure where he lives these days. Although...' She rose and crossed to a heap of newspapers on top of a cupboard. 'There was something in *The Messenger* a few weeks ago...'

Lincoln watched her back view as she lifted a few issues of the local newspaper aside, the muscles in her calves flexing as she shifted her balance, her skirt tight over her bum. Wanting her was like a thirst. His mouth was dry as oatmeal.

'How was France?'

'Seems like years ago now.' She didn't look round.

'Kate enjoy it?'

'Loved it. Talking French all the time, even now. Driving me up the wall, actually.'

He wanted to go on asking her about France, to find out if she'd met someone else, but she said briskly, 'Here you are – the issue for the first week of June.'

She flung open a double-page spread full of grainy black-and-white photos from thirty years ago.

"*Battle of the Beanfield*!" the headline blared. "*First of June 1985 – looking back to the day we hung our heads in shame!*" The feature was by Ian Marston.

A convoy of New Age travellers, on their way in caravans and buses to set up a free festival at Stonehenge, ran into police who'd been tasked with stopping them from getting within four miles of the historic stones.

When the travellers showed no sign of leaving the fields where they'd pitched camp, the police launched a pre-emptive strike, beating mothers and children with truncheons, and dragging pregnant women out of their caravans. Even though dozens of travellers witnessed these acts of police brutality, it took over six years for the victims to be vindicated. *The Messenger's* collage of archive photos and news clippings made shameful reading.

Lincoln looked up from the newspaper. 'But what's the Battle of the Beanfield got to do with Arlo James? He was hardly out of short trousers in 1985.'

'His father, Hugo, spoke up for the travellers, criticised police tactics, called them thugs with truncheons. Which they were.' She held her hands up. 'Just saying. You only have to look at cases like Ian Tomlinson, the police getting over-zealous when they're in a crowd situation—'

'Trish, no one was *killed* at the Battle of the Beanfield.'

'Maybe not, but you can't deny that the police used excessive force. All the travellers wanted to do was celebrate the start of summer at Stonehenge, but the police were out to stop them, whatever it took. Loads of people got hurt and your lot lost the public's sympathy.'

'My lot? Come on, half those coppers weren't even local. And you know as well as I do, journalists can never wait to have a go at us. Any other time, New Age travellers, crusties, hippies – they're scum of the earth.'

'Yes, well, you didn't come here to have a political debate, did you?' She took a big breath. 'Look – Arlo.' She pointed to a photo in a sidebar next to the main article.

Above a few lines about "what the Beanfield meant for my family", Arlo James grinned out. Late thirties, long dark hair, black eyebrows, a sensual mouth.

Even in this low-resolution photo, he exuded roguishness.

Lincoln could see the appeal, sort of. He remembered his own schooldays, when buccaneering boys like Arlo – rough, wild, swaggering – had girls swarming round them. Never mind that boys like that were heading for trouble – their allure was hard to explain, impossible to resist.

'And there's Hugo, Arlo's father.' A photo from 1985: a wild-haired man trying to reason with a truncheon-raising policeman. 'He was hit over the head during the Battle of the Beanfield and lost the hearing in one ear.'

At last Lincoln remembered Hugo James, the loony aristo. Always in the Sunday papers, money troubles, sex scandals. Then he cleaned up his act, found God in nature, and became an environmentalist, a bit of a hippy.

'Married a model, didn't he, or a starlet?' He could see Mrs Hugo James in his mind's eye, her long legs, coppery hair and outrageous outfits.

'That's right, Arlo's mother. Marietta Something. She killed herself while he was still at school. Hugo moved abroad years ago – not sure he ever came back. Arlo seems to share his father's political views but not much else.'

'None of this helps me find him.' The more he read about him, the more Lincoln doubted Arlo James was Emma Sherman's killer, but until he tracked him down and interviewed him, he couldn't rule him out.

'If you'd bothered to read to the end of the article…' Trish tapped the final couple of paragraphs.

Autumn will see Arlo James return to the semi-derelict farm he's restoring single-handed. Casual gardening jobs keep him going through the spring and summer, and he busks in the town centre.

Isn't this a bit of a comedown for the son of the Beanfield hero? *'I'd have it no other way,'* he insists. *'It's the simple life for me.'*

These days, while dad Hugo rubs shoulders with California's glitterati, Arlo, 38, lives in a caravan at Pine Point, in the middle of Greywood Forest near Barbury. A simple life indeed!

'Bullshit!' Lincoln pushed the newspaper away impatiently. 'So we should be up in the woods looking for a caravan, if we don't trip over him playing Donovan songs outside the Co-op.'

'I should've stayed in France,' Trish groaned, gathering the newspapers up again. 'Photocopy the article while I finish up here.'

A few minutes later, she was shoving him ahead of her out of the reference library, keen to get away. She paused to slip her jacket on and without thinking, he helped her on with it, letting his hands linger on her shoulders, smoothing the fabric.

'Thanks.' A quick smile as she pulled away. 'You know where Pine Point is, don't you? Where Arlo parks his caravan?'

'It could be a house or a hole in the ground for all I know.' He followed her down the wide staircase.

'Used to be a campsite years ago. Suki went up there all the time when she was in the Guides.'

'You weren't in the Guides?'

'You must be joking! I got chucked out of Brownies for being too disruptive.' She pushed the double doors open, stepped outside. 'Sure you can't tell me why you want to speak to him? I wouldn't say anything.'

'You know I can't.'

'Has something happened to him?' She stopped on the pavement, people having to sidestep her.

'No, but we need to find him. Apart from his father, has he got any family?'

'Not really. His brother, Kit, died when they were in their twenties. Arlo got married a couple of times. Not sure the second one was official. The wedding involved walking through an arch of oleanders or over a bed of hot coals – I forget which. No one could accuse him of being conventional!'

'Sounds as if you're still a little in love with him.'

She grinned wryly and started to walk. 'Arlo James was the local bad boy. With money. Fatal combination. We all thought he'd get a recording contract or make experimental films – something shocking but artistic.'

'So what went wrong?'

'He went off the rails when his mother died. She killed herself. He left uni, came home and sort of disappeared. Until I saw that bit in the paper, I thought he'd moved to the States with Hugo. Either that, or the drugs had caught up with him, the way they caught up with Kit – accidental overdose at twenty-four.' She stopped again, looking up at him appealingly. 'I don't know what you think he's done, but Arlo was never bad. Subversive, yes, a bit of a headcase, but he was never *bad*.'

'You knew him twenty years ago, Trish. People change.'

'Their circumstances do, but not their natures. Arlo's a good man.'

'We'll see. Got time for a coffee?'

'Sorry, I need to get back. Kate's got piano tonight. Maybe some other time?' And she headed for the car park.

As he lost sight of her, he remembered she'd said she needed his advice on something too. He'd been so intent on finding out about Arlo James that he hadn't given her problems a second thought.

He texted her: *U wanted some advice?*

Her reply buzzed back: *CU @ liby tomorrow 12pm. Tell U then.*

He smiled to himself. Whatever had happened in France, or whoever she'd met, they were still friends.

Lincoln had scarcely had time to sit down at his desk when Pam came over to him.

'We should talk to Crystal Sherman again,' she said. 'According to her sister, she already knew a boy was sexting Emma. All that shock-horror when she saw the photo of her and Tom together was an act.'

'Do the house-to-house tomorrow morning, see what you can pick up from the neighbours first, then go and see her.' He went over to the area map on the wall. 'You know where Pine Point is?'

'The old Scout camp? There's a road up to it from Speldon Magna.' She came over and poked a speck on the edge of Greywood Forest. 'Single-track, unclassified, enough room at the end to park a few cars. I've cycled round that way a few times. Why?'

'It's where Arlo James parks his caravan.' Lincoln traced the dotted lines of an unmetalled road, about a mile long, passing Mayday Farm and the old Scout camp before it petered out into a drove road through the forest. He'd been a keen weekend walker until a few years ago, and he really ought to take it up again. His old boots must be somewhere... 'Looks as if there's a track between Pine Point and his farm.'

'Yes, but he'd need an all-terrain vehicle to drive along it. We don't know what he drives but he probably didn't pick Emma up on a quad bike!'

'First thing in the morning, then, take Shauna and Dilke to Folly Hill Crescent, talk to the neighbours, find out all you can. Me and Woody will go in search of Arlo James.'

She grinned. 'You might need your wellingtons.'

Two hours later, Bella came marching in after a strategy meeting with DCS Youngman at Park Street. She disappeared into her cubbyhole, with no signs of flagging despite the late hour. She draped her jacket over the back of her chair and came out again.

'Still no luck finding Arlo?'

Lincoln directed her towards the map of Greywood Forest he'd stuck up next to the whiteboard. 'He parks his caravan at an old Scout camp. We'll go up there first thing tomorrow. Except, after finding out a bit more about him, I'm even less convinced he's a likely suspect.'

'For fuck's sake! He's a man of forty who's living rough, throwing drug-fuelled orgies and having sex with underage girls. What makes you think we've got this wrong?'

'I found some background material at the library and—'

'You put too much faith in what your librarian friend tells you. I read the file on the Holly Macleod case. Your Ms Whittington nearly derailed the whole investigation because the chief suspect was a mate of hers. Divided loyalties are dangerous. Did she tell you Arlo's father's got a record? Old Harrovian he may be, son of a baronet or whatever, but Hugo James was jailed for assault in 1986.'

'The Battle of the Beanfield?'

'Exactly! Assaulting a police officer. Criminal damage. Endangering life. Resisting arrest. He might be landed gentry, but Hugo James has got a violent streak.'

'Maybe we should be looking at Hugo for this, then, instead of his son.'

Bella's face clouded. 'You are sailing incredibly close to the wind, Inspector. I wasn't joking when I suggested you review your own career options when you're giving due consideration to Dennis Breeze's.'

With that, she spun round, stalked back to her cupboard and slammed the door. A moment later, probably realising it was her only means of ventilation, she cracked it open again, settling down to put in another couple of hours before she knocked off and went home.

Lincoln wouldn't keep her company for long.


At Presford General, weakened by years of drug and alcohol abuse, Liam Coe's heart failed him during surgery for the wound in his throat. He didn't regain consciousness. Jacqueline Walsh's charge of attempted murder was upgraded accordingly.

On the other side of Presford, her daughter Lorren was squeezing through the toilet window at her foster home and out onto the flat roof of the extension. In half a minute, she'd clambered down to the ground and was running towards a Ford Fiesta waiting at the kerb.

# CHAPTER 22

When Lincoln got home, lights were once again blazing from the back of Fountains. Two or three people were silhouetted on the patio, chatting and drinking.

He stared out of his French windows, mug of coffee in hand, his own lights off. He'd have to put some curtains up if the new owners planned to outshine every other house in the neighbourhood. In the glare, he caught sight of the stray cat that had taken to sleeping in the old henhouse at the bottom of his garden, tucking itself neatly into one of the few nesting boxes that were still intact. Every chance it got, it tried to get into the Old Vicarage, though once inside, it always turned tail and fled out again. He didn't mind these occasional intrusions, but he really didn't want the bother of looking after a cat. He trusted that some kind soul would take it in.

Losing his privacy dismayed him. For the whole of the summer, with Fountains empty, he'd cherished his seclusion. All that would change now. He wasn't a gregarious man, never would be. Okay, no man is an island, but he quite fancied being a spit of land, only occasionally accessible, on which few strangers set foot.

When he married Cathy, she was the only company he wanted. He lost the knack of making friends. But the marriage didn't last once they'd given up hope of having kids. Then she met someone else and wanted to move out. When she died only a year or so later, he felt as bereft as if they'd still been married, because he'd had no chance to make peace with her.

Trish was the first woman he'd been serious about since Cathy – but was he wrong about her too?

Bella clearly didn't agree with his assessment of Arlo James, but he could hardly blame her: Arlo's was the only name linked with Emma, though how and where they met were still a mystery.

What made him think Arlo was innocent? Gut instinct – and Trish's sympathy for her one-time heart-throb. But if Arlo hadn't killed Emma, who had? Tom Crane's alibi checked out. No other names came up in the course of interviews with Emma's school friends and family, although her phone records still contained a few unidentified, unidentifiable numbers – one of which could well be Arlo's.

The computer analyst, Raj, had taken a quick look at her laptop. The hard drive showed signs of a young woman who guarded her privacy, he said – she deleted files and cleared her internet search history regularly. He'd do his best to recover what he could, but so far he'd found nothing obvious.

Two steps forward and one step back.

Lincoln went to bed, but couldn't settle. Tomorrow, with any luck, he'd track Arlo down and decide whether or not he was a worthy murder suspect. He needed to solve the case but he was afraid he'd have to shatter Trish's illusions in the process. Bella's voice boomed in his head: *Divided loyalties are dangerous.*

At half past one, he got out of bed again and sat with some whisky and one of his Barrelhouse Women CDs of 20s blues, until he fell asleep at the kitchen table.

# CHAPTER 23

## WEDNESDAY 11TH SEPTEMBER

First thing next morning, Lincoln and Woody drove up the rutted lane from Speldon Magna to Pine Point on the edge of Greywood Forest. They parked where the lane petered out into a grass track. Where did Arlo park his own car, if not here?

A dog galloped towards them as they came in sight of Arlo's camp. Of an indeterminate breed – was "mongrel" one of those words you couldn't say anymore? – it had a rough, rust-coloured coat and wild brown eyes. Not a dog lover, Lincoln regarded it warily.

'Tiffin, here! Good girl.' A man he recognised as Arlo called the dog over and made a fuss of it when it lolloped back to him. He was even scruffier in person than he looked in his photos.

'Mr James? Barbury Police.' Lincoln showed his warrant card.

'Police? Oh man, what am I supposed to have done this time?' Less aggressive than resigned, he didn't sound like a man who knew he was wanted for murder.

'Let's talk about Emma Sherman.'

'Who?'

'Anywhere we can sit down?'

Arlo waved them towards a smouldering heap of ashy logs. 'Let's sit round the fire.'

Lincoln and Woody perched on a sofa in a patch of sandy soil. Smooth knobs of fresh horse manure steamed close by. The sofa felt more like an old car seat covered in a blanket. Indeed, Lincoln was pretty sure it *was* an old car seat covered in a blanket.

Arlo, meanwhile, sat down cross-legged on a leatherette pouffe and waited for Lincoln and Woody to tell him why they were paying him a visit.

Lincoln studied him. He might only be in his late thirties, but his skin was as weather-beaten as a much older man's, a testament to his years in the open air. His dark hair was wavy and thick, settling untidily on his shoulders and snagging on the intricacies of his lacy collar and embroidered waistcoat. Gypsy, buccaneer, highwayman – he looked like all of these, but without their vigour.

'Came up here to do our Woodlander badges,' Woody recalled,

nodding towards the log cabin that stood windowless and vandalised on the far side of the clearing. 'A few years ago now. Used to have Scout and Guide jamborees here.'

'I pitch the caravan here because of that cabin,' Arlo said. 'I can put Steptoe in there overnight if it's raining.'

'Steptoe?'

'My horse.'

Ah. Not the sort of caravan on the front of *Motor Home Monthly*, then. Lincoln looked round. In the shade of the trees he saw a caravan of the gypsy variety: horse-drawn, old and brightly coloured, wooden and tin, no doubt eco-friendly.

He tried once more to take up a dignified position on the slithery seat, and handed Arlo a photo of Emma. 'Recognise this girl?'

'Should I?'

'That's Emma Sherman. She's been front-page news for the last few days. Don't suppose you get the papers delivered this far out of town.'

'I keep in touch with what's going down. Things that matter.' He handed the photo back. 'What's happened to her?'

'She went missing a week ago. Turned up dead on Sunday, dumped on the golf course. We heard you two were an item.'

'Oh come on, man, who told you that? She may have come up here to make music but these kids, they all look the same to me.' He shook his head, bemused. 'They're fascinated, y' know? By the way I live, this way of life. The caravan, this place, the farm. We have great times here, no one telling us what to do.'

'What sort of great times, Arlo? What do you get up to here, with no one telling you what to do?'

He tipped his head back and shut his eyes again. He needed a shave. His hair needed washing. What did these youngsters see in him?

'This world, this time – they aren't forever. You have to live for today, y' know? *Carpe diem* – seize the day. This place where I live, this forest, it's been here for, like, millennia. Fucking millennia. Men have driven cattle and sheep along the tracks through these woods for centuries. Right up until – when was it? The Second World War. Thinking about it like that, you understand where you are in the universe, y' know?'

'No time for philosophy, Mr James, not today. The last time Emma was seen alive, she was supposed to be meeting you.'

'Really? Man, you have got that so wrong. When did you say?'

'Last Thursday evening.' Lincoln was running out of patience.

'Thursday? Cross my heart, she wasn't here. Not even sure where I was last Thursday.' He gave a half-smile, as if they'd share the joke.

Tempted to slap him, Lincoln took a deep breath and let himself slither back into the seat. 'Mr James. Arlo. You need to account for your movements on the night that Emma disappeared. And for the days after, right up until her body was found on Sunday. Not to put too fine a point on it, you are our main suspect right now, so you'd better start taking this a bit more seriously.'

'A suspect? Me?' Arlo pointed to his chest. He wore a ring on every finger, and his thumb. The gravity of the situation seemed to have hit him at last. 'How was she killed?'

'She was strangled.'

'That's terrible, man. I wish you hadn't told me that.'

Lincoln said, his jaw tense, 'You know what I think happened? I think when Emma came to one of your famous musical evenings up here in the woods, you took a shine to her, asked her out. And then Thursday night, you picked her up, brought her up here, things got out of hand and—'

Arlo's eyes sharpened, narrowed. 'Hey, man, I don't have a car. I haven't driven in years.'

Lincoln was thrown. He hadn't expected this. Still, it didn't mean Emma hadn't been here – Arlo could have got someone else to pick her up. 'What about Tom Crane – you know him?'

'Yeah, I know Tom. Brings his guitar. Used to come up here a lot, him and his brother, some girl or other, another guy. Not so much now.' He frowned. 'Brother died, didn't he? Smashed his car up? See, that's what I'm saying, man, you've got to live for the day.'

'Tom was probably here the first time Emma came up here, with some other kids from the drama group. Anything coming back to you now?'

Lincoln showed him the photo again and this time Arlo studied it more carefully.

'Ah, now I remember. Big voice for a little girl, yeah? Man, that's a shame, someone doing that to a kid with a voice like that.'

'I'll ask you again – where were you last Thursday night?'

'Most nights last week, I was over at Speldon Magna, the Two Magpies. Been clearing the beer garden for Billie. She's let it go over the summer so it's kept me busy.' He rootled in his waistcoat pocket, pulled out a crumpled business card, handed it across.

"The Two Magpies, manager Billie Wheeler". Landline and mobile. Facebook page. Twitter.

'Billie gives me a meal when I've finished and sometimes I stay over.' He shook his head regretfully. 'Man, you are so wrong about me and that kid.'

'What's your phone number?'

'Phone number?' He looked perplexed, as if Lincoln had asked him some complicated mathematical formula. Then he leapt to his feet, shoved his hand down the front of his jeans and pulled his phone out. It was a simple Nokia flip-phone – into the case of which he'd carved the number. He held the phone out. 'I can never remember it.'

'That's okay,' said Lincoln. 'Read it out and I'll write it down.'

'You gonna call me up and whisper sweet nothings?'

'The number, Mr James.' As soon as he'd written it down, Lincoln knew it wasn't in Emma's phone records; it ended in a distinctive 8888 which he'd have remembered, but he didn't want to let Arlo off the hook just yet. 'If we find out that Emma was up here on Thursday night, we'll turn this place upside down.' He struggled up from his seat.

Arlo shook his head. 'You've got it all wrong, Mr Detective. Now, unless you want to do something stupid like arrest me, you'd better go and look for the *real* murderer.'

There was a short silence broken only by Steptoe chomping on the lush grass at the edge of the clearing. The horse blew through his nose, lifted his giant head, shook his mane, ground his teeth and put his head down again.

'We'll be back,' Lincoln promised. 'We'll be back until we get the answers we need.'

'Or the answers you want.' Arlo wasn't Hugo James' son for nothing.

# CHAPTER 24

On the outskirts of Barbury, off the busy London Road, senior social worker David Black was arriving at the crematorium. He was so early, he nearly joined the wrong group of mourners. He didn't want to make the same mistake again, so he checked what looked like a fixtures list pinned up beside the main door.

"*East Chapel: 11.00 – Linus Aldo Bonetti.*"

He straightened his tie, smoothed his hair and looked round in vain for anyone he knew. Then he saw a knot of people, all in black, mostly dark-haired, at least partly Italian. Among them, he recognised Linus' father. They'd met a couple of times, in difficult circumstances – though none as difficult as this, the young man's funeral. As the mourners processed towards the chapel, each paused to grasp Mr Bonetti's hand or shoulder and hug his fair-haired English wife.

It took less than a minute for the group to reach him, but to David it felt more like half an hour. No escape. He had to face them.

Linus' father nodded curtly. 'Mr Black.'

'Mr Bonetti.'

'So here we are. At last.'

'At last. Maybe now...'

'Maybe now we'll bury the truth with our son, is that it?' Angelo Bonetti squared up to him like a bantam cock until his wife tugged at his jacket sleeve and tried to pull him away.

David spread his hands helplessly. 'If I could have done anything more... If only Linus had come to me sooner...'

'He could have come to you six months ago, and you still wouldn't have believed him. Instead, you people punished him, punished him for telling it like it is.'

'Come on, Angelo, let's go inside.' Mrs Bonetti took her husband by the elbow, steering him towards the door of the chapel. 'This isn't the time, not today. Today is about Linus.'

'*Every* day is about Linus.' Bonetti yanked his arm out of her grasp. 'Every day. Every night, Mr Black. Last thing before I put my head on the pillow.'

Me too, thought David. 'I dearly wish I'd been able to do more, but...'

'This isn't the end.' The little man in his over-large black suit, his funeral tie, his neat moustache and thinning black hair, wasn't going to give up. 'My son spoke out, that's what he did, and see what happened.'

David held his breath. Maybe he shouldn't have come to the funeral after all, but he felt he owed the Bonettis that much. He knew they must hold him largely responsible for what happened, but he refused to take all the blame.

A young and idealistic social worker, Linus had insisted that management failings were letting his clients down. He made constructive suggestions that were ignored, complained informally – to David and to anyone else who would listen – that council protocols weren't being followed.

Fault was found with his timekeeping. Errors were found in his expenses claims. Against David's advice, he complained formally about being victimised. His complaint was thrown out. Discrepancies were noted in his casework reports. A warning was issued. He was required to work under close supervision for six months – effectively on probation, with David as his line manager and mentor.

Then Linus talked to a journalist who approached David's own line manager for verification. The substance of his claims was never revealed and never published.

Eventually, Linus was suspended on full pay pending an inquiry into his disclosure of confidential and sensitive information.

Two weeks later, at the beginning of August, he was found hanging from a cross-beam in his parents' garage. The inquest was opened and adjourned.

Now they could have the funeral, and David was there in his interview suit and black tie, officially representing his department and trying in vain to think what more he could have done.

Too late now though, wasn't it?

The recorded organ music started up like a skirl of bagpipes. He straightened his tie again and slipped into the empty back row where a dozen orders of service lay scattered, a dozen Linus Bonettis smiling up at him, a photo taken in happier times.

Too late now.

# CHAPTER 25

While Lincoln and Woody were tramping away from Arlo's campsite, Pam, Shauna and Dilke were calling at each of the six houses in Folly Hill Crescent.

The house next door to the Shermans' was empty, a "To Let" sign jammed into its hedge. Pam made a note of the agent's name: Partingdale Flood.

The man who lived on the other side of the Shermans – late sixties, tweedy, possibly ex-military – was backing his car out of the drive.

'Running late for the London train so I can't stop,' he bellowed, 'but I can pop into the police station when I get back, if that's any use to you?'

Two doors along, Pam found Mrs Wragg, who'd lived in the close for forty years and made it her business to keep an eye on comings and goings – a one-woman, unofficial Neighbourhood Watch.

'Crystal's had a hard life.' The elderly lady slumped down at the kitchen table with its view down a wooded garden and a forest of bird tables. 'Derek was a lovely man. None of my business what went on with his wife, whose fault it was or anything, but she took the children and left and he moved Cryssie in. They got married, and he died not long after. Cancer, it was, of the pancreatic. Bit of a drinker, Derek was. That's what did it, I daresay, the circles he moved in. Business lunches.' She tapped the side of her nose. 'More booze than business, I bet!'

'Bringing a little girl up on her own can't have been easy for Crystal.'

Mrs Wragg grimaced. 'I brought up four boys, and I know which I'd choose! You know where you are with boys. Girls can be so devious.'

Pam sat up, interested. 'Was Emma devious?'

'I saw her in town a few weeks ago, outside the café, chatting to some lads. Tuesdays, she's got singing practice, so what was she doing making eyes at lads outside the café in the shopping centre, eh? Skirt all hitched up, load of make-up on. I thought, Well, that's not how your mother's brought you up to behave. So I said to her, to Cryssie, I said, "Do you know what your daughter's been up to?" and of course, she didn't. Terrible, what's happened, but that girl wasn't all she was cracked up to be.'

'Can you describe the boys?'

'One of them was good-looking, fair, quite smart. The other one, well, he was a bit on the heavy side, glasses. But there she was, making a right exhibition of herself.'

Pam cast her eyes round the sunny kitchen; a geranium on the windowsill, gingham tea towels hanging over the handle of the Raeburn. This house seemed so much homelier than Crystal's. Cheerful souvenirs from holidays and day trips were ranged along the dresser shelves. *Happy Birthday Nanna*! shrieked a clumsily-crayoned card stuck to the fridge.

Mrs Wragg dropped her voice. 'Of course, what with her trouble, I suppose she worries more than most, not being out and about the way any other mother would be.'

'Her trouble?'

'Angerphobic, isn't she? Doesn't go outside unless she's taken and even that's quite difficult. Been like it for years.'

'"Angerphobic?" What, like fear of confrontation?' Shauna grinned. 'Dunno why I'm laughing, mind. My mum was agoraphobic until she got some pills and had some counselling.'

They were in the car driving back, comparing notes.

'It'd explain all that tension,' Pam said, 'needing to keep things under control. How did you two get on?'

'I was talking to the guy who heard them arguing Thursday morning,' said Shauna. 'Confirms what Crystal's already told us: that she was having a go at Emma about her phone.' She sighed ruefully. 'I know what it's like – my Alfie winds me up something chronic. Neighbours hear me yelling at him, they must think I'm the worst mother, but when I lose it, Alfie just thinks it's hysterical.'

Pam glanced at her in the rear-view mirror, realising she didn't know much about her younger colleague. 'How old is he?'

'Coming up eighteen months. Knobhead's taking him to the park today. They've got some kiddies' activities going on.'

'Knobhead?' Dilke sniggered. 'You call your husband Knobhead?'

'Not to his face, unless things get really heated. And we're not wed. Don't go along with all of that. We share the childcare. He's got a job as well.'

'What does he do?' Pam asked.

'Does admin for the council at the local hub – housing, mostly, stuck behind a desk. Flexible hours, good pay, no nights.' She looked away out of the window. 'Fuck, I envy him sometimes.'

Lincoln was glad to be back in the CID room after his fruitless visit to Pine Point. He chucked his coat at the hat stand and watched, unsurprised, as it missed. He went over and picked it up, shook it out, dusted it off and hung it up properly. It smelt horsey with an undertone of mildew. Maybe if he put it on a hanger by an open window overnight...?

'Oh, you're back.' Pam looked round from putting the kettle on. 'Any luck finding Arlo?'

'We found him but he wasn't much help. Says he never met Emma on her own. Can't remember what he was doing last Thursday but he certainly wasn't with her. *Man*. Woody's gone over to some pub at Speldon Magna to check his alibi for the rest of the week.' He dropped his mobile onto his desk. 'What's more, he doesn't have a car, doesn't even drive. So either Tom's got it wrong or Arlo got someone else to pick her up for him. Anything from the house-to-house?'

'Crystal Sherman's agoraphobic – which would explain why she was shaking like a leaf when we took her to the mortuary. I put it down to shock, but she must have been scared just being out of doors.'

She dropped a teabag into her dainty cup, doled a heaped spoonful of coffee into Lincoln's mug.

'The house next to hers is empty,' she went on. 'I got on to Partingdale Flood, the agents, but the previous tenants moved out a few months ago – a couple called Miller, now travelling abroad. So we can forget about asking them for any information.'

'Could they've told us anything, d' you think?' In Lincoln's experience, in a close like Folly Hill Crescent, people generally kept themselves to themselves. He couldn't see Crystal telling her woes to her neighbours across the garden fence.

'Might've been worth a try but—' Pam broke off as her phone rang.

When she put it down, she looked like the cat that got the cream. 'John Spooner at Traffic Management. I asked him to go through the traffic cam footage covering Spicer Street and guess what – he's spotted Emma getting into a car at the back of the gym. Another camera's picked up the same car at the traffic lights. He's sending the pictures through to me.'

Lincoln felt like punching the air. He could hardly contain his impatience while they waited for the photos to arrive in Pam's inbox.

A few minutes later, they were studying three black-and-white prints: 7.14, Emma waiting on the pavement in Spicer Street at the back of Bods. A minute later, a dark-coloured car pulling up beside her. Twenty seconds after that, Emma clambering into the back seat, her bag hugged tight to her side.

As Tom said, Emma had swapped tracksuit and trainers for a tight T-shirt, skinny jeans and flat shoes. She'd untied her ponytail, let her hair hang loose. Only her sports bag was the same.

Pam frowned. 'Your boyfriend picks you up, you get in next to him, don't you?'

'Personally, no.' Lincoln grinned. 'But I see what you're getting at. She doesn't show any sign of knowing him, as if he's no more than a chauffeur.'

He shook his head at the photos, puzzled. What kind of man sends a car to pick up his fifteen-year-old girlfriend? A man who hasn't got a car and lives a long way off a bus route. Like Arlo James. He thought of Trish's insistence that Arlo must be innocent; tried to shut her voice out of his head.

Pam laid some more photos on the desk. 'The car stopped at the lights, junction of Spicer Street and High Street, 7.16. It's a Fiesta. I'll check the index number, see who's the RO.'

She was back a few minutes later. 'Registered owner's Ashley Tyler, the guy from the gym – but that's definitely not him driving it.'

It certainly wasn't. Lincoln peered at the close-up of the Fiesta driver waiting for the lights to change. This man was about Ashley's age – early twenties – but his skin was swarthy, his hair dark, his features well-defined as if he might be of Indian or Mediterranean origin.

Lincoln patted his jacket pocket for his car keys. 'I think we need another chat with Ashley Tyler, find out who was driving his car.'

His phone buzzed: a text from Trish. *Where were u @ 12?*

# CHAPTER 26

'Course I know Arlo. We're mates, me and Arlo.' Billie Wheeler gave Woody a dirty grin. 'Not like that. Just mates. I let him sleep in the back room sometimes in exchange for odd-jobbing, gardening, you know. Wouldn't think it to look at him, but he's strong as an ox. Good with the barrels. I pay him cash, let him charge his phone, have a bath, do his washing a couple of times a week.'

The landlady of the Two Magpies in Speldon Magna was probably about forty, with a forty-four-inch bosom and forty-eight-inch hips. Her waist was somewhere in between.

'Any idea where he was last Thursday night?' Woody perched on a bar stool, Radio 2 droning low in the background, the pub almost empty. He'd interrupted Billie doing the cleaning, so everything smelt of Flash, like at home.

'Thursday, he was here. Quiz night. Brings the punters in, quiet as the grave otherwise. This isn't anything to do with that Emma, is it? 'Cause that's when she went missing, isn't it, Thursday? Why d' you think Arlo had anything to do with that?'

'I just need to confirm where he was.'

'He was here all evening – all night, in fact, me and Arlo and Jock from across the road, all of us a bit the worse for wear.' She chuckled. 'Way into the early hours, setting the world to rights.'

Woody took down Jock's details. 'You ever see Arlo with Emma?'

'He never brings girls in here but I know he has quite a following for his *happenings*.' She made a wry face at the word. 'He gets his guitar out and the kids join in. She wanted to be a singer, didn't she, that Emma? It said, in the paper.'

'When was the last time you saw him?'

'He was in here Sunday evening. We were watching that quiz show, and he knew all the answers. He's clever, is Arlo. You can tell he went to university, even if they did throw him out.'

'You never heard him talk about meeting Emma, going out with her, taking her up into the woods?'

'Nah! She was just a kid. Arlo's nearly as old as I am!'

Woody put his notebook away. 'I'd best get back. You'll let me know if anything else comes to mind?'

'Course. It's a woman in charge this time, isn't it? It said, in the paper.'

He slid down off his stool. 'DCI Bax, yes.'

Billie beamed. 'She'll get it sorted. Always takes a woman to sort things out. Men make such a snoddle of the simplest things.'

# CHAPTER 27

The back office at Bods was hardly big enough to accommodate Lincoln, Pam and Ashley Tyler, especially when Tyler was puffed up with indignation. The photos of his Fiesta in Spicer Street sat on the table between them, but he insisted his car had been stolen and he hadn't got round to reporting it. And no, he didn't recognise the man behind the wheel.

'Looks like a Paki,' he said. 'I don't know any Pakis.'

'Know who was in the back of your car, Ashley?'

Tyler leaned his tanned arms on the table, looked down at the photos as if the answer might be written there in big letters. He shook his head, looked up.

'Emma Sherman.' Lincoln pointed to the figure getting into the back seat of his Fiesta. 'Found murdered on Sunday. Fifteen years old. There she is, last known sighting, getting into *your* car.'

Tyler's upper lip glistened. 'Not me driving, though, is it? Someone nicked it from outside my flat.'

'Come on, Ash, who'd want to nick a five-year-old Fiesta?' Lincoln shoved the photos at him again, their edges colliding with his bare arm. 'This a friend of yours, someone you trust? Or someone who twisted your arm to lend him your car?'

'I told you – someone nicked it. End of.'

When Lincoln and Pam returned from seeing Ashley Tyler, Woody was already back at his desk.

'Arlo's alibi for Thursday night is rock solid,' he said. 'He was at the pub all night Thursday, and apart from a couple of hours in the afternoon when he went into town, all day Friday.'

Lincoln wasn't surprised. He believed Arlo when he said he didn't really know Emma, and his number hadn't come up on her phone records.

'We now know that this bloke drove her away.' He showed Woody the traffic cam photos. 'Though he looks as if he's only a driver, not someone she knows.'

'Maybe other cameras have picked the car up after Spicer Street?'

'That's a lot of CCTV footage to trawl, Woody. Still, if the DCI doesn't like it, she can tell me how else we're going to solve this case.'

'By the way, Graham left a note on your desk. Something he found in Emma's phone records – reckoned you might be interested.'

'You want to speak to Maisie Finnegan?'

Bella was getting ready to leave for a meeting at Presford HQ, and Lincoln's presence in her cupboard/office wasn't helping. They shuffled around each other as she tried to stuff folders into her bag and put her jacket on without hitting him.

'She gave us a statement after she found the body. Why do you need to speak to her again?'

'Dilke spotted that Emma contacted her as recently as the beginning of August. If we'd known the girls had been in touch within the last few weeks, we'd have asked Maisie if she knew anything about Emma's love life.'

'We can't risk upsetting her after what she's been through.' Bella straightened her collar, tweaked her jacket down over her hips. 'You do know who Donal Finnegan is, don't you?'

'Probably the richest man in Barbury. Should we let that influence us?'

She snorted. 'Don't be naïve. A man like Finnegan will have his lawyers in here in a flash if he thinks his darling daughter's being accused of something.'

'I'm not accusing her of anything! I simply want to find out if Emma told her who she was seeing. If you're saying we can't question a witness just because her dad's a big noise in Barbury business circles—'

'Of course not, but...' Bella's briefcase sat ready and waiting on her desk. With a quick heave, she lifted it up and over, whacking Lincoln's elbow. Possibly by accident. 'Follow it up, but for Christ's sake, be diplomatic. Take Pam. She strikes me as being sensible. Can I at least rely on you to tread carefully?'

'Like I'm on eggshells.'

'They've got photos, your fucking mate driving my car! I told you, didn't I fucking say?'

'They arrest you?'

'Course they didn't arrest me!'

117

'No, because they've got no fucking evidence. Ash, they've got a photo of your car, someone else driving it. Which puts you in the clear if you stick to your story, don't cave in and balls it up. Okay, little bro? We clear?'

Ashley stared at the phone in his hand. *Call ended.*

# CHAPTER 28

Marsh Pulham Hall was a magnificent house, if you liked that kind of thing, and Lincoln didn't: far too showy, self-satisfied, smug. Donal Finnegan's mansion wore its market value like bunting across its Doric-pillared portico. A sporty white Audi stood on the drive. He might give generously to charity, but Finnegan clearly kept back a bob or two for himself.

Lincoln was surprised when the property magnate himself came to the door when Pam rang the bell, and not a butler or maid. He let them into an entrance hall so vast it seemed more fitting for an upscale office building than a family home.

Lincoln proffered his warrant card. 'We spoke earlier on the phone.'

'Ah yes. Come in.' Finnegan was a man in his fifties, barrel-chested but trim. His thick hair was swept back from a broad face as genial-looking as in his publicity photos. 'So what's this about? You said on the phone you wanted to speak to my daughter, but do you really need to quiz her all over again?'

'We need to clarify a couple of things with her, that's all,' Lincoln said. 'Shouldn't take long.'

'If you're sure that's all it is...' Finnegan smiled at Pam. 'We've met before, haven't we?'

'At Mrs Sherman's, yes.' She went a bit pink, much to Lincoln's disgust. Couldn't she see this bloke was a professional smoothie?

He led them down the hallway, the walls lined with huge black-and-white photographs of architectural details – Gothic windows, Georgian fanlights, Victorian brickwork. He paused at the foot of the stairs to call up to his daughter, before waving Pam and Lincoln into a kitchen-diner almost as big as the hallway.

'Coffee? Tea?' He put a bowl of fruit and a plate of shortbread on the breakfast bar.

'Coffee,' said Lincoln.

'Tea,' said Pam. 'Please.'

Maisie slipped into the kitchen as if she was expecting trouble. Slender, fragile-looking. Brown eyes big in an elfin face. Thick,

119

chocolate-coloured hair cut in a wedge, tousled as if she'd got out of bed and not brushed it.

'Coffee, Maize?' Her father drew her into his side, trying to jolly her along, but she pulled away.

'I only want juice.' While her father yanked open a glossy red fridge the size of a wardrobe, Maisie slid onto a stool as far from Pam and Lincoln as she could get. 'Have I got to go over it all again? I already made a statement.' She took the glass from her father and sipped as delicately as an invalid.

'We'll try to be quick.'

Late afternoon sun streamed into the kitchen, striking every gleaming surface. Lincoln decided he'd get more out of this encounter if he set his assumptions aside. Not all successful people make their money at other people's expense. Maybe the owner of Marsh Pulham Hall was genuinely altruistic, if not quite a philanthropist.

'You built this place yourself?' he asked, feigning admiration. 'It's an impressive house.'

Finnegan smiled. 'I trained as an architect. I love old buildings, hate to see them go to waste, but it's generally cheaper to build something new than to restore something that's already there. But my ambition was always to save what I could when I could afford to, and now that's where the money is – refurbish old buildings and treble their worth. Ah, but listen to me, giving you the sales *spiel!*' His eyes twinkled as he poured coffee.

Lincoln had to admit the coffee was delicious, and gone all too soon. He plonked his empty cup down. 'You want to give us the guided tour, Mr Finnegan?' He caught Pam's eye and, as they'd discussed on the way over, she took her cue.

'Er – I'll just chat to Maisie while I finish my tea,' she said, raising her cup. 'And then I'll catch you up.'

'It must have been a dreadful shock, finding Emma like that.' Pam put her cup down and reached for a piece of shortbread. She passed the dish across, but Maisie pulled her cardigan sleeves down over her hands and shook her head. 'You knew her, didn't you?'

'Only because Daddy's friends with her mother. When we were little we were at the same school but her mother moved her to Barbury Fields and we lost touch.'

Pam sipped her tea, taking her time, not wanting the girl to think she'd done anything wrong. 'When we spoke to you on

Sunday, you didn't mention you'd been friends.'

Maisie wound her hands tighter into her cuffs. 'Didn't get a chance. I was so upset. Daddy got me away from there as soon as he could. Anyway, it's hardly relevant, is it, being friends at school absolutely *years* ago?'

'But your mobile number came up in her records. She phoned you a few times at the end of July and the beginning of August.'

Maisie stared into her glass. 'Oh yes, I forgot. She wanted me to watch some play she was in, but I had something else on and couldn't go.'

'Did you talk about anything else?'

She shrugged. 'Holidays, exams, the usual stuff.'

'She called you three times,' Pam reminded her, disappointed by her evasiveness. Was she feeling bad for rejecting Emma's invitation to come to her play, an opportunity to renew their childhood friendship? How could she have known she'd never get another chance?

Maisie pushed her glass away. 'Like I said, she kept on about me going to her play.'

'Did she tell you she was seeing someone? Or that she'd fallen for someone?'

'*Fallen* for someone?' Maisie made a face, as if she wondered what planet Pam was on. 'She never said. Her mother was so intense. Emma could never have a normal social life.' She stared at her hands, her short nails painted blood red. 'She thought we could be friends again, but people change, don't they? You can't go back.'

Pam reached out towards her. 'Maisie, about last Sunday – if you need to talk to someone...'

'I'm fine.'

'Have you talked things over with Joe? But then, men always have to be so macho about everything, don't they?'

'Haven't seen him. Daddy says he's too old for me. What he really means is, he hates his little girl going out with someone from the council flats.'

'Dads always worry. My dad says it's in the job description.' When Maisie didn't offer even the ghost of a smile, Pam knew it was time to go. 'Look, here's my card in case you feel like a chat.' She left her card on the breakfast bar. 'Now, let's find your dad and my boss.'

The Finnegans' sitting room was furnished simply: a couple of sofas, bookshelves, a big coffee table with art books piled on it. Large canvas-mounted photographs hung on the walls in this room too, depicting rural scenes, as if Finnegan felt he had to emphasise his love of the countryside: one little girl throwing grain for a stream of eager hens; two even smaller girls giggling down at the camera from their lofty perch on the back of a carthorse.

He opened the French windows onto the terrace. Perfect lawns rolled away below the house, leaving behind the tobacco scent of freshly mown grass. River mist shivered above the reeds. Not another house in sight.

'Must take a lot of upkeep,' Lincoln said.

'I employ good people – all local.' Finnegan beamed out over his domain. 'No closer to an arrest, then?'

'Early days.'

'I'm not sure Crystal would be consoled by "early days".'

'You and Mrs Sherman are close?'

'Derek and I weren't just business partners – we were friends, pals. I owed it to him to look out for Crystal and his little girl.'

It crossed Lincoln's mind once more that this man – energetic, commanding, charming – was practically a stepfather to Emma. Had they clashed or become too close? Bella hadn't let him explore either possibility. 'So you've seen Emma grow up?'

Finnegan shook his head. 'Crystal and I were close when Emma was small, but the girls grew apart as girls do, and Crystal's such a private person. She didn't want to be blamed for breaking up another marriage. Not that we've ever...' He glanced across to make sure Lincoln understood. 'She didn't want people to get the wrong idea. But when Emma went missing, she needed support, so I've been doing my best to help.' He drew himself up. 'Which is more than can be said for you and your team. You treated her disappearance as if she'd thrown a tantrum and would be back when she'd calmed down.'

Before Lincoln could defend himself, the door behind them flew open. He spun round, expecting to see Pam and Maisie, but instead an unknown woman stood there.

Finnegan was suddenly affable again. 'Come and meet Inspector Lincoln, darling. Inspector, this is my wife, Lindsey.'

Shiny with money and expensive grooming, Mrs Finnegan was slim and smart in a body-skimming dress. She ran a hand through her coppery hair, a couple of diamond rings flashing. 'I'm on my way out.' She checked her watch. More diamonds. 'I need to catch the next train.'

Lincoln felt invisible, as if she might walk through him, rather than round him, to give her husband a farewell kiss. She smelt of lipstick and perfume, with minty breath. Then she strutted away, jacket draped round her shoulders, handbag and car keys in one hand, sleek briefcase in the other.

The door closed behind her, and Finnegan turned back to him. 'You did fuck all to find Emma. Those first few hours, you should've done more.'

Lincoln didn't argue. What was the point? He knew he'd been slow to act. 'If Mrs Sherman had given us a bit more information...'

'Don't blame Crystal for your own failings.' He stood looking up at one of his photographs: a mother reaching up to pick apples while her daughter gathered windfalls beneath her. 'Us poor parents. Protect your kids and you're accused of coddling them. Give them a bit of freedom and you're called neglectful. We can't win.' He glanced Lincoln's way. 'You've got kids?'

'No, but I can understand—'

'Ah, but you see, Inspector, you can't. You think you know what it's like to be a father, but you can't possibly know. Take that lad that Maisie was with on Sunday. He's twenty-something. My daughter's not quite sixteen. He lives in a rented flat overlooking the railway line. Maisie doesn't love him – she *pities* him.'

'Emma's mother probably knows more about the girl's love life that she realises, but she won't even talk to us.'

'Can you blame her when all you do is denigrate her daughter?'

Before Lincoln could defend himself, the door opened again and Maisie stood there, timid and mute, Pam beside her.

The visit to Marsh Pulham Hall was over.

Lincoln's mobile rang as he opened his front door at nearly nine.

'Where the hell were you?' Trish, irate.

He sank onto his uncarpeted stairs. 'I know what you're going to say, and I'm sorry. Trish, I—'

'You haven't got a *clue* what I'm going to say. You can't begin to guess how unsurprised I am that you *completely* forgot we'd arranged to meet at lunchtime. Neither can you guess how bloody *furious* I am with you. And with myself.'

Lincoln shut his eyes, her voice booming in his ear.

'You never learn, do you, Jeff? Jeff? Are you still there?'

'Yes, I'm here. And no, I never learn.' He sighed. Why did he have to sabotage himself every time? Just when he'd thought that row in July was history...

She sighed too, her anger spent. 'I'd tell you to come over but I expect something would distract you on the way and you'd go off somewhere *totally* different, leaving me wondering where you'd got to, and I'd have wasted another couple of hours waiting for you. God, I seem to have spent my whole *life* waiting for you.'

'You didn't mean that.' He couldn't help smiling.

'No, I didn't. Oh, you know what I mean. My whole life since I met you.'

He shut his eyes, imagined her getting more and more wound up. 'I'd like to think you really have been waiting for me your whole life.'

'Nobody's that special, Jeff. Not even you.' A pause. 'You could come over now?'

'Bit late. You should get some rest.' He crossed his fingers, both hands.

'I can get some rest later. Come over. Please don't make me wait.'

# CHAPTER 29

Weak sunlight trickled into the CID room, heralding a change in the season, a hint of autumn in the air as Pam flung the window open. Lincoln felt frustrated that a week had gone by since Emma went missing, and yet they were no further forward.

He gathered the team together for an impromptu brainstorming session while Bella was out of the building.

His head throbbed. Too much wine the night before, too little sleep in Trish's rumpled bed. Reluctantly he pushed aside the thought of Trish and sex, and took his team back to a time when Emma was still alive: Thursday evening, arriving at the Half Moon Centre for a dance class she planned to skip.

'She goes into Bods, changes her clothes. Tom Crane lets her out the staff exit. A few minutes later, she gets in the back of Ashley Tyler's Fiesta driven by a man of Asian or Mediterranean appearance. Tyler says the car was stolen from outside his flat.'

Another camera picked the Fiesta up ten minutes later, on the main road out of the town, signalling right to take the B-road towards Speldon Magna, the road running along the edge of Greywood Forest, a favourite destination for lovers – and murderers.

'That phone call she got as she was walking into town could've been the driver,' Dilke suggested. He put on a gruff voice: '"Hi, Emma, your mystery boyfriend has asked me to pick you up at quarter past seven. I'll be driving a clapped-out Fiesta." It'd explain why she got in the car so readily even though she didn't appear to know the bloke behind the wheel.'

Lincoln patted the photo taken at the traffic lights soon after the Fiesta picked her up. 'But we still haven't identified him. If we could find him, we'd find out who put him up to it.'

'Let's show the photo to the cab offices,' Shauna said. 'He could be a minicab driver.'

'In a Fiesta? That he's stolen?'

She shrugged. 'You've been out on the town and your shoes are too tight to walk home in, you're not fussy.'

'Worth following up, yes.'

125

Raj stuck his head round the door. 'Am I interrupting?'

Lincoln waved him into the room. 'Found anything on that hard drive?'

'Music downloads, and some videos Emma made of herself singing, as well as an audio clip – only very short – recorded in the first week of August, in which she's talking to a young man.'

Lincoln clapped him on the shoulder. 'You've found her mystery boyfriend?'

'Sadly, no. They're friendly but not *intimate*. You can hear for yourself – I've got it here.' He held up a memory stick, aimed it at Lincoln's computer. 'May I?'

A couple of minutes later, the room was filled with laughter: Emma and a teenage boy chortling over something.

'*That is not how it's meant to sound!*' Emma could hardly talk for giggling. '*I thought you said you knew how this thing worked, Dumbo!*'

'*I thought I did.*'

'That's Simon Lovelock,' Dilke whispered.

'*You were wrong!*' Emma honked and snorted. '*Let's try it again.*'

Half a minute ticked by: switches clicked, pages rustled, the youngsters moved round near the microphone, setting something up, plugging something in. Emma took a deep breath and a swell of music swamped the laughter, as she or Simon ran their hands over an electronic keyboard. A few chords and then a pause before her voice slipped out onto the surface of the silence.

She had a clear, ethereal voice – haunting, textured like silk threads twisting. The song was folky, something Lincoln vaguely recognised; something about a fine day, or a fine night, sung without accompaniment. Not a false note. Perfect pitch.

'*You could try to get an agent or something.*'

'*No I couldn't. Not the way she is.*' Emma, resentful.

Sounds coming in through an open window: children playing football in the street, the *Greensleeves* chime of an ice cream van.

'*Go to him, Em. He could help you. He must know people, all his London connections. What've you got to lose?*'

The football slammed against something metal and one of the children yelled.

Emma again: '*I'd feel so awkward, that's all.*'

'*Em, he owes you.*'

'*Yes, but she'd be so upset. God, is this still recording? I thought you'd—*'

Then nothing.

Lincoln turned to Raj. 'That's it?'

'Afraid so.'

'Sounds as if they're talking about Arlo,' Pam said. 'That he could get her an audition, maybe, with his connections? But why did he owe her something?'

Lincoln ejected the memory stick. 'Graham, go back and speak to the Lovelock boy again. Find out what they were talking about – and who. We need to know what Emma was up to.'

Her voice still echoed – in the room or in his head, he couldn't tell. *It's going to be a fine day tomorrow...*

# CHAPTER 30

'You didn't tell us you suffer from agoraphobia.' Hoping she'd get more out of her if they could chat more informally, Pam had come back to see Emma's mother on her own.

In the chilly beige sitting room, Crystal sat sideways on the sofa, rigid with tension, her hands clasped in her lap. 'It's not something you talk about.'

'Talking about it might help. Some people—'

'It's irrelevant. And private. Is there any news?'

Pam showed her the photos of Emma waiting in Spicer Street and getting into Ashley's car around quarter past seven, then the photo of the driver's face in close-up. 'Do you recognise him?'

Crystal stared at each photo in turn, as if absorbing every pixel. At last she cast them aside with a weary sigh. 'She must have thought she was getting into a minicab. I warned her time and time again...'

'A cab taking her where, though?'

'I have no idea. I thought I knew my daughter inside out, but that girl...' She gestured towards the photos. 'That girl's a stranger to me. All these secrets...' She rose, crossed to the window and looked away down the garden towards the distant summer house. 'Where did she meet him? When? I was so careful about her using the internet, all these stories about grooming. That's why her laptop was down here. What more could I have done?'

'You did the best you could.' Pam stood up. 'You don't want your sister to come over and keep you company?'

'Not now, no. It'd do more harm than good.'

Crystal could hardly wait to get the policewoman out of her house. She wanted to be on her own. If she couldn't be with Emma, she didn't want to be with anyone else.

That man in the car – who was he? Where was he taking her? She couldn't get away from it: her daughter had deceived her. She'd always known the time would come when her nerves would affect Emma too. When she was little, Tania and Todd had taken her places, but once she started wanting to go to concerts and gigs, even something as simple as looking round shops, life became more difficult.

'How am I ever going to *achieve* anything if I can't go anywhere?' she'd cry. 'I never go anywhere! Why can't we go on holiday like other people? Just because *you* don't like going out, why do I have to stay in all the time?'

Emma simply didn't understand. Nobody did unless they'd suffered the sort of panic attacks Crystal had when she was outside. The house would be burgled, the pipes would burst, she'd have left the gas on, the iron plugged in, a light on in the cupboard under the stairs... There was no end to all the dreadful possibilities. Much better not to go out, to stay in and watch for the next thing that would go wrong...

Crystal shut her eyes, willing her heart to stop racing. You don't wake up one day to find you can't leave the house anymore. It creeps up on you. All it takes is one incident out of the blue, like Stephanie's accident on top of all the hoo-ha with Derek's family, and bam! There you are, marooned, restricted to a few carefully planned outings, a hopeless succession of empty days. Bearable if you're on your own, but when you've imprisoned your daughter too...

Oh, the effort it took to go into the kitchen now, put the kettle on, reach down a cup and saucer from the shelf, make some tea! Crystal's legs felt like lead, her shoulders weighed down by a yoke of fear. Emma was gone but she still couldn't believe it.

How could anyone understand what they'd been to each other?

She used to think she'd been so lucky, falling for a man who gave her the love her father never could. She'd worked for Derek for years before he even noticed her, but once their affair began, they were inseparable. Then just when life couldn't be more glorious, he told her he had cancer, and that the next few months would be the last they'd have together.

In the next magical, crazy week, he made love to her with a kind of desperation, determined to create new life before he lost his own.

She lay with him at the end of that week, sore, aching, Dez taking her hand in his, asking her to marry him even though he'd always said he'd never marry again, not after what happened the first time; his terrible wife, the children he despised.

'This'll be different,' he'd said with a twinkle in his eye. 'This'll be forever.'

Only they both knew it couldn't be. Dez was dying before her eyes, living what little life he had left with such gusto it sickened her. A couple of months later, she told him she was expecting.

'A baby?' He'd held her, crushed her in his arms, proud, triumphant. He wouldn't die, not when new life was growing inside her.

She married him at Presford Registry Office. Peach two-piece, conscious for the first time that, in a fitted skirt, her bump showed. She didn't care, wanting the wedding to end so she could rush into the loo and be sick. Which to do first, have a wee or throw up, both urges equally pressing.

Twelve and a half weeks later, Derek was dead. She felt the imprint of his head on her belly where he'd lain down to listen. He'd been so sure she was carrying a boy. 'How's Junior doing?' he'd say, leaning his poor heavy head in her lap. In those last couple of weeks, his colour drained away, leaving his skin papery white. His hair thinned and lost its customary sheen. 'How's Junior doing?'

The memory gripped her now, convulsed her. What a useless mother she'd turned out to be! She went shivery all over; couldn't even pick up her cup and take it across the room to the table.

'How's Junior doing?'

Oh God! Oh God, Dez, I'm sorry!

She folded her arms on the worktop, laid her face on her arms and sobbed as if she'd never stop.

# CHAPTER 31

'We want to play you something,' said Shauna. 'See if you can explain it a bit.'

Dilke could tell Simon felt uncomfortable, and not only because his grandmother was in the next room. Looking apprehensive, he listened to the recording Raj had salvaged from Emma's laptop. At the sound of her singing, he looked down at the floor, his eyes glistening. He was clearly hurting but was damned if he was going to admit it.

'Who was it who had the London connections?' Dilke asked when it ended. 'Arlo?'

'Not Arlo, no. Mr Finnegan. Thought he might know someone, get her an audition. He used to be round her house a lot when she was little, so I thought he might feel, y' know, like family.'

'And *did* she ask him?'

'Don't think so. She didn't want to upset her mum.'

'Take a look at this.' Dilke flipped through his folder until he reached the close-up of the Fiesta driver. 'You know this bloke?'

Simon lifted his glasses to peer at the photo. He shook his head, let the glasses drop, handed it back. 'Who is he?'

'He's the guy who drove Emma away from Bods the night she was killed. You never saw her with him?'

'He looks a bit rough. She wouldn't go with someone like that.'

'What, because he's black?' Shauna's tone made Dilke cringe, even though he'd been wondering the same thing.

'Wouldn't call that black. Looks a bit dodgy, that's all. So – er – you haven't found out who she was meeting that night?'

Dilke put the photo away. 'Still looking into it. Had any thoughts? She ever go on about someone she'd met – boy, girl, man, woman?'

Simon blushed, but he shook his head. 'Doesn't matter now, does it?' he said. 'Nothing's gonna bring her back.'

# CHAPTER 32

'You scrubber, you're fucking screwing him!' Jess punched Lady's arm.

'Ow! No, I'm not, actually.' Lady put her nose in the air, grinning. 'Arlo and me are just good friends!'

The girls lolled on the squashy red sofa in Mokkery, the coffee shop that had replaced the Wimpy. Most of their friends still went to Starbucks or Caffè Nero, so they felt like trendsetters, making this very brown little café their new hideout. How long before the kids coming down into town from school discovered Mokkery and spoiled it?

'Honest,' Lady insisted, knowing that the more she denied it, the less Jess would believe her. 'Just good friends.' Lady smiled to herself. She had yet to let him inside her, but it was only a matter of time. 'Anyway, you can talk! You did it with him, didn't you?'

'We never actually, you know...' Jess put on a stupid angelic expression. 'I'm saving myself, like poor innocent little Emma.'

Lady shot her a look. 'Fuck you on about? You didn't even know Emma.'

'My sister did. Lexie was always on about her getting the best parts because the teacher fancied her. None of the other girls liked her. She was such a bighead. "Everyone will love me on sight! I'm so sexy."' Jess clasped her hands under her chin, fluttered her eyelashes. '"Boys will fall at my feet because I'm so beautiful and talented!" Yeah, love, but you've got to put out for them, too!'

'Yeah, like *you're* the expert.' And what did her stupid sister know about anything? Lexie always looked like she was brain-damaged. 'You shouldn't talk about Emma like that.'

'Can't hear me, can she?' Jess pulled her hair back from her face, lifted her arms.

'You got a new bra? Your tits look bigger.'

Jess beamed. 'It's not you who's supposed to notice!'

'Then stop showing them off to me.'

'Then don't look, you lezzie.'

'I'll fetch you such a slap in a minute, Jessica!'

They fell about laughing. 'So when you seeing Arlo again?' Jess asked.

'Saturday.' Lady tucked her hair behind her ears, felt his phantom embrace round her shoulders. 'Fuck, I wish it was tonight. I feel so frigging frustrated!'

Jess rolled her eyes again but Lady knew that, deep down, she was jealous as hell.

# CHAPTER 33

'You held a briefing without me?' Bella dumped her bag on her desk.

'I wouldn't call it a briefing,' Lincoln said. 'More a putting-together of heads.'

'That's right,' said Pam. 'Informal.'

'And you sent Hartlake and Dilke to speak to that boy from the drama group, is that right?'

'Simon Lovelock.' He told her about the snatch of conversation Raj had found that suggested Emma planned to approach someone who might help her, someone with London connections. 'But we still don't know who she was seeing.'

'I need to be kept fully informed,' Bella went on. 'I am in charge, after all.'

Philippa Giles, one of the press officers, hovered in the doorway: slim and blonde in a close-fitting zipped top over smart jeans. She hadn't been with them long but she seemed pretty competent. She was related to somebody senior in the local council – Lincoln couldn't remember the details.

Bella glanced round. 'Oh, hi, Pip.' She collected some papers from her desk and headed for the door. 'Jeff, I'll be in one of the interview rooms if you need me.'

A minute or two later, the Shermans' next-door neighbour turned up at the front desk, asking for Pam, and she went to fetch him.

Lincoln felt Oliver Spence was the sort of man you wouldn't mind having next door. Late sixties, respectable, respectful of your privacy but not afraid to question a suspicious-looking caller.

'I was on my way out when you chaps caught me yesterday,' he said, crossing his legs – immaculate tailoring, expensive trousers, Church's brogues. 'I said I'd pop in at the first opportunity, didn't I?' He flashed a quick, confident smile at Pam. A polished jaw, meticulously shaven. Teeth pearly white; a man with a good dentist.

'You've lived next door to the Shermans for how long?' she asked. They'd taken him into one of the more comfortable interview rooms: easy chairs, a coffee table, a potted plant suffering in the arid atmosphere.

'Twenty-two years.'

'So you knew Derek Sherman?'

'We used to pass the time of day. Pleasant enough chap, not a great talker. Meriel, his first wife, was still around then. She left him when she found out he'd been carrying on with Crystal. Huge row, took the children. Well, they were teenagers by then. Crystal moved in with him soon after. Speak as I find – she was always polite, and treated Derek very well. You could see she was devoted to him.' He rubbed his hand over his face. 'I still can't take it in, you know, someone hurting that little girl. Although...' He paused as if unsure whether or not to share a confidence.

Lincoln leaned forward, prompting him. 'Yes?'

'Crystal made such a fuss of her, there were bound to be consequences. Emma was pretty enough, but she wasn't what I'd call exceptional.' He spoke as if he were a connoisseur of pretty girls. 'Talented, of course, but not what I'd call gifted. But Crystal sent her to all these classes – dancing, singing, acting – filling the child's head with ideas...'

'We understand that Mrs Sherman doesn't go out very much. Were you aware of that?'

'The old panic attacks, you mean? Started not long after Derek died. Meriel gave her a pretty hard time – problems over the estate, who'd inherit what and so forth.' He shook his head. 'Vultures descending, that's what it was like. Took a couple of years to sort it all out. And no sooner had Crystal picked herself up from that, than her sister's kiddie had a nasty fall, nearly died, and poor old Crystal went to pieces. Nervous breakdown, I suppose it was.'

'Have you noticed any unusual comings and goings recently, anyone hanging around?'

'Nothing out of the ordinary. She has everything delivered, of course. Oh, and the gardener comes every couple of weeks, but no actual visitors. The uncle used to be round there all the time but not anymore. Tremlow. Nice enough chap but it always seemed strange...' Another eloquent pause.

'Strange?'

'That it was the uncle taking Emma out places and not the aunt.'

'Their daughter's never recovered from her fall,' Pam said. 'It won't have been easy for Mrs Tremlow to get away.'

Spence wrinkled his nose. 'Still think it's odd. Mind you, speak as I find, he always seemed a friendly sort. Must've filled a gap. I'd have done more myself but... There, it's easy to say these things after the fact, isn't it? What I found strange was, well...' He shifted in his seat and dropped his voice, conspiratorial. 'He was forever photographing her. All a bit excessive, I felt. Eva, my late wife, couldn't see any harm in it but I used to say to her, "Look, he's out there with his camera again!" Tremlow took an *awful* lot of pictures of her. Of her and the other little girl, dancing around, playing. Not saying there was anything sinister in it, but these days it's hard to resist the thought that...well, that there was more to it than met the eye.'

'The other little girl?' Pam asked.

'We're going back a few years. They were probably not long out of infants – no more than seven or eight, anyway. No idea what the other youngster's name was but she was a chubby little thing. They virtually lived in the summer house, those girls. That's what I mean, you see, thinking back, old Tremlow in the summer house with two little girls and a proper camera. Try as you might, you can't help thinking that there was more to it than you realised at the time.'

When Pam returned from seeing Oliver Spence out, Lincoln was already back at his desk, scanning the notes he'd taken. Was it possible that abuse committed seven or eight years ago might culminate in Emma's murder? It seemed unlikely and yet here was the first hint of something seriously amiss in the Sherman household, a possible reason for the estrangement between Crystal and her sister.

Lincoln wanted to hear what Pam made of it before he said anything. 'What do you think?'

She perched on the edge of the desk across from his.

'Uncle Todd Tremlow alone in a summer house with two little girls? Hard to avoid the obvious assumption, isn't it?'

'Could the other kid be Stephanie?'

'Not if they were both dancing around. I don't think Stephanie can even walk on her own, and anyway, Spence thought the girls were the same age, and Stephanie's two or three years older. More likely someone Emma was at school with.'

Lincoln tried not to jump to conclusions – especially since Spence was recalling something from years ago. 'Where was Tremlow Thursday night?'

Pam checked her notes. 'He and Tania were hosting a meeting at their house – a support group they belong to, parents of teenagers with special needs. You don't think...?'

In need of caffeine and sugar, he headed for the kettle. 'Could be a motive, say, if Emma was threatening to tell her mother. She's fifteen, starting to stand up for herself. Maybe she's kept quiet for long enough, wants to confront something from her past.' Although he hoped to God it was nothing like that.

'The boys from Board Treaders could've been encouraging her.' Pam followed him, teabag at the ready in her dainty china cup. 'That other little girl could be Maisie.'

'Christ, that's all we need – another reason for Donal Finnegan to be on our tail!' Lincoln spooned extra coffee into his blackened mug. 'The meeting at the Tremlows' house? Did the alibi check out?'

'The Tremlows gave us the names and addresses of everyone there.'

'Yes, but did you check them out?' He could tell from the sheepish look on her face that she hadn't. 'Then do it now.'

Pam went back to her orderly desk and found the list of parents straightaway. 'Todd would never hurt Emma, I'm sure. He seemed genuinely upset that Crystal had stopped them seeing her.'

'Yes, but men like that are expert at presenting themselves as loving and considerate.' Lincoln thought while he stirred his coffee. Maybe if Crystal knew they'd got suspicions about her brother-in-law, she'd open up – if only to defend him. Repeating Spence's allegations might prompt her to confirm or deny them.

'Tomorrow, Pam, go round and talk to Crystal again. Let her think we know more than we do, see if she gives a bit more away. Careful, though – Oliver Spence could simply have a vivid imagination.'

'If only she'd talk about Emma.' Pam sipped her tea as decorously as a spinster in a teashop. 'Still, if you've made someone the centre of your universe, you don't know where to turn when you lose them. What is it they say: "Grief is the price we pay for love"?'

Lincoln turned his face away. 'Something like that.'

# CHAPTER 34

'They think she was driven away by some Indian cab driver.'

'Who told you that?'

'They showed me a picture. She must have thought it was a taxi.' Crystal shut her eyes tight as she pressed the phone to her ear. She'd left the lights off, letting dusk spread through the house. Now she was scared to cross the room because of the shadows between her chair and the light switch. 'I told her over and over again about the dangers...'

'He'll be found, for sure.'

'But why would she do that? Where was she going in a taxi? She was meant to be at her dance class.'

'Crystal, she wasn't the little girl she used to be. Think of the way she changed in the last few months. You hardly knew her.'

She frowned into the darkness. He was right, but it wasn't his place to say it. 'We were as close as a mother and daughter can ever be.'

'And yet she was going out with this fellow, this Indian.'

'No, no, she thought she was getting into a minicab—'

'But she was going out with *somebody*, wasn't she? You must know, Crystal. You're her mother. How can you not know what she was getting up to?'

He was punishing her now, rubbing it in, making her feel even worse – if that were possible. 'I don't know!' The phone was shaking in her hand, shuddering against her cheekbone.

'You were meant to be protecting her, for pity's sake! Isn't that what a mother's supposed to do? Keep her children safe?'

'I tried! I did my best! It's my fault, I know it's my fault, but I did my best!'

'Your best wasn't good enough, was it?' He hung up, leaving her clutching the receiver, staring into a darkness that was taking shape around her, rearing up between her eyes and the light switch, blocking her way.

Her best had never been good enough. She'd always known that. She was a failure as a daughter and as a wife, and now as a mother. Emma was dead because of her, because she hadn't been good enough. He'd said it and he was always right, so it must be true.

# CHAPTER 35

## FRIDAY 13TH SEPTEMBER

'So we're okay?' His voice was muffled by the duvet.

Trish groaned. Two o'clock in the morning and he wants to know if we're back together again...

She kept her eyes shut. She didn't want to talk about this, not now, not with the Essex job in the offing, everything beginning to take off again. 'Yes, Jeff, we're okay.'

She felt him snuggle into her back and let him pull her into the heat of his lap. A few minutes later he was snoring.

Seven o'clock and she was up again, making coffee. Jeff appeared in the kitchen doorway, bleary, rumpled, checking his phone. 'Gotta go home and change before I go into the station.'

'At least have some coffee.' She thrust the big pottery mug at him: strong coffee, black, sweet. He added more sugar, as she knew he would.

'Breakfast?' She held a couple of eggs up. 'Scrambled okay?' She took butter out of the fridge, milk. Hunted for the mustard while the butter melted.

'You said yesterday you wanted to ask me about something.' He pulled a chair out and sat down at the big farmhouse table she'd never regretted cramming into the kitchen. She couldn't help thinking how comfortable it felt, having him sitting at her table again, half-dressed, hair awry, stubble darkening his chin. 'Remember?'

'Oh, it's one of my staff. Her little sister's got in with a bad crowd. She's only fourteen but she's going round with some older kids. She's fallen for a boy who sounds like trouble, and she may have been shoplifting. Has anything been reported, like teenagers stealing stuff in the Half Moon Centre?'

'Nothing out of the ordinary.' He took a big gulp of coffee. 'What's her name?'

'Anita Rani.'

'Indian?'

'Half. The father died. She's Selina's little sister.'

'Selina? With the long black hair?'

'Thought you'd remember her!' Smiling to herself, Trish stirred the eggs in a figure of eight, the way her mother had taught her. Funny how some things become rituals. Which of her own little habits would Kate take with her into the future? All those scraps of advice at which she now groaned, 'Oh, Mu-um!'

'I'll check on the Rani girl,' he said, tucking into his breakfast a few minutes later. 'But unless she's come across our radar officially, there's not a lot I can do.'

'Selina's afraid this boy's a bad influence on her.'

'Name?'

'No idea. He's nineteen or twenty, with a flat in Barbury somewhere.'

'You say she's been shoplifting?'

Trish told him what she'd witnessed in the shopping centre, Anita and Selina tussling over a Tarara carrier bag.

He frowned. 'Sounds as if she's spending money she hasn't got.'

'But she's not old enough for her own credit card, and Tarara's an expensive boutique for a fourteen-year-old.' She was about to pour him more coffee when his mobile began to dance around on the table.

'Sorry, better get this.' He answered it, his face telling her there was no time for that extra coffee. 'Bella wants a quick update before she heads off to a meeting. In person. In other words, it's nearly eight, why aren't I at my desk?' He tucked his shirt in. 'Where did I leave my coat?'

'You're going to need it this morning. It's been drizzling since we got up.'

Kate appeared in the kitchen doorway, Jeff's mac draped round her, her face full of disdain. 'This mackintosh is quite stinky,' she told him, sliding it off her shoulders as if it were a slimy dead animal. 'They do dry cleaning at Sainsbury's, you know. You can drop it off and pick it up next time you shop. Even with *your* erratic hours.'

'Kate!' Trish put her hands on her hips. 'That's not very nice.'

'I didn't mean to sound rude.' Her daughter's eyes were wide pools of innocence. 'I was trying to be helpful.'

He took the mac from her. 'You're right, Kate – it does smell pretty ripe.'

His mobile started buzzing again.

'Go,' Trish ordered. 'And get that mac cleaned before it walks into the dry cleaner's on its own.'

He hurried out of the house, squinting at the rain.

'Are you two back together?' Kate asked as he drove away.

'Not sure. Ish.'

Kate grinned. 'Ish will do. For now.'

Drizzle turned to heavier rain as Lincoln drove to Barley Lane. Pam should be on her way to Folly Hill Crescent – but would Crystal Sherman be willing to talk about her brother-in-law? Oliver Spence had done his best to describe the other child yesterday. Plumper than Emma, he'd said, darker, with thick brown hair in a pudding-basin haircut, boyish, 'like Christopher Robin in those children's books – but most certainly a little girl'.

Could that be Maisie Finnegan? She certainly wasn't plump these days but maybe she was when she was six or seven. After his encounter with Finnegan on Wednesday, Lincoln didn't fancy telling him his daughter might once have been molested by her best friend's uncle.

If only Spence had come forward years ago! But would Crystal implicate Tremlow or exonerate him? Either way, the closed and private world she'd guarded so zealously would be exposed.

Bella walked in, sweeping drops of rain out of her hair. 'It's bloody pouring out there!' She took her coat off, shook it. 'Any developments?'

'Pam's gone over to talk to Crystal Sherman again.' He relayed what Oliver Spence had told them, deciding against telling her the other girl might be Maisie – without proof, he'd be stirring up trouble. Least said...

'Child abuse? Oh joy!' She hung her coat up, shoved her wild hair back from her face. 'We need to be sure about this – it's not something we can throw out and then reel back in again if we're wrong.'

'Spence's convinced Tremlow was taking more than family snapshots.'

'Okay, but where's the evidence? And how's that connected to her murder?'

'She could've threatened to expose him – he'd want to get her out of the way.'

Her eyebrows went up. 'You're saying this guy who picked her up in the car was some sort of *hitman*?'

Lincoln shook his head, hopeless. 'I don't know. She got into that car as if she was expecting it to come for her. She could've been set up, told she was being taken to meet her boyfriend.'

'And ending up in the woods.' Bella pursed her lips, thinking. 'But we still need to find out who she *thought* she was going to meet,

141

because until—' She broke off to answer the phone on his desk. 'Hi, Pam, what's up? She's what? Fuck. Did she leave a note? Keep looking. We need to be sure... Yes, he's here. I'll tell him.' She dumped the phone down, her face grim. 'The Sherman woman's in intensive care, Presford General. Overdose. Pam's still at the house so if there's a note, she'll find it.'

'Christ, that's all we need. I knew she was fragile, but—'

'You'd better get over to the hospital while I brief the PR team. This one won't be easy to dress up.'

As soon as Lincoln drove into the car park at Presford General, he spotted Todd Tremlow ahead of him, recognising him from the photo Pam had brought back from Whitpenny. He had a bunch of flowers he must have picked up at a petrol station on the way but Lincoln doubted if Crystal was in a fit state to appreciate them. He just hoped she was still alive.

Tremlow's face was grey and unshaven. Had this insignificant-looking bloke been abusing his niece and maybe had her killed?

'Sorry to hear about Mrs Sherman.' Lincoln caught up with him at the automatic doors into the lobby. He introduced himself but Tremlow scarcely acknowledged him as he marched towards the staircase going up to intensive care.

'She doesn't show her feelings much. Bottles it up. My wife would've gladly stayed with her as long as she wanted but she sent her away. What can you do?' He grasped the handrail, hauled himself up, not a fit man, short in the leg, tending to stoutness.

They arrived at the reception desk together and announced themselves simultaneously to the two clerks who asked for their details.

'Tremlow?' one of them said, jotting it down with a giggle. 'I thought you said Tremeloes! Shows my age!'

'When can I see her?' Tremlow asked, but the clerk shrugged, pointing the back end of her ballpoint at a doctor emerging from a door down the corridor.

'They'll come and look for you when it's okay to see her. They'll come and find you when they need to.'

Covering either eventuality: Crystal surviving or not.

Minutes later, they told Tremlow he couldn't see her, so he left the flowers with the nurse and trundled off towards the exit.

Waiting on the bleak landing between Busby ward and intensive care, Lincoln felt in limbo, the investigation wrenched away from him just when he thought he was getting somewhere. Beyond the window, another wing of the hospital mirrored this one, a tower of brickwork and unwashed glass panels. Pigeons roosted on the parapets, defying rows of spikes sprouting like black plastic grass from every outcrop. You'd soon lose the will to live if you were cooped up in a place like this. Even the pigeons looked depressed.

Unbidden, a memory shot into his head: nearly twenty years ago, waiting for his mother to die, the terrible sense of his own life coming to an end, his own life as he'd known it – her death from an aggressive cancer that surged back after years in remission. The recriminations, the rows with his sister Ruth as they tried to track their errant brother down somewhere in Bolivia.

Ruth was thirteen years older than Lincoln, Paul nearly seven. By the time Lincoln was a moody teenager, Ruth was starting her first job as a social worker in Solihull and Paul was at university in London. Left at home like an only child, Lincoln had grown closer to his father, his mother preoccupied with her charity work, her painting and her beloved house. Lincoln Senior had been a gardener, a man who travelled far to watch cricket matches, who loved the sea on windy days, who valued his solitude.

Which is probably why he didn't live long after Ruth badgered him into selling up and moving in with her and Reg, into her grandpa annexe. Lincoln had never forgiven her and – reading between the lines – neither had Paul. She'd been in the States for ten years now, and Paul was – well, travelling abroad, in perpetual motion.

Woody arrived. He must've passed Tremlow without recognising him. 'Lucky Pam found her in time,' he said when Lincoln filled him in on what had happened. He gave him the gist of Oliver Spence's allegations as well.

Woody looked appalled. 'Reckon Tremlow was abusing her? Is that what this is all about? But then, if he's into kiddie porn, Emma's been too old for the last few years.'

'But old enough to tell someone what happened to her. Supposing he decided he couldn't take the risk of her telling her mum, of going to the police? He was hosting a meeting at his house the night she died but if he got someone else to get rid of her, he'd make bloody sure his alibi was cast iron, wouldn't he? And if he was abusing Maisie Finnegan as well, the case takes on a whole new dimension.'

Woody snorted. 'As if three dimensions weren't enough!'

The service lift opened and a trolley erupted onto the landing, two orderlies steering it, a small, thin, elderly woman, nearly bald, lying there under a mauve cellular blanket. She looked dead but the orderlies probably knew better.

Lincoln turned away. 'Crystal's been keeping Tremlow at arm's length for the last few months. Maybe she knew something went on years ago. She didn't want to make a fuss so she just kept him at a distance. Listen, there's no point both of us hanging around here. I'll see you back at the station.'

Not long after Woody left, Lincoln's phone rang.

'I'm still at the Shermans',' Pam said, her voice tinny over the network. 'No sign of a suicide note. I assume the summer house is off limits?' It sounded as if she was out in the garden. 'If we could find something that backed up what Oliver Spence told us about Emma and her friend playing there...'

'Don't even think about it! We'll need more than Spence's innuendo to get a warrant.' He stared out of the window, transfixed by the unrelenting brutality of Presford General's architecture. 'And nothing to suggest anyone else was involved?'

'No. She was lying on Emma's bed, all neat and tidy.'

'You broke in, did you?'

'No need. When she didn't come to the front door, we went round the back and found the door unlocked. Knowing how she never goes out, I was a bit worried, went upstairs and there she was. Looks as if she woke up this morning, swallowed a load of pills and lay down to die.'

She made it sound so easy. Lincoln hung up, anger growling inside him. Not so easy for the people who have to clear up after you.

He pondered again on Todd Tremlow taking photos of Emma when she was small. Before digital cameras were the norm, over-zealous processors in film labs would call the police after developing photos of children in the bath or naked on the beach – photos the kids' own parents had taken. The tabloids lapped up every tale of political correctness gone mad.

But exactly what was acceptable? Where did hysteria stop and justified concern begin? This case had gone from enigmatic to messy in the last twenty-four hours.

A few minutes later, he was heading for the car park, keen to get back to work. He'd just fed his parking ticket into the pay station machine when his phone rang.

Pam again.

He jammed the phone under his chin while he ransacked his pockets for change. 'Yes?'

'We've found something but I'm not sure we can use it.' He could hear the apprehension in her voice. Something was wrong.

The coins clonked into the box. His ticket shot out again and dropped onto the damp concrete before he could catch it. 'Damn. Sorry, not you.' He bent to pick it up. 'Tell me what you've got and I'll let you know.'

'Charlie unlocked the summer house and went in.'

'Christ. Didn't I tell you to stick to the house?'

'He'd got the key and gone in before I could stop him. He found some photos in a drawer. Emma when she was about six or seven. Posing.'

'Posing?' His heart raced.

'In a ballet dress, with make-up on. She's decent but it's obvious why the photos were taken. Charlie opened this drawer with a bit of a yank, it came flying out and everything went on the floor. The photos were in an envelope in amongst some seed packets. It doesn't look as if anyone's set foot in the summer house for years but once upon a time—'

'Those photos won't be admissible. You found them in an unauthorised search. Put them back exactly where you found them.' Though having to say that made him boil inside.

'I was afraid you'd say that.'

'And forget that Charlie ever set foot in that summer house.'

He rang off, opened his car door, took his mac off. A black Land Rover Discovery swept into the car park, Donal Finnegan at the wheel. It swerved to a halt and Finnegan wound his window down. 'Any news?'

'She's still unconscious. Not sure they'll let you see her.'

'Fuck it, Lincoln, I built half this hospital. I'd like to see them try and stop me!' And he put his foot down, shooting away into a space reserved for staff.

Back at his desk, Lincoln checked every possible database but Todd Tremlow wasn't on any of them. If he'd ever committed a crime, it couldn't have been serious enough to stay on file. Or else he'd never been caught.

If he'd been abusing Emma and her friend when they were six or seven, they might have been too embarrassed or confused to confide in anyone at the time. Then, over the years, they'd made themselves forget about it. Lincoln had come across plenty of cases where victims of childhood abuse had buried such memories, only to have them brought back to the surface later on through therapy or trauma.

Historical allegations of abuse always made the headlines – think Jimmy Savile, think dead Prime Ministers – but they were hard to prove because so little evidence remained. Only when other victims came forward with similar stories was a case likely to go to court, and even then, juries were reluctant to put too much reliance on recovered memories alone.

Was this what he was dealing with now? Emma, abused by her uncle, recalling years later what happened, forcing her mother and her aunt apart because of her allegations?

Lincoln felt as if he was clutching at cobwebs, strands tearing in his hands, nothing holding. Tired of searching databases, he shoved himself away from the computer.

Taking a break in the canteen, he saw Sergeant Bob Bowden. Bob knew everything there was to know about local villains – family connections, past liaisons, that blend of gossip and intel that never got officially logged.

'The name Todd Tremlow mean anything?' He took a seat beside Bob at a corner table. 'Lives with his wife in Whitpenny.'

Bob unwrapped a Penguin, snapped it in two and dunked one half in his tea while he ran Tremlow's name through his mental database. 'Private landlord, isn't he? Buys at auction, does them up and flogs them on.' He lifted a bushy eyebrow. 'Keeps a few as rentals, usually in the less salubrious parts of town. Can't be much in it for him, money-wise.'

'How d' you mean?'

'Well, you can't ask high rents for a flat round the back of the station, can you, or down in that dead end where the gas works used to be? Mind you, if you've got enough of them on the go...' He shrugged. 'Pile 'em high and rent 'em cheap.'

'Yes, but nobody's going to do up derelict houses out of the goodness of their heart, are they?'

'No, but if you've spotted a gap in the market, you're coining it! Wasn't there some scheme he was involved in...?' Bob frowned as he tried to recall it. 'No, it's gone. Sign of old age.' He posted the other bit of Penguin into his mouth. 'What was Ollie Spence doing in here?'

'You know him?'

Bob leaned back in his chair, dusted his fingers free of chocolate crumbs. 'Ollie's notorious. Always getting letters in *The Messenger*. World's going to hell in a handcart. Country's going to the dogs. Young people these days... You know the sort.'

'He's told us Tremlow took photos of Emma Sherman and a friend when they were kids – possibly dodgy. I thought we were onto something but now you're making him sound unreliable.'

Bob opened his hands imploringly. 'Don't shoot the messenger. I'm only telling you what I know. Doesn't mean it didn't happen – just that Ollie Spence is such an old bigot, he'd be easy to discredit in court. Think he's been kiddie-diddling, then, your Mr Tremlow?'

'Don't know what to think. There's something not right about this case, something we're not being told.'

'Scratch the surface in most families, there's dirt underneath.' Bob grinned, showing chocolatey teeth. 'I'll let you know if anything comes to mind.'

Back at his desk, the phone was ringing, and no one else was around so he picked it up. 'Hello? Lincoln here, can I—'

'Why's someone guarding Crystal 24/7?' A familiar voice. 'Is that the best use of your resources?'

'Mr Finnegan. It was decided that Mrs Sherman should be watched during hospital visiting hours, at least until we're sure she hasn't been the victim of an attack.'

'She tried to kill herself, for fuck's sake! Isn't that obvious?'

Lincoln shared Finnegan's reservations about watching Crystal all the time but it wasn't up to him. And he wasn't going to have the likes of Finnegan tell him what to do. 'Better to be cautious until we can be sure.'

The man panted against the mouthpiece, exasperated. 'And you badger my daughter when she's already told you everything. Know what, I don't like what I'm hearing.' His words were slurred, as if he'd been drinking since he'd got back from the hospital.

'Nobody badgered her, Mr Finnegan. We needed some clarification, that's all.'

A snatch of breath, a long pause. Then, 'You don't have children, do you, Inspector? None of your own, anyway?'

We've had this conversation, Lincoln thought. 'No, none of my own.'

'Then you can have no idea how hard it is to raise daughters.'

'My partner's daughter is only a bit younger than yours, so I'm—'

'Your *partner*? Huh! Took you for more of a loner.'

Something in his tone made Lincoln's scalp prickle. He didn't reply straightaway. Then, 'We're narrowing down our pool of suspects, Mr Finnegan. Acting in haste could jeopardise the whole investigation.'

'Acting in haste? Right now, you don't seem to be acting at all!' He hung up.

Lincoln cradled the receiver against his chest for a moment. He hadn't mistaken Donal Finnegan for an ally, but neither had he thought him an enemy.

Until now.


He arrived at Trish's a little before six, craving food, drink, company. The minute he was inside the front door, though, he knew he was out of luck.

'I've had to get a plumber in and he's turned the water off.' Trish looked frazzled. 'The pipe under the washbasin's blocked. And if that isn't the source of the pong in there, he'll have to pull the panelling off and poke around a bit.'

He was glad she'd already got a plumber in. He didn't mind trying his hand at most household tasks if he had to, but the day's events had already left him with a nasty taste in his mouth. He'd gladly leave sorting out stinky waste pipes to a professional.

'I'll come round another evening if—'

'No, no, as long as you don't mind waiting for supper. Kettle's on, though, so we can have some coffee. I'll go up and see how he's getting on.'

Kate wandered into the kitchen while her mother was upstairs. 'Hi.' She picked up an apple, looked in the fridge, didn't seem to fancy anything she saw and came and slumped down beside him. 'We've got the plumber here.'

'So I've heard.'

'Put your new bathroom in yet?'

'Not yet.'

'You still decorating?'

'I need you and your mum to give me a hand to help finish it off. You made a good job of decorating my living room, didn't you?'

'I didn't do much really, but yeah, it was fun. Haven't been round your house for ages. Have you filled it up with loads of stuff from Ikea?'

'Do I look like an Ikea man?'

148

'No, but you and Mum went to all those antique shops and car boots and you didn't buy anything there either.'

'Slight exaggeration.' But not far off the truth. Lots of window-shopping. Plenty of poking fun at other people's castoffs, other people's taste. Innumerable discussions about 'shall we, shan't we buy this couch/mirror/wardrobe/table'. Not many actual purchases.

'We might be moving.' Kate said it without looking at him, running her finger along the edge of the worktop.

'Really?' Had he heard her right? Trish loved this house despite its tiny garden and all the parking problems. Was she downsizing? 'Where are you moving to?'

'Like, moving *away*.' Kate caught his eye, as if she wasn't sure if he knew, but Trish came thundering down the stairs before he could ask Kate anything more.

'He's opened the pipes up and there's all this disgusting sludge! He's going to be ages.'

'Okay, look, I'll get on back. I can see it's tricky.'

'But I was going to make some coffee.'

'No, that's okay. I should be getting back.'

'If you're sure...' Trish seemed relieved that he wasn't staying. One less thing to worry about. 'He's a very good plumber. I'll give you his card. He could put your new bathroom in.' She riffled through a wooden bowl full of business cards and takeaway menus. 'I bet it's still in the garage, isn't it?'

'Yep.' He hadn't even taken the components out of their cardboard and shrink wrap. He took the card from her, slipped it into his pocket.

'Sorry about supper,' she said, coming out onto the steps with him. 'Have you got stuff in?'

'Yeah, I'll be fine.' He visualised the shelves of his fridge, imagined them bowing under the weight of food and drink. Knew they were empty. 'I'll be fine.'

Moving away? He drove home in a daze. Just when he'd thought they were getting back on track. There must be someone else. Then why invite him back into her bed? Was that a farewell fuck?

The fridge might be empty but he'd got plenty to drink. Plenty enough to get him through the night, at least.

# CHAPTER 36

## SATURDAY 14TH SEPTEMBER

When his mobile woke him at 7.30 the next morning, Lincoln took a moment or two to work out where he was – then realised he'd fallen asleep over his laptop at the kitchen table, a mug of cold coffee at his elbow.

He rubbed his eyes, the phone's display too blurry to read. He answered anyway, to hear Dilke greeting him sombrely.

'A body by the side of the road, boss, Langford Hill Lane. Young girl, suspicious death. I'm on my way there now. Shall I come and pick you up?'

'No, get over there as fast as you can. I'll meet you there.'

Five minutes; ten. Time to clean his teeth, spritz his underarms, change his shirt.

Stiff and clumsy, Lincoln put the kettle on before heading upstairs to freshen up.

The lane linking the villages of Langford St Catherine's and Langford St John had been blocked off, so it was eerily quiet apart from the occasional shrill of birdsong.

The dead girl wasn't very old – thirteen, fourteen? – but she'd been beaten and fucked and cut like a prostitute twice her age.

Lincoln shook his head in disbelief. 'Christ, look at the state of her.'

'I know this girl.' Dilke hugged himself against the chill of the morning and gazed down at the body a jogger had found in a ditch less than an hour earlier.

'You know her? How come?' Lincoln squatted on his haunches, careful not to disturb anything before the SOCO team arrived.

'I attended when her mum got arrested. Attempted murder. Murder, it is now. Stupid bugger died. The kid was there when it went down. Lorren Walsh. Social worker took her back to her foster home in Presford.'

Lincoln looked up into the young man's face; saw the clenched jaw, the bleak disappointment in his eyes. 'When was this? Sunday?'

'Sunday afternoon.'

'Wrapped up like Emma,' Lincoln noted. 'Not quite as carefully,

150

but the same sort of tarpaulin.' Lorren's shroud had fallen open, exposing her body – naked except for a thin vest top.

Her mouth was a bloody mess of pulp, her face swollen and misshapen. Clumsy tattoos decorated her arms and thighs. *LORREN* was inked crookedly on one forearm. The tats wouldn't be legal, probably done by friends or even the kid herself.

There, on the insides of her wrists and forearms, gleamed the sad marks of self-harm, irregular weals criss-crossing, one set hardly healed before the next set cut open the fragile skin to let tension out, to make the girl inside feel better.

She'd probably lain there no longer than a few hours. Her long hair was wet and matted. Hard to tell what colour it was – light brown? Auburn? Her ears were pierced, though one lobe had been torn bloodily open when the earring was ripped out. Her fingernails – fragments of old red varnish still clinging to her cuticles – were ragged as if she'd clawed at something in her struggle.

Between her hollow thighs, blood streaked her blotchy skin, stains still so vivid it looked as if she'd haemorrhaged.

What had they forced into her to do that much harm? Lincoln wanted to throw up or hit someone or walk away, to turn his back on this insult. He guessed that Dilke, who'd met the girl and tried to help her, felt even greater outrage.

Bella stumbled up the verge towards them and without thinking, Lincoln put out his hand to help her over the last few feet of sodden grass. She swatted his hand away, hauled herself up to stand over the dead girl.

'Oh fuck.' She frowned down at the body, as if disapproving of a wayward child. She craned forward to peer at the tattoos. 'That's her name? Lorren?' Her voice betrayed her distaste – of the name, its spelling or its depiction on the kid's skinny arm, Lincoln couldn't tell. Maybe all of those.

Dilke spoke up. 'Lorren Walsh. Fourteen. Her mother's in custody, murder charge last weekend.'

'Guy with his throat cut, yeah? Who found her?'

'Jogger over there, out for his morning run.' Dilke jerked his thumb towards the other side of the lane, where a man in a foil blanket was slumped against the garden wall of a flint-and-brick cottage, grey head bent. A paramedic was squatting beside him.

Bella struggled to keep her balance on the bank. 'Where the fuck are the SOCOs?'

151

'Waiting for us to finish up here and get out of their way.'

Arms flailing as she slid down the bank, Bella took an ungainly leap and landed more or less upright on the road. Lincoln hadn't really wanted her to fall on her arse, but part of him wouldn't have minded if she had.

He and Dilke slithered down after her and let the scenes of crime team move in. She strode back to her car.

'I called at the cottage,' said Dilke. 'They were still in bed. They didn't see or hear anything.'

'Then let's go and talk to our jogger.'

They headed for the man in the Bacofoil cape.

# CHAPTER 37

Bella stood in front of the whiteboard, where photographs of Lorren Walsh's bloodied body and tattoos had shunted aside the smiley school photos of Emma.

'Earlier today, this young female's body was found dumped in Langford Hill Lane. She was wrapped in a tarpaulin similar to the one found with the Sherman girl – which suggests the murders could be the work of the same person or persons.'

'The victims are quite different,' Pam countered. 'Apart from being teenage girls.'

Not so very different, Lincoln thought. Fatherless girls with dysfunctional mothers – Jackie was a wild alcoholic while Crystal was so tightly controlling that her daughter must have felt imprisoned. Lost girls searching for someone to love them for themselves.

Bella turned to the whiteboard, spun back again, her soles squeaking on the vinyl. 'Good point, Pam, but the type of tarpaulin used is a bit of a coincidence. However, we are keeping the connection – the *apparent* connection – absolutely confidential for now. We don't want the media starting rumours of a serial killer.' She began to roam the room. 'So what do we know about this kid? Graham?'

Dilke related what he'd learnt last Sunday when Jackie Walsh was arrested at her flat in Michaelmas House and a social worker took Lorren back to her foster carers. The row between Jackie and her boyfriend began when Lorren turned up at the flat unexpectedly. Liam was all over the girl, and Jackie, already drunk, started shouting and throwing things around. By the time the police responded to a neighbour's 999 call, she'd rammed a broken bottle into Liam's neck.

By Sunday evening, Lorren was back with her foster carers, Peter and Yvonne Spring, in Presford.

'So when did she go missing?' Bella asked.

Lincoln shook his head. 'We won't know until we've spoken to the Springs. She hadn't been reported missing.'

Dilke looked appalled. 'Wouldn't they have been worried if she was out all night?'

'Kids in care run away all the time,' Bella said. 'The Springs were probably fed up with reporting her. Different standards apply, Graham. If you haven't learned that yet, you soon will do.' A lift of her eyebrows showed that she was keen to move on. 'Forensics?'

'She hadn't been there long, and the tarpaulin,' said Lincoln, pointing to the crime scene photos, 'this sort of woven plastic stuff, may have picked up prints and fibres. The cause of death was probably asphyxia, although she'd suffered a number of violent blows to her face and body, as well as a pretty bloody sexual assault.'

Even as he finished saying it, his mouth went dry. A kid so slender a gust of wind could have sent her flying. Bones so small, too hearty a hug could have crushed her. Beaten up as if she could fight back, could be a threat to somebody. It didn't make sense.

Bella stepped aside, beckoned him up to the front. 'Any thoughts on the location, Jeff? You know the immediate area better than I do.'

Trying to seem calm, Lincoln grabbed a marker pen and approached the whiteboard.

'Langford Hill Lane is single-track after Langford St Catherine's itself,' he said, 'with only a couple of passing places. I'm guessing after he dumped her body, her killer turned round at the church and drove back the way he'd come. SOCOs are checking the roadside for any other evidence he might have left behind, but...'

As he jabbed at the sketch map of Langford Hill Lane, his eye caught the photos of Lorren Walsh's body, discarded – yes, that was the only word for it – *discarded* by the roadside. His mind froze, as if a shutter had clicked shut and taken a photo of him. A weird kind of selfie.

For a split second he saw with absolute clarity that what he was doing was belated and futile. He was meant to be fighting crime, yet here he was, calmly prodding pictures of places where people threw dead girls away.

He pulled himself together, carried on. 'Let's assume she'd have a phone, keys and purse with her at the very least – none of which have been found. We need to establish her last movements, who she went round with, where she hung out.'

'Who's going to ID her if the mother's in custody?' Bella clasped her hands behind her back, squared her shoulders. There was something so military about her, so tough.

'The foster parents have been informed,' he said, 'and Family Services.'

'So, you'll talk to the foster parents, get an idea of what this kid got up to?' She held his gaze as if she expected him to argue with her.

'I'll get on to it now.'

'Meanwhile, we can't let the Emma Sherman investigation go off the boil. We need to be seen to be doing something. Mike, I want you to take Graham over to Whitpenny and speak to Todd Tremlow. It'll be a good test of your diplomatic skills.'

Woody looked alarmed. 'What, bring him in for questioning?'

'No, no. Approach him as if he might be able to throw some light on the Sherman woman's overdose. What can he tell us about the family, et cetera, et cetera. We need to keep him on side.' She caught Lincoln's eye. 'I'm not convinced there's anything in these abuse rumours, Jeff, but we can't ignore them. Still, let's not forget this is a delicate issue – we can't wade in there accusing Tremlow of molesting his niece when we've got fuck-all evidence to back it up.'

Lincoln longed to have a go at Tremlow himself, but if Bella wanted Woody to talk to him, there wasn't a lot he could do about it. Did she expect Tremlow to give himself away during a cosy chat? He was too clever for that, for sure. The bumbling, inoffensive front was exactly that – a façade.

Yet if these two girls were killed by the same person, what was the connection between Tremlow and a runaway like Lorren?

Dilke cleared his throat. 'Er – I was hoping to follow up on Lorren Walsh myself, ma'am.'

'And why's that, Graham?' She gave him a look that could have boiled a frog in its skin.

'Because I was there when her mum was arrested. Because I talked to her myself.'

'Well, if he thinks you have any valuable insights to impart, I'm sure Inspector Lincoln will consult with you. For now, you are going with DS Woods to interview Todd Tremlow, and the inspector is going to make a few phone calls. Okay?'

# CHAPTER 38

Woody and Dilke took their seats at the table in the bay window of the Tremlows' living room.

'Any news on Mrs Sherman?' Woody asked.

Todd Tremlow beetled in from the kitchen with a tray of mugs, half a packet of biscuits, a bowl of sugar. The tray was mucky and he'd forgotten teaspoons but since none of them took sugar, it didn't matter.

'Still hasn't come round. They're letting nature take its course.' He put their mugs in front of them and picked up his own, cradling it as he sat down again.

'As if you didn't have enough to deal with, eh?' Woody said, trying to sound his most sympathetic. He could smell spirits and guessed Tremlow's tea was fortified with Scotch or brandy.

Emma's uncle stared gloomily into his mug. Red veins glistened on his cheeks and nostrils. His coarse hair was poorly cut, a bit too long over his ears for a man his age. 'It's how we'll cope when she's out of hospital that's bothering me,' he admitted. 'She'll need a lot of support. Now, what did you want to ask me about? I think we've told you all we can.'

'Had any more thoughts about Emma's friends, anyone she might have been close to? Someone she was friends with when she was, say, seven or eight?'

'That's a good few years ago. What's brought this on?'

Woody was about to explain when Dilke cut across him. 'We heard you took lots of pictures of Emma when she was little, Mr Tremlow. Dancing and that.'

'Pictures?'

'Photographs. When she was little. In her garden.'

'Oh, *those* photos.' He looked wistful. 'She loved being photographed, Emma did. Always a little star. Always a little show-off. "Look at me, Uncle Todd, look at me!" I won a prize for a picture I took of her when she was small, you know – she was on the front page of *The Messenger*, and in a couple of camera magazines. My word, she was chuffed!' He was grinning but his lip trembled.

'And this friend who used to come round to play with her – you don't remember her name?'

'We're talking a long time ago. My memory's not *that* good.' Then he put his mug down. 'Am I being accused of something? I know what you people are like, looking for ulterior motives. If I'd been Derek Sherman, you wouldn't have thought twice about me taking pictures of Emma. I'll have you know, I was like a father to that child.'

'But Mr Tremlow,' said Woody, sensing the interview was beginning to fall apart, 'you *weren't* her dad, and the quantity of photos you took of her makes us wonder if—'

'That's it!' Tremlow planted his hands flat on the table, pushed himself up. 'No more questions! If you're accusing me of something, I have every right to know what you think I've done. If you've got any more questions, then I insist on having a lawyer present. I think you should leave now.'

'But Mr Tremlow—'

'No, that's it. Please leave. Now.' And he stood up, pulling their mugs into the centre of the table as if he was confiscating them.

As they went down the steep front steps, an elderly Peugeot lumbered into the parking space beside Tremlow's van. The door creaked open and Tania heaved herself out.

When she caught sight of the two detectives, her jaw dropped. She began to climb hurriedly towards them. 'Has something happened?'

'We're just leaving.' Dilke stood back to let her pass.

'How's Mrs Sherman?' Woody asked.

'Still out of it. Not much point me being there, if truth be told, not until she comes round. I'm just hoping—'

'Come along in, Tania,' her husband barked. 'Come along in this minute!'

# CHAPTER 39

Even though she wasn't due to work that day, Michaela Stanley, Lorren Walsh's social worker, agreed to meet Lincoln at the girl's foster home at four o'clock.

'Like you lot,' she told him over the phone, 'some of us are never off duty, not really. You take it home with you, even when you've walked out the office. Oh, and everybody calls me Micky.'

They met on the pavement outside the pebble-dashed house of Lorren's foster carers, Peter and Yvonne Spring. Set back from the busy main road on the eastern side of Presford, it didn't look a lot like a happy family home. The front garden had been turned over to hard standing, and the greyish-greenish door could have done with a fresh coat of paint. Dingy net curtains veiled every window.

'Can't believe she's dead.' Micky shook her head. 'Things were bad enough this time last week, but I never thought... And no idea who did it?'

'Not yet.' Lincoln had to shout over the din of heavy traffic. 'I need to know all you've got on her.'

The social worker – early thirties, overweight and braless in a glossy V-necked T-shirt, jeans and sneakers – made a face, cynical.

'Where do I start?' She tucked her bulging organiser under her arm and led him up a side street where the noise was muted enough for a conversation – and where she could shake a Marlboro out of a soft pack and have a quick smoke.

She lit up, tilted her head back, savouring the first drag. 'Lorren's been in care off and on for years,' she said, leaning a chunky shoulder against somebody's gatepost. 'Jacqueline's had a drink problem, like, forever. Single mum, string of partners, not really fit to look after her. Jackie'd take her clothes off in the street for the price of a six-pack of Kestrel.' Micky drew on her cigarette, let out a fierce stream of smoke. 'I really thought I'd reached Lorren in time.'

'You saw her on Sunday?'

She nodded. 'The ambulance had just left when I got there. Liam didn't make it so now it's murder. The kid saw everything. It probably happened because she was there. Jackie going off on one because Liam

158

was paying more attention to Lorren than to her. Kid like Lorren, she plays up to the boyfriend without knowing what she's doing. Grownups know it's about sex but a kid just wants to be favourite.'

'A dangerous situation.'

'Not that Jackie ever did much to stop Liam coming on to Lorren.' Micky took another deep, greedy drag on her cigarette. 'Kid was only twelve when he started abusing her.'

'So when did you place her here with the Springs?'

'About eight months ago, middle of January. Needed to put some distance between her and Liam. Barbury was too close to home. The Springs are good people, not especially lively but you don't need lively when your mum's a one-woman freak show.'

Lincoln looked away down the side street, a terrace of tall Victorian houses in various states of disrepair, wheelie bins bulging, rubbish cast into the front yards. Some had their windows boarded up; some had metal grilles padlocked over doors and windows, a sure sign the place had been wrecked inside.

There was constant noise from the main road. This must once have been a peaceful haven on the edge of the countryside, but now the sprawl of Presford had engulfed it in traffic noise and fumes.

'Wasn't happy here either, was she?' He'd seen the reports on Lorren now. 'How many times did she run away from the Springs'? Nine? Ten?'

'There were ten unauthorised absences.'

'"*Unauthorised absences*"? Bloody jargon. She ran away ten times.'

Micky shrugged again. 'Tell me about it. You think Lorren's the only damaged kid I'm looking out for? We do our best, okay? We're all overstretched. You heard what happened to one of the younger social workers? Topped himself. That's how stressed we are. That's how tough it is.'

The suicide story had been in *The Messenger* and some of the nationals. Lincoln recalled a fresh-faced young man photographed with his parents at his graduation. An Italian name – Bonetti, like the old Chelsea goalkeeper.

The young man's suicide came after months of speculation in the local press about poor management in the council's Family Services department. Bonetti had called himself a whistle-blower, Lincoln remembered now, but his bosses described him as over-ambitious and idealistic – office-speak for troublemaker.

'You knew him?'

Micky waved smoke away. 'Course I knew him. Tried to get the twat to join the union but he thought he was better on his own. He was never going to get anywhere with his allegations, but none of us wanted him rocking the boat trying to prove he could.'

'Allegations of what?'

'All hush-hush. He was still working on this famous report of his when he decided he'd had enough. "Gathering evidence," he said. My boss, David Black, was trying to bring him in line but Linus was so stubborn...' She dropped her cigarette on the pavement and ground it out. 'In the end, he must've seen the odds were stacked against him. You don't take on the council and get away with it.'

Lincoln and Micky looked at each other, recognising a familiar despondency.

'Come on.' He started walking. 'Let's go and get some answers.'

Yvonne and Peter Spring were mournful but pragmatic. They'd done their best but Lorren was vulnerable. They'd always dreaded the worst.

'Can I see her room?' Lincoln asked, not sure what he'd learn but wanting some time alone with the dead girl's belongings.

'Of course.' Leaving her husband in the kitchen, Yvonne led the way upstairs.

Lorren's bedroom was like a room in a hostel. Divan bed, chair, table under the window, a wooden locker instead of a wardrobe, lino on the floor beneath a couple of cheap rugs. The walls were bare except for scribbled slogans inexpertly erased. The thin orange curtains needed washing.

Micky stood at the window, watching as Lincoln sized up the room and its contents.

'She never carried a bag,' Yvonne said as he worked his fingers into an uncooperative pair of latex gloves. 'Always stuffed her purse in her pocket and carried her phone around like it was stuck to her hand.'

She stared bleakly at the little heap of belongings he'd begun to assemble to take back with him. There'd be a more thorough search later, but for now he bagged some tablets, which he guessed were over-the-counter painkillers, and a notebook that Lorren had customised with ready-made sticky letters.

He did the bags up with plastic ties. 'Was there a boyfriend?'

'Some boy she called Scoot was trying to get her to move in with him,' Yvonne said.

'Scoot? Know anything about him?'

'Not much. He was all over her to start with, charming, flashy. She talked like he was the most amazing boy she'd ever met.' She rolled her eyes. 'But you know how they operate, these lads. Soon as she let her guard down, he was on to her, snap his fingers and she'd jump. Softening her up, that's all it was, so he could get her to work for him.'

'Besotted,' Micky agreed. 'She couldn't see for the stars in her eyes, poor kid.'

'We knew she'd had a rotten start,' Yvonne said, 'with that awful mother of hers. But the more we gave, the more she took. She said she ran away from the last foster home because a kid was murdered there, but it was a load of nonsense.'

'Murdered?' Lincoln spun round.

'All made up, of course. The story changed every time. Her imagination ran riot and she didn't have the gumption to see how daft her stories were. Lorren was a fantasist. A damaged little girl who was a fantasist.'

Yvonne sighed, her gaze following Lincoln's, travelling across the unmade bed, the messy pile of clothes on the chair, the tatty magazine flung down unfinished on the floor, open at a real-life story about a woman whose lover cooked and ate her baby...

Micky inched towards the door. 'How about making a cuppa and we can talk a bit more downstairs? Let the inspector go through things without us here, eh?' She gave Lincoln a meaningful look as she led Yvonne away.

Alone in Lorren's room, he opened her locker; found a collection of toiletries, make-up and cheap scent. Tissues, tampons, cotton wool, hairbrush, a comb, hair clips. Long strands of her auburn hair were snagged in a dirty brush. An old sweet tin contained jewellery – earrings, bangles, a silvery crucifix on a tarnished chain. His heart felt chilly as he shut the locker door. Such a little life.

Under her bed – apart from dust-balls the size of kittens – he found a balsawood gift box that had once held a selection of Boots bath products. She'd written *"My Tresaure Box"* in bright red felt-tip on the lid.

He flipped it open, and perfume wafted up, sweet as peaches. Inside he found a jumble of buttons, odd cufflinks, a frayed label torn from a garment, a couple of baby photos – impossible to tell if they were Lorren as a child or someone she knew. A £10 note and some loose change. Five ballpoint pens – including two Parkers and a Schaeffer.

A man's cotton handkerchief – creamy white, edged in silvery blue. A brown envelope labelled #3MH with a Yale key inside, wrapped in a strip of paper torn from a notebook: *With thanks* written with a flourish.

Keepsakes, mementoes of a short life cut shorter. His throat thickened with sadness. He snapped the box shut again and slid it gently into an evidence bag.

Half an hour and a cup of undrinkable coffee later, Lincoln and Micky were back out on the pavement and heading for the quieter side streets again. Fumbling for her cigarettes, Micky was doing her best to hide her feelings but Lincoln sensed the tearfulness beneath her tomboy swagger.

They stopped outside a derelict house while she lit up and took a calming drag.

'So this Scoot bloke was grooming her?'

She nodded. 'Before Lorren came here, she was in Presford House – a children's home, not the nicest of places – and she got in with a girl called Eily, a couple of years older. Eily was getting her to bunk off school, hang out with this guy Scoot in Presford, drinking, taking drugs. Not hard drugs, but that's how it starts. Even after she moved in with the Springs, she was going round to this guy's flat all the time.'

She shoved back from her forehead the only lock of her hair that had survived a harsh buzz cut.

'You know anything more about him?'

'Scoot, Scooter – she didn't seem to know his proper name. Had a flat in Presford, down near the bus station, behind Asda. Watkins Court, one of those old blocks the council got refurbed. He let the girls go round there whenever they wanted to. Then after a couple of weeks, he started bringing his mates round, expecting her to have sex with them.'

Lincoln let out a long sigh. 'Great.' Classic grooming tactic. String along a kid who's hungry for affection, who wants to belong. Ply her with food and drink. Spike something safe with something riskier, spike it some more... How he'd love to get his hands on men like Scoot!

'She tried to stand up to him,' Micky went on, 'but he started knocking her about. She told me what he'd done but she wouldn't press charges.' She shrugged, smoked, stared away down the road. 'I was scared she'd go AWOL if I went to the police, but I reported the assault to someone I know at Park Street police station – Liz Gregg.'

'She's a DI, isn't she?' Lincoln knew Liz slightly – recently promoted, eager to please but seldom one to speak up in meetings.

'Yeah. Known her for a while, knew she'd be discreet. Just wanted to make sure there was something on file about the assault. Had a bad feeling about the whole situation, that it wouldn't be long before Scoot started hitting her again. Didn't want to leave it till it was too late.'

She looked up at Lincoln. The irony wasn't lost on either of them.

'Micky, you did what you could.'

She flung her cigarette down, trod on it. 'Thought she'd settle down with Pete and Yvonne, stay away from Eily, get herself together but...'

'You say you reported this assault? I didn't find anything about it when I looked.'

'I asked Liz to log it but to keep it unofficial – seemed like the only way I could put down a marker in case anything else happened. She said there'd already been complaints from the guy who lived downstairs from Scoot – she'd gone round there sometime in May but there was no sign of Lorren. She promised to keep a lookout but I suppose without any evidence, not much she could do.'

Lincoln was puzzled. All he'd found on record were Lorren's "unauthorised absences". Liz Gregg had certainly kept the assault allegation unofficial – she'd kept it off the record completely.

'And then,' Micky continued, 'in June, I go to Greece for a fortnight and while I'm away, it all goes to cock. Eily talks Lorren into hanging out round Scooter's again, and she's brainless enough to go.' She shoved her organiser under her other arm, looked along the street, looked back. 'I let her down. I should have kept on at the police.'

'Sounds as if this Scoot character was clever enough to convince Liz and her team he was above board.'

'Obviously. Next thing I know, Yvonne's phoning to say Lorren's spending all day every day at Scoot's flat, only now he's moved to Barbury. Kid's talking about him like he's the love of her life. Tried getting back to Liz, but she was away. I'd have waited till she was back, but one or two of the punters Scoot was bringing round liked to knock the girls about as much as they liked to screw them.'

'You phoned Park Street?'

'Yeah, but like I said, Liz wasn't there. Woman I spoke to instead, I told her everything I knew about Lorren, about Scoot, the set-up at Watkins Court, the assault, the kind of punters he brought in. Told her he seemed to be starting the same sort of operation in Barbury.'

Lincoln couldn't understand why he'd found nothing on record about any of this. Okay, so information could all too easily get lost in the system – a wrong spelling, a data field left empty – but someone's sloppy inputting could have cost Lorren her life.

'Who did you speak to at Park Street when Liz was away?' He got his pen out, ready to write it down. 'And when?'

'It was a woman.' Micky scrabbled through her organiser, checked her diary. 'Beginning of July. Spoke to her myself. Yeah, here we are, I made a note: July 2nd. Spoke to DCI Bax.'

# CHAPTER 40

Shops in the Half Moon Centre were shutting as another Saturday afternoon drew to a close. In an hour or so, the clubs and pubs would start to get busy but for now there was a lull, not much open except a couple of coffee shops, a newsagent, and the Co-op on the corner opposite.

At last Simon caught sight of Tom striding across the concourse, his shift at Bods over for the day. 'Hi, Tom,' he said, blocking his path. 'You avoiding me?'

'What? Course not!' Big grin. 'Why would I avoid you, you great mutt? Trying to get on with stuff, that's all.'

'They came round to mine, Thursday. The same copper as came to Board Treaders, only this time he had some woman cop with him. I didn't know what to tell them.'

Tom patted his arm, like he was about to shoot off somewhere – can't stop, see you around, mate. But then he suggested coffee, 'Round that new one, if it hasn't been overrun by kids and grannies.' Another grin, another pat, Tom turning quickly and leading the way.

The new coffee shop was almost empty: wooden floors, exposed brickwork, big posters, coffee machines like steam engines.

'Mokkery?' Tom looked round, tutting, though Simon could tell he was impressed. 'Wankery, more like! This *boho* enough for you, Si? Is this *gay* enough?' He put his feet up on the low table between the red leather seats.

Simon flicked a sugar packet at him, which hit him on the cheek.

'Ow! Okay, Dumbo, so what did the cops want?'

'They had a picture of some guy who picked Em up that night. Looked Indian, but she didn't know anyone Indian, did she?'

Tom shrugged and started to pick the edges off the sugar packet. 'Probably a minicab. They're all Indians or Muslims.' Golden grains spilled out. He threw the empty packet on the table and slouched back into the squashy armchair. His polo shirt was open a little at the neck, a few soft black hairs showing. His skin glistened there, hot, damp.

'Who did it, Tom? Who killed her? You think it was Arlo? I mean, it could've been an accident, couldn't it?'

'An accident? You didn't see what they did to her! They fucking beat her up!'

Shit! Simon didn't think Em was lying there like that old painting of Ophelia, all dreamy, surrounded by flowers, but he didn't know she'd been beaten up. '*They*? What d' you mean, *they*?'

'He, they, whoever.'

'How do you know she was beaten up? The cops tell you?' Simon's scalp began to sweat.

'Joe told me.'

'Joe?' He shoved Tom's feet off the table.

'Joe Day. Rich's friend.'

'Oh, the one...'

'Yeah,' said Tom quietly. 'Joe was in the car with Rich, only Joe was wanky enough to put his seatbelt on.'

They hadn't talked much about last December's car crash, except how Joe and Tom's big brother Rich had been stoned when it happened. Rich had been flung out of the driver's seat and across two carriageways. He'd left one of his shoes behind. Simon had always wanted to know which shoe, left or right, but never liked to ask.

'It was Joe and his girlfriend that found Emma,' Tom went on. 'He phoned me, wanted someone to talk to. Girlfriend's dad wouldn't let her out so he called me.'

'You can say her name, y' know. I know it's Maisie.'

Tom looked guilty, like he thought he'd got away with it. He'd fancied Maisie from when she first went to Board Treaders, and she'd seemed to fancy him, but then she started going out with Joe and Tom went off her. She hadn't been back to drama group since the crash. 'Sorry, Si. Didn't think you'd remember.'

'My memory's fine, mate. I haven't caught Alzheimer's off my nan. It's not infectious, you know.'

Tom grinned. 'Might be – all these old people could be catching it off each other.' He looked away out of the window as he sipped his coffee.

Simon remembered Emma coming to his house a few months ago so he could help her set something up on her new phone. In his bedroom, she messed around on his electronic keyboard, got him to play "*Chopsticks*" with her until he was scared Nan would thump on the kitchen ceiling with the broom, make them shut up.

Then she went round opening all his drawers and cupboards and going through his stuff. It was like being touched by her, something intimate, arousing even though he didn't fancy her. Not like that.

'They're just cupboards, Em,' he'd said, teasing her. 'You've probably got some just like them at home.'

'Yeah, but I'm not allowed to go through things at home. It's like it's all secret and private and out of bounds. You know *The Tale of Two Bad Mice*?'

'No.'

'Well, there's these two mice, and they get into the dolls' house and all the food looks so delicious they can't wait to eat it. Only it's really made of plaster so they can't eat any of it! Well, I live in a house full of cupboards and drawers and cabinets that might as well not open. Everything's locked or I'm not allowed, and if I move anything she knows exactly what's different and screams at me for touching things.'

'You could come and live with me.' He hadn't meant it but for a little while they'd giggled, plotting how she could secretly move into his house. 'Nan already thinks you're the bee's knees!' he told her, and even that crap expression made her fall about.

Simon's eyes watered now. 'You think this guy she was meeting sent a cab for her?'

Tom shrugged. 'All she told me was that she had to be out on Spicer Street, 7.15.'

'And you really don't know who she was seeing?'

'I told you, he was her Great Big Secret – like I gave a fuck!'

'So the guy who gave her a lift... Maybe he never took her to meet her boyfriend that night. Or else he took her there but when he came to collect her, he didn't drive her home.' He didn't suggest the other possibility: that her boyfriend was the one who killed her.

Tom laughed, kind of cold, sarcastic. 'Well hel-lo? Isn't it pretty bloody fucking obvious that's what happened?' He leapt to his feet. 'You wanna play Simon Lovelock, Boy Detective, go ahead, but I'm sick of the whole fucking thing!'

And he stormed out of Mokkery, knocking a pile of leaflets off the counter as he went.

By the time Simon had scrabbled round picking them up, Tom was striding along the street. Something made him stop, turn, come back.

'Sorry, Si.' He stuffed his hands in his pockets. His face was wet.

'It's all right.'

'Text me if you hear anything, okay?'

# CHAPTER 41

Back at his desk, Lincoln inspected the evidence bags of Lorren Walsh's possessions. The notebook was covered in cheap wrapping paper, the corners deftly mitred. Shop-bought stickers spelt out *LORREN* on the padded front cover. She hadn't got the second 'R' quite straight, and it tilted into the 'E'.

Inside, she'd written her name at the top of the first page, then all the addresses where she'd lived in the last couple of years – ten in all. The most recent was Presford House, the children's home, and before that, Michaelmas House, where her mother had let her be abused by Liam Coe. She hadn't got round to writing the Springs' address or Scoot's.

She'd torn the first few pages out of the notebook, and the rest was blank. He put it aside, disappointed.

His mobile rang: Shauna Hartlake. She must still be at the hospital. His first thought was that Crystal's condition had deteriorated. Why did he always assume the worst?

'Shauna? Any news?'

He could hear her grinning. 'Old friend of Mrs Sherman's turned up at the hospital earlier on. We got talking when she was having a quick fag. Name's Gaynor Rees, lives in France. She's gone off to find a hotel for the night but it sounds as if she can fill in quite a few of the blanks.'

'Great! How did she find out about Crystal?'

'You can't turn the telly on without seeing something about it, can you?' A pause, another audible grin. 'Sorry, course you haven't got a telly, have you, boss?'

Moments after Shauna rang off, the door opened and there was Bella. She glowered at Lincoln as she headed for her cubbyhole. After a couple of minutes, he got up and followed her.

'Can I have a word, ma'am?'

'Jeff?'

'You already knew about Lorren, didn't you?' He chucked the dead girl's skinny file onto her desk.

She looked up, irritated. 'Lorren? Lorren who?'

168

'The girl found dead in Langford Hill Lane this morning. You were contacted about her weeks ago, told she was at risk.'

'No idea what you're talking about.'

'You got a call about her being groomed by a man who was offering her to his friends for sex – but I can't find any mention of her on the database, apart from the times she was reported as a runaway.'

'I really don't know what—'

'Wouldn't you have written it down, put it on record?' He was pleading with her to tell him he'd missed something.

'If there's nothing on file, it's because I was given bugger-all information to record.' She sighed hugely. 'I don't have time to play games. Give me a clue.'

He'd been expecting a fight but she was blocking him. He hadn't got his facts straight so he was the one in the wrong.

But he wouldn't give in. 'Michaela Stanley? Micky? Social worker based in Presford, responsible for Lorren Walsh?'

Bella's face was a blank, as if he was speaking a foreign language. Maybe Micky had got it wrong after all.

'Where are you going with this, Jeff? You're not making sense.'

'Lorren was being groomed by a man known as Scoot or Scooter. He beat her up, and Micky reported him to your team. She was told they'd already been round to his flat to investigate a complaint but found nothing. When Lorren told her he was moving to Barbury, Micky phoned Park Street because it was Liz Gregg who'd looked into it originally.'

Bella pursed her lips. 'Then maybe it's Liz you should be hassling over this.'

'Micky didn't speak to Liz that time. She spoke to *you*.'

She stood up, heading for her filing cabinet to put some paperwork away. 'Well, she obviously didn't speak to me personally.'

Lincoln pulled his stomach in to let her pass. She didn't look round from the open drawer, intent on reinserting a folder in the correct place in the sequence.

'No doubt whoever took the call said they were passing her on to me, but some other woman answered. That's why this Micky person assumed it was me she was speaking to.'

That made so much sense, it hurt. And it would explain everything.

'Who else might she have spoken to, then? Who else would've picked up your phone?'

Bella slammed the drawer shut, turned round. 'How the fuck

would I know? Without checking the duty rosters for July, I really can't tell you. I certainly can't give you an answer off the top of my head!' She sat down again. 'Okay, I'll ask Park Street to look into it, see if they can unearth anything for you.' Like she was doing him a huge favour.

'This kid was being groomed,' he said, feeling as if he had to spell it out in big letters.

'I heard you. I'll get someone to look into it. But you know as well as I do – kids in care are always trouble.'

'That's a bit sweeping.'

'Trust me. I've worked more child abuse cases than you have.' She flipped her wrist over, checking her watch. 'Autopsy's scheduled for Monday morning.'

'Not till then?'

'Not blaming me for that too, are you?' She looked up, fixing him with a warning glare. 'Watch your step, Inspector. You're not in charge now. I'd appreciate a little more respect, okay?'

'Ma'am.' He hung his head.

'So, have we tracked down her killer yet?'

'A full search of her room's arranged for tomorrow, but I brought a few items back with me – a notebook and a box of odds and ends.'

'Anything useful?'

'I haven't had a chance to go through it properly.'

'Well, if she was already on the game, the field's wide open.' She turned her attention to her paperwork, a page of figures she seemed impatient to get on with.

'The kid was being exploited,' he said. 'She wasn't out on the streets selling herself. Men were being brought to the flat and—'

'This pimp of hers – is that what we're saying here? This Scoot guy? Acting as her pimp? Do we know anything about him? Is that a good place to start, a bit of background?'

'I'll get on to it, but—'

'Go on, then, and tell me when you've got something solid to work on.' She shooed him out with a flick of her hand.

It was only when he was driving home that he realised what she'd said about finding out who took Micky's call: "*Without checking the duty rosters for July, I really can't tell you.*"

He hadn't told her when Micky phoned. If she knew it was July, she must remember the call. Why pretend she didn't?

His thoughts returned to that pathetic heap of belongings he'd retrieved from the girl's room at the Springs': her box of buttons, baby photos, pens, a handkerchief. She hadn't asked for much out of life – safety, understanding, love. How little was left of her!

He put his foot down, the faster to reach home, the sooner to be back between his own four walls.

# CHAPTER 42

'Thought you and Jess weren't mates anymore?'

'Who told you that?' Lady reached past her mother to grab her jersey, snatch her bag off the back of the chair.

'Saw the two of you coming out of that new coffee shop.'

'Fuck you doing down town? You're supposed to be resting.' She hated the idea of her mother being pregnant, having a baby that would disrupt Life As They Knew It.

'Can't stay in all the time. Get stir crazy.'

'Better get used to it. Once this baby comes along, you're gonna be a prisoner in your own home.' That's what having a kid was all about. Lady didn't need to read the magazines at the checkout to know that motherhood was a bloody nightmare. Who the fuck chose to have a baby?

'So you off out with Jess tonight?'

'Probably. Not decided.'

'You heard there was a girl found? Another one?'

Lady checked she'd got her phone, door key. 'How d' you mean?'

'Dead. Out Langford St Catherine's. It was on the news.'

'That's miles away. You're not wanting me to stay in because of that?'

'No, but—'

'I can take care of myself, Mother. I'm a big girl now.'

A couple of hours later Lady was resting safe in Arlo's arms.

'Glad I got you to keep me warm now the evenings are chilly.' She snuggled tighter into him.

'Summer's over, that's for sure.' He pulled her closer under the blanket. She couldn't help longing for a duvet, something softer than the rough khaki blanket he'd thrown over them as they lay beside the dying campfire. The blanket smelt as doggy as Tiffin, who was stretched out in the shadows, whiffling in her sleep.

'You angry with me?'

'Me? Angry? Why should I be angry with you? You're my delicious Lady. I could eat you all up.' He ran his tongue up from her collarbone to her earlobe, snagging on her earring. She shuddered, a pulse between her legs thudding, shaking her, passion chasing through her like the shivers you get after a fever, only stronger.

'I'm on the pill but I can't risk, you know...' She hadn't been on it long enough for things to settle down. Her mother had warned her. The first couple of months, you're all haywire. Don't take any chances.

And if anyone should know, it was her mother.

Arlo stroked Lady's fringe back from her forehead. She wanted to sleep. Maybe it was the weed that was making her so sleepy. She'd be up at three, her stomach winding itself up with hunger.

'Next time, okay, my Lady?' He lifted her chin with his fingers. 'What you did was very sweet and considerate. You have a beautiful mouth.'

'And you have a beautiful cock, my lord.' She giggled, nuzzled down against him, blushing. Her lips were still sticky with his cum. Her throat ached. But she'd done it! And he didn't know she'd never done it before!

'You'd better be getting home, my Lady. Your coach and pair will be here any minute and we don't want to keep the driver waiting.'

She punched his chest lightly, giggling. 'I need a pee first.'

'Take the torch.' He shoved the big flashlight at her.

Lady stood up, staggering a bit, and headed along the path behind the cabin, the strong beam of the torch lighting the way to the patch they used as a toilet. She pulled her jeans down, peed, pulled them up again. Dizzy as she stood, she steadied herself on Arlo's dustbin until her head stopped reeling. As she straightened up, the bin tipped against her legs, its lid rolling off, its contents spilling quietly into the grass. She pointed the flashlight downwards.

A tracksuit top, hooded. Grey with pink trim on the shoulders. All scrunched up.

A shiver coursed down her back: fear, not passion. Terror.

A twig snapped behind her. 'Long time pissing, your ladyship?'

'Look.' She held the tracksuit top out to him. 'I found this.'

'Oh, Lady,' said Arlo. 'I really wish you hadn't.'

# CHAPTER 43

## SUNDAY 15TH SEPTEMBER

Woody rang him early. 'Seen the papers?'

Lincoln could barely see the screen on his phone. He rubbed his eyes, shoved the bedclothes back, swung his feet out. 'Don't get the papers. What've I missed?'

'Front page of the *Mail on Sunday*. Listen to this: "*Tragic Emma not my sister. Dad was not her father, says Mark Sherman, speaking exclusively about the murdered teen. Businessman Mark, 32, claims that dad Derek's second wife duped him over the paternity of her unborn child...*"'

Lincoln groaned. That's exactly why he didn't get the papers. 'Pretty callous, washing the dirty linen now.'

'Think we need to talk to him?'

'I'll run it past Bella, but she'll probably say it's low priority.'

'What's that noise?'

'It's what would've woken me up if you hadn't got to me first. New neighbours. Hammering. And there goes a buzz saw. Hear that?'

A chuckle down the phone. 'Hoping for a lie-in, were you, boss?'

As soon as Woody had hung up, Lincoln wrenched the back door open, stumbled over the threshold and blundered down to the end of the garden. The door in the wall wouldn't budge, but he could see over the top where the brickwork was crumbling. Still fuzzy-eyed, he tried to make out what was going on at Fountains; what was so urgent they had to wake him up on a Sunday morning to fix it.

They were building a pergola – is that what you call it? – a wooden monstrosity taking up more than its fair share of the back garden. Who in their right mind...?

A couple of men were working on it but they were making such a racket, they were oblivious to his presence – just as well, since he was wearing only his shorts and the old plaid shirt that doubled as a dressing gown.

He'd bought the Old Vicarage on impulse, letting his heart rule his head after he rejected everything else he'd been shown. He'd fallen in love with it the way you fall in love with a woman you can't resist, even though you know she'll never make you happy. He hadn't known what

174

he was looking for when he had to move out of his bedsit last year. Looked at flat after flat, house after house, realising in the end that he was searching for a neat three-bedroom semi like the home he made with Cathy. Except that ideal had been spoilt the day she walked out on him, and searching for it again had been madness. Madness.

And now this untidy, sprawling, lunatic wreck of a former vicarage was going to have lunatic neighbours, and every day, every night, he'd know buying it was a mistake.

He gazed back up his garden towards his house with its peeling paintwork and wonky sash windows. The veranda still had more gaps in its roof than glass. The back door stood ajar onto his primitive scullery, and the scullery door stood ajar – well, the door was jammed on a broken flagstone so it had no option but to stand ajar – so he could see through into the unmodernised, barely functional vicarage kitchen with its shelves and mesh-fronted meat safe and ceiling hooks and...

And he fell in love all over again.

# CHAPTER 44

Trish liked working a Sunday shift. Alternate weeks, ten till four. Until students started to trickle in, the library was quiet, so she had a chance to check the timetable for her trip to the Charles Lundy Library on Wednesday – tour of the library, meeting with the trustees, interview. They'd notify the successful candidate within twenty-four hours.

'Call for you!' Briony stuck her head round the partition between Trish's local studies area and the general enquiry desk. 'Sounds like Selina. Sounds like trouble.'

'Selina, I'm on duty – which means on duty upstairs in the library, not down here in the street.' Trish pulled her cardigan round her shoulders, shivering in the chilly outdoors.

'Sorry, but I didn't know who else to call. It's Anita. She came home really late last night, kind of spaced out. This morning, it took me ages to wake her up. I think she's taking drugs. But while I was getting breakfast, she slammed out of the house and she's not answering her phone.'

'Listen, you need to talk to your mum.'

'Mum can't cope with anything else. And Nita won't tell me anything. I'm caught in the middle, lying to Mum, shouting at Nita—'

'Your mum's got to try and get her act together. She's got a responsibility to both of you. You shouldn't have to shoulder all of this on your own.'

'Mum doesn't even get out of bed some days. She's on that many pills...'

'Not setting Anita a very good example, then, is she?'

Selina turned away, despondent. 'I thought you'd understand.'

'Selina! Listen!' Trish grabbed the girl's arm, regretting her harsh words. It couldn't be easy for her mother, bringing up a couple of spirited teenagers alone. 'You need to go home and wait for Anita to come back. Did she tell you where she was last night?'

'No, but I bet she was with this guy she's fallen for, the one I told you about. Scoot, she calls him. Her and this girl she's taken up with,

176

they go round his flat all the time. That's probably where she is now. What can I do, Trish, what can I do?' She turned back, tears on her cheeks.

Trish looked up and down the street as if the answer might be there, but all she saw were dreary queues at bus stops, wheelie bins of trade waste, a row of traffic cones marking off the roadworks that were taking months to finish. 'Okay, where does this Scoot boy live?'

'Finisterre Street, somewhere near the Methodist church. Over some shops, she said.'

'You know what he looks like?'

'I've only seen him from across the street, when I saw her and this girl hanging out with him. He looks Indian but she'd have said if he was, so I'm thinking he's Greek, maybe? His skin's dark, and his hair, but his eyes are blue or grey, which is weird, isn't it? Slim, five-tennish. His hair's kind of shaved over his ears, long on top.' Selina gasped. 'You're not going looking for him, are you?'

'Of course not, but I could drive down that way later, see if I can see her anywhere. But Selina, you *must* go home and talk to your mum. I'll try and find out where this flat is, at least get an address.'

'You're not going to tell your policeman friend, are you?'

'If I do, it'll be unofficial, okay?' And she let Selina go, wondering what on earth she'd let herself in for.

'Where did you get to?' Briony grumbled as Trish got back to her desk. 'People have been queuing!'

'Arlo! What the fuck's happened to you?' Billie Wheeler dragged him through to the kitchen of the Two Magpies before her Sunday lunchtime drinkers could see him. 'Look at the state of you!'

'Some bastard smashed me over the head last night. Woke up with Tiffin in my face, everything going round. I tried to sleep it off but when I woke up... Man, you really do see stars when you get hit over the head.' He was pale as a dishcloth except for the blood all over his shirt.

'Come through, strip off, get in the shower.' She pushed him away from her so she could inspect him better. 'Is all that blood yours?' She reached up and ran her hand tentatively across the top of his head, searching for a wound that would have produced so much blood. Found a lump, a graze that was crusting over, but no cut deep enough to bleed like this. What the fuck had he been up to?

'I've done something terrible, Bee,' he whispered, trembling. 'I think I've killed someone.'

# CHAPTER 45

'Suki doesn't mind you coming out for a drink?'

'Long as I'm back by two.' Woody checked his watch. 'Ages yet.' He hunched forward over the picnic table in the garden of the Bull Terrier. 'You heard what happened when we went to see Tremlow? No more questions without his lawyer there.'

Lincoln sighed, exasperated. 'He's not doing himself any favours, suddenly getting defensive. Makes him look guilty.'

'Yes, but he's not daft. Reckon he guessed where we were coming from – pretty niece, he took lots of photos of her when she was little, stands to reason he's a paedophile. You can't blame him for wanting some backup.'

'You're right. We need to get the facts straight before we accuse him of anything. Although, when I think about the photos Charlie found in the summer house...'

'Which we aren't supposed to know about.' Woody popped a few peanuts into his mouth. 'And maybe Pam overreacted. The kid had her clothes on, didn't she? They weren't *nude* photos, were they?'

'That makes it okay?'

'I'm only saying...we haven't seen them for ourselves.'

'Charlie seemed as shocked as Pam, but you're right, we can't be sure.'

Lincoln sipped his drink. Sergeant Bob had raised doubts about Oliver Spence's reliability, so he was reluctant to jump to conclusions. Tremlow's photo sessions with Emma and her friend could have been perfectly innocent. Better to keep an open mind until more evidence turned up.

'A friend of Crystal's showed up at the hospital today. Gaynor Rees. Might be able to give us a bit of the background.'

'Shame she wasn't here to stop Crystal taking an overdose.' Woody took another slurp of his Mole Catcher.

'There's something I want to run by you, now we're here.' Lincoln leaned forward, lowering his voice. 'It's about Lorren Walsh. According to Micky, her social worker, she was being groomed by a bloke called Scooter.'

'Groomed? Like, for sex?'

Lincoln nodded. 'Micky had a quiet word with Liz Gregg at Park Street, found out there'd already been complaints about him, but nothing worth following up. Beginning of July, she tried to contact Liz about him again, but Liz was away, so she got put through to Bella, told her all about it.' He shifted his glass on its mat. 'Thing is, when I checked, there was nothing on file about any of this, and yesterday, when I asked her about Micky phoning her, she said Micky must've spoken to somebody else.'

'She could be right,' Woody said with a shrug. 'The DCI isn't the only woman at Park Street.'

'So how come she knows *when* Micky called her? I didn't tell her the date. Either she remembers that phone call or she doesn't. And either way, she didn't put anything on record at the time. *Nobody* did.' He took another thirsty mouthful of beer, keen to blunt the edginess he'd felt since he realised that Bella Bax was lying to him.

Woody put his glass down, dabbed at his moustache. 'You think she's covering for someone?'

'Who's she covering for but herself? When she took that call from Micky, she should have taken it up the line to decide what action to take. It's serious stuff, sex abuse, underage kids. It's where so many runaways end up, being groomed, exploited – which is all the more reason to deal with any allegations properly, not pretend you haven't been told!' Lincoln heard himself getting evangelical, giving Woody a lecture he didn't need. 'Whatever else you do, you don't turn a blind eye.'

Another long draught of beer began to work its magic. Lincoln felt his shoulders growing heavy, his heartbeat slowing.

Woody plonked his empty glass down. 'Reckon if this Scooter bloke's known, he'll be on the system somewhere.'

Lincoln knocked back the last of his beer. 'I'll drop by the station on my way home. The sooner I start looking for him, the better.'

# CHAPTER 46

Lincoln could find nothing on file about anyone nicknamed Scoot or Scooter. He checked Lorren Walsh's name once more in case he'd missed something but he found nothing new. Taking a chance, he phoned Park Street to ask which team dealt with allegations of sexual abuse, and was put through to DC Alan Hayes.

'Why, you have something at Barbury?' Hayes sounded interested, and had a soft Scots accent.

'Might have. I'm trying to identify a male, IC 2 or 4, nickname Scoot or Scooter, late teens, early twenties, allegedly grooming underage girls in Presford. Wondering who'd be the best person to speak to.'

'That'd be DCI Bax but she's covering your patch just now, isn't she?'

Lincoln faked a groan. 'Damn. Trust me to want some intel on her day off!'

'I'll see what I can do. What was he calling himself?' The reassuring sounds of a keyboard being hammered. Lincoln told Hayes what little he knew, listened as keys clicked, wondering what database he was searching – evidently one to which Barley Lane nick had no access. 'Aye, here we are… That'd be Zakariah Scotson. We went round there a couple months ago but it was just him and his girlfriend. End of story.'

'What? Where?'

'Watkins Court, Presford. Girlfriend's a lassie called Eily Quinn.' Hayes spelt it out. This must be the girl who'd befriended Lorren at the children's home. Now Lincoln had her surname too. 'She's been in care but she seemed settled with him. Seventeen. Nothing we could do if she was there of her own volition.'

'Any mention of a girl called Lorren Walsh being there too?' Lincoln spelt her name out in case she'd been recorded as Laura, Lauren or Welsh.

'No, sorry.'

'And when did you go round to Watkins Court?'

'Er – May 27th. A neighbour complained to the council, lassies hanging around, men coming and going all hours. The council asked

180

us to take a look.' A few more key-clicks. 'Nothing incriminating observed on the premises but we didna have a search warrant so we were a wee bit limited in where we could look.'

'You went there yourself?'

'Not me personally, no. I can only tell you what's on my screen and what I recall of the debrief after. It was a non-starter, lassie saying she was fine, nothing to worry about, difficult situation at home, better off with the boyfriend. The usual story.'

'And that was it?'

'Like I said, she was happy, he seemed clean. I heard the place was a bit of a tip but apart from that... No evidence of men coming and going. Concluded the neighbour downstairs didna like the colour of Scotson's skin, wanted rid of the guy.'

'Not black, is he?'

'Mixed race.'

'Know anything about him moving to Barbury?'

Click, click. 'Nothing logged, sorry. You want me to send you the info I've got? It may give you a bit more to work on.'

'Great, thanks.'

'You're welcome. Aye, and give the boss my love when you see her.'

Lincoln could tell from his tone that Hayes didn't mean it.

As he put the phone down, he saw Sergeant Bob Bowden heading his way, tea and cherry Bakewell in his hands.

'Charlie Trufitt pass the message on?' Bob took a sip of tea. 'That Fiesta you're looking for. Patrol found it burnt out up Steepleton Pits.'

Steepleton Pits were disused chalk quarries three or four miles out of Barbury. Mesh gates across the entrance were supposed to keep intruders out but they'd been vandalised into something more like modern art than a security fence. Cars, fridges, building rubble and the like were always being dumped there because the site was unsupervised with no cameras.

Bob chomped on his cherry Bakewell, scattering crumbs. 'They're going over the car in the morning but don't get your hopes up. Not much left of it.'

'Damn. Could they tell how long it had been there?'

'Still warm. Probably torched last night.'

And with it, any chance of forensic evidence linking it to Emma.

'Thanks, Bob. While I think of it...does the name Zakariah Scotson ring any bells? Around twenty, mixed race, been living in Presford?'

Bob pursed his lips, flipping through the Rolodex of his memory.

'There was a Della Scotson here in Barbury years ago, used to work round Back Market Street when it was the red light district. You'd never guess these days, mind, now it's been *gentrified.*' He scoffed. 'Good-looking girl except one of her eyes had a turn to it. She was half-Greek or something. Maltese? Zakariah could be her boy.'

'She still in Barbury?'

'Been dead a while now. Roughed up by one of her customers. She had a kid, I remember, but whether that's this Zakariah you're asking about...'

'Rumour is, he's set himself up in Barbury now. Young girls and lots of visitors, if you know what I mean.'

'We don't want that sorta thing in Barbury, do we?'

As Sergeant Bob ambled back to the counter, Lincoln tried to get hold of Gaynor Rees. Shauna had been trying her all morning but her phone was off, so he was surprised to get through straightaway.

Her voice was deep, husky, a smoker's voice. She and Crystal had been at school together, she said. Although she lived in France now, she kept in touch by following the English news online. When she saw that Crystal had been rushed to hospital, she'd come over as fast as she could.

'I'm at the hospital now, getting a breath of fresh air.' It sounded more as if she was having a smoke.

'How is she?'

'Puh! They won't tell me anything. I'm not family.'

'Can we meet? I'd like to ask you—'

'What can I tell you that you don't already know?'

'The more we can find out about Emma, the better.' The truth was, he was clutching at straws. 'Barley Lane police station, tomorrow morning?'

She sighed. 'Okay.'

By the time he got back to his desk with a cup of coffee, a file was sitting in his email inbox. Alan Hayes, the Scottish detective, had been as good as his word.

Lincoln took a welcome mouthful of coffee and clicked "*Download*".

# CHAPTER 47

Every big town must have a Finisterre Street, Trish thought as she steered her Mini slowly along its messy length. A street that looks as if someone's tipped the town up so that anything that isn't well-established has rolled down the slope and ended up, a tumble of dregs, somewhere near the railway station or the council dump.

She drove past the Methodist church, a Chinese takeaway, an Indian restaurant, an off-licence, a chippie – all shut, mid-afternoon on a Sunday, their windows protected by grilles that were padlocked and sprayed with graffiti.

None of these premises seemed to have flats above them, but a run of shops and a kebab house across the street looked more promising. She tucked her car in behind Barbury A1 Tyres and, trying to look nonchalant, walked back past the shops. Three of them were closed but the one on the corner was open – and above its door was a peeling sign: *STAIRS TO FLATS.*

She climbed the steps to a walkway that ran past four front doors. One door was mostly chipboard and another was all metal. The other two doors looked less forbidding. Did either of them belong to Scoot or his family?

*What am I doing here? Do I have any idea what I'm walking into?* Lincoln's voice in her head, quizzing her, warning her. A bad sign, that, your conscience talking in someone else's voice.

'Looking for someone?'

Trish spun round. A young man, twenties, slim, black hair shaved short over his ears, long on top. Was this Scoot? Black eyebrows, olive skin. Dark T-shirt, faded jeans with a big buckle. Timberland boots. And light grey eyes, just like Selina said. He had a paper bag of takeaway food in one hand, a beer bottle in the other.

'Can I help you at all?' He gestured with the bottle as if he was offering her a choice of the four doors: *See one you fancy?* As he swept his arm out, she saw a tattoo inside his wrist: ZAK in big letters, red and purple. Initials, or his name?

She swallowed hard, her mouth dry. 'I'm looking for – for Jeff. Jeff Smith. Someone said he lived over the shops.'

He shook his head, made a face. 'Never heard of him. These flats? You sure?'

'Um – are there any other flats over shops round here?'

'Fuck I know! You not got an address for him?'

'No, he's a bit vague like that.' She realised that this sturdy young man, this Scoot, stood between her and the only exit down to the street. 'Sorry, I must have got the wrong block. Thanks for your help.'

She moved to pass him but he stood his ground, challenging.

'You from the Social, lady?'

'What? No! Look, I'd better track my friend down before he gives up on me!' She forced a laugh, put her head down and pushed past him before he could stop her.

'Guy in the corner shop – he'd know,' he called after her. 'Ask him, yeah?'

She jogged down the steps to the street and, keeping up the pretence in case Scoot was watching her, she hurried into the corner shop.

A tall man behind the counter – Greek, Turkish – looked up from his newspaper. 'I help you?'

'Some chocolate, thanks.' She picked up a slab of Bourneville, hands trembling, and somehow managed to extricate the right coins from her purse.

She slid back into the car and drove off, chuffed that she'd tracked down Anita's erstwhile boyfriend. Chuffed but shaking. She wasn't cut out for intrigue.

# CHAPTER 48

Lincoln downloaded the document Alan Hayes had sent him and began to go through it on screen. According to the Park Street team's report on 7 Watkins Court, the first-floor maisonette was "a Revyve property", whatever that was.

Mr Armitage, the tenant in Number 6 on the ground floor, had complained to Housing Services about constant noise as people stomped up and down the stairs all night. At the end of May, housing officers decided to involve the police after Armitage alleged that 'schoolgirls' hanging out at Number 7 kept throwing rubbish out of the windows and into his front garden.

DS Gregg and PC Cotton visited the flat and found Zakariah Scotson, aged twenty-one, and Eily Quinn, aged seventeen, a girl already known as a persistent runaway. She was adamant that she was Scotson's girlfriend, and that no other girls were living there.

According to Liz Gregg's report, the flat was untidy with few items of furniture, but there was no evidence of drug-taking or other illegal activity.

Scotson had a criminal record, which Liz had pasted into her report with his mugshot. He stared out from the screen, his hair poorly defined in the photo as a dense, dark slab. His complexion looked sallow, as if he didn't get out much, his eyes greyish blue. He classed himself as "mixed race/other ethnic" – a tick box that covered a host of possibilities.

He'd had two cautions for smoking pot in public, and last December he'd been arrested in Presford after crashing his employer's van into a row of bollards while he was stoned. He was banned from driving for a year.

After Liz Gregg dropped in on him in May, he must have decided it was time to leave Watkins Court and move on. If, as Sergeant Bob suggested, he was Della Scotson's son, he'd know Barbury well – but exactly where had he gone to ground?

When he tried to print the report, Lincoln realised the printer was off and there was no paper in it anyway. It could keep till tomorrow. He'd found out what he needed to, although he was surprised and

185

disappointed that Liz Gregg – who'd been promoted to detective inspector since the report was written – had taken Scotson at his word and dismissed the neighbour's allegations.

A headache was building behind his eyes. He should have eaten at lunchtime as well as having a pint. The sanctuary of the Old Vicarage beckoned.

He might have made a bit of progress towards finding out what happened to Lorren, but was he any nearer to uncovering Emma's killer? Might Gaynor Rees be able to fill in any blanks in the Shermans' story? He got in his car and sat with the key in his hand for a few minutes, staring out at the brick walls of the yard.

If Emma Sherman was killed by the man driving the Fiesta or a boyfriend they had yet to trace, her uncle's obsession with photographing her was irrelevant. Pursuing Tremlow was a waste of time.

And yet he couldn't help thinking the photos in the summer house were significant. Bella's warning voice boomed in his head: *Going off-piste again, Inspector?*

What about Mark Sherman's tabloid revelations? Did it matter that Derek Sherman might not have been Emma's father? If Mark's claims were true, whose daughter was she?

Lincoln got home to find construction work on the pergola at Fountains had stopped. Someone was noisily jet-washing the patio. So much for peace and quiet!

His groin vibrated, his mobile ringing. Dilke's turn to be on call this Sunday.

'Graham?' His headache thudded. 'Is it urgent?'

'Could be.' Dilke's voice was grim. 'Fifteen-year-old reported missing from Barbury Down. She hasn't been home since last night.'

'Shit. Text me the details.' Lincoln tossed back a couple of painkillers and went out again. He hadn't even taken his jacket off.

# CHAPTER 49

'I'd kill myself if anything happened to her.' Polly Burnie was propped up in an armchair against an assortment of cushions, her fist full of tissues. Early thirties. Wispy brown plaits, dull skin, glasses. Puffy wrists and ankles, the sour smell of unwashed hair and clothes. Heavily pregnant.

'Tell us what happened,' said Pam, squatting on a footrest close to Polly's chair while Lincoln hunted round for something to sit on. Every chair and horizontal surface was littered with clothes, junk mail and dirty crockery. He lowered himself gingerly onto a wonky-looking stool. 'Take us through Saturday.'

'I went to my mate Becky's yesterday evening. She's only round the corner. Lady—'

'Lady?' Pam's pen hovered over her notebook. 'Spelt the way it sounds?'

Polly looked sheepish. 'It's Elaine really, but when she was little, we called her Lainey and she turned that into "Lady" and it sort of stuck.'

'Sorry. Just wanted to get that right. Carry on.'

'And she said she was going out with Jess and she'd be back by ten. I didn't call her because she never answers when she sees it's me. And before I left Becky's, I went to the toilet and I was coming down the stairs and I felt the most horrendous pain, you know, all up through. And I thought, Oh no, what's happening? Next thing I know, everything's going round and then Becks is calling an ambulance.'

Lincoln remembered Cathy's second miscarriage. She'd stood up from taking washing out of the machine, then doubled up in agony, bleeding. She'd felt fine until that moment. She lost the baby, nothing anyone could do to save it – and nothing either of them could do to save their marriage in the long months that followed.

'You're okay now?' Pam asked.

Polly nodded. 'Pressure on my bowel,' she said, sparing them the details. 'Need to rest a bit. Except how can I? I got back here two o'clock and she's not here, the bed's not been slept in. I phoned her friend Jess and she said Lady was meeting some boy Saturday night, only she didn't know his name.'

'Would any other friends know who she was seeing?'

Polly shook her head. 'Lady only goes round with Jess these days. Don't know why – she's always slagging her off.'

'We need to speak to her. Have you got her address?'

At first, Jessica Merritt insisted she didn't know who her friend was meeting but then her mother, petite and perfumed, put a hand on the girl's arm. 'It's silly to protect Lady, Jessica. The police need to find her. No one's going to blame you if you tell them what you know.'

'His name's Arlo James,' said Jess. 'He lives in Greywood Forest, at Pine Point, in a caravan. That's where she's been having *sex* with him.'

Her mother tutted and frowned, pushing Jess' fringe out of her eyes before showing Pam and Lincoln out.

Lincoln phoned Bella as he walked back to the car, fuming that he could do nothing without her authorisation. Supposing Lady ended up dead like Emma because he had to wait for the DCI's permission to go looking for her?

'No answer.' He stuffed his mobile back in his pocket and turned to Pam. 'You know where Her Majesty lives?'

Ten minutes later, they were swinging into Bella's road, a crescent of Edwardian houses backing onto the grounds of the convent – a smart address even on a DCI's salary, and with a smart price tag. Lincoln was pretty sure she hadn't got a rich husband.

While Pam waited in the car, he hurried along to Bella's house, passing a car he recognised, a VW Beetle convertible, its top down. Philippa Giles, Pip, the media relations officer, had one just like it. A resident's parking permit was jammed inside the windscreen. Did Pip live in this crescent, too? PR must pay better than he thought.

It took a few minutes and three rings to bring Bella Bax to her front door. In a long, loose dress and with her frizzy mane tucked away under a big blue scarf knotted turban-style, she looked strangely Bohemian and about five inches taller.

'Jeff?' She seemed reluctant to let him in, holding the door open only a few inches.

'Sorry, ma'am, is this a bad time?'

'It's not the best time, certainly. Hang on.' She shut the door and went back inside. He heard a murmur of voices down the hallway.

Impatient, he paced up and down the path and was about to check his phone for messages when a figure darted out from the far side of the house and through the side gate.

A blonde in skinny jeans, short tweed jacket, smart red trainers. Pip Giles, the one whose brother held some important post in the council.

He pretended to peer at his phone, pretty damn sure he wasn't supposed to see Pip fleeing. The front door opened again and Bella ushered him in. The Beetle started up in the road, whined and shot away.

'Okay, so what do we know?' In the dim living room at the back of the house, the DCI sank onto a sofa of well-worn leather, a tartan blanket thrown across its back. At least here at home she had room to spread out.

He stayed standing while he told her about Elaine Burnie.

'Pick Arlo James up,' she said. 'As soon as you've got him in custody, I'll get over to the station. Anything in these allegations in the papers, Emma not being Sherman's kid?'

Lincoln shrugged. 'The son's taken long enough to come up with it. The tabloids have simply pounced on a bit of scandal.'

'Better follow it up, just to be sure. You still convinced Arlo James isn't behind Emma's murder?'

'Less convinced than I was,' he conceded. 'But he can't be working alone because he needs transport and he doesn't drive.'

'The Fiesta driver?'

'The car's been dumped at Steepleton Pits, burned out.'

'Fuck. No trace evidence.' She showed him out. 'If we can get Arlo to talk—'

'We've got to find him first. And the girl. That's the priority.'

'Of course, of course.'

He paused on the step. 'Was that Pip I saw leaving?'

'Pip? Er – yes. We were working on the next press release.'

'I guessed it was something like that.' When did he become such a good liar? He hurried back to Pam, waiting in the car.

Four uniforms, Lincoln, Pam and Charlie reached Pine Point by twenty to seven. Tiffin the dog didn't come rushing to greet them this evening and even though dusk was falling, it was easy to see that neither Lady nor Arlo was within a hundred yards of the caravan.

It wasn't locked. He hadn't cleaned up. The brightly painted caravan was messy, with empty spirit bottles and food wrappers lying around inside. Lincoln and Charlie did the first sweep, bumping into each other in its cramped confines.

They stripped the thin quilt from the shelf-like bed, searched round every sparse piece of furniture and pulled back curtains over cubbyholes. No trace of Lady or her clothes, her keys or her phone – according to Polly, such a bright shade of pink it made your eyes hurt.

Charlie shone his torch onto the floor. 'Stains. Looks like blood.'

Lincoln followed the torch beam to the corn-coloured rush mat between the bed and the bench. Dark brown splodges spread across it.

'Blood? Could be, but it's not fresh.' He crouched down, ran his fingers over the mat, testing the coarse texture, recalling the autopsy findings – friction burns on Emma's back and shoulders, possibly from sacking or a sisal mat...

A chill ran through him. Was this where Emma was killed? How could he have been so wrong about Arlo? How many other girls had suffered here?

They climbed back down the steep wooden stepladder.

'Oh fuck, what I have trodden in?' Trufitt danced around on one leg while he tried to see what was on the sole of his other shoe.

'Could be anything round here, Charlie.'

Trufitt shone his torch into the grass. 'Yuk, a dead rabbit with its fucking head ripped off. Ter-rific!' He scraped the mess off his shoe in a clean patch of grass.

They both took a look at the animal's stiffened corpse, gobbets of congealed blood in the grass around it. Its head had been tossed into a nearby bramble bush. Tearing a rabbit in two didn't seem Arlo's sort of thing.

His horse was grazing contentedly a few yards away, but of Arlo himself, there was no sign.

'You'll want to see this.' Pam's face was grim. 'I took the lid off a bin round the back of the cabin and look what I found.'

Even in the dim light, Lincoln recognised the T-shirt and tracksuit top Emma was wearing when she left home on Thursday night.

'Don't touch anything else,' he shouted to the rest of the team. 'We need to get forensics in. This is a crime scene now.'

As dusk became darkness, Lincoln rang Bella to update her.

'No sign of Arlo or the girl. I'm suspending the search until first light.'

'He's definitely not doing this alone, is he?'

'Doesn't look like it.' Rain began to fall, quietly rinsing away

190

potential clues. 'I've sent Woody over to the pub where Arlo works – he may have gone to ground there.'

'Wrap things up ASAP, and get off home. Early start.' She hung up.

For a couple of minutes, he sat with the phone in his hand, angry with himself for getting Arlo so wrong. And then Woody phoned from the Two Magpies to say that Arlo, riding an old bike, had turned up at the pub last night as Billie was closing.

'She said he was a bit agitated,' Woody went on. 'Told her he had to go away, didn't say why, and could she lend him some cash? She tried to get him to stay but he was in a right state, wouldn't listen. Left his dog with her. She lent him fifty quid out the till.'

'She won't see that again.' And we won't see Arlo again for a while, Lincoln added silently. The case against him was building up: Emma was meeting him, Lady was meeting him. Emma was dead, Lady was missing. Arlo on the run. How far could he get on a rickety bicycle and fifty quid?

'Go home, Woody, we'll be out at first light in the morning.'

Trish sounded tired when he phoned, even though it wasn't much after ten.

'Busy day,' she said. 'Sundays, my body wants a break, not five hours answering enquiries and catching up on paperwork. This better be important.'

'Problems with your friend Arlo. Any idea where he might run to if he was in trouble?'

'Come on, I haven't set eyes on him in twenty years!'

'What about family? You said he was married.'

'Once upon a time, yes, but...' She sighed. 'I can't do much now but I'll have a look first thing in the morning, see if I can find anything out. It's not like he's on Facebook.'

'You've checked?' Jealousy prickled, taking him by surprise.

Trish sighed again. 'There may not be much to find. He's not high-profile like his father. Hugo's got a whole Wikipedia article on him but Arlo's just a stub. And please don't tell me you don't know what that means. I'll call you in the morning when I've had a chance to check the newspaper files, okay?'

He turned his phone off. Of course he knew what a stub was – when the Wikipedia people only know enough about a topic to write a couple of lines. Was Arlo James' fame – or notoriety – about to eclipse his father's?

# CHAPTER 50

## MONDAY 16TH SEPTEMBER

Monday morning, and Bella had gone over to Presford for Lorren Walsh's autopsy, leaving Lincoln to hold the fort. A sweep of the woods around Arlo's caravan was already underway and Woody was leading a search of Mayday Farm. Arlo was on the run, so the search was for Lady now, dead or alive. So far, there'd been no sightings of a hyped-up hippy on a bicycle.

Woody rang at 9.15. 'Nothing here at the farm, boss. Doesn't look as if anyone's been near the place since we were here on Tuesday.'

No sooner had Lincoln put the phone down than it rang again. Gaynor Rees had arrived.

Crystal's friend was slender, neat. There was something French about her style – the tousled dark hair, the olive skin, the pout, the cloud of expensive perfume. Black leather jacket, woollen polo neck, corduroy skirt, thick tights, ankle boots – clothes that seemed too autumnal for September. Perhaps she felt the cold.

'Take a seat.' He moved a chair nearer his desk. Pam joined them, notebook in hand, looking wary of this new arrival. Introductions made, Lincoln asked Gaynor about her friendship with Crystal.

She blinked up at him. Dark brown eyes, owlish behind horn-rimmed spectacles. 'We've been friends for a very long time. Grew up on the same street, went to school together. She was Crystal Clark then.' She shrugged. 'Not a happy childhood. Her father was as strict as a regimental sergeant major. No talking at mealtimes, no telly after ten even when the girls were teenagers. Always finding fault with the way they dressed, things they said – you know the sort.'

'Religious?' Lincoln wondered.

'Self-righteous. You don't need church for that. And their mother was house-proud to a fault. She put these thick polythene covers on the three-piece suite, I remember, and all the bookshelves had glass across.' Gaynor gestured with her hands. 'Everything in its place and a place for everything. I hated going round there. Always afraid I'd get told off.'

'You knew Tania too?'

'Oh yes. She's a year or two older. So different, those two. Tania

192

always looked a mess, whereas Cryssie – well, she looked like she'd been to modelling school, and she was always singing, dancing. Loved performing. I used to say to Em, "I know where you get that from!"' Her face fell and she looked down at her hands.

'Did Crystal go to drama school?'

'Huh, her dad wouldn't have let her go even if she'd wanted to. And the only time she was in a school play, she was crippled by stage fright, couldn't go on.'

Pam looked surprised. 'So she had nervous problems even then?'

Gaynor nodded. 'Her dad was always running her down, making her feel she'd never achieve anything.' She fidgeted with her chunky bangle, turning it round and round on her wrist. 'Doesn't do a lot for your confidence.'

'A lot of stars have had unhappy childhoods,' Pam pointed out. 'A bad start can make you strive all the harder.'

'Well, it didn't work for Cryss. They made her leave school and get a job as soon as she could. She went to night school, did business studies. Then she landed a good position with Derek's firm, worked her way up to be his PA.' She opened her hands, her bangle clattering on the table. 'And they fell in love, even though Dez was in his fifties and Cryss wasn't even thirty.'

'Big age gap,' said Lincoln.

'He gave her the security she needed, even if she was only "the other woman". His wife walked out and Cryss moved in with him. They got married when he found out he had cancer but as you probably know, he died not long after. He never got to see Emma.'

Lincoln leaned back in his chair, hoping to put Gaynor more at ease. 'And Tania's husband – does Crystal get on with him okay?'

'Todd? Haven't seen him in years.' She broke off, looking for something in her bag. 'God, I'm dying for a cigarette. Where can I smoke?'

'You'll have to go outside,' said Pam.

Lincoln stood up. 'We'll go out into the yard. We can carry on talking out there.'

'And I'll put the kettle on.' Pam flung her notebook down as he went by.

A chilly breeze buffeted the smoking area outside the back door. Undeterred, Gaynor dug around in her shoulder bag, coming up with a tobacco tin and papers. Eventually, she got her cigarette rolled and lit, smoking irritably for a minute or two. When at last she spoke, her eyes were brimming with tears, and she raked through her bag for a tissue, churning up a mobile, an iPod and a crumpled map of the Paris Métro in the process.

'Crystal's my oldest friend,' she said. 'I don't want her to die. Seeing her like that's really tough, y' know?'

'Are you surprised she tried to take her own life?'

She shrugged, snatching a quick drag on her pinched and papery roll-up. 'After what she's been through the last couple of weeks, is it any wonder?'

'Suicide's pretty drastic. Didn't she want to see Emma's killer brought to justice?'

'You don't get it, do you? Cryss lived for that kid. The last few months, she got really low because she couldn't take Emma places or see her perform. Em tried to understand but she was only a kid. She started rebelling the way kids do, seeing what they can get away with.' She lifted her chin and blew smoke away. 'I told Cryss she'd get over it, but she was scared she'd lose her – so she got even more protective and made things ten times worse.'

They stood a little while longer in silence. Gaynor finished her cigarette but made no move to go back inside.

'When was the last time you heard from Crystal?' Lincoln asked.

'July, early August? She emailed me. Em had done really well in this play of hers and was desperate to try for drama school. I think they both realised that if she was going to succeed, she'd need someone to take her to auditions. Cryss couldn't do anything like that. Something had to change, but Cryss couldn't – *can't* – do anything about her agoraphobia. She felt like she'd failed Emma – the one person in the world who meant everything to her.'

Lincoln could imagine the tension between mother and daughter, Emma desperate to move on with her life, Crystal unable to, neither of them wanting to hurt the other. And lurking in the background, never mentioned, those photos taken in the summer house years ago. No wonder Emma felt the need to break away.

'We still don't know who Emma was meeting the night she disappeared,' he said. 'Did she ever talk about any boy in particular?'

'No, and Cryss didn't either. Not that she was emailing me all the time – it was usually me making the first move. God, listen to me, talking about her in the past tense!' She shoved her hair back, wiped away a tear and hugged herself, feeling the cold. 'Can we go back inside?'

Lincoln held the door open for her, followed her along the corridor.

They were soon sitting down having the coffee that Pam had made, the atmosphere a little more relaxed, as he'd intended. He didn't want Gaynor to feel she was being interrogated, but he sensed that she held vital clues to the relationship between Emma, her mother and the Tremlows.

'How well do you know Tania?' he asked. 'Was she good at music like her sister?'

'Tania, good at music? God, no! Quite the opposite. It was science she liked, maths, computers...'

'Computers?' Pam sounded as surprised as Lincoln was. Hadn't she and Dilke told him Tania was clueless about computers?

Gaynor nodded. 'Even before it was fashionable. Both she and Crystal had a flair for figures, but Tania did a proper IT course at Barbury Tech and went to work for a computer firm in Presford. That's how she met Todd. She set up a property database for him when most landlords were still working with boxes of index cards. She put him ahead of the game – for all the good it did him.'

'How do you mean?'

'There was some trouble a few years ago, but...'

Lincoln sat up. 'Trouble?'

'Between Todd and Derek. They did a lot of work together but then Dez went into partnership with somebody else and Todd felt sidelined. Tania always had to have a little dig about it, forever reminding Cryss how badly Dez had behaved, going behind Todd's back. She could never let it drop.'

Pam pushed her cup and saucer away. 'Has anything happened more recently to drive Crystal and Tania apart? Their relationship seems to have soured lately.'

Gaynor looked awkward but then said dismissively, 'Sibling rivalry – you know how it is. My girls fought like cat and dog when they were small, and even now it doesn't take a lot to set them off. It blows over soon enough.' She pulled her jacket into her lap, straightening it. Reached for her bag, edgy, keen to get up and leave.

Lincoln didn't want to let her go yet, though. 'Has Crystal ever expressed concern about the amount of time Emma spent with Mr Tremlow?'

'With Todd? What are you getting at?' Gaynor fidgeted with her bangle.

'He took a lot of photos of her,' Pam said, 'from when she wasn't much more than a baby. We wondered if—'

'Well, he would, wouldn't he? Dez wasn't around anymore so who else was going to take them? Cryss couldn't.' Gaynor's treacle-dark eyes narrowed. 'What are you trying to suggest?'

Lincoln leaned in towards her. 'His behaviour might be construed as suspicious.'

'Hark at you! "Construed as suspicious" – God, and I thought *I* was the one with the dodgy English!'

He decided to change tack. 'Have you seen what Mark Sherman's told the Sunday papers?'

'I saw the headlines. Mark's out for what he can get and the papers are lapping it up. That's one of the many things I hate about this country – the tabloids and their so-called exclusives. What does it matter who her dad was?' She snatched up her coat and bag and got to her feet. 'Right, now I need to get back to my friend's bedside, if that's okay with everyone.' Before they could even thank her for coming, Gaynor Rees had stormed out of the office.

They watched her go.

'That went well,' said Pam.

'Don't you start.'

It was one of those rare times when Lincoln wished he had a proper office, or even a cupboard, with a door he could slam.

Gaynor could hardly bear to see how much Barbury had deteriorated. Apart from an annual flying visit, she'd been away for over ten years. The ring road had been widened, demolishing more old buildings, destroying even more greenery. And for what? She'd called a cab outside the police station half an hour ago and had got nowhere.

The taxi driver cursed the traffic as they sat immobile on the bypass. He caught her eye in the rear-view mirror. 'Here on holiday?'

'Mercy dash. An old friend's in hospital.' She toyed with her tobacco tin, longing for a chance to light up. The dashboard clock showed they'd taken fifteen minutes to crawl about a hundred yards. 'Is it always this bad?'

'Schools are back, aren't they? Always bad when the schools are back.' He ran a hand over his oily hair. 'Your friend in Presford General?'

'That's right.' She didn't want to talk. She was too angry, too sad. Bloody Mark Sherman! All Em wanted was to belong and he'd turned her away. "*You're not my sister.*" Thank God Cryssie hadn't seen the headlines!

The traffic began to shunt forward. Gaynor gazed out of the window at a town she'd always hated. It was worse now, the old brick terraces giving way to sordid blocks of concrete flats and cottagey houses with no front gardens. Road signs obliterated every vista towards the abbey. Pylons she couldn't remember marched across the downs. Everything was ugly, spoilt, tampered with.

'Why can't people leave well alone?' she cried out without meaning to.

The taxi driver cast a look behind him, probably thinking she was on her mobile. Let the handbrake off. Inched forward.

# CHAPTER 51

'Any news on the Burnie girl?' Bella slipped her jacket and shoes off and came padding out to Lincoln's desk. After several hours at Lorren's autopsy in Presford, she looked tired.

'Nope, but no news is good news. If she'd been killed at the campsite, SOCOs would have found evidence by now.'

She made a face, not entirely convinced. 'And I take it that bloody hippy hasn't turned up?'

'Not yet, but he can't get far on a bike.'

She flipped open her notebook. 'Lorren Walsh's autopsy. Cause of death was asphyxia – something shoved down her throat until she ran out of air. Eleven violent blows to the head and torso. Evidence of long-term sexual abuse. Scars from self-harming. If she was taking drugs, she wasn't injecting. She'd had sex with three different men the night she died. Might get a match if we're lucky. She'd been sexually assaulted with something – Ken's guess was one of those beer bottles with the china stopper on a metal clip. Can you imagine?'

He could, but didn't want to. 'Go on.'

'Not all the blood was hers – chances are, she bit one of her assailants, sank her teeth into his hand or maybe into something softer...' She smiled coldly. 'And if we find a likely crime scene – those blue fibres on her vest and in her hair were from a cheap nylon carpet.'

'Anything useful from the tarpaulin?'

'Still working on it when I left. Everything takes so long...' She was about to shut her notebook when she added, 'Oh yes, and there was something in her stomach – something she'd swallowed or been forced to swallow.'

She grabbed her phone, turned it towards him, a quick photo she'd taken.

'A cufflink?' He took the phone from her, zooming into the photo until it blurred. Two golden discs the size of 5p pieces, linked with a tiny bar. He thought of the contents of Lorren's treasure box: buttons and coins, easily swallowed for retrieval later...

Bella snapped her notebook shut. 'Real gold with initials on, some fancy monogram, hard to decipher with the naked eye. They'll clean it up, look more closely, give us a better idea. Where are we with Emma Sherman?'

He told her about Gaynor Rees and her dismissal of the allegations against Todd Tremlow.

'Doth the lady protest too much?' She folded her arms, sceptical.

'Seemed pretty shrewd but she can't know for sure – she's lived abroad for some years, seldom visits.'

'Let's keep on trying to identify the Fiesta driver. What about Indian groups, Muslim associations? Isn't that what we think, that he's Pakistani, Asian, black?'

'Dilke asked round the cab offices. One bloke recognised him as someone he's seen hanging around in town late at night – certainly not a cabbie. He had him down as a pusher. Not much to go on.'

'You need to be pursuing this one, Jeff, trying every angle – if only to keep Donal Finnegan happy.'

Before he could argue, she'd retreated to her cubbyhole.

His phone rang – Bob Bowden on the front desk warning him he had another visitor. A moment later, the door flew open and there was Trish.

'Don't you *ever* answer your phone?' she snapped. 'I've had to come over in person because you never pick up.'

'I was in a meeting. You find out anything about Arlo?'

'Not a lot. His second wife emigrated to Australia years ago, so if he's gone into hiding, it's not with her. Which I could have told you half an hour ago if you'd left your phone on.'

'Sorry.'

Mollified, Trish let out a long breath. 'Ah well, I needed to get away from the library anyway, before I lost my temper with Selina. You know I told you about her little sister?'

'Annette?

'Anita. Stayed out overnight, mother doesn't even know and Selina's not going to tell her. I said to her, suppose something had happened to her? But she can't see it like that. Now the kid's home again, all Selina cares about is keeping it from her mum.'

'So where was she? She's only fourteen, isn't she?' He thought of Lady Burnie, of Lorren Walsh and Emma Sherman.

'Probably spent the night at Scoot's flat, although he was on his own when I bumped into him.'

'Did you say *Scoot*?' His heart skipped a beat. Anita, fourteen, bunking off school, hanging around with an older boy, a young man, in a flat in Barbury. A kid spending money she didn't have.

'I found out where he lives,' Trish went on, clearly oblivious to his concern. 'He's got a flat over a kebab shop in Finisterre Street.'

'How the hell...?' He was on his feet and round the other side of the desk in a flash.

'Selina told me where she thought he lived and I went round there yesterday afternoon. I was hoping to find Anita or at least get an address so—'

Lincoln grabbed her by the arm. 'Didn't it even cross your mind this bloke could be dangerous?'

Trish tugged away from him. 'I wanted to help.'

He pulled a chair out for her – the one so abruptly vacated by Gaynor Rees – and she took it, her gaze roaming the room while he prepared to take some sort of a statement. When he looked up, she was staring at the whiteboard.

'There he is,' she said. She got up and crossed to where the three traffic cam photos were pinned up in a row. 'That's him there.'

She pointed to the close-up of the Fiesta at the lights, the shadowy face of the driver. 'That's the man I met on the walkway over the shops, exactly how Selina described him. He's got ZAK tattooed on his arm – d' you think that's his name or initials of some sort?'

Lincoln leapt to his feet again, strode across.

'*This* is Scoot?' He laid his hand across the photo. 'The man in this car is the man you saw in Finisterre Street?'

'Yes. Isn't it obvious?'

In the only mugshot they'd got of him, taken months ago, the harsh lighting had made Scotson look sallow but Caucasian. Now that Trish had identified him as the man behind the wheel of the Fiesta, the likeness was obvious. His hair was longer now and a close-cropped beard shaded his jaw – but of course it was him!

'Trish, this bloke is wanted in connection with Emma Sherman's murder.'

She gasped. 'Selina's going to have to listen now.'

'We need to talk to Anita.'

'Jeff, you can't! Her mum doesn't even know she was out all night.'

'She's been to a flat that's being used for sex. With underage girls. We need to find this bloke before anyone else gets hurt.'

Woody came in, surprised to see his wife's sister in the CID room.

Lincoln slapped the whiteboard. 'She's only come face to face with Zakariah Scotson! It was *Scotson* who picked Emma up that night. Trish, we've got to speak to Anita.'

'No! Listen, I can tell you where the flat is, what Scoot looks like. But I can't get her involved. She could be in danger if he found out.'

Lincoln squeezed himself into Bella's office. 'We've got an address for Scotson,' he said. 'And we've found out he was the one who picked Emma up in the Fiesta.'

'That was Scotson? You think he was grooming the Sherman girl?'

'Doubt it, but maybe he was paid to pick her up and take her up into the woods.'

'By Arlo James?'

'Possibly.' He didn't want to admit he'd been wrong about Arlo, but it was looking that way. 'We need to pick Scotson up.'

'On what grounds?'

'He's been driving while disqualified.'

'How do you know that?'

Lincoln hesitated. He only knew because Alan Hayes had secretly sent him Liz Gregg's report. But Bella wasn't to know that. He carried on. 'So we could bring him in for that and then once we've got him in here...'

She reached for the phone. 'I'll organise a warrant and get a team together to go round there first thing, before it's properly light.'

'Let's go round there now. Arlo might be there, and the Burnie girl. Those few hours could make all the difference.'

'Okay, okay.' She punched the numbers in. 'Donal Finnegan's been on the phone – he wants to offer a reward for info leading to the conviction of Emma's killer.'

'Shit, that's all we need.'

'I told him to contact the chief constable.'

Lincoln snorted. 'Anyone putting up a reward for Lorren Walsh?'

'Probably not.'

'Wasn't really a question, ma'am.'

'Get over yourself, Jeff.' She waved him out of her cubbyhole, pushed her door half-shut.

His phone rang – Maureen from the lab. 'That tarpaulin,' she said.

'What've you got, Mo?'

'I should really speak to DCI Bax.'

He glanced back over his shoulder. Bella was still on the phone. 'Tell me and I'll pass it on.'

'The tarpaulin from the Walsh murder was the same as in the Sherman case.'

'What?'

'It's one tarpaulin, cut in two with something like a Stanley knife. We spread the pieces out and fitted them together. When we cleaned it up, we found a logo stencilled on it: FPD – Finnegan Property Development.'

# CHAPTER 52

'We've met before, haven't we, Inspector?' Steven Short waved Lincoln and Woody into his office on the top floor of Finnegan Property Development. 'At Southlawns?'

Lincoln recognised the man who'd rescued him from Nigel McTimothy's presidential pomposity. 'Yes, of course. I was grateful for your help that day.' He sat down, while Woody strolled across to look at the view across Barbury marketplace.

Short perched on the edge of his desk. 'Did the clubhouse security cameras give you anything?'

'Unfortunately not, but thanks anyway.'

'Poor old Nigel hadn't quite grasped the urgency of the situation.' Short smiled down. 'I take it you're not here to talk about Southlawns.'

'Yes and no. I understand you're operations manager here?'

'For my sins. How can I help?'

'The tarpaulin recovered that day...'

'You mean the one the Sherman girl was wrapped in? I saw the body. When Maisie came rushing into the clubhouse, the first thing I did was get her to show me what she'd found.'

'But you probably didn't see that your company logo was printed on it.'

Short looked horrified. 'Are you sure?'

Lincoln pulled out the photo Maureen had sent across from the lab: FPD inside two concentric circles. 'Is this the logo of Finnegan Property Development?'

'You know it is.' After a few seconds, Short handed the photo back. 'But y' know, these tarps go missing all the time. They get stolen from our building sites, end up on allotments, in back gardens. We're working on properties all over Barbury so we've got goods and equipment parked all over the place.' He crossed to a display board on the wall and waited for Lincoln and Woody to join him. 'You can see for yourself. Our Revyve project.'

A cartoon strip charted the fate of a house that had been neglected. Its owners stood on the front path, wringing their hands and peering up in despair at a roof that was clearly in need of retiling. Rescue came in the form of a man in a green-and-yellow striped van, who shook hands with the elderly couple before setting to work restoring their home to its former glory.

Lincoln thought back to the clubhouse at Southlawns that Sunday afternoon. Tables heaped with leaflets, badges, jotter pads. A couple of young women grudgingly untying strings of green-and-yellow bunting and repacking boxes of goody bags...

'You do up empty houses, don't you?' Woody put in. 'Refurbish them? An old chap in our road – you've been doing his place up.'

Short brightened. 'We're in partnership with the council. We fix up houses that owners can't afford to maintain, move them into more suitable accommodation – which in turn helps the council keep its housing waiting lists down.'

Lincoln snorted. 'Sounds too good to be true.'

Short spread his hands, disappointed by such cynicism. 'Donal has quite a job convincing his critics that he's doing this to give something back. He's got to make money – he's running a business, after all – but he wants to help people too.'

'Old Arthur along our road certainly needed a bit of help,' Woody agreed. 'There's another phase planned, isn't there?' He sounded quite the expert. 'That parade of shops on Market Row? My wife's been campaigning. Doesn't think they should be converted into flats.'

Short grinned. 'Sounds as if *you* think they should.'

Woody grinned back. 'If shops are closing because no one's using them, reckon it makes sense to turn them into homes. That's what there's never enough of.'

'Exactly.'

Unimpressed, Lincoln turned away and went over to retrieve the photo of the tarpaulin. 'So you've no way of knowing if you're missing a tarp like this one?'

Short shook his head. 'I wish I could help, but when so many go missing...'

'We'd like a list of your employees, anyone who might have access to tarps like this.'

'That's impossible, I'm afraid. Revyve's got its own refurbishment team, but we subcontract most of our work.'

When Lincoln and a team of officers arrived at Finisterre Street a few hours later, the flat was empty. Empty at least of Zakariah Scotson, empty of any of the girls he'd kept there, groomed there. Empty of any of the men who'd dropped in for a quick fuck with an underage runaway.

'Damn.' Lincoln gazed round in despair at the bare floors, the wrinkled sleeping bags on filthy mattresses, the abandoned drugs paraphernalia. 'Someone must've tipped him off.'

The kitchen looked as if it had been stripped back for an overhaul that never happened. In the living room, a torn sheet had been thrown over the window pole in place of curtains. The bathroom stank and the lavatory was stained as if it got backed up as a matter of routine. Just as well there was no bulb in the ceiling light: after dark, you wouldn't see what a cesspit you were pissing into.

Woody cast a disgusted gaze over what was left of the bedding. 'Reckon they'll get plenty of forensics off this lot.'

Who else had been here with Scotson? Lorren? Selina's little sister? Lady Burnie? And if Lady was here, had Arlo been here too?

Woody stood, hands on hips, looking round. 'You think this is where the Walsh girl was killed?'

'Place is such a mess, it's hard to tell.'

And then Lincoln saw bloody fingerprints high up on the edge of the kitchen door frame – thumb and forefinger, probably, where you might put your hand out to steady yourself stepping over something in the doorway. 'See that?'

Woody grinned. 'That'll do nicely.'

'Let's get the SOCO team in here. We need to get everything sealed off ASAP.'

The flat reeked of weed, mildew, cigarettes – and air freshener, the powdered sort you sprinkle onto carpets and then vacuum up. Yet the floorboards were bare except for a fragment of blue nylon carpet held fast by the metal strip in the doorway – just like the fibres on Lorren's vest top. The rest of the carpet must have been ripped up and thrown out.

'How did Scotson know we were onto him?' Woody scratched his head.

'Trish turning up on his doorstep might have unsettled him a bit.'

'She spooks me sometimes.'

'Did you see any cameras in the street? Could give us something. And we'd better search the bins downstairs while we're at it.'

Behind the Aziz Kebab Shop, they found several pieces of blue carpet stuffed into a trade waste bin under a mess of food scraps. Even in the fading light, Lincoln could see the carpet glistening red.

And beneath the carpet, a Grolsch beer bottle, swing-top lid, streaked with blood.

Zak Scotson was on the run, possibly with Arlo James. Where would they go now, these unlikely partners in crime?

Lincoln and Woody watched while the area behind the kebab shop was taped off for the SOCO team to do a thorough search. Woody nodded towards the gigantic wheelie bins that lined the alleyway. 'You think the Burnie girl's in there somewhere?'

'Let's hope not.' Lincoln didn't voice what he was thinking: *Be glad your sister-in-law didn't end up here, Woody.* The thought of losing Trish creased his heart. 'Better get back to the station.'

# CHAPTER 53

The room was swimming round her. Sound flowed towards her, then away again, like a tide. Not a dream. A nightmare, then. For real.

The big guy was there, half-turned away. Lady recognised him now, seeing him from behind and sideways; bald, hefty like a bouncer. Arlo's driver.

'Why you keeping me here?' Her ankles were bound together with duct tape, the insides of her knees sore from being pressed together.

'Shut the fuck up. Won't tell you again.'

'I wasn't going to say anything about the top, honest.'

'You found it. That's enough.'

'Was it Emma's?'

'Who?'

'Arlo wouldn't kill her. He's not like that.'

'It's Arlo that wants you out the way, you stupid cunt.'

Bloody fucking Arlo. Bloody fucking shitting pissing Arlo. Was this how Emma was killed? Held here, wherever it was, until they were done with her? Poor cow. Poor stupid, spoilt little cow.

Lady's head throbbed like she was having a brain haemorrhage. Her lip hurt, there was a deep cut in the middle. She'd be scarred for life! Her mouth was so dry, she couldn't swallow. They'd given her something to knock her out and she'd lost track of time. Her bones felt like they'd been filled with grit, itching from the inside.

Wasn't anyone looking for her? Fuck, the things she'd worried about! The baby, her mum all over the place, a little kid taking over the flat, wet washing, nappies, the stink of poo all the time... What wouldn't she give to get through this, to get back to her mum!

Tears smarted behind her lids. 'How long've I been here?'

'Long enough to get on my tits.' He didn't look up. 'Sooner we get shot of you, the better.' He was checking his phone, his face blue, white, yellow, then blue again from the screen colours as he scrolled. A fat face, thick neck, shaved head.

Patrick. The guy who'd driven her to and from Arlo. Never said a lot and she never knew what to say. While he drove, she'd sat behind him and studied the tattoo on the back of his neck, watched it stretch or shrink as he moved his head. It all but disappeared into the folds of fat at the base of his skull when he tipped his head back to check his mirror. A mermaid surfing his flab.

She shut her eyes, trying to work out how long she'd been here. How many times had he brought her water? How often had he picked her up and carried her across to the toilet whether she wanted to go or not? How many times had he stuck that needle in her arm?

She worked out she'd been here two nights. Must be Monday. She couldn't see out, couldn't hear anything from outside. Patrick's voice echoed like they were in a cave, stone walls, hollow, underground.

'Where is he?'

'Who?' The big guy didn't even look round. It was too dim to see the mermaid stretched out and basking.

'Arlo.'

'Fuck I know? Fucker's long gone.'

Her heart shifted in her chest. Had Arlo buggered off, left her to this moron? Or did he mean...? 'Haven't hurt him, have you?'

A nasty laugh. 'That'd give me so much pleasure.' He didn't even look up from his phone. Pressed a button, waited for his contact to pick up. 'Yeah, mate, it's me. What you want me to do with the package? Want me to send it off or—' His horrid little eyes flicked her way. He chuckled, sharing a joke. 'Yeah, we'll see about that! See you when I see you.' His phone went quiet and he put it in his pocket. 'Get up.'

'Don't want to.'

He came closer, bent over her, a gust of sweat and aftershave and tobacco and disgustingly bad breath, like his mouth was full of vomit.

'Get up.'

He reached behind her, pulling on her arms. The next thing she knew, her head was spinning and her arm was stinging from a needle and she was going under, going under, down and down...

# CHAPTER 54

Trish phoned late. 'Listen, Jeff, er – I need to tell you something.'

'If it's about you moving house...' Lincoln put his glass down, took the phone into the kitchen where he was reheating some risotto in the microwave.

'How did you...? Did Kate say something? Listen, I was going to tell you when I could get you alone but it's been impossible to find the right time. And we're not moving house, not unless I get this job, and there's only an outside chance I'll get it. I need to stretch myself, that's all, branch out a bit. I see other people moving on and I realise how stuck I am, no chance of a better job here or even elsewhere in the county...'

'It's okay,' he said before she could bombard him with any more rehearsed excuses. 'I understand. Go ahead and apply for this dream job of yours.'

'I already have. The interview's Wednesday.'

The blood boomed in his ears. So she was serious. 'Oh.'

'It'll be good experience, the interview, I mean. I haven't a hope in hell of getting the job, but...'

'You'll be fine.' He took his plate out of the microwave. The risotto was reduced to a heap of crispy grains and desiccated vegetables.

'Jeff, I don't want you to think—'

'Just do it.' Nothing he could say was going to stop her, no matter how much he wanted her to stay.

'You're still angry with me, aren't you, about going round to see Scoot? If I'd had any idea...'

He thought again of the bins behind the kebab shop, that stab of terror when he'd realised how close she'd come to danger. Mortal danger.

'You were lucky, Trish. But if I need to speak to Anita Rani, I'll go ahead whether you like it or not.'

'I know. Just tell me first, okay?'

'No promises.'

'Okay. You've had something to eat?'

He looked away from the charred remains on his plate. 'Yes, thanks, a bit of rice. Sleep tight.'

# CHAPTER 55

Next morning, Lincoln received a preliminary forensic report on Scotson's flat. Woody leaned over his shoulder while they read the clinical findings together. Neither said a word, each reconstructing the events leading up to Lorren's death.

In the two or three hours before she was killed, she had sex with at least one man on the bed and two men on the carpet. The blood on the carpet and on her vest top was mostly hers but a few drops were from one of her assailants. The prints on the Grolsch bottle that had been repeatedly rammed inside her were Scotson's.

Without more tests, it was impossible to conclude who'd finally choked her to death, but Lincoln's money was on Scotson.

'Any other prints in the flat?' Woody asked, scanning the screen.

'Mostly too messy to interpret. The only prints that were clear enough to identify belonged to Lorren, Scotson and – oh shit.' Lincoln put his hands on his head and shut his eyes. 'How did we miss that?'

Woody craned closer to the screen. 'Patrick *Tyler*? Aged twenty-nine. Reckon he's Ashley's older brother?'

The mugshot confirmed it: Patrick Gerard Tyler, a shaven-headed, slope-shouldered hulk, Ashley on a bigger scale. Convicted of assault ten years ago, sentenced to six years, released after four. The bloody fingerprints on the edge of the door frame were his.

'Why didn't we know about him?' Lincoln stood up, drawn to the whiteboard, where Patrick Tyler was conspicuous by his absence.

'He's not on the sex offenders register so his name didn't come up when Emma went missing, did it? Ashley was never a suspect – he came forward to see if he could help – so we never asked him about his family. We can't do background checks on everyone, boss.'

If Patrick Tyler was in the flat around the time Lorren was killed, he and Scotson must be working together. When they needed a car to pick Emma up, Tyler didn't think twice about borrowing his kid brother's Fiesta.

'I need to tell the DCI.' Lincoln picked up the phone, hoping to reach Bella at Park Street where she was briefing DCS Youngman. He tried her mobile, got voicemail and left a message to call him ASAP.

210

He felt useless and marooned, unable to act without her permission. If it was up to him, he'd be tearing round to arrest Tyler straightaway. But it wasn't up to him, not any more.

Anyway, chances were the big bastard would've made himself scarce now the Finisterre Street flat was out of bounds and Scotson had gone to ground. The Tyler brothers both lived in Chartman Way, separate addresses some distance apart.

'Let's hope Shauna and Graham have found some CCTV cameras,' Woody said. 'If we can get some footage of the street below Scotson's flat, we should be able to spot some of the punters, see if Arlo was there too.'

'His prints weren't.'

'They might've been, just too messed-up to identify.'

'Messed-up like this whole situation.' Lincoln halted by his desk, gazing at the mugshot of Patrick Tyler that scowled out from his screen. His mobile rang – Bella calling back. He put her in the picture and waited for the explosion.

'And this is the guy whose brother you interviewed a week ago?' she shrieked. 'Why the fuck's it taken you this long to find out about him?'

'Ashley came forward voluntarily – maybe to throw us off the scent. Never mentioned a brother. We can't do background checks on everyone.' He caught Woody's eye as he said it.

'I'd better come back to Barley Lane pronto,' she snapped, 'before anything else gets screwed.'

Meanwhile, in the vicinity of Zak Scotson's flat in Finisterre Street, Shauna and Dilke were finding that most of the CCTV cameras they'd spotted were either dummies or dead.

'Nearly lunchtime,' said Shauna. 'I'm starving. Fancy a kebab?'

They went into the Aziz Kebab Shop and queued while the man behind the counter laboriously sliced fatty leaves from a revolving cone of grey meat.

'Actually, Shaun,' Dilke said after a couple of minutes, 'I'll just pick something up at the paper shop.'

As he came back across Finisterre Street with a packet of Hula Hoops and a can of Fanta, he spotted the eye of a lens above the door of the off-licence.

'You've got a camera.'

The man broke off from stacking cans of a beer Dilke had never heard of. 'Camera?'

'Over the door.'

'Is upstairs,' the man said, getting the gist. 'Is club upstairs.'

Shauna joined Dilke as he knocked on the street door beside the off-licence. "*Diego's*", it said beneath the knocker on a tarnished metal sign.

A few minutes later, they were climbing dark stairs to the first floor.

Diego's was a two-room drinking club for retired cab drivers. Ostensibly. It was only open four nights a week so the cameras were only running from midday on Thursday to midnight on Sunday, recording onto old-fashioned VCR tapes. The earliest recording ought to show comings and goings the day before Lorren died.

'We need to take these away,' Dilke said. Probably relieved they hadn't asked to check the club's fire certificate, the burly man in charge of Diego's made no protest.

They took the tapes back to the car.

'Might get something off these, yeah?' Shauna chomped on her kebab, wet strands of crinkled lettuce escaping from her pitta and tumbling down her chin. She picked tomato pips off her chest. 'The camera should've picked up anyone visiting Scoot's flat.'

'Let's hope so.' Dilke thought back to Langford Hill Lane and the sight of Lorren Walsh's ruined face. 'If the images are clear enough, we can nail the bastard.'

'Don't get your hopes up, Gray. It's a camera outside a drinking club, not Quentin Tarantino.'

'We can bring Scotson and Tyler in on suspicion of murder,' Bella said, 'if they haven't already gone to ground.' She paced back and forth between her cubbyhole and Lincoln's desk. DCS Youngman had probably given her a bollocking for failing to make an arrest. All too easy to make judgements when you're ensconced in an ivory tower. 'And I'm bringing someone else in to take over the Elaine Burnie case – DI Liz Gregg. I'm sure you'll give her every assistance.'

Never mind that it was Liz Gregg who'd let Scotson off the hook only weeks ago...

'Of course,' said Lincoln, making an effort to hide his resentment. 'I'm sure we'll work well together.'

'Take a team over to Chartman Way and pick Patrick Tyler up – though I doubt if he'll be hanging around waiting for us.'

*

Bella was right. No one came to the door when they called at Tyler's top-floor flat but they went in anyway – with the help of a team of uniforms using an Enforcer to smash the door open. The kitchen was a mess of takeaway debris, empty beer cans and unwashed plates, the fridge empty, cupboards likewise. In the bathroom they found no more than a few basic toiletries on a mucky shelf. The bedroom smelt of stale sweat and trainers, and was kitted out with only a mattress, a couple of pillows and a sleeping bag.

The only signs that Tyler had been home recently were the sell-by dates on the milk and bread slung into the fridge.

Woody came out of the second bedroom, holding up a bunch of payslips bearing a now-familiar logo: FPD.

'So that's who he works for,' Lincoln said with bitter delight. 'Donal bloody Finnegan.'

The woman who picked up Steven Short's phone would have made a good spy: under interrogation, say nothing. Mr Short was away from the office for a couple of days, she said, but she'd tell him Inspector Lincoln had called.

'I can't wait for him to get back,' Lincoln said. 'I need to find Patrick Tyler, one of your employees.'

After several minutes of prevarication, she told him Tyler was a member of the refurbishment team, currently employed on the cemetery redevelopment.

'How do you redevelop a cemetery?' Lincoln wondered as he and Woody drove towards it.

When they got there, they saw that only the cemetery superintendent's detached 50s house was being redeveloped. Green-and-yellow logos were dotted around the site: a child's drawing of a house, a speech bubble billowing like smoke from its chimney, rejoicing that *"I'm being Revyved!"*

Some adjacent outbuildings once used for storage – of what, Lincoln didn't like to think – were being gutted "for upgrade into two desirable dwellings finished to an exceptional standard."

The foreman steered them away: they were hatless in hard-hat territory. Tyler had phoned in sick at the start of the week, hadn't called since. 'In trouble again, is he?'

'Again?'

'I know Pat's got a record,' the foreman said, 'but the boss believes in giving people a helping hand, get them back on the straight and narrow. Mr Finnegan gave him a chance when any other boss would've turned him away.'

'He ever mention a girlfriend, somewhere he might go if he doesn't go home?'

'A closed book, is Pat. Never says a lot. So no, sorry.'

'If he turns up or you hear from him, let us know. Urgently.'

They trudged back to the car. 'Can't seem to get away from the saintly Mr Finnegan,' said Lincoln.

Woody slid behind the wheel. 'Must be a big-hearted bloke, though. Bit of a risk, employing convicted offenders like Patrick Tyler.'

'Easy to be magnanimous from a distance. Finnegan's not the one who's got to work with him.'


'Watching this footage is boring my arse off.' Dilke moved his chair along so Shauna could see the screen. 'I'm only up to Thursday evening and my eyes are out on stalks.'

'You can't fast-forward?' Her fingers hovered over the button.

'The tape's poor quality. Everything smears.'

'We've just gotta press play and sit here? I'm going for a pee first, then. You want me to bring you back a coffee? It's all right, I'll wash my hands in between.'

A few minutes later, she was back, and they began to watch together.

Diego's CCTV camera was hardly state-of-the-art, but as well as commanding a view of the street outside the club, its lens saw anyone coming and going from the flats where Zak Scotson lived, even though the walkway was partly obscured by a brick parapet and everything was in black and white.

By the time the screen clock was showing 20.15 last Thursday, they'd seen three drug deals going down in the doorway of the kebab shop, and a scuffle between a couple of teenagers.

Then, at 20.17, a balding man, middle-aged, heavily overweight, suit and tie, crossed the street and disappeared behind the shops. Thirty seconds later, his head and shoulders appeared above the parapet. Scotson's door sank open and Balding Man was silhouetted by a dim light from the hallway. The door shut.

Scotson himself, slim build, black hair, came out onto the walkway to have a smoke. He kept looking down into the street as if he was waiting for someone. Then Dilke spotted someone else he recognised hurrying along the pavement alone.

He jabbed the screen. 'There she is.'

Lorren Walsh in a tiny skirt over leggings, a skimpy jacket and white trainers, going up the steps to the flat. She wasn't tall enough to appear over the parapet, but after a few moments, Scotson flung his cigarette down into the street, opened the door of his flat and shoved her inside.

Dilke watched, his breathing shallow, tense.

Balding Man emerged after less than twenty minutes, aiming a key fob at a car out of shot. Five minutes later another man turned up: leather jacket, jeans. Door open, dim light shining, door shut.

Nearly an hour went by before Leather Jacket came down, got in his car, a white or silver Astra, and sped away. Dilke stabbed the pause button, froze the car's licence plate.

'Write it down.'

'Say please.'

'Please, Shaun.'

'Bastards,' she muttered, scribbling. 'Bastards in suits and leather jackets.'

Sergeant Bob went by on his way to the lockers.

'Patrick Tyler,' said Lincoln. 'Know anything about him?'

Bob rubbed his chin. 'Bit of a heavy, isn't he? Got in trouble a while back, far as I recall – paid to scare the shit out of some fella and nearly slaughtered him! What's he done now?'

Lincoln told him about the bloody fingerprints in Scotson's flat.

'You had his brother in here the other day, didn't you?' Bob said. 'Ashley? I was going to say something to you about Pat but it went out of my head. One of the perils of getting old. I bet that's Della's boy, that Zak. Practically brought up in a knocking shop!'

'And now he's running his own – except it's kids he's selling.'

'So how did the Sherman girl get mixed up with him, eh?'

'I'd love to know. But she got into his car that night without a second's hesitation.'

Bob sighed. 'Teenagers! But what can you do? It's my grandchildren I'll be fretting about next, few years' time.' And he ambled off, his shift over for the day.

As he watched the older man depart, Lincoln wondered what Scotson said to Emma, in that one and only call to her, that made her climb into his car a few minutes later without a qualm. Climb in and let him drive her away. Drive her away forever.

# CHAPTER 56

As soon as the library was quiet again, Trish checked her mobile, expecting a good luck text from Jeff. Nothing. Surely he hadn't forgotten her interview was tomorrow?

'I wonder if you can be of assistance?'

'I'll certainly try. How can I help?' She looked up into the brown eyes of a man about her own age. Waxy hair and tinted half-moon glasses. A smile that would melt butter.

Letting the broad strap of his laptop bag slide off his shoulder, he sat down and thrust a card at her. "*Ian Marston. Freelance journalist.*"

She recognised the name: he'd done regular features for *The Messenger* in the last year or so, including the article on the Battle of the Beanfield that she'd unearthed for Jeff only a few days ago.

Marston lowered his voice. 'I'm looking into the case of Linus Bonetti.'

'Linus Bonetti?' Oh Lord... 'You're welcome to look at our back file of local newspapers, and of course the nationals covered it after the inquest but—'

'I really wanted to speak to someone working for the council. Your colleagues in Social Services?'

'You need to go through Corporate Communications – er, the press office at County Hall. Although...' She glanced up at the clock: 4.48. 'There'll be someone there till five, so if you try them now—'

'Been there, done that. Not very helpful.'

'They'll have told you all they can.' Trish knew the protocol: council officers talk to journalists at their peril. Linus Bonetti had made that mistake, wanting to bring the press in, going on Twitter, stirring up the shit.

Marston leaned forward, his chin almost grazing the top of her screen. 'You know he was under investigation?'

'I know there were some issues.' She stared beyond his shoulder, willing a queue of customers to form behind him, but no importunate readers came to her rescue.

'He was a whistle-blower,' Marston went on. 'He was in discussion with me about exposing some scandalous practices.'

Trish tried to suppress the panic fluttering in her chest. 'I'm aware that he'd raised some concerns. Er – the council's whistle-blower policy is available to download from the website, if that would be of any use to you?'

God, why was she applying for a job in Essex? With such skills of diplomacy she could easily land a job in Corporate Comms here!

'Thanks, but I was hoping to speak to someone who knew him.'

'Why come to the library, then? You'd be better off talking to people who worked alongside him.'

'Because I know you helped him, Ms Whittington.' Marston's steady gaze defied her to deny it. 'You were helping him with his research.'

# CHAPTER 57

Shauna had finished for the day, leaving Dilke on his own in front of the video screen.

Lincoln sat down beside him. 'Any sign of Patrick Tyler?'

'Nope. Three punters Thursday night, stayed thirty minutes, an hour. One of them, guy in a leather jacket, drives an Astra registered to the council.'

'Huh, he's hardly going to be calling at Scotson's on council business at that time of night!'

'We got another index number – a BMW registered to Colin McTimothy. Arrived at ten, left ten to eleven.' Dilke consulted his notes. 'Aged thirty-six. No record, nothing on file. His address is an apartment at the Old Art School.' He pushed a screen print across to Lincoln.

On the way back to his car, McTimothy had paused on the kerb long enough for the camera to make sense of his features. Clean-shaven. Light-coloured hair swept back from a high forehead. Heavy-rimmed glasses. A pale tailored mac over a dark open-necked shirt.

Lincoln recalled Nigel McTimothy, the bumptious golf club president at Southlawns. Could Colin be his son? 'So where are you up to now?'

'Friday afternoon. Not long before Lorren was killed.'

'Seen her yet?'

Dilke passed a couple of stills across. Skinny kid down in the street, short skirt, short jacket. 'She turned up Thursday evening. Haven't seen her leave yet.'

'Get off home now, Graham.' Lincoln patted the young man's shoulder. 'This can keep till the morning.'

As he rinsed his mug under the tap in the cloakroom a little later, Lincoln realised tomorrow was the day of Trish's interview. Supposing she got the job, left Barbury? She couldn't have many reservations about breaking up with him, applying for a post so far away.

Could you break up, though, if you weren't really together?

He leaned his head against the tiles over the sink, relishing the cold pressure on his forehead, the icy shiver down his back. He didn't want to lose her, but was scared he was about to. Why was he so pathologically unable to commit himself?

Back at his desk, he texted her: *Good luck for tomorrow. You'll knock their socks off. Xx.* Nearly sent a follow-up: *Not that I want you to, of course!*

But that would've been selfish, even if it was closer to the truth.

# CHAPTER 58

Angelo Bonetti stood in his son's bedroom, the lights off, the house quiet, no sound apart from his breathing. Linus' absence seemed to fill the room.

He'd made them so proud, coming along when they'd given up hope of having children. Such a handsome child! He didn't make friends easily – too quick-tempered, too sensitive, a solitary boy. He was moody – aren't all teenagers? He'd sleep whole days away, then walk to Stonehenge and back without telling them where he was going.

Angelo and Linda were so pleased when he went into teaching, even though he wasn't paid much and could only afford a small flat on the outskirts of Birmingham. But they were shocked when he told them what he had to put up with – children with no respect, useless parents who blamed the teachers, supervisors determined to find fault.

He left after clashing with his head teacher, decided to be a social worker instead. Newly qualified, he moved back home to Barbury and got a job working for Family Services based at the local hub.

Social work he enjoyed, seemed cut out for – except he worried all the time about getting it right, being the best. Soon he was having run-ins with his bosses, arguing, squaring up to them. Fighting his corner, Linus called it. Belligerent, his bosses said. He got warnings, interviews with boards of this and that.

'They're covering things up, Dad,' he kept saying. 'You and Mum, you have no idea what's going on. Kids are being taken out of these homes and driven to sex parties in some big house somewhere. And if that isn't bad enough, at one party a kid got *killed*!'

Linda had put her knitting down and looked up at him. 'Linus, you can't believe everything these kiddies tell you. They'll say anything to get your attention. It would've been on the news if something like that had happened.'

'You just don't get it, do you? You're just like the rest of them!' He'd slammed out of the house, upsetting his mother, too headstrong to realise how hurtful his rage could be.

Angelo's thoughts returned to the funeral and David Black, Linus' supervisor. Made out he was on his side, but he wouldn't risk his own job to save someone on a lower grade, would he? Black had wanted Linus to take sick leave, plead stress, but what kind of blot would that leave on his record? Who'd employ him then?

From the shelf beside his son's bed, Angelo took down the old tartan biscuit tin Linus used to keep his swimming medals and certificates in. He set the lid aside and sifted through the little scrolls and diplomas with their illuminated headings, their old-fashioned signatures.

But what...? Underneath them lay a jumble of buttons and pens, a tie clip – whose? Linus never wore ties; few men did these days – and a snapshot of a baby, huge eyes, wispy hair.

His heart pounded. Surely Linus hadn't...?

He turned it over. *Lucy-Jane – July 1994*. It wasn't even Linus' writing. Angelo's pulse quietened. But why was all this junk mixed in with his medals?

'It's a scandal, Dad,' Linus had said, standing on the hearthrug, filling the living room with his indignation. 'They're putting people into flats who haven't been on the waiting list two minutes. And then they're gone again.'

'You must tell your managers, son. Let them sort it out. It's not your responsibility.'

'You ought to find a nice girl,' Linda would say. 'Settle down, have some children.'

'Not gonna happen, Mum. Not yet.'

And now it never could. Too much worry for one man to bear. For even Linus to bear.

Angelo was about to tip everything out of the tin and throw the junk away when he heard Linda's voice from the kitchen, calling him down. He shut the tin, restored it to its shelf among the swimming trophies Linus had won at Barbury Fields.

'Angelo?' She was on the stairs now, wondering where he'd got to. As if she didn't know.

# CHAPTER 59

Headlights raked the ceiling above Tom's bed. A couple of minutes later, he heard the clatter of his mother's car keys on the hall table.

He pulled his boxers up, tugged his T-shirt down, slid back under the duvet. Not that she ever stuck her head round the door to say goodnight like she used to. She hadn't done that since Rich was killed.

The sheet was sticky against his thigh. He'd been fantasising about Board Treaders, all the girls there, which of them he'd have and how. Stupid really because he didn't fancy any of them, not even Fifi with nipples like jellybeans.

He listened for the *thwop* of the living room door opening, a blast of music – Rachmaninov, probably, his father's favourite. Quiet when the door shut again.

And then the voices going to and fro, her and then him, *bap-bap-bap-bap, waw-waw-waw, bap-bap, waw-waw*. A thud as one of them slammed the door and stormed into the study.

His mother was seeing someone – Miles, the guy who owned the riding school where she helped out with the disabled children once a week. The bastard was rolling in dosh, earls in the family or something.

Tom found out about the affair before his dad did. Sent home from Forrester's early one day in February because the classroom pipes had burst, he'd come in the back way, up the lane and through the garden. Voices from his parents' bedroom had surprised him. Not a row this time, but groans and gasps. He'd felt disgust, curiosity, embarrassment. His dad must have taken the morning off. Did they often do this when he was at school, fuck each other's brains out?

But then his mother had yelled out, 'Oh, Miles, please, now!'

Miles? She was up there with Mr Riding School? And yes, there was Miles' jeep, parked where his father's car ought to be. Tom had sloped back into town, kicking his heels in the library and Starbucks until it was time to go home.

How soon after that had his father found out? It was unspoken between them that they both knew about the affair. His mother spent a lot of afternoons at the stables now instead of being at home.

222

Probably once Tom went to uni, she'd fuck off and leave them both. Probably thought she was owed something after Rich got killed. No wonder his dad... No, don't even go there.

Tom dragged the pillow over his head, trying to blot out the thoughts tumbling in his brain. He wanted to tell someone all about it, about everything, but there was no one he could talk to, not even Simon.

And Scoot, picking Em up in his car that night. Why was she going anywhere with that pothead? He was the *last* person she'd go with. Tom giggled at that: the *last* person she'd go with.

I didn't mean it, Em, not like that!

He snatched his pillow up, punched it, lay down again.

The *bap-bap, waw-waw* started up again, doors banging, Rachmaninov surging up the stairs, full volume. Somebody threw a plate or a cup or one of those pottery vases his mother kept buying, except she never bought flowers to put in them. If she went to live with Miles, she could take those ugly monstrosities with her. They'd have the house to themselves, him and his dad.

The Subaru started up. His dad had had enough and was going off somewhere, leaving Tom behind as if he didn't count, as if he was the last person either of them thought about.

It should've been him in that car with Joe Day, not Rich. It should've been him that got killed. Then they'd be sorry!

# CHAPTER 60

Bella introduced DI Liz Gregg to the team first thing next morning before whisking her off to an interview room for a briefing. Ten minutes later, when Lincoln saw Liz departing with an armful of paperwork, he followed Bella into her cubbyhole.

'Are you expecting her to lead this from Park Street?' He was furious that the Lady Burnie case had been taken away from him and given to someone who wasn't even in the same station.

Bella met his anger with calm reason as she squeezed behind her desk. 'Liz has got her own team there. She'll come over here when she needs to. We need to make some progress. I'm meeting the DCS shortly but fuck knows what I'm going to tell him.'

'The tarpaulin's the same.'

She looked up, stunned. 'What?'

'Forensics called. Emma and Lorren. Wrapped in two halves of the same tarp. From Donal Finnegan's firm. Patrick Tyler works for Finnegan and he's a mate of Zak Scotson's – assuming you'd only ask a mate to help clear up after a fourteen-year-old got murdered in your flat.'

'Jeff—'

'Embarrassing for Mr Finnegan, a mate of one of his men driving Emma Sherman away.' He expected Bella to argue or prevaricate, to accuse him of being vindictive, but she didn't.

'Find Tyler and Scotson,' she said. 'Fast.' She shooed him out.

'That council car that Leather Jacket was driving,' Dilke said as Lincoln got back to his desk. 'It's allocated to a woman called Marianne Mearns who works at the Presford hub, facilities management. She hasn't reported it stolen so she must have lent it to Leather Jacket even though she's not supposed to let anyone else drive it.'

'A ticking-off from her boss'll be the least of her worries if she's married to one of Scotson's punters.'

'I Googled Colin McTimothy, our Beemer driver. He's got his own company and a shop in town. Golfing supplies.'

'Must be related to Nigel – too much of a coincidence.' Lincoln could only guess McTimothy Senior's reaction when he found out his son was paying to have sex with underage girls. 'Spotted Eily Quinn yet?'

'Eily Quinn?' Dilke looked blank.

Then Lincoln remembered: he'd told Woody about Liz Gregg's useless visit to Scotson's old flat, but nobody else. 'Eily's the girl who introduced Lorren to Scoot. She was living with him when he had a flat in Presford.' And he outlined what he'd learnt from DC Alan Hayes.

'You mean Park Street already knew Lorren was at risk?' Dilke said. 'And they didn't do anything?'

'Not a lot they could do, based on the evidence. Micky tried to get them to follow it up but no one took her seriously enough to log it. Look, read the report for yourself. Fresh pair of eyes, you may spot something I've missed.' Lincoln hunted round on his desk for the report Hayes had emailed him. 'It should be here somewhere...'

'You're thinking, if Eily was recruiting for Scotson in Presford, she'll be doing the same here?'

'Exactly. If we could get hold of her, she might talk.'

'Big if.'

Bella reappeared as Lincoln was raking through his in tray. She shrugged herself into her smart jacket. Even the most expensive tailored garments looked a tad too tight, a shade too short on her. 'Right, I'm off to Park Street.' She glanced across at Dilke. 'Still going through the tapes?'

Dilke jabbed his pencil towards the shabby videocassettes waiting beside the monitor. 'Slow going, ma'am. I don't want to miss anything.'

'Where've you got up to?'

'Friday, not long before Lorren was killed.'

She raised an eyebrow. 'That must be the last VCR player left in the county. And those tapes look like they're on their last legs.'

'I'm being very careful, ma'am.'

'I'm sure you are, but we all know how unreliable videotape can be.' She picked up her paperwork, jangled her keys, turned to Lincoln. 'Find Scotson and Tyler.' She lowered her voice to a whisper. 'And keep the Finnegan connection to yourself for now.' She strode towards the door. Her jacket collar was tucked in at the back but he wasn't going to tell her.

Lincoln breathed out as the door closed behind her. 'Now, Graham, if I could only find that bloody report...'

'Can you email it to me?'

'Better not. Not sure anyone outside Park Street was supposed to see it. Hang on, maybe I didn't actually print it out. I'll do it now and you can see what you think. Just don't leave it lying around on your desk.' Lincoln glared across at the printer, which took three minutes even to acknowledge his print job. Someone somewhere else in the building was probably printing off their timesheet or a fifty-page memo.

Dilke chuckled. 'You know what they say about a watched pot, boss.'

'I want it to print a three-page report, not make the bloody tea!'

'Talking of which – do you want a cuppa?'

By the time Dilke was back with Lincoln's coffee and a mug of builder's tea for himself, the Presford report was churning out of the printer. Lincoln got up to retrieve it.

Dilke took it from him, sat down to read it through. 'On paper, you can see why Park Street took no further action, but... The guy downstairs from Scoot – did Liz Gregg really think he'd make up stuff about schoolgirls being there? He'd get his door kicked in for less.'

'Or his face.' Behind him, Lincoln could hear the printer rapidly spewing out more paper. 'Now what's the bloody thing doing?' He snatched four blank sheets from the tray, dumped them into the box lid they kept for scrap paper. A short pause and then the printer was off again, more slowly this time. 'Oh, for crying out loud!'

Dilke didn't even look up. 'Probably someone's routed something to our printer by mistake. Wouldn't be the first time.'

Lincoln skimmed the pages as they came sliding out, recognising sentences from Alan Hayes' report – but it was only when the printer had produced another three sheets that he could see what had happened. Someone had amended the report on the visit to Scotson's flat in Watkins Court – but instead of overwriting the old version with the new, they'd left it tacked on at the end, separated by a few page breaks.

Hayes had sent Lincoln an edited version of the original, but he hadn't realised he'd sent him the *unedited* version as well.

Or had he?

Dilke looked up. 'Wrong printer?'

'No,' said Lincoln with a wicked grin. 'Wrong report.'

# CHAPTER 61

She was running for the train when her shoe flew off and skittered along the platform. A girl stopped to pick it up and handed it over with a laugh.

'Thanks. Serves me right for trying to run in high heels.' Trish crammed the shoe back on and clambered aboard.

No seats, and her feet were killing her. Why hadn't she thought to wear walking shoes for the journey, carry her heels in a bag? She sat herself on a tweedy ledge outside the toilet. The door kept flying open, sending out gusty smells of disinfectant and diarrhoea.

Onwards into Essex. She dived for a proper seat the moment it was free, slipped her shoes off, settled back.

Possible interview questions went through her mind, and she scoured the Charles Lundy information pack again for crucial dates and figures. She reread her application, feeling a bit smug at how well she'd presented herself. She had to be in with a chance.

She was beginning to relax when, along the aisle, she saw an elbow sticking out, a sleeve, a mac the same colour as Jeff's. She could only see the back of the man's head. He was reading a book propped up on the table in front of him, tugging on his earlobe the way Jeff did when he was concentrating. His dark brown hair was peppered with grey like Jeff's, a few white strands starting to show above his ears.

It wasn't Jeff, of course, but Trish felt suddenly ambushed, reminded of him as the train drilled deeper into the makeshift countryside of Essex.

An unfamiliar landscape jogged past the grimy window – flat and untidy, pretty in places. She looked forward to being closer to the sea – even if she'd be a little way up the estuary. But where would she go for a landscape as expansive as the plains and downs round Barbury? For fields and forests, for the green rivers that soothed her?

Oh, but it'd be wonderful to run her own library, to put her stamp on such a neglected collection of books and papers.

She took her phone out, checked for messages. Nothing from Jeff. A text from Kate: *Good luck xxx*. She smiled. The two of them, starting a new life here. Her and Kate.

New voicemail. She called it, waited.

'Listen,' Jeff stammered, 'you know I'm crap at this sort of thing but, well, look, I hope it goes all right and I know this is something you've always wanted to do so... Well, good luck. Hope it goes okay. Um. And if it doesn't, well, you know I'm here and... Um. Anyway, you know who this is, so I'll leave it at that. Bye. Catch up when you're back.'

*End of messages. To listen to the menu again, press...*

Trish shut her eyes. When she opened them again, the man down the train had moved his elbow off the armrest and vanished from view.

The train began to slow. She shoved her feet into her punishment shoes again and stood up.

# CHAPTER 62

'You've heard that reporter's snooping round again? Marston?'

David Black looked up from his screen to see his boss standing there with her hands on her hips. 'The one Linus was talking to?'

'That's the one. Bloody Bonetti. Why the fuck did we take him on? Subversive little prick. If Marston comes anywhere near you, Dave, tell him he's got to go through Comms.'

'It's okay, I know the rules.'

'Bonetti miss that training session, did he?' She dumped a wodge of papers in his tray. 'Rundown for the Paragon launch.'

'You make it sound like the bloody space shuttle.'

She smiled coldly. 'It's less than two weeks away and your presence is required at lift-off. So dig out your smart suit, Dave, and make sure you're there.' She swept off again.

David skimmed the programme for the laying of the foundation stone of Barbury's new arts centre, but the return of Ian Marston was more pressing. He glanced around the office to make sure he wasn't being observed before locating *MichaelmasHouse.docx*. He'd saved the file on his hard drive in defiance of corporate regulations. He tapped in the password to open it.

The document was a report Linus had done – off his own bat, unofficially – on the former Ash Tree Commercial Hotel, sometime a bail hostel in the back streets of Barbury.

Gutted and transformed under the Revyve banner and renamed Michaelmas House, it had opened a year ago as twelve self-contained flats. With great fanfare, Donal Finnegan and the head of Housing Services, Fergus Gee, had cut the green-and-yellow ribbon to signify the public/private partnership that would return the old hotel to the community.

Linus' document included a list of the twelve families selected to move into the flats in August and September last year. He'd tabulated the scores awarded to each one based on their housing needs prior to selection – alongside the scores he felt they *should* have received.

In every case, there was a significant discrepancy between the scores they'd been awarded and Linus' own assessment. He'd emailed

David the list, adding *DAVE – YOU CAN SEE HOW THESE SCORES HAVE BEEN INFLATED! THIS CAN'T BE RIGHT!!!!*

David had summoned Linus to his office as soon as he'd got the email, frogmarched him into one of the small meeting rooms. Easter time, a burst of warm weather, the room hot from the radiators that wouldn't go off until the 1st of May.

'Linus, how the hell did you get access to that information?'

'People leave doors open,' the young man had said smugly. 'I don't mean office doors. I mean digital ones. People come out of the system without logging out properly. You just need to know where to look.'

'What you've been doing is—'

'What I've been doing is trying to expose what's going on.'

'Linus, Michaelmas House was a key project for the council, for Revyve. Everyone wanted it to work because it was a pilot. Fergus and his team worked for months to put everything in place. After all that build-up, they couldn't risk it failing. For all we know, those families were chosen because the assessors thought they'd be model tenants, even if they weren't the most deserving. Window-dressing, a public relations exercise, okay?'

'All single mums? All with one or two kids under twelve? Come on, Dave! You know what? I think someone was up to something. In fact, I *know* they were.'

'Linus, don't go down that road. This project—'

'You know how long some of my clients have been waiting to move, Dave? Fifteen years. People with breathing problems from living in mouldy bedsits, families having to sleep in shifts because they haven't got enough beds. And then some twenty-year-old with a baby and a toddler gets a two-bedroom flat in Michaelmas House after fifteen *weeks* on the housing list. Where's the justice, Dave? Where's the fairness in that? And you think Michaelmas House is the only place it's going on?'

'You don't mess with the policymakers.' He'd patted Linus on the shoulder. 'Let's just stick to doing what we're paid to do, eh?'

'I'm not letting this go.' Linus had shrugged him off. 'I'm gathering evidence to prove it!' And he'd flung open the door and rushed out.

Now, nearly six months later, David stared at *MichaelmasHouse. docx* one more time. Closed the file, highlighted it in the short list of files on his hard drive.

Deleted it.

# CHAPTER 63

The lounge bar of the Rising Sun was quiet apart from the whoop of the gaming machines, but it seemed the ideal place for Lincoln to meet up with DC Alan Hayes, the Presford detective who'd sent him the report on Watkins Court.

Once he'd read the original report Hayes had sent him – tacked on at the end of the edited version – Lincoln knew he had to meet him urgently, to get to the root of what looked like a cover-up.

Hayes had insisted on meeting well away from Park Street, and this dim pub near Barbury's central car park fit the bill. Its tables were sticky and its upholstery smelt like old men's trousers but its draught beers and a choice of three single malts redeemed it.

He fidgeted with his whisky glass. 'I shouldna be talking to you.'

Lincoln took a sip of beer. 'Listen, Alan, you can trust me. I want this cleared up as badly as you do. Thank you for sending me that report – *both* versions,' he added wryly.

'I was expecting you to get in touch sooner, to tell the truth. Thought you must've taken it up the line already.'

'Sorry if I gave you a few sleepless nights. I didn't see the unexpurgated version until I printed it off this morning. So, why was the Walsh girl written out of the official version?'

Hayes hunched forward over his drink. A detective constable, mid-forties, little hope of promotion, the way things were going. Scared of losing his job, Lincoln guessed. Unsure how much he should disclose.

'End of May, it was. Liz Gregg – she was still a DS then – and a uniform, Tony Cotton, went round to Watkins Court, request from the council because a tenant was complaining about the guy living above him. The wee Walsh girl was there at the flat. Tony knew her from when he'd had to pick her up before, take her back to her foster home, knew she was only fourteen. The other lassie, Scotson's girlfriend, made out Lorren was her wee sister. Liz didn't know how to handle it and when Scotson started talking racial harassment, she backed off, took Tony away back to the station.'

'Pretty feeble response.' Lincoln banged his glass down. 'If she'd stood up to him then...'

'Aye, well, there's more.'

'Go on.'

'Liz wrote it up, Tony put his notes in, thought no more about it. NFA, no further action, report filed, though he wasna happy, thought Scotson had made fools of them. When Tony heard the Walsh kid'd been found dead, he looked her up, couldna find anything about the Watkins Court call. Came to me, knows I know my way round the databases better than he does. I dug around a wee bit and found the report I sent you. Whoever "corrected" it hadna the brains to delete the original before they uploaded it to the system. Looks to me as if someone wanted to write Lorren Walsh out of history, like she never existed.'

They sat for a while drinking, two men wishing they could rewrite history so a vulnerable fourteen-year-old wasn't dead.

Lincoln drained his glass. 'You know who corrected that report – or tried to?'

Hayes knocked back the last of his Talisker. 'DCI Bax,' he said. 'Seems like she's shite wi' computers.'

# CHAPTER 64

Dilke took a break from watching the videos to look for a photo of Eily Quinn, but the most recent he found was at least a year old, from when she was last reported as a runaway.

By the time he got back to the VCR player, Shauna was there too. 'Seen this Tyler prick going in yet?' She pressed play. 'You think he killed Lorren?' She unwrapped some chewing gum, offered Dilke a piece but he shook his head.

'His prints were in her blood and he's done time for beating someone up. What do *you* think?'

'Maybe he was just clearing up. "Taking out the trash" – isn't that what they call it? Hey, who's that?'

A slender girl, a little taller than Lorren, a little older, came out of Scotson's flat and went down to the street. Cropped jacket, dark leggings, knock-off Ugg boots with heels that slid sideways under the soles of her feet. A scrawny ponytail erupted from the top of her head and, phone in her hands, she was texting as she walked.

She came across the street towards the camera, heading for the off-licence below it. For a long moment, she looked straight up into the lens, a moment Dilke froze with the pause button. 'That's her. That's Eily Quinn.'

'Who?'

'The girl that got Lorren into this in the first place.' He took his finger off pause, let Eily go into the off-licence and emerge two minutes later with a six-pack of lager. The wayward boots made her hips swing as she walked, a kind of tottering dash across the road.

So this was the girl who'd taken Lorren under her wing, delivered her to Scotson, abandoned her. He stared into the screen, watching the door of the flat open to admit the girl and the booze. Last Friday evening, nearly nine o'clock.

Then Eily ventured out again, quickly disappearing from view along the street.

When she came back a few minutes later, she wasn't alone. Another girl, plump, straight dark hair, over-large jumper, baggy trousers, jostled against her as if using Eily for cover as they went up to the flat.

'That kid's never sixteen,' Shauna snorted. 'She doesn't even look as old as Lorren!'

Dilke bit his lip, concentrating on the scene unfolding before them. Two underage girls in the flat with Eily Quinn and Scotson.

Five minutes later, Leather Jacket turned up. Husband or partner of Marianne Mearns, driving her Astra against council regulations. At 9.15, Colin McTimothy arrived. High forehead, glasses with heavy frames, light-coloured mac.

Two men in a flat with two underage girls, Scotson and Eily Quinn. After less than half an hour, Leather Jacket trotted down the stairs.

'Fuck, he's still zipping himself up!' A man who could have sex as casually as he might take a leak.

McTimothy still hadn't come out when a third man went up to the flat, at nearly ten o'clock. Slightly built, five-seven, five-eight, with short fair hair, he wore a T-shirt and chinos with a loose jacket, as if smart casual would help him blend in.

The door opened a crack, stayed ajar for almost a minute, but Smart Casual wasn't let in. The door shut and he stomped off along the walkway. On the pavement, looking rattled, he paused to check his phone.

'I know that guy,' Shauna said, leaning into the screen. 'He works for the council. His sister's our press officer, Pip Giles.'

'Are you sure?' Dilke craned forward.

'Course I'm sure! He's Knobhead's boss. That's fucking Fergus Gee!'

Lincoln sat at the VCR machine, playing one of the Diego tapes, stopping, rewinding, playing it again. Men arriving at Scotson's flat, leaving after thirty minutes, an hour.

Or in the case of Colin McTimothy, eighty-three minutes, the last minutes of Lorren Walsh's short life.

Dilke and Shauna were long gone and the CID room was quiet, only a couple of desk lamps on, when Bella came in.

'Still here, Jeff?'

'Going over the CCTV footage, who was coming and going from the flat.'

'Ah.' She went into her cupboard, dumped her stuff on the desk; came out again. 'Anything useful?'

He turned the machine off. 'Dilke and Shauna have written up what they've seen so far. A number of men visited the flat while Eily

Quinn and Lorren Walsh were there, along with a girl we haven't identified, clearly underage.' Probably Anita Rani, but he didn't want to tell Bella – and certainly not Trish – until he was sure.

'Patrick Tyler there?'

'Haven't seen him yet but maybe he only came back later to help clear up.'

'What about the punters? Any more names?' She stalked over to the VCR player, arms folded.

'Still waiting to identify someone driving a council car.'

She frowned, concerned. 'Someone working for the council?'

'Car's assigned to a woman called Mearns, manager at the Presford hub. Bloke in the leather jacket's probably her husband.'

She waved a hand at the dead screen. 'You think one of these men killed the girl?'

'Or saw her being killed. Either way, we'll need to interview them as potential witnesses. They'll be facing charges of sexual activity with an underage girl at the very least – possibly sexual assault or rape charges too.'

She pursed her lips, stalked back across the room. 'As soon as you've gone through the rest of the tapes, I'll speak to the DCS, give him a heads-up on the scale of things. I can't act on this without his say-so – it's way above my pay grade. We need to be absolutely sure of our ground.'

'Of course. These are men with reputations to protect, so it could get messy.'

'Then we need to be one hundred and *ten* per cent sure we're right. Get this wrong, it'll be more than a bit of an embarrassment.' She checked her watch. 'It's late, Jeff. You should be getting home.'

He grabbed his jacket. 'See you in the morning, ma'am.'

In the corridor he paused, listening for the sound of Bella turning the VCR player on. How long would it take her to reach the bit where Fergus Gee arrived at the flat where a fourteen-year-old runaway was being got ready for him? Fergus Gee, head of Housing Services, brother of her housemate Pip.

When he'd waited long enough, Lincoln pushed open the door and went back in.

Sitting in his kitchen a couple of hours later, cradling a big glass of Jameson's, the microwave clock his only source of light, he thought through what had happened.

He'd gone back into the CID room to find Bella yanking the tape out of the machine – though despite her best efforts, she'd failed to damage it. She wasn't to know that the tape showed Scotson turning her housemate's brother away at the door. Bad enough that Gee was there at all, but a good solicitor could explain it away.

'Why are you trying to protect him?' Lincoln had held his hand out for the tape, as if she were a naughty schoolgirl caught with a forbidden plaything.

'Fergus is Pip's brother. Half-brother. They're very close.'

'Bella, he's paying to screw little girls.'

'Hardly a little girl! She was fourteen. That kid knew exactly what she was doing, mixing with the likes of Zak Scotson!'

'I know the report on Watkins Court was doctored. Lorren was there at Scotson's flat when your team called round, but someone wrote her out of the official version. I think that someone was *you*.'

She must have realised making excuses for Gee or herself was pointless, but she needed to explain. 'Fergus met some girl in a club a few weeks ago, went back to her flat. Watkins Court.'

Lincoln didn't think Eily was the sort of girl to hang out in clubs. More likely, she was on a street corner when Gee came cruising by in his car. 'Eily Quinn?'

'Sounds like it. She had the Walsh girl with her and...he didn't know Lorren was underage. These kids put a load of make-up on, dress themselves up...'

Bella had got up, begun to pace back and forth as she carried on explaining. 'Then Fergus heard his own staff had brought us in to investigate what was going on at the flat. He was afraid we'd interview Lorren and she'd land him in the shit. So he asked Pip if... if I could limit the damage. Simplest solution: take the kid's name off the record. If we didn't know she was there, we couldn't interview her, could we?' She'd sighed, pleading for sympathy. 'How was I to know things would escalate the way they have?'

Lincoln's temper had roiled in his chest. 'So when you saw her lying dead in Langford Hill Lane, her name on her arm... You knew even then who she was?'

'Yes, but if I thought Fergus had anything to do with her death—'

'He did! Every one of the men who fucked that poor kid had something to do with her death!'

'Oh, don't get political on me, Jeff.' She'd stopped pacing, had stood in the doorway, head down. 'I'll take myself off the case. Conflict of interest. Fergus is involved either way, bound to be interviewed, if only as a witness. Pip's a close friend of mine so I can't be impartial. That's all the DCS needs to know.'

'We'll need a different press officer too, then, won't we?'

She'd cast him a bitter look. 'Maybe Youngman will assign Bryn Marshall to replace me. That's who you wanted from the start, wasn't it?'

'Not if it meant evidence was tampered with, I didn't.'

She'd held her head up like someone noble going to their execution. 'You want to make something of it, I can't really stop you, can I?'

'No,' he'd said, wishing he'd never started this. 'No, you can't.'

He'd watched her gather her belongings together and leave her cubbyhole for good. Watched her march out of the CID room.

So here he was now, hours later, nursing a whisky. He'd caught her out and she'd fallen on her sword. Yet he felt not even a weak thrill of triumph, only a sense of loss.

After watching the tapes for hours, Dilke had made a disappointing discovery: minutes after the camera caught McTimothy leaving Scotson's flat, it abruptly stopped filming. Easy to imagine some sinister hand at work but Lincoln guessed someone at the club inadvertently threw the switch, or the crap tape jammed.

Whatever the cause, any hopes of seeing Lorren being taken away – dead or alive – were dashed. Instead of a week's worth of action, the camera had captured little more than a day and a half.

If the filming had stopped only a couple of hours earlier, they wouldn't even have Fergus Gee on film, and all Bella's fears would have been groundless. As it was, though, Pip's half-brother was caught in more ways than one, his downfall assured. If he didn't face prosecution – and surely, he should – he'd have to resign from his post.

And Leather Jacket, driving Marianne Mearns' leased Astra. Lincoln could put a name to him too, now. A bit of a surprise, that one, and not in a good way.

He stood at the window gazing down into his tangled garden. He'd probably got rats in it now, all that undergrowth. Certainly foxes in the bank under the hedge, with their eerie, keening bark in the small hours. No sign of the black-and-white cat.

The lights were on at Fountains. Must cost them a bloody fortune and they weren't even there all the time. A couple of cars were parked there tonight, an estate car and a 4x4, Land Rover, one of the fancy ones.

His mobile rang. Trish.

'Jeff, can you come over?'

He looked at the glass in his hand. Put it down. He'd only had half a tumbler. 'Twenty minutes.' Where the hell had he kicked his shoes off? And where'd he chucked his trousers when he got home? 'How'd the interview go?'

'I'll tell you when you get here. Just get here. Fifteen minutes?'

'Ten.'

Lincoln groaned. 'Sorry.'

Trish rolled away, flung the covers back. 'No, it's me.' She slid out of bed and pulled her T-shirt on again. 'My mind's elsewhere.' She headed for the bathroom.

He stared up at the ceiling rose that had been painted so many times, it was like a swirl of soft ice cream threatening to melt over the bed.

His mind, too, was elsewhere, frames of video sliding across it: Colin McTimothy, Leather Jacket, Fergus Gee. The men calling on Zak Scotson, two underage girls and Eily Quinn. Was one of those girls Anita Rani? From what Trish had told him about the kid's mother, barging in with questions wouldn't elicit the answers he needed.

Tomorrow, a new SIO would be brought in – with any luck, Bryn Marshall.

He sat up. 'You haven't told me how things went today.'

Trish flopped onto the bed, hugging her pillow. 'Terrible. The board all sat there with a collective frown on their faces. They want a *publicist*, not an archivist, someone who'll raise the profile of the collection, attract more funding. "Develop new income streams", the phrase was. They weren't interested in conservation or cataloguing or improving access to the collection itself. It was a disaster. How could I have got it so wrong?'

She must've set her heart on Essex. He really hadn't grasped how much it meant to her. 'Something'll turn up,' he said lamely.

'Thank you, Mister Micawber.'

'How does Kate feel about it?'

'Haven't told her yet. She was already having second thoughts. She and Charlotte are so close, moving away would be a real wrench, and I know she'd miss Dad...' She pressed against him, comfortingly familiar. 'How's things with Bella?'

He daren't give too much away. Christ, Trish worked for the same council as Fergus Gee, probably knew him. 'She may have to stand aside. Conflict of interest.'

'Will you be taking over?'

'Not sure I want to, not the way this case is going.' And he knew he wouldn't be asked.

Then she wrapped her arms around him, pulling him in, and soon he didn't care.

# CHAPTER 65

## THURSDAY 19TH SEPTEMBER

Bella was right: Chief Superintendent Youngman wasted no time in replacing her. When Lincoln arrived next morning, DCI Bryn Marshall was already inspecting her cubbyhole.

'They tell you I'm taking over from Bax?' As tall as Lincoln and two stone heavier, the Welshman was just a few years older, with a rugged energy.

Lincoln grinned as he shook the rain off his mac and hung it up. 'Not officially. Welcome to Barley Lane.'

'I can't work in this bloody toilet cubicle, though. Any suggestions?'

'There's a spare desk out here – unless you want your own private space?'

'That'll do lovely.'

Lincoln helped him shift folders from Bella's desk in the stationery cupboard to the desk next to Pam's – Breeze wouldn't be back for another week.

'You heard the good news?' Bryn asked. 'Credible sightings of our missing girl.'

'Elaine Burnie?'

'In Southampton, catching a ferry to the Isle of Wight with a chap old enough to be her dad – probably your Arlo James. Red Funnel Terminal 2, quarter to eight Monday night.' Bryn rubbed his hands in glee before scouring the room for a spare office chair. 'Thought they'd have told you already.'

'Liz Gregg's the first point of contact now.'

Lincoln was annoyed with himself for feeling sidelined, but at least Lady was still alive. With the cash he'd borrowed on Saturday night, Arlo must have lain low with her on Sunday, then made a dash for it on Monday. Why go to the Isle of Wight, though? Once there, he'd be trapped. Why not head for London, a place where he and Lady could easily lose themselves?

'Good start, eh?' Bryn hovered by the kettle. 'What do you chaps do for drinks round here?'

'Help yourself. I can't offer you milk but you're welcome to some of my coffee.'

'I drink it black. And sweet. Can I nick a bit of sugar?'

We're going to get along fine, Lincoln thought, smiling to himself. A man after my own heart.

Less than thirty minutes later, Bryn introduced himself to his new team.

'Most of you will have heard of me, some of you have already met me, I've even had a drink with one or two of you...' A rumble of laughter, the atmosphere easing. 'DCI Bax is taking some personal leave, and then she'll be back at Park Street, so you're stuck with me for now.' He grinned round the room.

Parking one meaty hip on the edge of the desk in front of the whiteboard, he embarked on his first briefing. 'There's good news and there's bad. Elaine Burnie's been spotted on her way to that romantic Shangri-La, the Isle of Wight, in the company of Arlo James.' Surprise and relief ran round the room. 'Our colleagues on the island hope to track them down very shortly. But – we've still got two murder investigations to crack.'

He drew a vertical line down the whiteboard, separating Lady from Emma and Lorren. 'So let's give it all a bit of a reboot, eh?'

# CHAPTER 66

165 miles away, Peterborough police were searching the bungalow of Terence Sweet, a man who liked to sit on a bench in the kiddies' playground for hours, watching the children on the swings and the roundabouts.

He'd been dismissed as harmless, a bit simple, fifty-something, unmarried, dependent on benefits – but now a seven-year-old girl called Leah was claiming he'd grabbed her hand as she sat next to him, waiting her turn on the swings. He had his trousers open, she said, with something sticking out.

He was arrested, his bungalow searched. He had two computers – an old PC and a laptop. The hard drives were chock-full of images of young girls, mostly prepubescent.

In a cupboard in his hallway, Sweet also had a stack of box files brimming with photographs, many commercially produced and probably purchased in the 1990s from suppliers all over the country and abroad.

Two box files, though, labelled "Little Innocence", were devoted to photos of just one girl, from when she was a chubby toddler in a tutu until her graceful emergence, at seven or eight, in a leotard and tap shoes, her soft, wavy hair piled high on her head or trailing down her back. The background in the photos was always a garden or a summer house.

Sometimes she was joined by a plumper girl of a similar age, whose thick, straight hair was cut into a distinctive pageboy bob. Mostly though, the little dancer was pictured on her own, always clothed, always demure. The picture of innocence.

Amongst Sweet's papers was a padded envelope, postmarked August 2011, containing a dozen photographs of a little girl – possibly but not conclusively the same girl – fellating an unidentifiable man. The return address: "*T. Tremlow, Riverside, Brook Lane, Whitpenny*".

# CHAPTER 67

Bryn went through the evidence they'd gathered on Emma Sherman's murder.

'So, bare bones, Zakariah Scotson picked her up in town, drove her up to Pine Point and attacked her in Arlo James' caravan. Probably killed her in the forest. Yes? Then he wrapped her in a tarp and dumped her on the golf course. Right so far?'

Lincoln nodded. 'But Arlo's got an alibi for that night, and he doesn't drive. As far as we can tell, Emma didn't know Scotson. She got into the back of the Fiesta as if it was a cab she'd sent for – except we know she didn't call a cab. It must have been prearranged. She was expecting that car to come for her at 7.15.'

'But no idea who this mystery lover is – boyfriend, girlfriend, whatever?' Unbuttoning his cuffs and rolling his sleeves up, Bryn frowned across at the whiteboard. There was a big gap where the face of Emma's mystery date should be.

'None at all. But there is another angle.'

'Oh?' His eyebrows went up, rising even higher as Lincoln outlined Oliver Spence's allegations about Todd Tremlow.

'Not that we've got any proof Tremlow abused Emma,' Lincoln stressed, 'and Spence could be exaggerating or misremembering. However, Pam and Charlie found some pretty explicit photos of Emma in the summer house – except, because of a mix-up, they weren't authorised to search there and had to leave the photos where they were.'

Bryn frowned. 'Pornographic photos, were they, Pam?'

'Suggestive,' she said. 'Emma was covered up but you could tell why they'd been taken.'

Charlie snorted. 'Every paedo's wet dream.'

'You think she'd decided to tell the world about what happened to her?' Bryn asked. 'And the nasty card and the newspaper photo you found – they were some sort of warning to keep her mouth shut?'

'Nah,' said Shauna, 'they're more like you'd expect from another teenager. And I expect Tremlow can spell!'

Bryn nodded. 'So probably unrelated. See, we need to concentrate less on why Emma was killed and more on who killed her. Scotson drove the car, you've got this Patrick Tyler character as his associate for the Lorren Walsh murder – not much of a leap to guess one kills and the other cleans up.' He sighed. 'Nice couple, eh?' He pointed to the photo of the tarpaulin, the FPD logo in close-up. 'But you can see how this is going to look, can't you, Tyler working for Finnegan?'

'It gets better.' Lincoln crossed to the whiteboard, jabbed one of the stills of Leather Jacket leaving Scotson's flat. 'I recognised this bloke last night when I was going through the tapes again. It's Steven Short, Finnegan's ops manager.'

Bryn gaped. 'You're sure? Embarrassing, that.'

'More than embarrassing, Finnegan's right-hand man having sex with fourteen-year-olds!'

'Let's see that footage again.'

They crowded round the screen to watch the comings and goings outside the flat in the crucial minutes before Lorren died.

'Steven Short left the flat first,' Dilke said, 'the one we've been calling Leather Jacket – leaving Colin McTimothy inside. Then Fergus Gee turned up but Scotson sent him away without letting him in.'

Bryn nodded as he studied the screen. 'Suggesting something had already gone wrong. Lorren must've been with McTimothy when she died. How long was he there?'

'Nearly an hour and a half.'

'Men like McTimothy think they can get away with anything.' Shauna chucked her pen and phone down on her notepad. 'Just because they're loaded.'

'There's something in that, yes.' Bryn leaned back to see her more clearly. 'Shauna, isn't it?'

'Shauna Hartlake, yeah.' Her scowl softened.

'We're talking about men who get a thrill out of taking risks, see, Shauna. Slumming it with girls who are little better than street urchins. Nothing new. But these days, the kids are being groomed, doped into submission. They're not out on the streets getting paid a fiver for handjobs in parked cars but they're just as much at risk.'

Lincoln stood up. 'Have we got enough to bring McTimothy in?'

Bryn shook his head. 'Let's talk to Steven Short first. See if we can get him to admit he was in the flat and that McTimothy was there too. With any luck, he'll be keen to tell us he'd already left before anything nasty went down.'

'And Scotson and Tyler?'

'We've issued an all-ports warning but I doubt they've gone far, either of them.'

The briefing broke up, everyone scattering to their various tasks.

'I'm cancelling the watch at the hospital,' Bryn told Lincoln. 'Waste of resources. If someone was trying to kill the Sherman woman, he'd have tried to get at her before now, agreed? So, let's get Steven Short in here, see if we can crack this thing.'

# CHAPTER 68

As Tom wheeled his bike past the kitchen window, his mother came out of the house in her pyjamas and the old quilted coat she wore to walk the dogs. She hugged herself as if she was about to go all caring on him.

'Why don't you give that job up, Tom, come and work round the yard instead? Miles would find you something to do. Probably pay you more, too.'

'Thanks, Ma, but I detest horses and I'm not particularly fond of Miles.'

'You hardly know him.'

'Neither do you.' Though that didn't stop her sleeping with him.

'Just be careful on the roads.' She stomped back inside.

At Bods, Carol was on about the girl who'd gone missing, yattering on about how it was on the news that she'd run away to the Isle of Wight with an older man. She had the television on in the back office, switching between the news and the CCTV feed. For the first time, Tom recognised Elaine, the missing girl, only he knew her as Lady, a kid who hung around with Jess, drippy Lexie's sister. And then the guy's face flashed on the screen, the man they were looking for, and it was Arlo.

What was Arlo doing on the Isle of Wight with Lady? She was fifteen, younger than Jess, but surely he wasn't stupid enough to...? Fuck!

'They've found them?'

Carol looked round, a spoon in her mouth from where she'd been scoffing yogurt. 'Phoo?'

'The police. Have they found them?'

She pulled the spoon out, leaving a cum-like blob on her lower lip. 'No, some woman spotted them getting on a ferry but that was days ago. They'll have holed up somewhere, gone to ground. Evil, men who do that sort of thing. Mind you, she's old enough to know better, and her mother looks a right slop-cabbage.'

Tom went on staring at the screen. He'd felt bad about landing

Arlo in the shit over Emma. He wasn't even sure they were an item but he'd always blame Arlo for what happened to Rich. It was Arlo's weed he'd been smoking the night he crashed his car and it was fucking strong stuff.

'You're on cleaning.' Carol nodded at the plastic buckets and cloths stacked in the corner beside the desk. 'Better get your skates on.'

'Thanks for nothing.' He felt like stuffing a manky dishcloth – a whole bunch of manky dishcloths – down Carol's wrinkly old throat. He picked up the bucket, imagining himself picking up a bucket of horse shit at Miles' stable yard, sweeping up dung, swilling rancid horse piss away down the drain...

His whole life seemed to be one foul stink after another.

How could his mother let that bloody stable boy maul her? How could she love his father if she could let that fucking jockey screw her? Women made no sense to him.

'You've forgotten the antibacterial.' Carol jabbed a thumb towards the spray bottle.

And at that moment, Tom could see no earthly point in carrying on. He slung the bucket and the cloths back into the corner and stormed out of the office. At the service door, he swiped his card and buzzed himself out into the cool, dull shadows of the yard, relieved to find it was raining. He turned his face up into it and stood there for ages getting wet, relishing the rain on his skin, his hair, his clothes, getting soaked until he was shivering.

He thought of Emma, lying out there in the long grass, dew beneath her, rain drenching her from above. He could see tendrils of her hair clinging to her cheeks, to her forehead, her clothes plastered to her body.

Except she wasn't wearing any. That's what Joe said. Only her bra.

Who would do that to her? Who could hate her enough to leave her out in the rain, night after night, exposed, unprotected?

He couldn't bear to think that it was somebody he knew.

# CHAPTER 69

Steven Short arrived at Barley Lane with Harry Pinker, his legal representative. After they'd gone through the formalities, Lincoln presented the case against him.

'Mr Short, you were filmed going into Flat 3, The Parade, Finisterre Street, Barbury, where we have reason to believe you engaged in sexual activity with one or more underage females. Would you like to tell us—'

'Filmed?' Harry Pinker raised his fountain pen. 'If you're referring to the camera across the street from the premises in question, it was installed without notifying the Information Commissioner's Office, and was thus filming in breach of the Data Protection Act. Therefore, any images obtained from it are inadmissible. You have no valid reason for detaining my client.' He began to put his pen and notebook away in his briefcase.

'Wait.' Lincoln spread his hands on the table. 'Mr Short. Steven. A fourteen-year-old girl died in that flat. Lorren Walsh. Steven, you must have seen who was responsible. Please help us resolve this.'

Pinker began to stand up, but Short didn't budge, tempting Lincoln to think his conscience had got the better of him.

'What happened, Steven?' he asked. 'What happened to Lorren that night? We need to find Zak Scotson before another girl ends up dead.'

Short blinked, sighed. Then stood up and followed Harry Pinker out into the corridor.

They'd lost him.

'So now what?' Lincoln nursed his coffee mug, despondent. It was the end of the afternoon, rain streaming down the windows, and he, Bryn and Woody were sitting round Bryn's desk. 'We've no idea where Scotson and Tyler have run to, there's been no news from the Isle of Wight... We're up shit creek without the proverbial paddle.'

'Before we even attempt to bring McTimothy in on suspicion of murder,' Bryn said, 'we've got to build a stronger case. So far all we've got is circumstantial evidence. If the men we're dealing with can afford briefs like Harry Pinker, then we need a lot more to back it up.'

The phone rang, and within a few minutes, everything got turned upside down.

# CHAPTER 70

## FRIDAY 20TH SEPTEMBER

'What am I doing here?' Todd Tremlow asked as he gazed round the interview room.

Lincoln sat himself down, took a minute or two to organise his notebook, pens, some beakers of water and the tape recorder, while Woody peeled the shrink-wrap from a fresh pair of cassette tapes.

'We all ask ourselves that question from time to time, don't we, Mr Tremlow?'

'Yes, but...' Tremlow's face was flushed and sweaty. 'Am I under arrest?'

'No, but you have agreed to answer some questions for us.'

They got settled: Lincoln, Woody, Tremlow and his solicitor, Ben Blake.

'Mr Tremlow,' Lincoln began, 'a man has been arrested in Peterborough and charged over the possession of indecent images. Many of those images are of children. Can you explain why that man was in possession of obscene material sent from your address?'

'But I've never been to Peterborough!'

'That's what the postal service is all about, Mr Tremlow. You can send things to people in Peterborough without having to go there yourself.'

Lincoln laid two photos on the table. One showed a padded envelope addressed to Terence Sweet at an address in Peterborough, while the other showed the back of the envelope with a label bearing the return address: "*T. Tremlow, Riverside, Brook Lane, Whitpenny*". 'Is that your home address?'

'Yes but—' Tremlow picked the photos up, his fingers leaving misty imprints on them. 'I don't know anyone called Sweet.'

'If we were to search your house, Mr Tremlow, what do you think we'd find? Indecent photographs? Camera equipment? Kiddie porn on your laptop?'

Tremlow's face ran with sweat. He undid his collar button, loosened his tie. 'I don't have a laptop. Yes, I've got a camera but I haven't used it in a long time. Never even got round to going digital. Doubt if you can still get film for a camera like mine.' His mouth twitched in a brave little smile, but Lincoln didn't smile back.

'You used to take photographs of your niece, Emma Sherman, didn't you?'

Tremlow looked up at him, imploring.

'Is that a yes, Mr Tremlow?'

'Yes, but—'

'Do you admit that you took photos of Emma when she was a child?'

'Well, yes, but—'

'Was she always fully clothed?'

'I can see what you're doing here – trying to catch me out. Define "fully clothed".'

'Did you ever take photos of Emma in which any part of her torso was exposed?'

'You're asking if I took dirty pictures of my niece. The answer's no, categorically no.'

Late the previous afternoon, Peterborough police had sent through some of the images they'd seized at Sweet's house including a sequence showing a little girl – recognisably Emma, aged six or seven – peeking coquettishly over her shoulder, her back to the camera. All she had on was an enormous sun hat. Among them, Pam recognised copies of the photos Charlie had found in the summer house. There was little doubt about the photographer's motivation.

'So can you describe some of those photos to me, the ones you took when Emma was a little girl? What she was wearing, how she was posing?'

Tremlow's eyes were squeezed tight shut and his pudgy hands were balled into fists on the tabletop. 'It wasn't like that. It was never like that. You don't understand.'

Lincoln sat back. 'Then explain it to me.'

Tremlow looked to Ben Blake, looked to Lincoln, to Woody. 'I've always taken photos. It was a hobby from when I was a boy. I've always had a camera. I've won competitions. She was so pretty, a real natural. My sister-in-law asked me to take photos of her. My wife did too. My photos of Emma won prizes! "Little Miss Innocence". They published them in *The Messenger*, and in *Amateur Photographer*. There was nothing dirty about the photos I took. I'd never do anything to hurt that girl, never.' His face took on a hurt expression, no doubt designed to make them feel sorry for him. 'What proof have you got that I've done anything wrong?'

Ben Blake leaned forward and pushed the photo of the envelope back across the table. 'The envelope was found in the home of a gentleman who allegedly possessed pornographic material,' he said flatly. 'According to the postmark, this envelope was sent to the gentleman in question several years ago, allegedly by my client. There is no way of establishing without a doubt the nature of the contents of this envelope when it was sent to the gentleman in question. Unless you have proof that my client sent him pornographic material, there is no case to answer. Do you have such proof?'

Lincoln saw it was useless.

Blake pulled his hands back, folded them calmly, waiting. The overhead lights shone on his glasses, making his eyes invisible. 'Thought not.' He rose, bidding his client do the same.

Fuming, impotent, Lincoln watched the overheated Tremlow scramble to his feet and follow Blake out of the interview room.

Unable to contain his temper indoors, Lincoln strode out into the yard without waiting to tell Bryn how the interview went. He had to get outside before he exploded.

He could understand why people smoked: an ideal excuse to get out into the fresh air for ten minutes. If you didn't mind the cigarettes.

'Hang on! Boss!' Someone was running along the corridor behind him: Pam, chasing after him with a sheet of paper, her face flushed.

'Let's go for a walk.'

'But boss, aren't you supposed to be—'

'They can ring if they need me. What's up?'

'There's good news and bad.'

The footpath that skirted the police station yard climbed towards a stand of pines, and Lincoln strode along, Pam tagging after him. A large Victorian house used to shelter against those pines. Demolished a year or so ago, it was being replaced with two blocks of posh apartments. He'd rather have had the house. Did that make him old-fashioned, a conservative, a radical? He just didn't see the point of pulling down buildings with a bit of history in their brickwork, even if that made him an idealist.

He was puffing a bit by the time he got to the top. He stood looking down on Barley Lane's hotchpotch of rooftops, then lifted his gaze to the distant chalk downs on the western edge of the town, imagining himself striding over them, not a care in the world...

'Bloody Tremlow,' he muttered as Pam caught up with him.

'Bloody Blake.' Only then did he turn to her. 'Okay, give me the good news first.'

'The couple who lived next door to the Shermans, the Millers. Moved out a few months ago, went travelling. They got my message and Mrs Miller phoned back just now. She remembers Emma and another little girl spending a lot of time in the garden with a man taking photos – just like Oliver Spence said. The girls would disappear into the summer house with this guy and it would all go quiet.'

'She remember when this was?'

'Eight years ago – she remembered because it was when their daughter had her first baby and they'd all sit out in the garden.'

'We've got him then – two independent witnesses saying they saw Tremlow taking photos of the girls.'

'And now for the bad news.' Pam took a big breath. 'It wasn't Tremlow.'

'What?'

'Six foot, dark-haired, trim, in his forties.'

Tremlow was no more than five foot seven and stocky, with mousy hair. 'They're sure?'

'They knew Tremlow, didn't have a bad word to say about him, how he used to look after Emma when she was small, always there for Crystal... They know it wasn't him.'

'Then who the hell...? They know who this other kid was?'

'Definitely not Stephanie. Same uniform as Emma, Abbey School. And a pudding-basin haircut, same as Spence told us. Sounds more and more like it was Maisie.'

'Afraid you'd say that.' He began the descent to Barley Lane, his spirits sinking.

Pam followed him down. 'The Tremlows might know, but in the circumstances... Shame we can't search the summer house, find those photos again.'

'We'd never get a search warrant.' His mobile rang as they were crossing the yard. Micky Stanley. He let Pam go indoors ahead of him. 'Hi, Micky, what's up?'

'Linus Bonetti. Remember? Social worker that killed himself? Some journalist's been back, asking questions about Revyve.'

'Revyve? The housing project, Donal Finnegan working with the council?'

'Uh-huh. I can't stop, about to go into a case review but... Listen, Linus was onto something, who gets council flats and where.'

Lincoln was suddenly more interested. 'People paying to jump up the waiting list, you mean?'

'Something like that. You might want to look into Revyve, that's all. Before the tabloids do. Gotta go, sorry.'

As soon as he got back to his desk, he rang Trish at the library. 'What can you tell me about Revyve?'

'Not wanting a council flat, are you?' She still sounded cross with him. They'd argued before breakfast over whether or not he'd need to speak to Anita Rani. He'd said he'd have to; she'd dared him to try. He'd stormed out, no breakfast, not even coffee.

'Revyve's the big success story,' she said now. Even over the phone, he could hear her cynicism. 'Donal Finnegan's brainchild. Repossessing empty properties and tarting them up, letting them back to the council. Haven't you seen the dinky little signs everywhere? *This property has been Revyved!*' Actually, you and Donal have got a lot in common, rescuing houses that are falling down.'

'Ha ha. But what's in it for Finnegan? Not doing it for free, is he?'

'He keeps some of the properties for private rentals, sells a few to fund the next lot. And I daresay his planning applications sail through committee without a hitch.'

'This Bonetti bloke that died – what did he think he'd uncovered?'

'Linus?' She sounded worried now.

'Trish, I can keep your name out of it, if that's what you're afraid of.'

'It's not that, but you see...'

He heard the lengthy pause, knew what it meant. 'Okay, Trish, what aren't you telling me?'

# CHAPTER 71

Trish shut herself in her office with Lincoln, leaving a resentful Briony to hold the fort.

He pulled out a chair. 'Heard from Essex yet?'

She shook her head. 'I won't hold my breath – I did a terrible interview. You asked me about Revyve.' She brightened as she pushed the council's quarterly magazine across to him, open at a double-page spread: *"How your council helps house the homeless – Fergus Gee, head of Housing Services, explains a new initiative guaranteed to cut waiting lists and bring empty properties back to life – thanks to local businessman, Donal Finnegan."*

Finnegan beamed out, eyes twinkly, that heavy cowlick of greying hair swept back from his genial face.

'Okay, so Saint Donal's a cross between God and Richard Branson, but what was Linus Bonetti up to?'

Trish took a big breath and explained. 'Linus was angry about the way council properties were being allocated. You know there's a points system, based on your circumstances, your needs? Well, Linus was convinced that less-deserving cases were being housed ahead of families who'd been waiting for years.' She stopped, looked wary. 'His death wasn't suspicious, was it? That's not why you're asking about him now?'

Christ, as if he needed any more complications! 'No, no... Just something one of his colleagues said. So what came of it? Did he find anything out?'

'He was told to look at the bigger picture and get on with his job. Linus was a bit of a hothead, no diplomatic skills.' She grinned. 'Like someone else I know.'

He rose, rolled the magazine up and shoved it in his pocket. 'Thanks for this – a bit of background's always useful. Listen, about this morning, about Anita, I'm sorry if I said anything—'

'Actually, everything's okay. Anita and a girl in her class have been experimenting with alcohol. She wasn't drugged some mornings – she was hung-over! She hasn't been anywhere near Scoot for the last two or three weeks.' She made a face, apologetic. 'You were counting on her, weren't you, to tell you what happened to Lorren?'

He nodded, disappointed. 'I was pretty sure the girl we saw going into the flat was Anita, but obviously not.' He headed for the door. 'So, Linus Bonetti – where was he going with these concerns of his? The union? The newspapers?'

Trish held up her hands. 'He didn't say and I didn't ask. He was on a crusade. Crusades always end in bloodshed.'

Lincoln's mobile rang as he was about to leave the library, and he paused in the entrance hall to take a call from Pam.

'I've been going over some of the notes Dennis took when Emma first went missing,' she said. 'I think we may've missed something.'

'You mean Breezy missed something in his rush to leave for Spain? Go on.' He stared at the library bulletin board, where a poster announced the launch of the Barbury Paragon building project, the town's first dedicated arts centre. The laying of the foundation stone was less than a fortnight away.

'The Shermans had another gardener.'

'What?'

'Dennis spoke to Gordon Judd, who's been doing the Shermans' garden for the last few months. Judd told him he replaced another man called Collins, who'd had a fall and had to give up.' She paused. 'It doesn't look as if Dennis got round to speaking to this Collins guy. I suppose at the time, when Emma was still only missing, it didn't seem relevant.'

Lincoln hurried outside, heading for his car. 'Well, it's certainly relevant now!'

# CHAPTER 72

Collins' Plant Nursery was on the edge of Barbury, on Old London Road. With summer over, it was winding down, though something told Pam it had been winding down all year.

She showed her card, introduced herself to the woman behind the counter. 'I need to speak to Burt Collins.'

'You've had a wasted journey then. He's been dead nine months.'

'Oh. I'm sorry.' No wonder Breezy hadn't spoken to him. Would've been nice if he'd put in his notes why not. 'You're Mrs Collins?'

'Sandra Collins, yes. Hang on.' The woman went down the end of the shop and had a muttered exchange with an elderly man who was sweeping the floor. He followed her back, taking her place behind the counter. 'Won't be long, Dad.'

She led Pam into a messy side office. No chairs. An old adding machine sat on the desk amidst a slew of water-stained paperwork. Crumbs of old compost littered every surface, and packets of birdseed sagged on a shelf, long past their sell-by date. Business didn't look good.

'So, what's this about?'

'We think your husband may have witnessed a crime in the course of his work.'

'A crime?'

'Probably without even realising it. Did he ever talk about gardening for Mrs Sherman in Folly Hill?'

Sandra shrugged, perching her behind on the edge of the desk. 'Never much of a conversationalist.' She was a thin-faced woman in her late forties, with home-tinted brown hair in need of a top-up along the parting. Her apron covered a brown T-shirt and khaki shorts. 'But yes, she was one of his first customers, through Donal.'

'Donal?'

'Donal Finnegan, the developer. Used to do Donal's garden, him and Kyle – that's my eldest. Donal was friends with Mrs Sherman, said she needed someone. Donal put Burt in touch with her. Ten years ago now.' She looked away for a moment. 'The summer Kyle left school.'

'And Burt was doing her garden right up until his accident?'

'Yeah.' She paused, looked down at her apron lap. 'Broke his back rock climbing. Bloody fool. He was in hospital six months. Came home for Christmas, got pneumonia, and that was it. A relief, really. No sort of a life.' She sniffed. 'He liked working for the Sherman woman. She paid well, left him to it. Some people are out watching you all the time, fussing, finding fault, but she stayed indoors, let him get on with it. He was up at Folly Hill most weeks for at least a few hours.' She narrowed her eyes at Pam. 'You said he may have witnessed a crime?'

'We're looking into an allegation that something happened to Emma, Mrs Sherman's daughter, when she was a child. About eight years ago.'

Sandra sat up. 'You think Burt did something to her? Is that what you're saying? You're saying he molested her or something?'

'No, but he might have seen someone acting suspiciously when Emma and another little girl were playing there. Did he ever mention seeing anyone else in the garden or the summer house, taking photographs?'

Sandra sat without speaking, watching Pam's face. Even as the seconds tocked by on the smeary clock above the woman's head, Pam could hear, too, the sound of a can of worms being opened.

'Mrs Collins?'

'It's a big garden,' Sandra said quickly, standing up and brushing her hands over the seat of her shorts. 'He always wore ear protectors when he was using equipment. And goggles. Wouldn't have noticed anything that'd be any use to you. And nobody'd get up to stuff with the gardener about, would they?'

She began to head out of the office, obliging Pam to step aside to let her through.

'Is there anyone else in the family he might have told? Your father, perhaps?'

'Don't bring my dad into this! Him and Burt never got on. Dad's only been round here since the accident.'

'Times must have been tough, losing your husband like that.'

'Tougher when he was alive, believe me!' Sandra pushed ahead, expecting to be followed, but Pam hung back.

'Might he have told Kyle what he'd seen?'

'Wouldn't have told him anything like that. Anyway, eight years ago, Kyle would've been away at college. Didn't come home much. Like I said, my husband wasn't the easiest man to live with.'

'And you've got a younger son? I noticed the chopper bike outside.'

'Max. He'd only have been a kid himself, so there's no point asking him.'

'Well, if you think of anything else—'

'I won't.' Sandra was about to see her off the premises when the phone on the counter rang and her father, dealing with a customer, was too far away to answer it.

'It's okay, Mrs Collins, I'll see myself out.'

As Pam went out through the sweaty warmth of the cyclamen house, a teenager appeared in the doorway ahead of her. Hands in pockets, he was trying to look casual even though he must have been waiting to waylay her where Sandra couldn't see him.

'You must be Max.'

'Is this about Emma?' A gangly redhead of fifteen or sixteen, he was thin-faced like his mother, with a fuzz of fair hair on his upper lip and cheeks. T-shirt that needed washing. Armpits ditto. He breathed through his mouth as if his nose was blocked.

'You knew her?'

'Used to play in her garden.' He sniffed noisily. 'Is this about the photos?'

The can opener completed its jagged circuit and the lid came off. Pam could hear the worms jostling to be tipped out.

# CHAPTER 73

'Isn't this a bit cloak-and-dagger?' Trish pushed her coffee cup aside, wondering why she'd agreed to an impromptu meeting in the middle of the afternoon in this awful café, a greasy spoon that left you smelling of chips. She'd almost given up on him and gone back to work, but then the door had opened and there he was.

David Black took a seat across the table from her, his dark hair steely grey now, much shorter than when she'd first known him. These days, of course, he had to look the part of local government manager: corporate, authoritative – yet his bright blue eyes could still make her pulse quicken.

She'd nearly had a fling with him fifteen years ago, her first Christmas with the council. They'd got chatting in the staff canteen, flirted with each other, gone for drinks, coffee, lunch one Saturday when Vic was away for the weekend. She enjoyed the riskiness, the romance. Then she'd overheard a couple of library assistants giggling about seeing her and David together, and in an instant, their relationship seemed tawdry.

She'd backed off, and let David do the same. No drama, no showdown. Their friendship cooled and their career paths diverged. She rarely saw him these days.

Until today, when, out of the blue, he'd phoned to ask if they could meet at Nell's Caff.

'Cloak-and-dagger? Trish, I just need to talk to someone.'

'Tried the Samaritans?'

'Not funny. Especially in the circumstances.'

'Sorry.' She noticed he'd cut himself shaving: beads of blood had dried along his jaw. He still smelt of vetiver aftershave and – faintly – of cigarettes, but his lean cheeks had filled out. Probably given up playing football. She grinned encouragingly. 'Fire away.'

He hesitated, turning to check they couldn't be overheard. 'Linus Bonetti.'

'What about him?'

'I was put in charge of him when his probationary period was extended.'

'I know. He told me how much he appreciated your support.' But Linus hadn't trusted anyone, not even David.

'Trish, did you help him with some research?'

She pulled the coffee cup back, fidgeted with it. 'I looked at some minutes of council meetings, local newspapers from the archive. I'm an information specialist. It's what I do.' She paused. 'What's bothering you?'

'Know anything about the allegations he made?'

'Not in detail, no.' She kept her eyes on her cup, its chipped saucer, the tarnished spoon. 'Does it matter now? He's dead.'

'I know he's dead – I went to his fucking funeral!' He lowered his head onto his clasped hands. She longed to stroke the back of his head, the smooth nape of his neck, to soothe him as she'd soothe Kate, as she'd soothe Jeff when he let her.

But David wasn't a child. He wasn't Jeff.

'Tell me, then.' She rested her hand on his sleeve. His breath warmed her fingers until he lifted his head, turning those blue eyes on her, troubled.

He went on to explain how Linus, inexperienced and keen, had followed up a councillor's complaint about housing waiting lists. 'He should've passed it straight on to Housing, of course, but he didn't like to say no.'

She too had been eager to please the politicians when she was new. She'd soon learnt that most councillors are fickle and transient. 'Go on.'

She let David tell her what she already knew. Points allocated unfairly, selected applicants – usually vulnerable single mothers – getting pushed up the housing queue.

She kept quiet as David reeled off one example Linus had told her about. Patsy, a young single mum with a ten-year-old daughter, was living with her parents in a three-bedroom house in Presford – not ideal, but certainly not in urgent need. Within a month of being assessed, however, Patsy and her daughter were among the first tenants to move into Inglefield Court, an Edwardian mansion block rescued from squatters and refurbished under the Revyve banner.

'Linus was sure the assessor was on the take,' David said. 'Awarding points in exchange for cash.' He sat back from the table, studying her suspiciously. 'Didn't Linus tell you any of this?'

She lifted her cup, changed her mind about drinking from it. Put it down. She couldn't look him in the eye. 'No, he didn't. As I said,

I simply dug out some background stuff on local housing associations, building projects, Revyve—'

'Why was he so fucking interested in Revyve?'

'Revyve *is* social housing locally, isn't it? For now, at least.' She hesitated. 'Is there a problem with Revyve?'

'Of course not! But Linus wanted to blame Revyve for what was going wrong – when it was simply one bad assessor letting people buy their way up the waiting list.'

'Linus thought he could put things right, single-handed.' You were like that once, Dave, she thought. But then you grew up. Linus never got the chance to.

'Thing is, Trish, we don't want the newspapers getting hold of it. You've talked to some journalist called Marston...?'

'Well yes, but—'

'Listen, it'll be best if we handle the situation in-house, discreetly take this dodgy assessor to one side, offer him a chance to resign, go quietly. We don't want a scandal.'

'I told Ian Marston to speak to the press office. I assume that's what he's done.'

David relaxed a little. 'Good, good. You know how the media like to sink their teeth into the council. And I don't want Linus' failings raked over yet again.'

She reached down to pick up her bag. 'Feeling better for our little talk?'

'Absolutely.' That grin, that half-regretful sparkle in his eyes. 'You were always good at calming my nerves.'

She stood up and slipped her jacket on. 'Honestly, Dave, Linus really didn't tell me much.' She grinned at him, the man for whom she'd nearly risked her marriage. 'I won't go running to the *Daily Mail*, if that's what you're scared of!'

'You'd be a fool if you did.'

A chill ran through her when he said that, the ground tilting a degree or two beneath her feet. She tugged open the door of Nell's Caff and breathed fresh air for the first time in half an hour. Over her shoulder she gave him a cool smile before hurrying across the street to the library.

Back at her desk, Trish opened her inbox, her heart sinking at the number of new emails that wouldn't repay the time spent reading them. Her eye was caught by one from the Charles Lundy Library

Trust: the evaluation she'd requested at the end of her disastrous interview. Not that she needed their feedback – she knew only too well how badly she'd done. She'd look at it later.

She opened Word and searched for the folder she wanted. Glancing round to check Briony wasn't hovering, she clicked open the first file in the folder: *MichaelmasHouse.docx*.

# CHAPTER 74

'I hear you used to go gardening with your dad.' Lincoln plonked a cold Coke in front of Max Collins. Beads of moisture trickled down the sides of the can.

'Yeah, when I was a kid.'

'He took you to Mrs Sherman's house in Folly Hill and you used to play in the summer house – is that what you told DC Smyth earlier?' He sat down across from the lad. Max had bad breath, dark shadows under his eyes, a chin bumpy with pimples. 'And you'd have been how old? Nine, ten?'

'Nine.'

'And you found something in the summer house, is that right?'

The boy didn't even look at Kyle, his big brother, who sat tense and silent in the corner. 'Dirty photos. Loads of them.'

Lincoln's heart raced. Pam had given him the gist of what Max had told her, but this was better than he could have hoped for. 'Where exactly did you find them?'

'There was some drawers in there with gardening stuff, y' know? And packets of photos. Girls with no clothes on. Younger than me.'

'You okay, talking about what was in the photos?'

'Yeah.' Max rubbed his chin, the soft rasp of down that hadn't yet coarsened into bristles. 'We was always passing rude pictures round in class and after school. Magazines we got hold of, stuff off the internet. But this was different. This was little girls.' He said it with a mix of disgust and relish. 'I used to go in the summer house and look at them while Dad was gardening. Like a ritual, y' know? Always afraid they wouldn't be there when I looked, but they always were.'

A secret smile softened his bony face. Lincoln remembered the agonies of his own puberty, the insatiable curiosities of body and mind, the wonders and the terror.

'Did you recognise anyone in the photos?'

Max fixed his gaze on the tabletop. 'I didn't know who it was at first, only where. That cabin.'

'The summer house?'

'Yeah. There was these chairs with stripy cushions, and the same curtains, with big flowers on. And then after a bit, I found out who it was.' He looked round at Kyle, back at Lincoln.

'Go on.'

'See, Mrs Sherman used to make us a jug of squash. This one time, Dad told me to take the tray back. She didn't hear me knocking on the back door so I went round the front. She opened the door and asked me to bring the tray through to the kitchen. Everywhere you looked, there was all these pictures of her, the girl in the photos, in school uniform or in her dance dresses. And I knew it was the same girl. Her daughter.'

'So you're saying the girl was Emma Sherman, is that right?'

'Yeah. So it was weird,' Max went on, 'seeing all these other photos of her, because it was like I knew her already. Like we was friends.'

'Do you know what happened to the photos you found in the summer house?'

Max hesitated. 'I took a few, about ten. Or maybe twenty. Didn't think anybody'd notice.'

'And you've still got them?'

He shook his head. 'Dad found them in my room, said he'd have to get rid of them. But he didn't. Used to take them in the bog for a wank.'

Kyle tutted.

Was Pam right about Burt Collins? Was he the man who watched little Emma dancing? When he was meant to be gardening, was he taking photographs, confident that Crystal wouldn't step outside to inspect his handiwork? He could have hidden the photos of Emma in the summer house, thinking it was safer than keeping them at home, never expecting his son to go poking around inside.

'Did you ever see Emma in the garden or the summer house when you were there with your dad?'

Max shook his head. 'Never met her for real till Barbury Fields. Couple of years below me. Funny seeing her round school with her clothes on, knowing what she looked like underneath.'

'You ever go out with her?'

'Nah! Right little cow, she was.' His face clouded. 'It's the end-of-term dance, right, a few weeks ago, and I'm stood next to her. Never been up close till then. And I said to her, "You remember me?" and she looked at me like I'd crawled out from under a stone. Stuck-up little cunt. "Oh yes," she goes, "the gardener's boy." Like I was a piece of shit. In front of my mates. Like I was a fucking nobody.'

People have killed for less. Lincoln could smell the boy's sweat, breath like vinegar. 'You must've been angry, all those years you'd had fantasies about her and she snubbed you when you actually got to meet her.'

'Got my own back, didn't I? There was a few photos Dad didn't find, that I still got. I scanned them, sent them to her in a text.'

Lincoln held his hand out. 'Are they on your phone now?'

Max passed the phone over. It was hot, damp from his hands. 'What were you going to do? Threaten her? Blackmail her?'

'Dunno. I was angry. Teach her a lesson, I s'pose.'

Lincoln opened the gallery, thumbed through till he found the sequence of photos Max had scanned.

A little girl of six or seven. Emma lying back on a striped cushion, sunshine streaming across her from behind the photographer. Shadow of a window frame falling across her long pale hair, stray tendrils loose around her face. A teddy bear nestled in the crook of her arm, just like in the photos the Peterborough police had sent them. Almost certainly from the same sequence as the photos Charlie saw in the summer house.

Legs wide apart.

She was wearing ballet shoes, the ribbons criss-crossing the soft contours of her ankles. She was wearing a tutu with a shiny bodice, stiff net frills.

No underwear.

Legs wide apart.

In the last photo, she was joined by the little girl Oliver Spence had described. Naked, she was hugging Emma, the photographer's left hand on her hip. In this photo, she had two black holes for eyes, like on the newspaper cutting they'd found in her locker.

Lincoln kept his voice steady even though disgust thickened his tongue. 'Did she know the photos had come from you?'

'I put "*From the Gardener's Boy*" so she'd know I hadn't forgotten, even if she had.'

The phone felt heavy in Lincoln's hand, weighed down by the photos Max had sent in an impulsive act of spite because Emma showed him up in front of his mates.

'Did you send her anything else? A good luck card, maybe?'

Max went red. 'I was angry, y' know? Her, thinking she was so special, like she was gonna be famous because of some shitty play.'

'Did you show these photos to anyone else? Tell me the truth,

Max, because if you've been passing these round, or uploading them onto a website—'

'No!'

'Did your father have anything to do with these photos being taken?'

'Shit, no! I told you, I found them, in the summer house. He didn't know anything about them till he caught me with them in my bedroom. Anyway, he never had a camera. Didn't even use the one on his phone except by accident.'

Lincoln wanted to believe him but so much of the evidence pointed to Burt Collins – possibly aided and abetted by Todd Tremlow.

But if Burt had never even had a camera... Pam might have thought she'd found the mystery photographer but Lincoln wasn't so sure.

Max put his head down and covered it with his arms as if to ward off blows. 'I should've left them pictures where I found them,' he moaned. 'Then none of this would've happened.'

While Dilke took Max home, Lincoln did enough checking to convince himself that Burt Collins wasn't the man the Millers had seen taking photos in the Shermans' garden. The climbing club website had a tribute page to him, picturing him over the last couple of decades. He was average height, slightly built, with wispy red hair and – during the last few years – a bushy red beard.

'I should've realised it wasn't him,' Pam said, disappointed. 'The Millers would've known Collins – he was next door doing the garden often enough.' She sighed. 'Back to square one.'

Shauna grinned across at her. 'Yeah, but at least now we know who sent Emma those sexts and the newspaper cutting – a nasty-minded little boy who can't spell.' She chuckled. 'Private and fucking confidentical... And there we were, thinking it was Tom sending her pictures of his willy.'

When Dilke returned an hour later, he brought a bundle of photos – all that was left of the snapshots Max had found in the summer house all those years ago.

Lincoln spread the photos across the desk. 'Pam, are these like the ones you and Charlie saw?'

She sifted through them. 'The same sequence, certainly – the big hat, the make-up... And it's definitely Maisie in this one, isn't it?'

'This is real film,' Shauna said. 'None of your digital stuff. This guy's got to have his own darkroom.'

267

Lincoln flipped the prints over but found only that they'd been printed on Kodak paper. 'Tremlow told us himself, he's never gone digital.'

'But the Millers are adamant it wasn't Tremlow.' Pam went back to her desk. 'We're going round in circles. No denying who that other child is, though. I saw a photo when we did the house search, Emma and that little girl in some ballet show. Never thought at the time – "Em and M" on the back. The M was for Maisie.'

'I just had a thought,' said Dilke. 'When Shauna and I talked to Simon, we asked him about the photo Emma was sent – the one cut out of *The Messenger*, with her eyes poked out.'

Lincoln tapped the photos into a neat stack. 'And?'

'Well, to start with, Simon said something like, "You mean a photo of when she was little?" Why would he say that unless he knew about these photos of Max's?'

'Emma must've told him,' said Shauna. 'Someone sends you stuff like that and you can't tell your mum – you're gonna tell your bestie instead. And I bet that was Simon.'

'Then we need to talk to him again.'

She took her chewing gum out and squashed it between her fingers. 'Tremlow still needs to explain why this guy in Peterborough's got an envelope of stuff he sent him in 2011.'

'Sweet's got an *envelope* Tremlow sent him, yes,' said Lincoln, 'but it could've had postcards of Basingstoke in it, for all we know.'

'Basingstoke?' Shauna lobbed the nugget of gum into the bin.

'Figure of speech. I need to call Bryn and let him know where we've got to.'

The DCI was at Park Street, some update session about the search for Lady. He'd said as he left that Liz Gregg would be going over to the Isle of Wight to liaise with the local force.

'Rather her than me,' Bryn had laughed. 'Not much of a sailor, me.'

He wasn't answering his phone so Lincoln texted him instead: *Still no ID on photographer. Other kid = Maisie.* Should he say it was *probably* Maisie? He turned to Pam.

'You're sure it's Maisie?'

She nodded, her face grim. The implications were clear to all of them. When Donal Finnegan found out his daughter had been abused, there'd be all hell to pay.

If he didn't know already...

# CHAPTER 75

Simon and Tom were the only customers in the Mokkery coffee shop. Somebody'd left a copy of the *Daily Mail* behind, Arlo James and Elaine Burnie on the front page, fuzzy photos from the ferry terminal CCTV, and Simon was flipping through it.

'Doesn't even look like him, does it?' He held it up for Tom to see but he could tell he wasn't really interested.

'Listen, Si, I'm kinda busy, so make this quick, okay?' Tom looked awkward, like he didn't want to be seen with him. Was that why he'd suggested they met here instead of outside Bods? Was he afraid of bumping into his mates when he was with his Fat Gay Friend From Drama Group?

Simon chucked the newspaper aside. 'How did Arlo get to Southampton if he can't even drive?'

Tom shrugged. 'He's got people who'll drive for him.'

'What, like that guy who picked Emma up?'

'Yeah, like him.' Tom peered at his phone, looking up at the wall clock as if he needed to keep an eye on the time. 'You said you wanted to ask me something...?'

'Need a favour, that's all.' Simon hauled his messenger bag onto the low table. 'Em asked me to look after this for her.' He pulled out a silvery memory stick. 'Only, my computer's so crap, I can't open any of the files to see what's on it. They're spreadsheets.'

Tom took the stick from him. 'Spreadsheets? She hated maths.'

'Yeah, but you don't only use it for maths, do you? Maybe it's a list or something.'

'List of what?' Tom spun the stick round on the tabletop in amongst the slopped latte and the cookie crumbs. Simon couldn't take his eyes off it, scared Tom would ruin it.

'I could tell you if I could open the fucking files! You've got newer software, though. You'll be able to see what's on there.'

'Suppose it's something disgusting?' Tom waggled his eyebrows, Groucho Marx-style.

'Just see what's on it, okay? It must have been something important or she wouldn't have asked me to look after it for her.'

'Okay, but if I find it's only her fucking maths homework...' Tom glanced at his watch. 'Shit, gotta go or I'll be late.'

Simon watched him shove the memory stick into his jacket pocket, stand up and head quickly for the door without saying what he'd be late for or who he was meeting. Already Tom was growing away from him, going places he didn't tell him about, with friends he didn't name.

'You'll tell me what's on there, yeah?' Simon called after him. He knew that once Tom had opened the spreadsheets, he'd want to look at all the other files too.

# CHAPTER 76

Lincoln looked forward to seeing Trish at the end of the day. He tried to avoid talking shop when they were together, but he was desperate to run his suspicions past her if only to hear her reassure him he'd got it wrong.

Supposing the mystery photographer was Finnegan? Was it because of those photos that Simon, in that audio clip, told Emma that Finnegan owed her something? Was Shauna right about Emma turning to her Board Treader buddies – rather than her mother – when Max sent her those ugly photos?

He phoned Trish as he headed for his car, asked her if he could come over.

'Not tonight,' she said, sounding as if she was in the middle of something in the kitchen. 'I'm taking Kate over to Charlotte's for a sleepover and I won't be back till late.'

Disheartened, he drove home, stopping off at Sainsbury's on the way, picking up some bread, a bottle of Scotch and something he could sling in the microwave.

He'd been indoors twenty minutes when the squawk of his front doorbell echoed through the house. His first thought was that Trish had changed her mind, but the silhouette in the frosted glass of the front door was way too big to be hers.

His instincts told him to be wary – but then the handle turned, the door opened and Bryn stuck his head round. 'You in there, Jeff?'

'Glad we work so well together.' Bryn drained his second glass of Famous Grouse. 'Not easy having someone else brought in as SIO over your head. When you're used to being in charge, it's tough when some other bastard's telling you what to do.'

Lincoln grinned. 'I've come to terms with it.' He held the bottle over Bryn's glass.

'No thanks, this'll do me. You've got a good team at Barley Lane, and I'm glad of the opportunity to work with you. Park Street was getting on top of me.' He paused. 'You know I lost Jean last year?'

Bryn's wife had been deputy head of one of Barbury's bigger junior schools. Breast cancer, aggressive, quick. A eulogy in the local paper, emails round Park Street and Barley Lane raising funds in her memory. Their daughter, Lucy-Jane, in her twenties now, was a teacher in Wales somewhere, probably not home much.

'I heard, yes. Must've been tough.'

'You bet. But you know that yourself, Jeff. How long since Cathy died?'

Lincoln took a sip of Scotch. 'Nearly three years. We'd been apart a while when it happened but that didn't make it any easier.'

'Hit-and-run, wasn't it?'

'Joyrider lost control of his car. Ran into her as she was walking home from work.' He didn't want to talk about it, not even now. 'Saddest part, another week and she'd have been on maternity leave.'

'I didn't realise...' Bryn glanced across at him. 'But the baby...?'

'Cathy'd moved in with a bloke who teaches at the tech.'

Bryn didn't need to know Andy Nightingale's name or how useless he'd made Lincoln feel, fathering the child Cathy had yearned for so much – a yearning that had strained their marriage to breaking point. Neither did Bryn need to know about Lincoln's own indiscretions.

'Seems a long time ago now.' He was afraid he'd start talking about her for real, something he hadn't done even to Trish. Best stop now.

Bryn encompassed the Old Vicarage with a wave of his hand. 'No significant other yet?'

'Er, Trish and I – we've been together, on and off, best part of a year. She works at the library.'

'Ah, I never use the library. All that shush.'

'Not so much shush these days, but I know what you mean.' Lincoln sat back. 'So, you've got some news? You didn't drop round just for a heart-to-heart.'

'You left me a message. Maisie Finnegan.'

'I didn't mean for you to come out of your way. It could've waited till the morning.'

'Well, I'm here now. What's the problem?'

'How the hell do we find out who took those photos of her and Emma? We can hardly ask her outright, can we? She probably doesn't even remember them being taken.'

Bryn made a face. 'Peterborough police don't need anything more from us to secure Sweet's conviction, see. What purpose does it serve, stirring up nasty childhood memories?'

'But Sweet getting hold of those photos from Tremlow – that suggests there's a network, some outfit circulating pictures of the girls

272

along with a whole load of other child porn. Who else has got copies that we don't know about? We can't just let it go.'

'Burt Collins is dead. He's the only one who could tell us where he sold his photos. So it ends with him.'

Lincoln was speechless. Why this sudden change of tack? At last he found his voice. 'Bryn, Collins didn't take those photos. Sounds like he enjoyed them in the privacy of his own bathroom but someone else took them. He looks nothing like the man the neighbours saw and neither does Tremlow. Damn it, Donal Finnegan fits the description better than Burt Collins does!'

There was a horrible silence. Bryn pushed his empty glass across the table and stood up. 'Take my word for it, Jeff, this one's run its course. Not relevant to Emma's murder, not relevant to the murder of the Walsh kiddie. It's historical, see. No reliable witnesses, no halfway decent suspects.'

'Getting cold feet, Bryn?'

'No, Jeff, I'm pulling rank.' And Bryn snatched up his jacket and left.

Lincoln took his coffee down the garden after Bryn had gone. He stood staring out towards Fountains, which had gone quiet again. The thicket he'd been clearing the day Emma was found dead had already sprung back as tall as ever, as if he'd never raised a mattock to it in anger. In the end, was anything he did really worthwhile?

*Damn it, Donal Finnegan fits the description better than Burt Collins does!*

The expression on Bryn's face: dismay, alarm. The possibility that Finnegan abused Emma and his own daughter, yards from the house where Crystal waited for them all to come in to tea...

Bryn, pulling rank. Nice privilege to have. You don't like what you hear, you ignore it. Who could Lincoln trust, if he couldn't trust Bryn? Of all people, he'd expected Bryn to see this through, but either he'd taken fright or he'd been persuaded to keep things quiet.

He tramped back into the house. How the hell could he prove that Donal Finnegan was the man in the summer house all those years ago? And where would he go with that proof when he found it? *If* he found it...

Then just as he was putting a packet of Uncle Ben's in the microwave, his mobile rang: a number he didn't recognise, landline, local. Who the...?

'It's me,' said Arlo James. 'And I'm nowhere near the Isle of Wight.'

'He's in here.' Billie Wheeler led Lincoln into the lamplit snug, where a crumpled figure huddled in the corner. 'You want a cup of tea? The kettle's just boiled.'

'Coffee, please. Black, two sugars.'

Arlo looked up. 'Inspector.'

Lincoln pulled out a chair, sat down across from him. 'So, no Isle of Wight ferry for you after all.'

Arlo nodded at the floor. 'Been down the beer cellar most of the time – until I felt like the walls were closing in on me. Lady – I think I hurt her.'

'You *think* you hurt her? She's missing. If you're not on the Isle of Wight, neither's she. She hasn't been home since she went to meet you Saturday night. That's a week ago. What the hell happened?'

Billie bustled in with two mugs of coffee. 'Aren't you going to caution him?'

'Should I?' Lincoln sat back as she dumped the mugs down. 'Tell me what happened that night and I'll decide what happens next.'

Arlo put his head in his hands and shut his eyes. He looked pallid and grubby. He might have taken refuge at the Two Magpies, but he clearly hadn't availed himself of the pub's washing or laundry facilities.

'Saturday night, Lady's getting ready to go back into town with Pat – he drives for me sometimes. She shows me these clothes she's found. Then I'm waking up, no sign of her, and oh man, my head's like it's splitting open, blood all over my hands, my clothes. Pat told me to get out, and he'd take care of everything. And now I've got Bee in the shit because this was the only place I could think the fuck to go.'

Billie stroked his shoulder. 'Never mind that, love. We'll get this sorted.'

That dead rabbit Charlie trod on by the caravan – did Tyler spatter Arlo with its blood while he was out cold to make him think he'd hurt Lady? 'How come you're mixed up with Patrick Tyler?' Lincoln wanted to know.

'He's a good customer.'

'Customer? What are you selling?'

Consternation flickered over Arlo's face. 'Weed, man. Didn't you find my grow-room? At the farm?'

'What? Whereabouts at the farm?'

'In the cellar. Thought you'd be sure to find it.'

In his mind's eye, Lincoln saw the blue tarpaulins over Arlo's unfinished renovation work. Christ, how could Woody and his search team miss a room full of cannabis plants? 'So how did Emma Sherman's clothes get in your bin?'

'I put them there. Got back to the camp one night and there was this holdall under my caravan. Recognised the clothes from the film they kept showing on the news, what she was wearing the night she went missing.'

'You didn't wonder how her holdall came to be under your caravan?'

'Sure, but...whatever I did would look suspicious to you lot, wouldn't it? You gonna believe me if I come and tell you I found it? You'd arrest me first, ask questions after. Man, I know how these things work.'

Lincoln sipped his coffee. Billie must have put three or four sugars in. At least. 'So Pat Tyler buys his weed off you. What about Zak Scotson? He another customer?'

'Scoot? That nutjob? Pat brought him up the camp a couple of times. The guy's off his head.'

'We think Emma Sherman was in your caravan.'

Arlo shook his head emphatically. 'Not when I was there, man, but anyone who knows me knows I never lock it. Nothing to steal. Shit, you think she was killed in my van?'

'The attack on her may have started there, yes. She was probably killed in the woods.'

Arlo ran his hands through his greasy hair. 'Pat's a cold bastard. I wouldn't give him the time of day if I didn't need him to market my product for me.' As if pushing weed was as innocent as being an Avon lady. 'But he wouldn't kill a little girl like that.'

'You think Scotson would?'

'Scoot loses control, y' know? Man, has he got a temper! Fuck, I hope he hasn't got his hands on Lady.'

'So do I.' Lincoln tilted his coffee mug, watching the syrupy dregs slump into the bottom. 'You know Lady's only fifteen, don't you?'

'I do now, now I'm supposed to have *eloped* with her. Fucking Isle of Wight! Thought she was sixteen, like Jess. Tall for her age.'

Lincoln snorted. 'We're still going to charge you. You can keep your excuses for the courtroom. Did you know Scotson was keeping underage girls in his flat, selling them for sex?'

The shocked look on Arlo's face told him he hadn't got a clue.

'Was there anything else in Emma's holdall?'

Arlo pushed his mug away. 'Didn't look. It was dark when I found it. I took it to the farm, left it in the cellar. Thought it'd come in handy for carrying stuff.'

'Anything else you can tell me about Tyler?'

'You know he works for Donal Finnegan?'

'Part of the refurbishment team, isn't he?'

'Not just that. Finnegan pays him to take care of business.' Arlo grinned a knowing grin, as if Lincoln was in on the joke. 'These old people with houses falling down round their ears – you think they all want to move into a bungalow so Mr Big Money can do their houses up and make a packet?'

'Finnegan uses Tyler to get people out of their homes?' That wasn't in Revyve's sunny propaganda.

Arlo nodded. 'Bastard like Finnegan wouldn't get his own hands dirty. He pays Pat to handle the nasty stuff for him. He tells Pat what needs fixing and Pat fixes it.'

After he'd driven a very subdued Arlo to Barley Lane, Lincoln drove up to Mayday Farm, even though it was nearly midnight. If he could find Emma's holdall, he might also find her phone. He parked where he and Woody had parked before but it was only when he reached the farm gate that the beams of his flashlight lit up a white van in the cobbled yard.

That definitely hadn't been there last time.

He sneaked across to it. The radiator grille was still hot and its tyres were chalky. Was this the van that dumped Emma and Lorren? What wouldn't he give to get a forensics team onto it!

He crept towards Arlo's half-finished cottage. Lit from below, the tarpaulin draped across the doorway glowed blue in the darkness. At the sound of a voice, he halted. A man was barking into his mobile.

'No, you listen, shit-for-brains, I need to get moving on this one. I'm holed up in this fucking dungeon...' Bulky, shaven-headed, tattooed, the man swiped the tarpaulin aside and stepped out into the open, phone clamped to his ear. Patrick Tyler. 'Sooner she's away from here, the better. Give me that address, okay? Stop fucking me about.'

He rang off, jabbed his phone into his back pocket and began to swing his arms, warming himself up in the chill air. He suddenly stopped and leaned forward into the shadows as if checking for intruders, before slapping his way back through the tarpaulin.

Lincoln went after him, easing the tarpaulin open, his eyes dazzled

276

by arc lights. When his vision cleared again he saw that the cottage was little more than a shell, with two rooms opening off a central hallway. At the far end of the hall, a trapdoor was propped open above a flight of steps down to the cellar. The musky pondweed smell of a hothouse rose from it: Arlo's grow-room. No wonder Woody and his team didn't find it when they came looking – the trapdoor would've been easy to miss in the unlit hallway.

He groped in his pocket for his phone and realised he'd left it in the car. Lincoln knew he was no match, physically, for a man built like an ox.

Tyler loomed out of the shadows. 'What the fuck?'

Lincoln pulled his warrant card out, put it away again before Tyler could see his hand was shaking. 'I'm looking for a girl who's gone missing. Wouldn't know about that, would you?'

A whimper from the cellar made both of them look towards the steps, but that split second's distraction was enough for Tyler to lunge forward, grab him round the back of the neck and slam his face into the door frame. Stunned, Lincoln couldn't stop himself being dragged down the slippery stone steps into the cellar. The walls glistened in the light of lamps trained on enough cannabis to keep Arlo's customers mellow for the foreseeable future. At the end of the cellar was a small room. A cell.

'Take a look,' Tyler said, lifting a panel in the top half of the door.

Head reeling, Lincoln peeped through the aperture, making out the shape of a young girl curled up on a mattress. Then something colossal hit him from behind and everything went black.

# CHAPTER 77

## SATURDAY 21ST SEPTEMBER

'Why the hell didn't you call for backup?' Bryn was seething and had little sympathy for Lincoln's battered face and chipped tooth.

'There wasn't time. I went looking for Emma's bag and walked straight into Tyler. But at least we know Lady's still alive.'

While Lincoln was out cold, Tyler had taken Lady Burnie and fled. With any luck, his van would be spotted, picked up by a number plate recognition system or by good old-fashioned police work. For now, though, he and the girl could be anywhere. Liz Gregg was on her way back from the Isle of Wight and Ashley Tyler's flat was being watched in case his big brother tried to take refuge there.

Arlo was locked up downstairs, awaiting a lawyer, and yet another search of Mayday Farm was being organised.

By the time Pam brought Lincoln back from A&E, the team had found Emma's Nike bag – empty except for a white sock and a plastic hair clip with a few strands of her soft, fine hair still trapped in it. But no phone.

The litter of needles and food packaging in her cell suggested that Lady had been kept sedated since her abduction, with no washing facilities and only a bucket for a lavatory. She'd subsisted on petrol station sandwiches and cola.

'And now the whole thing's gone arse over tit because you uncovered a bloody cannabis farm!' Bryn took his jacket off, rolling his sleeves up as he went over to turn the kettle off and make coffee for them both. 'You heard Crystal Sherman's out of hospital?'

Lincoln rubbed the back of his neck, wondering if he'd got whiplash. Early afternoon and he hadn't eaten since this time yesterday. 'Thought they were supposed to let us know when she came round.'

'They phoned Park Street but the buggers there didn't think to pass it on. I only found out because Donal Finnegan phoned me. Furious, he was. Went to visit, they said she came round two days ago. Discharged herself yesterday afternoon. They wouldn't say who came to collect her but she's not gone home.'

'She's probably gone to ground until she can face going back to the house,' said Lincoln. He knew more than Bryn did. Gaynor had texted him a few hours ago while he was at the hospital waiting to have his split eyebrow sutured. *Taken Cryss away for a few days. Be in touch.* He wasn't ready to share that with Bryn just yet. 'You'd think Finnegan would understand what Crystal's been going through.'

Bryn shrugged. 'Need to mend some fences there, Jeff. Best let me deal with Donal in future.'

'Off limits now, is he? What's this all about, Bryn? Arlo told me Finnegan uses scare tactics to get people out of their houses if they won't sell up.'

'And how would that bloody hippy know?' Bryn stirred sugar into both mugs.

'Tyler told him.'

'Your friend Arlo's hoping we'll go easy on him in exchange for information. He's playing you.'

'I know when I'm being played.'

The men stared at each other for a moment or two until Bryn handed the coffee over. 'Still mad at me for letting Tremlow go, Jeff? Like we haven't got enough dirty bastards to deal with.'

Lincoln dumped the mug down, slopping hot coffee over his hand. 'Those pictures of Emma could be the tip of a massive iceberg.'

'That's for Peterborough to find out. Here.' Bryn passed him a cotton handkerchief, nodding at his hand. 'Least you won't need to go to A&E for that.'

'Thanks.' The cool fabric soaked up the coffee and soothed his burning skin. Lincoln felt foolish and clumsy.

Then Bryn's phone rang, his expression changing from expectant to grim as he listened. He hung up. 'Scotson's turned up at Steepleton Pits. Head bashed in. Doesn't look like an accident.'

'Scoot screwed up.' Lincoln grabbed his jacket, picked up his phone. 'And he's been punished.'

# CHAPTER 78

'Did we have to come so far away?' Crystal hung back from the window, overwhelmed by the acres of lawn stretching away beneath her. The sight of all that empty land made her feel dizzy, swamped by space. The Orchard Hall Hotel was nearly an hour's drive from Barbury and ever since they arrived, she felt as if she'd been cast adrift with nothing to hang on to. She'd got tablets to take but the only effect she'd noticed so far was that the roof of her mouth felt coated with animal fur. 'I hate not knowing what's going on.'

'God, Cryss, you've had a week of not knowing what's going on and you've survived. It won't kill you to distance yourself a bit longer.' Gaynor perused the menu propped on the dressing table. 'Look, we can get room service if you can't face the restaurant.'

'I'm really not hungry. Why don't you go down and—'

'No, no, I'll explore later.' Gaynor tossed the menu aside and disappeared into the bathroom to fill the kettle.

Crystal shut her eyes. When had she last stayed in a hotel? Probably when Derek took her away to Bristol for a couple of days after he'd told Meriel he wanted to end their marriage. The trip hadn't been the romantic getaway she'd hoped for – he'd spent all day with Todd, inspecting a building project in one of the poorer parts of the city – but she'd been thrilled by the prospect of staying in a hotel with him, away from people who knew them.

Typical Todd, sure he'd found the next big thing, picking up condemned properties at auction and restoring them. He'd tried to persuade Dez it was the way to go, doing up places no one else wanted. A friend of his was gutting a dilapidated Victorian terrace in St Paul's and Dez had agreed to go along and see what all the fuss was about.

Over coffee in the hotel bar that evening, though, after Todd had hurried home to Tania, Dez had been dismissive.

'Wrong end of the market,' he'd said. 'But you know what Todd's like, wants to rescue these old terraces when it's much more cost-efficient to knock 'em down, build new houses from scratch. You're never going to make your fortune doing renovations unless you've got capital behind you.'

She smiled bitterly to herself now. If Todd's idea was so flawed, how come Donal had picked up on it? *Hijacked it*, that's what Todd said. Donal had stolen his idea. And that was even before the Revyve project took off. If Dez could've seen then how good Todd's idea was...

Instead, they'd returned to Barbury disappointed, the Bristol trip a waste of time. Two days later, Derek started divorce proceedings. Less than two years after that, he was dead.

'English breakfast or mint?' Gaynor was holding a teabag in each hand. 'Probably both as weak as the proverbial.'

'I need to lie down.' Crystal tried to pick her feet up high enough to cross the room, but it was as if she hadn't really emerged from her coma and was still swimming somewhere below the surface of consciousness, her legs caught in the undertow, her lungs bursting. 'Don't think I'm not grateful, Gaynor, but...'

She stretched her arm out towards the bed just in time to stop herself from falling, falling through space, drowning in the air that pressed down on her like seawater.

Death would have been so much easier to bear.

# CHAPTER 79

Lincoln and Woody stood over Zakariah Scotson's body, a few yards from where the Fiesta had been torched days earlier. Car parts and droplets of melted glass still littered the chalky ground.

He'd been dead only a few hours, the back of his head a congealing mess of shattered bone and matted hair. A wheel wrench could do that sort of damage in the right hands. His grey T-shirt was torn at the neck, his jeans bloodstained and soiled. The lace of one trainer was undone, trailing over the ankle of his other foot. Lincoln could hear his own mother's voice in his head: "*Tie that shoelace properly, Jeffrey, or you'll go flying.*"

Scoot had indeed gone flying, coming down to earth with a bump.

Lincoln recalled the chalky tyres of Tyler's van. No prizes for guessing who'd dumped Scoot here before driving to Mayday Farm to check on Lady.

'Our prime suspect bites the dust,' said Woody.

'If I was Eily Quinn, I'd be shit-scared.'

'Scared enough to turn yourself in?'

'Let's hope so.' Lincoln unwrapped Bryn's hankie from his hand. A patch between his thumb and forefinger had turned a livid red but the skin hadn't blistered. 'She could be the only witness to what happened in that flat the night Lorren died.' He tucked the coffee-stained hankie into his pocket and cast his gaze round the unofficial rubbish dump that was Steepleton Pits.

He could think of better places to die.

'What about the Indian girl?' Woody signalled to the SOCOs to take over. 'The girl you *thought* was the Indian girl, I mean. Any idea who she is?'

'Maybe Micky Stanley would recognise her.' Lincoln wondered how he'd get the image from the CCTV tape across to her, to see if she knew who'd been with Eily that night. They began to walk back to the car. 'That chap in your road – Arthur, was it? Did you say he got rehoused by Revyve?'

'That's right. Lost his wife last year. Suki used to pop round, keep an eye on him but it was a big house for a man on his own. They got

282

him into one of those retirement flats near the leisure centre.'

'And he just upped and moved?'

'Reckon he needed a bit of persuading,' Woody recalled, getting into the car. 'Him and Sheila'd lived there forty years. But he kept having accidents, forgetting to light the gas, leaving windows open in the rain, you know how they get, a certain age. And then one night his shed caught fire. Kids, probably. Reckon the final straw was losing the dog – well, it was Sheila's, really. Postie must've left the gate open and the dog ran off. Found it down the road full of airgun pellets. Had to have it put down. Bloody kids.' He slammed the car door shut, started the engine. 'Old Arthur couldn't wait to get away after that.'

Lincoln clicked his seat belt shut. Little accidents, incidents you could blame on kids, and you get to snap up an old man's house for the price of a one-bed retirement flat. Not so much Revyved as stolen.

Donal bloody Finnegan.

# CHAPTER 80

Sally Page and her husband lived on the outer fringes of the Barbury Down estate, in a prefab semi the council put up after the war.

'Actually, Micky, I was about to call you,' Sally said, brandishing her phone as she led Micky and Lincoln into the living room.

'What's up? Is Cookie okay?'

'I think so but... I'd better tell you what happened.'

While Micky sat on the sofa, Lincoln sank into the deep armchair by the window. Behind him in the kitchen-diner, a meal was cooking – soup or a stew, spicy, rich – making the whole house feel cosy and warm.

Two hours earlier, he'd shown Micky the CCTV image of a girl being hurried along Finisterre Street by Eily Quinn the night Lorren died – the girl he'd feared was Anita Rani.

Micky recognised her straightaway. 'That's Cookie Carmichael. Sweet kid but she's got learning difficulties. Her mum can't cope so she's been fostered with Sally for the last year or so. God, if she's got in with Eily...'

'We need to talk to her. She's our best hope of finding out what happened the night Lorren was killed.'

'She's only twelve.'

'She's all we've got.'

'As long as I can come with you.'

So here they were, Sally explaining how Cookie and Eily had met. Cookie had been browsing in Accessorize in the Half Moon Centre, August Bank Holiday, when an older girl snatched a load of earrings off a stand and stuffed them into Cookie's bag. If they didn't make a dash for it, she said, they'd both be done for shoplifting.

'She's only twelve, and of course, she went along with it. This girl took her round to her flat, somewhere down near the Methodist church, one of those back streets.'

'Finisterre Street?' Lincoln asked.

'That's right. Cookie went round there a few times before I even knew. Eily's boyfriend lives there too. Scoot, she calls him. Friday before last, Cookie didn't come home. We were about to call the police when she turns up on the doorstep. A taxi dropped her off, she said. Nearly midnight. She wouldn't say what she'd been up to, only that she hadn't realised the time.' Sally smacked the arm of her chair. 'So we grounded her – straight home from school, no treats.'

'That would've been the 13th?'

'That's right. Since then, she's been good as gold...until last night. Walked in at nearly eight. When we read her the Riot Act, she broke down and it all came out. That other Friday, there was another girl at the flat. Lorren. We were wondering if that's the girl who – oh, there you are, love.' Sally put on a broad smile as her foster daughter jogged down the stairs. 'We're having a chat about you and Eily.'

'Eily's my best friend.' Cookie flopped heavily onto the sofa next to Micky. 'She bought me an ice cream and a lipstick and a Beanie bear.'

'Tell us about that Friday when you had to hide in the bathroom,' Sally said.

Cookie giggled, screwing up her eyes. 'That was funny. Colin got mad, right? And Eily made me stay in the toilet for ages, and when I came out, Colin was gone and so was Lorren.'

'What's Colin like?' Lincoln asked.

She pondered. 'He's got glasses. He likes Lorren, only he got mad at her that night and so did Scoot. Scoot got super-mad. Lorren doesn't go round Scoot's anymore.'

'Why did Colin get mad at her?' Micky asked.

'She cut things out of his coat. Scoot said he'd have to teach her a lesson.'

Lincoln shot a look at Micky. 'Cut things out of his coat?' He thought of Lorren's box of treasures.

'Like, with scissors. And Colin said she'd stolen his cup link.'

'Cup link?'

The girl nodded, her fine straight hair shifting like dark silk. 'Like, you know, on his sleeve? He said it was gold.'

'You mean a cufflink, Cookie!' Sally held her own arm up, pinching the sleeve of her blouse. 'To fasten his cuff.'

Cookie's eyes gleamed as she giggled, both hands over her mouth. 'I thought it was cup link!' She turned her face up to Micky's, delighted with her mistake.

Lincoln thought about the cufflink Lorren had swallowed. Fancy initials, Bella had told him after the autopsy. Hard to decipher. Now he could make an educated guess. 'The night Colin got angry with Lorren, do you know what happened to her?'

'I was in the toilet so I didn't see. Maybe she went somewhere with Patrick? He's Scoot's best friend.' She tucked her hands under her thighs and rocked against Micky. 'I heard him come in. Eily said he came in specially to clean the flat 'cause Colin likes things nice and it was all a mess. But Patrick wasn't there when I came out of the toilet and Lorren wasn't either so maybe they went somewhere together.'

Lincoln took a deep breath. 'Can you tell us anything else about Lorren?'

She shook her head. 'You think Patrick was taking Scoot to see her yesterday?'

'Yesterday?'

Sally leaned forward. 'You met Eily and Scoot yesterday, didn't you, Cooks? Outside the chip shop. That's why you were late back.'

Cookie nodded. 'Eily, right, she said to come home with her and Scoot. But then Patrick came up in his van and said Scoot had to help him with something. Scoot didn't want to go but then he changed his mind and got in the van after all. Eily kept phoning him 'cause he didn't give her the money for the chips but he didn't answer his phone so she said for me to go home.'

If Scoot had waited for his chips instead of getting in the van, he might still be alive.

Lincoln showed Cookie photos of Arlo and Tyler, and the CCTV prints of Colin McTimothy and Steven Short. The only man she didn't recognise was Arlo.

'Do you know where Eily's living now, Cookie?' Micky asked. 'She's not at Scoot's anymore.'

'She was going back to see her mum, she said, and then up to London. With Patrick.'

'Did she say whereabouts in London, or how she was getting there?'

'Just London. Patrick had to deliver something. They're going in Patrick's van. You think Scoot's going too? They wouldn't go without him, would they?'

Pam and Shauna couldn't get any sense out of Eily Quinn's mother at the mobile home park. Her daughter ("that crazy little junkie") had stopped by only long enough to pack a few things in a bag and ask for some money. She had no idea where the girl was now.

'Fuck she thinks I'm gonna give her money for, anyways? Fucking need every penny for myself.'

286

Pam turned the car round, started back up Solent Road towards Barley Lane.

'Stop, stop, stop!' Shauna slapped the fascia and Pam slammed the brakes on. 'There! That's her!'

A skinny girl, her dirty blonde hair wrenched into stringy bunches, was hobbling along the pavement, a bulging laundry bag under her arm. One of her boots had shed its heel and the bag was throwing her off-balance.

'Are you sure it's Eily?'

Shauna snorted. 'I've watched those bloody videotapes often enough. Course I'm sure!'

Pam pulled up beside her and Shauna got out of the car. Eily put her head down and tried to run but her treacherous footwear and the bulk of the bag tripped her up. Literally. She went sprawling on her hands and knees, the bag breaking her fall.

Shauna helped her up. 'We've got some questions need answering, Eily. Get in the car.'

In the interview room, Eily sat rubbing her arms, looking round her like a nocturnal zoo animal caught in daylight. She needed a fix.

'Thanks for coming in.' Lincoln dumped a thick folder on the table between them. Only a few pages related to the murders of Emma and Lorren, but she wasn't to know that.

'You bin in a fight?'

Lincoln ran a tentative finger along his eyebrow. 'Tripped when I was out for a run.'

'Looks painful.' She scratched the side of her neck. 'You got Taff here now then?'

'Taff?'

'Taffy. The Welsh one. Usually over Park Street, isn't he?'

'DCI Marshall, you mean?' Odd that Bryn hadn't said he knew her.

She grinned. 'Nice fella, Taff. Not like some of them, treating you like dirt.'

'I'll be a nice fella too, Eily, if you tell me what I need to know.' He patted the folder. 'What happened the night Lorren died?'

She rolled her skinny shoulders, then told Lincoln pretty much what he'd pieced together from the forensic evidence and Cookie Carmichael's account of Lorren's final hours.

'So how did Colin McTimothy's blood get onto Lorren's top?'

'Colin went fucking ballistic when he saw what she done to his coat.

Then when she put his cufflink in her mouth, he tried to get her to spit it out and she bit him.'

'Did Colin McTimothy kill her?'

She frowned, hesitated, sighed. 'No, it was Scoot. He beat her up in front of Colin to show he don't put up with bad behaviour. Teach her a lesson, he said. Don't know his own strength, though, Scoot. Pat's different. Pat's cool. Cold. Like, when we was cleaning up afterwards, it was like he was doing a bit of housework.'

'You saw what Scoot did to Lorren?'

She couldn't look at him. 'He kept on hitting her and she was screaming, and he shoved this bottle into her, really hard, y' know? There was all this blood... And he put his hand over her face and she went all quiet. And when he finished, he turns to Col and he goes, "Happy now?" And you know what that fucking arsehole said? "You didn't get my cufflink back."' She pitched forward against the table edge, looking past him as if she thought Bryn was watching her from behind the glass, though Lincoln knew he wasn't. 'Tell Taffy I need protection.'

'Protection from what?'

'Pat Tyler. And all the bastard punters Scoot brought round.'

Lincoln flipped open the folder, made a show of consulting the first couple of pages. 'They were customers though, weren't they? Steven Short. Fergus Gee.' He watched her face to see if she recognised the names, but all she did was blink slowly.

He was beginning to think he'd got it all wrong when she sat back and clamped her hands tightly between her knees. Her thighs were quivering.

'And the rest,' she said. 'I can tell you how Lorren's mum got her flat, too, if, y' know, you give me a bit of a break.'

'We'll come to that.' He shuffled the papers in his folder. 'Did Scoot ever talk about Emma Sherman?'

She took her time answering. 'Someone paid him to set her up.'

The skin on the back of his neck prickled. 'Set her up how?'

'To get rid of her. Get her out the way.'

'You know who?'

A bony shrug. She started kicking the table leg very lightly. 'Someone'd took photos of her with her clothes off and she was gonna make a fuss about it. Scoot got paid to take her up the woods.'

So it was true. Lincoln's pulse throbbed. 'Who paid him? Todd Tremlow?'

She shook her head.

'Donal Finnegan?'

'Didn't say, only that he picked her up in Ash's car, took her up the woods to, y' know, shut her up, and someone paid him to do it. Cash.'

'How was Pat Tyler involved?'

'Pat helped him clear up. He's good like that.'

'Pat takes girls up to London, doesn't he?'

'Nothing to do with me.'

'But you know it's what he does. We need to find Elaine Burnie before he takes her up to London too.'

Eily chewed her fingernails ravenously. Then at last she said, 'There's this man, right? Like a businessman, local? He pays Pat to look out for girls, young girls, to go to parties. Boys, too, only Pat prefers the girls. The girls, they get paid really well, and they get put up in really nice hotels.'

Yeah, right...

'And is that businessman Donal Finnegan?' He pulled a photo from the folder. She stared at it as if she was wondering how to respond. She wasn't stupid but she was desperate and distracted, aching for a fix.

'He's took her to Lucette's.'

'What?'

'Patrick. He's took that girl to his mum's farm, one of them villages on the plain. There's some old barns there. He's took girls there before.'

With a lot of prompting and peering at maps, Eily remembered the name of the village, the name of Lucette Tyler's farm. But she wouldn't say whether the businessman involved was Donal Finnegan.

'Let's hope for your sake we find that girl in time. You've got yourself in with a pretty dodgy crowd.'

Wide-eyed, Eily began to pick at the underside of the table. She let out a sudden horrified howl. 'Euw, that's disgusting! Someone's left their snot under here!'

Lincoln felt vindicated. Scotson might be dead, but someone else was involved in Emma's murder apart from him and Tyler. And even if Eily wouldn't confirm that Finnegan was behind it all, Lincoln was sure he was.

Within a few hours, Liz Gregg had taken a team up to Lucette Tyler's farm, more of a smallholding really, where they found Lady Burnie drugged and dehydrated in an outbuilding. While the girl was on her way to hospital, Lucette was arrested and taken to Park Street. Of her elder son, there was no sign apart from some chalky tyre marks in the yard.

Bryn agreed that Eily's information gave them more than enough to bring Colin McTimothy in for questioning. 'Let's hope we have more luck than we did with Short,' he said. 'Colin's dad will get him the best brief in the county, I bet.'

Lincoln kept quiet about the part Finnegan may have played in Emma's murder, his possible involvement in buying and selling young girls 'for parties'.

Until he could be sure whose side the DCI was on, the less he told Bryn, the better.

# CHAPTER 81

## SUNDAY 22ND SEPTEMBER

Sunday morning, and Golf Kit Depot – wedged between a barber's called Number Two and a shop that sold nothing but beads – should have been open. Instead, Colin McTimothy's shop lay unlit behind a metal window mesh, and mail lay strewn on the floor inside. He wasn't answering his phone and his voicemail was turned off.

When they got no answer at his classy loft apartment in the Old Art School, Lincoln and his team roused the concierge.

He'd last seen McTimothy setting off for work on Friday morning at the usual time, he said. He'd got his sports bag and laptop with him. 'Think he goes to the country club after work most days. Nothing out of the ordinary. You got a warrant?'

He let them in. The apartment was sparse and impersonal, obsessively neat. No evidence of hurried packing or the destruction of anything incriminating.

Lincoln stared into the fridge: immaculate but empty. Another man living alone. Yet the kitchen cabinets were crammed with tins and packets of convenience food, neatly lined up, strictly arranged in order of size and – a quick check revealed – sell-by date. A man living alone who had to be in control.

They found three external backup hard drives hidden behind a stack of shoeboxes in the walk-in wardrobe. Their neat labels suggested they contained images of "children", "older children" and "pre-teens".

'Reckon he could've gone home to Daddy?' Woody picked up a sealed white envelope from the kitchen counter, addressed to Nigel at Bracken Cottage, Langford St Catherine's – not far from where Lorren's body had been found.

A little later, when they marched up the brick path of the cottage, an elderly woman, her hair as white and fluffy as a dandelion clock, poked her head up over the top of the dahlias that crowded the garden. Could this slender woman with the apple cheeks and tentative smile be Colin McTimothy's mother?

'May I help you?' She emerged with shears, which would have

seemed threatening if she hadn't been wearing polka dot gardening gloves.

'Is Mr McTimothy in?' Lincoln flashed his warrant card. 'This is quite urgent.'

'Is this about my grandson?'

'Your grandson?'

'Colin. We've been so worried about him. He seems to have gone off somewhere.' She actually said "gorn orf". Did people really talk like that?

'If we could speak to Nigel McTimothy...?'

'Oh yes, yes, do come in.'

# CHAPTER 82

Bryn finished reading Colin McTimothy's letter. 'Sounds like a suicide note.'

Writing to his father, McTimothy blamed himself for Lorren's death, even if someone else ended her life. He didn't name names but the forensic evidence was already conclusive: Scotson's assault on the girl was the last, not McTimothy's. Still, remorse clearly weighed heavily upon him.

'He must've realised we were catching up with him,' Lincoln said. 'We had Short in here, we raided Scotson's flat. Only a matter of time before we'd be knocking on his door. And now Eily Quinn's agreed to tell us all she knows...'

'Won't come across as reliable, though, will she,' Bryn argued, 'a girl who brought runaways home so her boyfriend could pimp them out?'

'She'll give us names, dates, places. Short and McTimothy may have slipped through the net but they won't all be so lucky.'

'Or have such expensive lawyers,' Pam put in.

'So where is she, the Quinn girl?' Bryn studied the whiteboard. The events of the last forty-eight hours had forced some hasty rearrangement of names and faces.

'Family Services have put her into emergency foster care until we interview her formally.'

'Foster care?'

'She's got nowhere else to go. Officially, she's still their responsibility. And thanks to her, we got to the Burnie girl before she ended up in London at some sex party or other.'

Bryn nodded glumly. 'Saw Lady's mum on the telly last night. Furious, she is, us taking so long to find her daughter. You'd think she'd be grateful to get her back in one piece!'

'It'll all blow over.' Pam switched the kettle on. 'The media will be chasing a different story tomorrow.'

'Something else Eily told me,' Lincoln said, 'makes a lot of other things fall into place. Lorren's mother got her flat in Michaelmas House in exchange for "services rendered".'

Pam grinned. 'That sounds like a euphemism.'

'It is. Jackie got the flat in exchange for sex with the housing officer allocating tenancies there – and anyone else he sent along to her. Worse than that, Lorren was part of the deal.'

'God, how could someone make their own daughter...?'

'Do we know who this housing officer is?' asked Bryn.

'No, but I'm guessing Linus Bonetti did.'

'Bonetti?'

'Social worker.' Pam spooned coffee into mugs. 'The council suspended him for going on Twitter to air his grievances instead of going through the proper channels.'

'I remember now. Killed himself, didn't he?'

'Unfortunately.' Lincoln thought back to Lorren's box of trinkets as he sipped his coffee. Wasn't there a door key in amongst the other bits and pieces? 'Be back in a minute.' He parked his coffee, headed out of the office.

A few minutes later, with Pam watching him, intrigued, he was riffling through the box he'd retrieved from the evidence locker.

'*TRESAURE BOX*?' she read, smiling at Lorren's misspelling. 'What a weird lot of keepsakes!'

'If that's what they are.'

Lorren in a hurry, armed with nothing more lethal than a pair of nail scissors, attacking a jacket draped over the back of a chair, snipping off a cuff button here, a tailor's label there. Teasing baby photos, a fiver or a credit card receipt out of a wallet while its owner was in the bathroom. Scrunching up a cotton handkerchief, slipping it under a pillow till later. Tugging a St Christopher from a key ring. Items their owners wouldn't notice right away; wouldn't make a fuss about when they did notice.

Colin McTimothy's cufflink probably wasn't the first keepsake she'd swallowed so she could retrieve it later when nature took its course.

'I assumed these were mementoes from Lorren's childhood,' Lincoln said, turning the St Christopher over in his hand. 'But I was wrong. She was gathering evidence.' He picked up the envelope labelled "#3MH". Pulled the Yale key out and unfolded the scrap of lined paper wrapped round it: *With thanks.* Flat 3, Michaelmas House.

'Evidence? To blackmail the punters?' Pam poked the contents with the end of her pencil. 'You think we could get prints off any of these things?'

Bryn shook his head. 'Most of it's too small to pick up even a partial, and I doubt many of the punters were men with records. Waste of resources, see, now we know who killed her.'

Lincoln took a last look at Lorren's haul. 'You're right. A waste of resources.'

'I'll put that box away for you,' Bryn offered. 'And I'll need an address for the Quinn girl. DCS Youngman likes to be kept in the loop, see.'

Lincoln hesitated. 'The fewer people know where Eily is, the better.'

'Come on, Jeff, I'm your bloody SIO!' A grin, not warm enough to be reassuring. 'I need that address.'

# CHAPTER 83

The darkroom door was ajar and the light was on. Safe to go in. Tom's father was sorting through chemicals and equipment.

'Dad?' Tom took a deep breath. 'I know about you and Emma.'

His father paused for a moment before carrying on. 'Not a lot to know.'

'You took photos of her.'

'Yes, for her portfolio, something she could send to agents. That's all.'

'Were you sleeping with her?'

'What? She was just a kid.' Duncan began wiping the shelf he'd emptied. 'First time I ever met her was when I did the photos for that bloody play – at your suggestion, if I recall.'

'So when did you start taking photos of her on her own?'

His father swung round. 'Hey, Tommo, why the interrogation? If you must know, I went backstage after the performance to tell her how well she'd done, see if I could do anything to help.'

'Why would she need *your* help?'

'You were the one who kept on about how her mother never did anything for her. I thought a bit of moral support would be appreciated. If you hadn't bailed out of Board Treaders halfway through the term, you'd have been there and seen all this for yourself.'

Tom watched him putting bottles and cans back on the shelf, shaking each in turn, consigning the empty ones to the waste bin. 'So that's all it was, some photos?'

'Of course it was.' Duncan held a plastic bottle up to the light, then chucked it away with the rest. 'Why are we even discussing this? Listen, nothing happened.'

Tom's knees were rigid with tension. Like a twat, he'd opened the files on Emma's memory stick. Spreadsheets, like Simon said, lists of what she had to revise, when she had to rehearse...

And all the photos his father had taken of her, revealing her for the little show-off she was. There were even two sly shots she'd taken of Duncan with his own camera, when he was fiddling with the lighting set-up.

'Was that why she phoned the house? To talk to you?' No point in his father denying it; why else was their landline number in her phone records?

'I suppose so. I didn't want to give her my mobile number. I knew how it would look if…if your mother found out.' Duncan chucked some offcuts into the bin before facing him properly at last. 'Okay? Satisfied? I took a few photos of her, as a favour, but I sensed something about her…' He reached out to him, but Tom shoved his hand aside. 'I didn't want to get drawn into anything. Listen, Tommo, that girl had some serious issues.'

'Did you kill her?'

'What the…is that what you've been thinking? Christ, Tom—'

'You were supposed to pick her up outside the gym.'

'What? Don't be ridiculous! I was teaching that night. And I'd never…' He turned away, shaking his head. 'I can't believe you've been thinking that.'

'Does Ma know?'

'Of course not, and she can hardly complain…'

'You disgust me!' Tom slammed out of the room and out of the house, hauled his bike out of the garage, not knowing where the fuck he was heading or if he was ever coming back.

Later that day, a white van mounted the verge outside a house in Meehan Close. According to a man walking his dog, a big bodybuilder type got out and approached the young blonde who was having a smoke in the garden. She didn't seem too pleased to see him but in less than a minute, he'd wrapped his arms around her, lifted her off her feet and bundled her into the back of the van.

Her cigarette was still smouldering on the concrete path when the woman who lived in the house came out to look for her.

By the time Lincoln had spoken to the dog walker and checked the index number the man had memorised, he knew the van was registered to Patrick Gerard Tyler. He also knew he'd lost his best chance of bringing charges against Steven Short, Colin McTimothy and Fergus Gee.

# CHAPTER 84

## MONDAY 23RD SEPTEMBER

'But how did Tyler know where she was?' Woody scratched his head. 'You wouldn't even tell *me*!'

'Good question.'

It was Monday morning and Lincoln was filling him in on Eily's abduction – if that's what it was. Maybe she'd decided she was better off with Tyler after all, putting up a fight for the sake of appearances – except she probably wasn't that good an actress.

Woody looked downcast. 'And we didn't even get to interview her.'

'Not formally, no, but she gave me plenty to go on.' Little of which would now be admissible in court, although, as Bryn had warned, Eily wouldn't have made a very credible witness anyway. Lincoln picked up his car keys. 'I've got to see Micky Stanley.'

He found Micky in Coronation Gardens, sitting on the curved back of one of the ornamental benches, her feet, in cherry-red Doc Martens, plonked on the seat.

'How did Tyler know where she was?' she wanted to know. 'She wouldn't have called him. Jane, the foster mum, said Eily was shit-scared he was after her.' She took a sip of the coffee Lincoln had brought her from the kiosk.

He took the lid off his coffee, gave it a stir. 'Tell me about Michaelmas House.'

'Not sure I should.'

'How were those flats allocated? Linus Bonetti was building a case, wasn't he? And he was using Lorren to help him.'

Micky set her mouth in a hard, thin line. 'He shouldn't have done that. She was fourteen. He had no business...' She ran her hand over her bristly scalp. 'Okay. He heard a housing officer had boosted his girlfriend's points to get her into Michaelmas. She told a friend who approached the same housing officer, asked him what it'd take to get her into Michaelmas too.' She snorted. 'She soon found out that flats in Michaelmas cost a bit more than a one-off blow-job.'

Eily had told Lincoln that's how Jackie Walsh got her flat: sex on demand, the housing officer, his friends, friends of friends... He hadn't

298

wanted to believe it. 'And that's how it all started? Women put into the flats if they were willing to trade? And their kids?'

She nodded. 'Thought Linus was exaggerating at first, all his little hints. Held on to his secrets, Linus did, didn't like to share. And then dragging Lorren into it...'

'And the officer behind all of this?'

'Gone already, I bet. Resign, keep your mouth shut and don't expect a reference.' She downed a bit more of her coffee. 'The Revyve crew, the guys who did the places up, they brought the punters in. They'd text their mates with the addresses, who'd do what for how much. Some women've already moved out but most of them don't have any place else to go. Or they put up with it, back to what they were trying to escape from.'

Lincoln had put too much sugar in his coffee but a whole bag of sugar wouldn't take the bitter taste away. 'Lorren was still gathering evidence,' he said. 'The night she died, she swallowed a punter's cufflink. She must've thought one of you would carry on with what Linus started, see it through.'

Micky sighed. 'As if. Poor kid.'

'What about the stories Lorren heard about a foster kid being murdered?'

'That's all they were – stories.' She looked away.

'Sure about that?'

'There were rumours, okay, about kids from one of the homes being taken off somewhere to sex parties, some rich bloke's mansion. Things got out of hand one time and one of the kids died. But that's an urban legend, a scare story the older kids tell the younger ones to wind them up.' She drank.

'Ever hear Donal Finnegan's name linked to those rumours?'

'Donal Finnegan?' She made a face, dubious. 'Like I said, it was guys on the Revyve makeover squad who were bringing the punters in, but nobody ever said Finnegan knew.'

'But Fergus Gee knew?'

She crushed her empty cup. 'Course he knew. We all heard the rumours about Michaelmas House but we didn't believe them. Didn't want to. And by the time we found out they were true, it was too late. We'd seen what happened to Linus.'

He stood up. 'Anyone you know who'd make a statement about any of this?'

Micky looked up at him, her eyes bleak. 'You're kidding, right?'

# CHAPTER 85

As Simon slipped the padlock off the door of his shed, he saw Tom loping down the garden path towards him, hands in jacket pockets, hair a matted thatch. He looked a mess.

'So, Dumbo, this is where you hide.' Tom grinned, though it seemed a bit fake. 'You can even lock yourself in.'

Simon held the padlock up: heavy-duty, weighty in his palm, reassuringly strong. 'That's for locking everybody else out. You okay? You look kind of—'

'Like I've been out all night? Stayed the night at Joe's. Bit of a bust-up at home.'

Joe Day again. Richard's friend. Maisie's boyfriend. 'You fall out with your dad?'

'You're a piece of work, you are, Simon-All-Innocent! You knew what was on that fucking memory stick. Spreadsheets? Bollocks! You're a fucking creep, you know that?'

'Not out here! You want to have a go at me, let's go in the shed.' Simon held the door open, his hand trembling as Tom shoved past him, elbowing him in the belly as he stepped inside.

The instant the door was closed, Tom tore into him. 'I used to think you were my friend. When did you find out about my dad and Emma?'

Simon had wanted Tom to learn the truth but he hadn't expected him to react like this. He'd never understood what Emma saw in a geeky twat like Mr Crane, who looked like Cary Grant in those old films: thick-rimmed glasses like a professor, no sense of humour. Tom was supposed to be grateful that he hadn't told the cops, not angry like this.

'Em asked me to keep hold of that stick for her in case her mum found it,' Simon explained. 'August sometime. I looked to see what was on it that was so special.'

'And you assumed my father was screwing her, yeah? Well, you got that wrong, didn't you, Dumbo?'

Simon was confused. 'Wasn't it your dad she was meeting that night?'

'Fuck no!'

'Sure? Wasn't that why you dumped your precious Arlo in it? Tom, he's in trouble now because of you.'

'Arlo's in trouble because he didn't tell the cops what happened to that girl he was screwing. Lucky for him she's turned up, but you can't blame me for any of that!'

'You haven't answered my question. Was Emma meeting your dad that night?'

Tom seemed to grow inches taller in his fury. 'No! He was teaching and he's got twenty fucking students to give him an alibi!'

Simon let the dust settle for a minute or two. 'So if it wasn't your dad she was meeting, who was it?'

'Doesn't matter now, does it?' Tom shifted his weight, like he was keen to leave.

'Your dad gonna tell the cops he took photos of her?'

'Are you mental? How's that gonna look? People'd get the wrong idea and he'd lose his job.'

'And so he should, leading her on like that.'

'*Him* leading *her* on? That's a joke!'

Tom was right. The way she flirted with Mr Crane when he was taking the photos for *Our Town* was – what was the word? Outrageous. Em fell for him from Day One, her eyes on him in every shot, putting on her posey face. Simon teased her about it and she went red and punched him, but that didn't make it go away. But couldn't Tom's dad see how fragile she was, how breakable?

'Em was fifteen, Tom. Your dad's old enough to know better.'

'And you're a fat poofter! Mind your own fucking business!' Tom's arm went back and his fist came up, and Simon felt as if his nose had been crushed. Everything went red, a blast of crimson light, and he brought his hand up, the one that had the padlock in it, and clocked Tom in the side of the head.

And then they both went quiet.

# CHAPTER 86

Lincoln ran into Liz Gregg when he got back from seeing Micky. 'How's Lady?' he asked. 'Elaine, I mean.'

'Still sedated. All she can remember after Tyler chucked her into his boot is a couple of phone calls he made. Seemed to be fixing up to deliver her to someone in London but she couldn't catch any details. Your intervention,' she added, as if he'd turned it into a proper balls-up, 'forced him to change his plans and move her to his mother's place first.'

'From where she was rescued. If he'd got her as far as London, we'd have lost her. You get anything out of Lucette Tyler?'

'Poor cow's doolally. And the brother says neither of them knew what Pat was getting up to.'

'Don't take people like that at face value, Liz. If you'd leaned on Scotson four months ago, we wouldn't be where we are now.'

Her colour rose. 'And you're such a shrewd judge of character, are you?'

'I like to think so. I certainly wouldn't have let the likes of Scotson scare me off.'

'Let's hope I won't either when I've been in the job as long as you have.' She flashed him an angry smile and marched off.

He cursed himself as he watched her out of sight. He'd been in the job long enough to know when a bit of diplomacy works better than a ticking-off.

Pam looked up as he came in. 'Gavin Lyons just popped up on my screen. Only he isn't Gavin Lyons.'

'What?' He came round to look. The Peterborough team had identified fingerprints found on some of Terence Sweet's material as those of convicted paedophile Perry French. Released on licence in 2011, French had since gone AWOL from his Trowbridge flat, slipping quietly through the administrative net.

'Peterborough sent us French's mugshot because he's local,' Pam said, 'but that's definitely the man we know as Gavin Lyons, isn't it?'

'How the hell did he get a job managing Bods?' Lincoln guessed if Perry French could change his name, he wasn't above faking some references too. A job behind the scenes at the gym probably meant less stringent criminal record checks than if he was one of the trainers.

'You think he came to Barbury because he knows Tremlow – through Sweet, say? Or because of Emma?'

'He definitely didn't come here for Emma.' He pointed at her screen. 'Mr French is into little boys.'

'Oh God, that little ginger-haired boy he brought with him when he explained the swipe-card system to us!'

Lincoln nodded, thinking too of all the impressive electronics in the security box: high-spec scanners, heavy-duty printers. 'If you've got a collection of dirty photos but you've only got prints, what would you need to circulate them to other people?'

Pam ticked them off on her fingers. 'Computers, obviously. Scanners, printers, access to the internet…' Her face lit up. 'God, he had all that expensive kit! Right under our noses!'

'We need to talk to him – French, Lyons, whatever he calls himself.'

'We can't – Bryn's closed the case, hasn't he? He said to let Peterborough handle anything to do with Tremlow and the kiddie porn.'

Lincoln went back to his desk, eager to track down the erstwhile gym manager. 'If French went AWOL from an address in Trowbridge, then he's *our* responsibility. Unless Trowbridge switched counties and nobody said.'

A wary deputy manager at the gym gave them an address for "Gavin Lyons". It turned out to be a rented starter home on the Southampton road.

'He's gone on his holidays,' his neighbour told them when they got no answer. 'Left this morning, bit of a hurry. Plane to catch, he said.'

'Does he live on his own?' Lincoln asked.

'Yeah, but his brothers are always popping round with their kids. Gav's got loads of nephews!'

One of whom probably had a ginger Afro and a serious expression. 'What time did he leave?'

'Early, so's he could get a head start on the motorway, I s'pose.'

'Did he say where he was going?'

'No, but he likes a bit of sunshine.'

Bryn was reluctant to pursue Perry French, but Lincoln managed to talk him round. Before long, a search of Bods' security box was underway.

Dilke rang from the gym to say he and Raj had accessed one of the computers – the password on a Post-it note next to it – and found hundreds of pornographic images and video clips of children.

'French has been scanning old-style prints so he can upload them as digital images and distribute them,' he said. 'Some of the photos are like the ones Charlie found in the summer house – Emma, big hat, no knickers.'

Lincoln was furious with himself. He and Pam had chatted to "Gavin Lyons" while his cache of child pornography was on a computer a few feet away. And then he'd had a go at Liz Gregg for taking people at face value! The irony filled his mouth with a metallic taste.

'How's he distributing the images?'

'Probably through the dark net,' said Dilke. 'People use bitcoins as payment, no bank details, no personal details. Stuff gets bounced around, computer to computer – almost impossible to trace without a lot of hard work and more expertise than we've got. French is probably one contributor among many.'

Lincoln sighed. 'Well, wrap things up there as soon as you can. We'll need to get the equipment checked out thoroughly. Good work, Graham.'

Bryn came over. 'What's the latest?'

Lincoln relayed what Dilke had told him. 'We need to find out who else was in French's distribution network, who else was getting those summer house images.'

'Jeff, we don't have the resources for this.'

'The man behind Emma's murder could be involved. Are you saying we can't afford to find out why she was killed?'

'Zakariah Scotson picked her up, took her into the woods and killed her. Now he's dead too. Case closed.'

'Is it? Is it really?'

'I'm handing this off to Peterborough as part of their investigation of Sweet. A force like that, see, they've got the resources.'

Lincoln leapt up. 'We're letting this go?' Out of the corner of his eye, he saw Pam pretending not to listen as she worked on a report.

Bryn held his hands up, trying to calm things down. 'We're letting someone else follow it up. We don't have the expertise to take those computers apart and we've got other cases to wrap up. Poking around in the bloody dark net isn't going to help us find Patrick Tyler, is it?'

Lincoln pointed at the whiteboard. 'Eily Quinn told me Scotson was paid to get rid of Emma because she was going to make a fuss about some photos that had been taken of her. Max Collins sent her some of those "Little Innocence" photos and a few weeks later, she's dead. Isn't that a bit of a coincidence? I think she threatened to expose the man who took them and he had her killed.'

'You'd trust the word of a little tart like Quinn? Look at the facts, Jeff. Show me the evidence. I'll bet you Scotson was Emma's bit of rough. Things got out of hand and he killed her. He's no threat to anyone now. Why can't you let it go?'

'When Max sent Emma those photos, I think she remembered who took them and confronted him. I don't know whether she wanted money from him or an apology but she'd had enough of keeping quiet. He got someone to shut her up for good.'

Bryn sighed in exasperation. 'Bloody hell, Jeff, why can't you accept that Emma went on a date that went wrong?'

'But she got into the back seat of that car,' Pam argued, 'as if she didn't know him.'

Bryn shrugged. 'They could've been playing some stupid sex game. "Pretend to be a cabbie," she says, "and I'll be your passenger. Our eyes'll meet in the rear-view mirror..." Oh, come on, you chaps. We're never going to know for sure, so what does it matter now?'

'It matters,' said Lincoln. 'Whether we think it's Todd Tremlow or Burt Collins or your precious Donal Finnegan who took those photos, we've settled for an easy solution – her killer's dead, end of story. I'm convinced the man who paid to have Emma silenced is also linked to this network of Perry French's. Those same "Little Innocence" photos keep turning up.'

'You're speculating, Jeff. We can't act on speculation.'

'We're copping out.' Lincoln snatched his jacket off the back of his chair. '*You're* copping out, Bryn.'

And he strode out of the building, his heart battering inside his chest, sweat prickling across his back.

# CHAPTER 87

'Just as well you've got thick hair.'

Tom leant his head back against the car seat. He didn't want to talk. He'd wasted hours sitting around in A&E and now he just wanted to get home. His mother kept trying to catch his eye in the rear-view mirror but he wouldn't play. His head was throbbing and his eyes were whizzy like he'd been playing computer games too long.

'What were you boys up to, anyway?'

'I slipped. Banged my head on the shelf.'

'Not sure Simon needed to call an ambulance. Better safe than sorry, I suppose.' Another attempt to catch his eye. 'Tom, I need to tell you something when we get home, but it can wait.'

'What?' He gripped her headrest and shook it. 'What?'

'Your dad's moved out. Only temporarily. Give us a bit of breathing space.' She waited to turn off the main road towards Amberstone. 'Let things settle down a bit, see how we are.'

'Right.' Tom shut his eyes, his head spinning. All this lying, all these people not being who you thought they were. Life used to be simple. He wasn't sure he could wait another year before going away to uni. He opened his eyes again, his heart pounding. 'They didn't call the cops, did they, the hospital?'

'"The cops"?' She smiled in the mirror. 'The police, you mean? No, of course they didn't call the police. It was an accident. Wasn't it?'

'Course,' said Tom, shutting his eyes again. 'I told you.' He never wanted to see Simon Lovelock again, ever.

# CHAPTER 88

Tania Tremlow folded the last of the clean towels and put them in the airing cupboard. Todd had hardly spoken to her in the last few days. When she asked him why he'd gone to the police station last week, he said there was some trouble with one of his tenants and the police needed to talk to him. She wasn't sure what to think. He normally let the solicitors take care of that sort of thing.

And now he was upstairs, rummaging around in his darkroom, shifting boxes, opening drawers and slamming them shut. She'd have gladly helped him but he never liked her going in there – too many chemicals, he said, and they'd be getting in each other's way.

That's all she seemed to be doing these days, getting in his way. Getting in Crystal's way, too, it seemed.

She put the kettle on, wiped the worktops down while it boiled. God knows where Cryss had gone off to! Couldn't even leave the house most of the time so she must've had help. That friend of hers from down the road when they were kids... Gaynor. Spiky little thing, she was – bossy, possessive, as if friendship trumped family.

Tania was making the tea when Todd came thundering down the stairs and out into the garden. He was carrying a cardboard box overflowing with paper and photos, mounts, binders.

She plopped the cosy over the teapot, followed him out. He was trying to get the lid off the fire bin without spilling everything. She reached forward to give him a hand but he shoved her away.

'I was only trying to help.' She hugged herself, hurt.

'Well, don't. You've done enough damage already.'

And she watched without a word as he dropped the first of many boxes of his photos into the bin and set them alight.

# CHAPTER 89

That evening, Bryn phoned Lincoln at home. 'Bit of good news,' he said. 'Hospital's discharging the Burnie girl tomorrow afternoon. She'll need some counselling, of course, but at least she'll be home.'

'Thanks for letting me know.' Lincoln felt ashamed of himself now. He shouldn't have taken Bryn to task in front of Pam and he shouldn't have walked out like that. 'But nothing more on Tyler's whereabouts?'

'No, and his mam's no help. Says she thought it was *puppies* he was keeping in the shed.'

'But the gym manager – Perry French? No sightings at the airport?'

'Nothing. Probably flew out before we started looking for him.'

'Or else he's gone to ground closer to home. Can't believe his whole operation was right in front of me in that security box and I missed it entirely.'

Lincoln caught sight of himself in the mirror over the empty hearth. Bags under his eyes. Too hurried a shave this morning. Hair badly in need of a trim, suddenly looking properly grey.

'Don't beat yourself up over it, Jeff. He fooled plenty of other folk in the last couple of years.'

'Sorry about earlier. This case has got to me, that's all.'

'Stressed out, that's what you are. It's a killer, stress. A break is what you need.'

'When we've got this cleared up.'

'Jeff, you're no good to me burnt out. You're no good to *anybody* burnt out. Take tomorrow off. Compassionate leave, I'll put it down as, give you a chance to recharge your batteries. Have a day out. Go to the seaside, change of scenery. We've got this under control.' And he hung up.

# CHAPTER 90

## TUESDAY 24TH SEPTEMBER

Lincoln felt ill-prepared for a day off. In the weeks after Cathy left him, he'd often taken himself away somewhere, driving without a destination in mind. Sometimes he'd stay overnight at a B&B, coming into work in the same clothes as the day before – which must have set tongues wagging.

He'd find himself in Torquay or Fishguard or Oxford, stopping for coffee at Little Chefs or service stations, eating sandwiches as he stared at views he hadn't seen before, would only vaguely remember, would never see again.

Today, though, awarded a day off by Bryn, he didn't know what to do with himself. He spent the morning clearing up in the garden but his heart wasn't in it. He kept thinking of Emma getting into that car, letting Scotson drive her away – to what? Where did she think he was taking her? Who did she think would be waiting for her when they got there?

When he took a break for lunch, he realised a day off-grid was an ideal opportunity to follow something up.

He phoned Pam, asked her to get him an address without letting Bryn know – 'In case it doesn't pan out...' Before long, he was on his way to London, coming off the M25 at Maple Cross and cruising down into the commuter-belt town of Rickmansworth.

The huge chalet bungalow had fewer flowers in its garden than a garage forecourt, and a lone bay tree stood marooned in its tub on a calm sea of beige paving. A young girl let him in, eight or nine years old, with straight brown hair and pale blue eyes.

'I'll tell Daddy you're here,' she said, but even before she'd finished speaking, Mark Sherman appeared in the hallway behind her.

'Wondered when you lot would get round to talking to me,' he said. 'Alice, make yourself scarce.'

# CHAPTER 91

'Damn it, Steven, I thought I could rely on you. We're about to launch the Paragon and you're caught with a fucking fourteen-year-old!'

Donal Finnegan marched across to the window of his office. The marketplace stretched away beneath him, flat and empty. The view troubled him. He'd hoped to get the go-ahead on a pair of Edwardian office buildings opposite – semi-derelict, Tudorbethan, huge potential for the most astonishing apartments – but now his bloody ops manager had put all that in jeopardy.

'They can't verify any of it,' Steven Short said. 'They can't use the CCTV in court.'

'They won't need to. If they're sure it's you, they'll get you some other way.' Finnegan thrust his hands deeper into his trouser pockets and glowered out at the skyline. 'That's not all. Some reporter's been snooping round, freelancer name of Marston.'

'You want me to...?'

Finnegan shook his head. 'Too late for that. He's been truffling for anything he can use against us. He's found out about the discounts.'

'But how?'

'One of the other bidders is challenging the council's decision. Bloody Corporate Audit's got involved. If we can't buy materials at the price we agreed, our profit margin's fucked.'

Finnegan needed a way out of this mess. The council had gone out to tender at the start of the year, offering a lucrative five-year contract for the supply of building materials. The process took months, from bidding to evaluation to the award of the contract, and there'd been a lot of competition.

For the past five years, the council's supplier had been Pegg Hosier, who'd also offered Finnegan's firm – off the record and against regulations – the same very generous discounts. They'd seemed likely to win the contract for a second five-year term.

In April, however, while the bids were being evaluated, Finnegan heard on the grapevine that, because of a poor safety record, Pegg Hosier might not even make the shortlist.

He was horrified. He'd never secure such good terms if another firm won the contract. He asked Steven to take care of it.

He hadn't asked for details – something about changing the weighting of health and safety factors – and nor did he ask who Steven had persuaded, and how. Nevertheless, in July, to his relief, the council awarded the contract to Pegg Hosier.

Now, though, if some rival firm's sour-grapes challenge meant the evaluations were subject to scrutiny by the auditors... Well, he'd say he knew nothing about it. Let them try to prove otherwise!

And if Steven had been caught screwing a fourteen-year-old, that was *his* funeral.

Still, especially with the Paragon coming up, Finnegan couldn't afford to go elsewhere for his materials and equipment. Pegg Hosier simply *had* to keep the contract.

He turned back to the graphite-and-mercury landscape of his office. 'Steven, who do we know in Corporate Audit?'

# CHAPTER 92

Mark Sherman's house was as dull and cheerless as his stepmother's. No offer of either a seat or coffee. The men stood in the oatmeal-coloured study while daughter Alice slipped noiselessly upstairs.

'Mr Sherman, when did you last hear from Emma?'

Feet apart, arms folded, Mark looked athletic, early thirties, self-sufficient. 'Not sure. June? July? Said she felt it was time she made contact with her family.'

'And you told her – what? That Derek wasn't her father?'

'Listen, my father left his bitch of a mistress everything when he died. Oh, pardon me, of course, he *married* her, didn't he, so he could *really* stitch us up.'

'Doesn't sound as if the passage of time has made it any easier to bear.'

'You can patronise me all you want, Inspector – that neurotic secretary didn't ruin *your* home life. Listen, when I wasn't much older than Emma, my father announced to me and my sister that Mum was taking us and moving out so his mistress could move in. How d' you think that made us feel?'

That sounded pretty cruel. Everyone spoke of Derek Sherman as a good man who'd made a bad marriage, but maybe he wasn't such a saint after all.

'So who do you think her real father was?'

Mark made a face. 'Not many candidates. Crystal was besotted and Dad lapped it up. But she must've found some fool desperate enough to screw her because Dad was having chemo when she got pregnant. That usually makes you sterile.' He paused. 'My money's on the guy who was Dad's business partner. Mum wouldn't have him in the house after – well, let's just say there was an incident.'

'An incident?' Lincoln was all ears.

'I caught him in the summer house with my little sister, Georgia – trying to put his hands up her dress. Made out she'd fallen over and he was making sure she hadn't hurt herself. Georgia said it had happened before but she'd been too embarrassed to tell anyone. Of course, Dad preferred to believe she was making it up. What kind of father puts his business interests before his family?'

'And you think this man was Emma's real father?'

'Yes, but I didn't tell her that. Just said she'd have to look elsewhere for her family because she's certainly not a Sherman.'

'So who is he, this man?'

'The guy who bought Dad out before he died. Finnegan. Donal Finnegan.'

Lincoln couldn't get back to Barbury fast enough. He had Georgia Sherman's address in Bristol and her brother's grudging agreement to make a formal statement about Finnegan molesting her. Their testimony would surely be sufficient grounds to bring him in for questioning, along with Lincoln's suspicions about who took the photos in the summer house.

The miles ticked by as he tried to put himself into the mind of a distraught fifteen-year-old. Once she'd got over the shock of being told Sherman wasn't her father, would Emma have approached Finnegan, told him she thought she was his daughter? How would he explain to his wife, the lovely Lindsey, that while she was in the early stages of pregnancy, he made a baby with his business partner's mistress?

Was that a more compelling motive for murder than fear of exposure as Emma's abuser? But what man would kill his own daughter?

No, Lincoln couldn't get back to Barbury fast enough. His phone kept chirping with text alerts but he was in too much of a hurry to stop and check them.

Only when he slowed to turn into the narrow lane to his house did he see blue lights swirling. Every window in the Old Vicarage was lit up, people moving around inside.

*Uniforms* moving around inside.

He could hardly breathe. An accident? A break-in? A fire? He drove on past his turning, pulled over a hundred yards down the road. Checked his phone. A text from Pam, mid-afternoon. *Theyve sealed your desk. Whats going on?*

A text from Woody, two hours ago. *DCI got a tipoff. They took yr computer. At yr house next. Where R U?*

'Am I under arrest?' I know this script, Lincoln thought bitterly. Only this time I'm the wrong side of the table, a Police Federation rep at my elbow.

'No, but you're suspended from duty pending an investigation.'

DCS Youngman opened a file and slid five pictures out: images of child abuse, amateur footage, grainy, old. 'We found these and a great many more like them on your laptop at home this afternoon.'

Youngman reeled off the provisions under which the Old Vicarage had been searched. He explained that DCI Marshall had received an anonymous phone call earlier in the day, alleging that Lincoln had downloaded obscene images from various websites and stored them on his computer.

A search of his house had found the evidence.

Lincoln didn't recognise the pictures. Nothing to do with Emma. Probably copies of material seized in some other enquiry, grabbed at random and dumped on his laptop while he was driving to Hertfordshire and back. Someone must have been watching the Old Vicarage, waiting for him to follow Bryn's advice and go away for the day.

'Convenient, this,' he said, holding Youngman's gaze. 'I get within an inch of pinning charges of child abuse on one of Barbury's most prominent businessmen and...' He lifted the prints up and dropped them again. 'And these turn up on my laptop. Coincidence? Or just bad timing?'

'You're a single man, with urges like the rest of us. Understandable you need an outlet. If you were accessing porn channels on your television, we wouldn't give a shit, but this is kiddie porn, Lincoln. Not forgivable.'

'These weren't on my laptop last time I used it. I'm being set up.'

Youngman's eyebrows arched. He patted the prints together, returned them to the folder. 'As of now, Lincoln, you're suspended on full pay pending an investigation. You will not speak to the media. Co-operate with the investigating team at all times. If you ignore this advice, you will only make a bad situation a great deal worse. Are we clear on that?' He folded his hands, bumped them up and down on the folder a couple of times waiting for a reply.

So much needed saying, but it was useless. Youngman wasn't ready to listen. No one was.

'Yes, we're clear.' Lincoln got to his feet and barged out of the office.

Now what? He was out on the street, trying to remember where he'd parked, before he took another proper breath. He called Trish, but she wasn't answering. When voicemail kicked in, he hung up. Woody would tell her what had happened, or she'd hear it from her sister. Christ, she probably wouldn't even let him in the house if she thought he'd been downloading child porn. But no one who knew him would believe he'd really done that, would they?

He started walking, moving fast through the cold rain that had drifted in during the evening. Autumn was definitely on the way. Before long, he found himself in a pub, somewhere they didn't know him, where he ordered a Scotch and then another before trudging back to wherever he'd left his car.

He got home to the Old Vicarage to find it violated. No longer a place of safety, the house felt alien, as if he hadn't lived in it for the past six months. He went from room to room seeing – as if for the first time – the extent of his folly. What had possessed him, in a moment of madness, to buy a money-pit like this?

A line from the letter Colin McTimothy wrote to his father stood out: *I went into that flat in a moment of madness.*

Had Donal Finnegan molested Georgia Sherman in a moment of madness? Was it in a moment of madness that he'd taken his camera into the summer house a few years later and persuaded Emma and Maisie to undress for him?

Before he knew what he was doing, Lincoln was charging out of his detestable house, leaving the lights blazing, the doors unlocked. It took him nine minutes to reach Marsh Pulham Hall, to draw up outside Finnegan's palatial wrought-iron gates. He turned his engine off.

Security cameras swung jerkily round to peer down at him, quickly losing interest and swinging upwards and away again.

What the hell did he think he was going to do? Go in there and confront the bastard?

He drove back into town, found a different pub, drank some more, got talking to a woman he didn't know and went home with her.

315

# CHAPTER 93

'I can't believe the boss would do that.' Pam stared at her screen, unable to take anything in.

'I wouldn't have thought so, but...' Woody looked as perplexed as she felt. 'But they found a load of pretty nasty stuff on his laptop.'

Bryn had been out at Park Street for most of the morning, discussing how media relations were going to handle Lincoln's suspension. Pam had heard "misconduct" being bandied about, a cover-all that skimmed over details.

She got up and stood over Woody's desk. 'Isn't there something we could be doing?'

'Liz'd welcome a hand following up the paperwork they found at Mrs Tyler's farm.'

Pam looked down the room. Liz was on the phone, her pencil flicking in the air as she talked, a grin becoming a laugh, oblivious to the impact of what had happened to Lincoln.

Pam pulled her bottom drawer open and retrieved the framed picture of Todd and Tania with Emma. 'Since Emma's case is closed,' she said with some bitterness, 'I'll take this photo back to the Tremlows.'

Tania had the vacuum cleaner out, the power lead stretched between two armchairs like a tripwire.

'Hate hoovering,' she said. 'Blessed thing stops picking up after a couple of minutes and I'm just putting fluff back down again. I've heard the bagless ones are best. We'll upgrade to one next time we change.'

'Mr Tremlow not around?' Pam had brought the photo back as an excuse to see him again. What good she'd do, she wasn't sure – unless he broke down at the sight of her and confessed.

'Todd? No, he's been out all day – problem tenant.' Tania pulled the plug out, started to wind the lead up. 'No fun being a landlord these days. The more you do for them, the more they expect.'

Pam laid the photo down carefully on a side table. 'You've heard your sister's out of hospital?'

'So I gather. No one told us, of course. Todd went over there to see her and the bed was empty. Imagine how he felt! And not a word from her since. Still, one day at a time, eh? That's what I say to Todd, but he's not what you'd call an optimist.'

Tania led Pam through to the kitchen, but instead of offering her a cup of tea, she flopped down at the table and put her head in her hands.

'I've done something terrible,' she said, tears suddenly welling up. 'It was a long time ago but it's come back to haunt me. To haunt all of us. And I don't know how to put it right before he destroys everything.'

# CHAPTER 94

Lincoln couldn't remember where he'd parked his car. Probably somewhere near the last pub he'd called at, wherever that was.

He'd spent the night in a maisonette on the Barbury Down estate, and the long walk into town gave him time to get his head together. He didn't feel so much hung-over as exhausted, and not because Debbie – was that her name? – had worn him out, because she hadn't.

He'd felt this way after Cathy left him. He'd come home to an empty house, not even a note on the kitchen counter, just a message on the answerphone to call her as soon as he got in. He'd feared that something had happened to one of his in-laws, bracing himself for a drive to a hospital somewhere but no – Cathy wanted to tell him she was moving out for a while, see how things went, no rush decisions...

How long had it taken her to decide she wasn't coming back? Three days? Four? She'd already made up her mind, already fallen for Andy bloody Nightingale.

Lincoln felt now as he'd felt then: as if he'd been hit full-on by a truck, all the energy knocked out of him. Only this time, he was suspended from the job he loved, barred from the station, unable to face going home.

His phone parped. A text from Pam. *U OK?*

He didn't reply. Nothing from Trish.

Someone had broken into his house to plant those files – though "breaking in" was a joke. How often had Trish let herself into the Old Vicarage and surprised him because he'd forgotten to turn the key in the lock or draw the bolt across? He didn't always bother, even late at night, like the time Bryn dropped by.

Bryn. His steps slowed. Bryn wanting to wind everything up unfinished or palm it off onto another team, another force. His stubborn refusal even to consider the possibility that Emma had been deliberately and callously silenced. Lorren's treasure box, everything spread out like one of those party games where you have to memorise a tray of objects and then work out what was taken away while your eyes were shut. Among the coins and buttons: a handkerchief, white cotton, blue edging.

Just like the one Bryn lent him the day he slopped hot coffee over his hand.

"*Got Taff here now, then?*" Eily, a cocky grin. Eily, who knew that someone paid Scotson to set Emma up. Bryn's insistence on having the address of her emergency foster home.

No one else at Barley Lane knew that address.

Lincoln had got too close to the truth, whatever it was. Should he feel flattered that they thought him such a threat?

He stopped walking and took his phone out, scrolled back through his messages. Dialled.

# CHAPTER 95

Soothed, Tania Tremlow sipped the tea Pam had made for her and started to explain.

'Emma was only about six or seven. Todd won a magazine contest with a photo of her. "Little Miss Innocence". It got reprinted in the newspapers. She looked so sweet! Half a dozen letters came, through the magazine, asking for copies.' She hugged herself, a plump, plain woman so different from her sister. 'We sent them off, thought no more about it. Then a few more letters came, direct this time. "We've heard you've got some photos of a pretty little girl" – that sort of thing.'

She broke off, sat back, toyed with her over-bleached hair. 'I expect you'll think me naïve, Pam, but it never occurred to me why they wanted them. Not then, anyway. Todd didn't want to know, not after those first requests. But they were willing to pay, you see, willing to pay quite a lot, and I was here all day on my own, looking after Stephanie, and the extra money – well, it seemed such an easy way to earn a bit more. No harm done. Easy enough to make copies with my scanner.'

Pam took her notebook out, began to jot things down. 'Did you keep a list of the people who asked for copies?'

'Oh yes, it's all in my database.' She said it so glibly, this woman Pam had thought unversed in IT.

'Tania, you weren't to know some of those men had ulterior motives.'

'But it didn't end there. I haven't told you all of it.'

'Go on.'

'About four or five years ago I was round my sister's, giving the summer house a bit of a going-over – she's kept it locked up for years and it seemed such a waste. I found some old photos, loose, in a drawer – little Emma half-undressed. How do you think I felt, knowing Todd used to snap her all the time when she was small? My sister would've had a fit if she'd seen them.' She pushed her cup away, stared out of the window. 'I decided no good would come of stirring it up again.'

'But if you thought Todd had been abusing Emma...'

She sat up primly. 'I've never doubted my husband. He always doted on that child. And I thought, well, you hear of these little girls leading men on... It wouldn't take a lot, and if he took some pictures of her being saucy, that's *all* he did. So when I got letters asking for her photo, I sent some of those saucy ones off as well.'

Pam's pen faltered. 'You realise what you did was illegal, never mind the moral—'

'It was only half a dozen photos, to a handful of people. But by then, I suppose I knew what they were after. At the time it seemed only right, after what Emma did to Stephanie...' She stopped herself.

'What did Emma do to Stephanie? Tania?'

She clenched her hands on the table, kept her gaze on them. 'It was when they were small, playing in Crystal's garden. From the start, Emma always got her own way. Stephanie was on the swing, Emma wanted a go and she pushed Stephanie off. We think the swing came back and hit Stephie in the head as she was trying to stand up again. She was every bit as pretty as Emma until that spiteful little madam shoved her in a fit of temper.' She looked Pam in the eye. 'Don't get me wrong – I've had sleepless nights since, and I'm glad I'm telling you now because it's weighed on my mind something terrible since Emma died but... Sometimes it's the little slip-ups that come back to haunt you, isn't it? The little things you do in the heat of the moment.'

Pam put her pen down. 'Was Terence Sweet one of the people you sent photos to?'

'I remember the name, yes. You would, wouldn't you, a name like that? Bit of irony there, I expect.' She smiled weakly. 'I've been a very stupid woman.'

# CHAPTER 96

'You found us, then.' Gaynor Rees rose from her seat in the bar and strutted across the hotel lobby towards him. 'You weren't supposed to.'

Lincoln shrugged. He'd heard a receptionist answering the phone in the background when he'd called her earlier. 'Not many Orchard Hall Hotels hereabouts.'

'Nice detective work.' She smiled coldly. 'You've wasted your time, though – she won't talk to you.'

'Is that Crystal's last word or yours? I need to see her. If she wants me to find out what happened to her daughter, then she's got to help me.'

Crystal was dozing in an armchair with the curtains drawn. She seemed to have shrunk since he'd seen her last. Had she left her hotel room at all since Gaynor brought her here?

'Tell me about Donal and Emma.' He swung a chair round and sat very close to her.

'There's nothing to tell.'

'Someone was taking photos of her and Maisie down in the summer house when they were only seven years old. Sometimes with their dance dresses on. Sometimes not. It was Donal, wasn't it?'

'What are you saying?' Gaynor hissed at him. 'How can you...?'

Crystal didn't say a word but the look on her face – resigned, crushed – told him he was right.

'I've seen the photos, Crystal,' he went on, ignoring her friend. 'And so has Max. Remember Max? His dad did your garden for you? Burt Collins?'

Crystal searched for words like a stroke victim. 'What photos?'

'Emma didn't show you the photos Max sent her, with her eyes blacked out? Photos of her and Maisie, arms round each other, no clothes on?'

'Please, please!' She twisted away, trying to fend him off.

'Isn't that why you keep the summer house locked up – because of what happened to Emma there? Except I can't understand...' He seized her by the shoulders, pulled her up, forcing her to look into his face. 'I can't understand why you let your daughter's abuser come into your house whenever he wanted. How do you explain that, Crystal, a caring mother like you?'

'Stop it, stop it!' Gaynor pummelled his back, his arms. The toe of her boot dug into his calf. 'Leave her alone!'

He let Crystal slump back into the chair. She kept shaking her head, saying over and over, 'I didn't know, I didn't know.'

Gaynor hugged her, glaring up at him. 'Can't you see what you're doing to her? Please go, before you upset her even more!'

But he stood his ground. 'I need answers.' He jabbed his finger at Crystal. '*You* need answers.'

Gaynor sprang up and bundled him towards the door. 'Give us a few minutes,' she said. 'Wait downstairs.'

He paced the hotel lobby, went outside and paced the driveway, his eye on the door. A family piled out of a huge Audi: parents, two sons, a daughter of about fifteen. She had soft fluffy hair piled high, tendrils escaping. Coltish legs in skinny jeans. Sweatshirt swamping her narrow frame. An instant reminder of Emma. Just as well Crystal didn't leave her room.

Then Gaynor was there, shoving open the swing doors, her jacket on, already reaching for her tobacco tin. 'Where are you parked?'

# CHAPTER 97

Trish marched through the open-plan office to David Black's desk, panting because she'd jogged across the town hall complex to the main building, where most of the other council departments were based.

'Dave, we need to talk.'

His shoulders sagged. 'Is this about Linus again?'

'It's about what Linus found out.'

He held his hand up, cutting her off. 'Not here.' He grabbed his mobile and led her to a small meeting room at the far end of the office.

As soon as they were alone, she told him she knew about Linus' allegations: extra points awarded to certain housing applicants to bump them up the queue and into prime properties.

'And please, Dave, don't give me the guff you gave Linus about handpicking the best tenants to get Revyve off to a flying start.'

Neither of them had bothered to sit down, Trish perching on the flimsy table while David leaned against the window blinds, his face showing little emotion. 'I don't know where you're going with this, Trish.'

'Some big names have been caught screwing a kid who's meant to be in council care – a girl whose mother was one of the first tenants in Michaelmas House. That little girl's been murdered, and a good friend of mine's been dumped in the shit because some of those big names are involved. How does that sound, Dave? Is that good PR?'

'For God's sake, Trish!'

'What did they have on Linus?'

The question caught him out. 'Come on, you can't expect me to tell you that. It's more than my job's worth! I've got my family to think about.'

'And how old are your kids, Dave, your precious girls? Ten? Eleven?'

'Thirteen and twelve.'

'Hmm, just the right age for Fergus Gee.'

From the horrified look on David's face, she knew Linus had been right. 'You can't go anywhere with this, Trish. You know you can't.'

'God, Dave, you used to have principles. You used to stick up for what you thought was right.'

324

'I can't afford principles these days.' He took a deep breath. 'The Paragon project's about to be launched, the biggest partnership project we've ever had. It's so high-profile, the bloody *Guardian* is covering it. You think I'm going to jeopardise that? They'd do to me what they did to Linus, and I can't take that risk.'

'*What* did they do to Linus?'

He began to usher her out of the cubicle. 'I've already said too much. This isn't a game, Trish. Knowing you, you'd love to play Superwoman and vanquish all the baddies, but sometimes you simply have to accept the way the world really works.'

When he'd herded her as far as his desk, she turned on him. 'You are such a coward! I can't think what I ever saw in you! To think I nearly—'

'But you didn't, did you?' He regarded her with cold amusement. 'You had enough sense to walk away and save your marriage. Now have enough sense to walk away from this. Please.' He pulled his chair out, sat down.

'So that's it? You just wash your hands of it and carry on?'

'You want to know what happened to Linus? He was a bit economical with the truth when he applied for his job here. When he started sounding off about the council, personnel did a bit of digging into his background. You know why he left his teaching post in the West Midlands? He accused some kid's father of child abuse. The guy accepted an apology from the school but Linus was forced to resign – only he didn't declare any of that when he applied to work here. Grounds for instant dismissal. End of story.' He reached for the phone. 'You can find your way back to the ground floor?'

# CHAPTER 98

Lincoln drove back along the A36 towards Barbury until Gaynor told him to stop in a big layby off the main road. A man in a converted 50s coach was offering *HOT SNAX, HOT DRINX,* but they weren't interested.

Gaynor got out and lit up. The layby overlooked the valley where a lake had been turned into a nature reserve. She leaned on the fence and gazed across at a crowd of Canada geese, a pair of swans drifting aimlessly on the silvery water.

'Used to come here at weekends,' she said, blowing smoke away. 'Used to go riding in the next village. Cryss wasn't allowed.'

'I need to know what was going on with Emma. I'm betting she told you more than she told her mother.'

She nodded. 'The last few months, Em began to realise how trapped she was. Her mum couldn't leave the house, so who'd take her places, auditions, performances? Todd and Tania weren't helping out anymore and she couldn't rely on someone else's mum or dad offering her a lift.' She hung her head. 'I knew she'd contacted Mark. I should've said before. He told her Cryss got herself pregnant by some other man, to trick Dez into marrying her.'

'Emma must've been devastated.'

'To start with, yes, but after a couple of days dwelling on it, she got all excited because her real dad could still be out there somewhere, very much alive, still able to help her. A dead dad's not a lot of use to a fifteen-year-old.'

Lincoln leaned in next to her. 'Who did she think it was?'

'Donal's the only other man who's ever been close to Cryss. Myself, I've never taken to him, but...'

'Mark caught Donal assaulting his sister.'

She shuddered. 'Cryss wouldn't have given him the time of day if she'd known that. I've never understood the hold he has over her. Maybe she feels she owes him because he was there for her when Dez got sick and she was left on her own. But if she thought he'd ever done anything to Emma...' She hugged herself and he realised she'd left her jacket in the car. 'Em made up her mind that Donal was her dad.'

'Did you know about the photos Max texted to her?'

'That kid's a pervert. What normal boy defaces photos like that?'

'Did Emma tell you about them, or Crystal?'

She looked up, alarmed, still so anxious to protect her friend. 'Cryss doesn't know, does she?'

'She knew someone sent Emma a sext.'

'Not the same as knowing what was in it, is it?' She finished her cigarette, flung the dog-end into the undergrowth and began to head back to the car. 'Em wouldn't have dared show her those photos. She'd never have heard the end of it.'

Maybe that's what the row was about, the day she disappeared – Crystal knew she'd had a text that upset her, something explicit, but Emma wouldn't let her see it.

Gaynor leaned against the car while Lincoln walked round and opened the door. 'She forwarded them to me, see if I thought they were Photoshopped but you could see they weren't. That little pervert had messed around with the eyes but everything else looked real enough.'

They got into the car but Lincoln didn't start it right away. 'Did she remember the photos being taken?'

Gaynor shook her head. 'That was the thing – she hadn't remembered any of it until Max sent her those photos. And that's scary at any age, a gaping hole in your memory. But you know what she felt most of all? Shame. That girl felt *ashamed* of something some bastard made her do when she was seven years old.'

Lincoln felt a chill in his stomach, a shiver in his blood. 'Did she remember the name of that bastard?' He watched her face, the guardedness in her dark brown eyes, the way she pouted as she made up her mind how much to tell him.

'Bits and pieces came back to her, she said – the costumes, the music they danced to – but she didn't remember who took the photos.' Gaynor sighed heavily. 'But I could tell she knew it was Donal.'

'Did she confront him? Go to his office, his house?'

She stared out across a landscape Lincoln guessed she hadn't seen in a while. He could pray his hardest but not even this woman, close to Crystal and her daughter alike, had all the answers. 'I doubt it. She'd just found her real dad, and that was more important to her than anything that might've happened in the past.'

'You think Finnegan knew that?'

'You mean he was afraid she'd tell Cryss about the photos?'

'And not just Cryss – someone at Board Treaders, her mother, the police...' How ironic that Finnegan had least to fear from the person he feared most.

Gaynor seemed only then to understand what might have happened. 'You think Donal had her murdered?'

'Do you?'

'You said the case is closed.'

'Officially it is.' He started the car, pulled out onto the road.

'But you want to keep it open.'

'I want to keep it open until I get to the truth. Except now I'm suspended, with my laptop in pieces on somebody's workbench and a house that no longer feels like home.'

'They got to you.'

'Yes.' He put a bit of speed on, desperate to shed his frustration. 'They got to me.'

'I know we're not supposed to contact you, boss, but you'll want to hear this.'

Lincoln had just ordered himself an all-day breakfast at the diner next to the motel when Pam rang. 'Go on.'

'It wasn't Todd Tremlow distributing those photos of Emma. It was Tania.'

'What?' He listened while she explained, his sympathy for Emma's aunt evaporating at once. 'So the photos of Emma that Lyons – French, I mean – put on the internet had come from her?'

'Yes. She's kept a list of who bought them – Todd's photos as well as the obscene ones she found in the summer house.'

A waitress in a red pinafore slid a platter of fried bread and baked beans in front of him. 'Any sauces?' she wondered.

He shook his head and she slipped away. 'Pam, the photos we think Finnegan took – has the Tremlow woman still got any of them?'

'Not anymore.'

'Damn.'

'Because she gave them to me.' He could hear the smile in her voice. 'And guess what – one of them's got two fingerprints on it, right there on the image, made when it was developed. If those prints are a match for You Know Who...'

'We took Finnegan's prints for elimination when Emma went missing. They should still be on file.'

'But if Bryn's closed the case—'

'I've got an idea. Don't tell anyone else you've got those photos, okay? They could be our only proof.'

'I'll guard them with my life. By the way, Trish has been trying to get hold of you. She says you aren't taking her calls.'

# CHAPTER 99

'I need your help.'

'My help?' Bella waved Lincoln towards her baggy leather sofa. He'd expected her to slam the door in his face, so he was relieved to have made it over the threshold. 'With what?'

'I need to check some fingerprints.'

She sat across from him, casual in jeans, T-shirt, old sandals. 'And how do you think you're going to do that now you're suspended? What did I say about going off-piste?'

'There wasn't really a piste to go off.' He told her everything he dared to, then waited for her reaction.

'You'll need more than a fingerprint match on some old photo to catch Finnegan out. It might prove he took dirty photos of Emma but it doesn't prove he had her killed. You know the pictures upset her but you don't know that she threatened him or tried to blackmail him. That's your missing link.'

She was right. After talking to Gaynor, Lincoln wasn't even sure Emma approached Finnegan – either to ask for his help or to threaten him with exposure. If Finnegan didn't know she was a threat to him, why did he have her killed? Lincoln instinctively distrusted businessmen in Finnegan's position and he'd let that distrust influence him. He'd tried to build a case on too shallow a foundation and it was all tumbling down.

He leant his head back against the sofa. 'How come Fergus Gee hasn't resigned?'

'There's no case. Scotson's dead and you saw that letter McTimothy wrote to his father – he as good as confessed to murdering that runaway in Scotson's flat.'

'The runaway's name was Lorren.'

'Lorren, then. McTimothy's gone AWOL and no one's going after the other men who were there, that night or any other time. Sorry, Jeff.'

Lincoln shut his eyes, Lorren dissolving into history as he'd feared she would. No charges brought. No further action. All wrapped up. 'Pip can't persuade her brother to do the decent thing and come clean? It's going to come out eventually.'

'Pip's moved out.'

He opened his eyes, sat up. 'Sorry.'

'Forget it.' She shrugged off his sympathy. 'Fergus will brazen it out, move on to another authority, hope the past doesn't catch up with him.'

'Meanwhile, kids like Lorren...' He shook his head, depressed by the injustice of it. 'What do you know about Bryn Marshall?'

Bella sat back in her armchair, crossed her legs. 'Thought you ran his fan club.'

'Used to be on the same wavelength, me and Bryn. He always seemed like a man of integrity but these days—'

'There are no men of integrity, Jeff, not anymore. They've all sold out – present company excepted. Bryn was probably warned off, same as I was. Donal Finnegan's untouchable.'

'You mean he's got something on someone?'

'On everyone who matters, probably. I'm handing in my notice. You should do the same.'

'What, just give in?'

'There's no shame in admitting defeat when you're up against men like Finnegan. And I want to get back up to London. I hate it down here, bloody sheep everywhere, bloody fields.'

'I need to find out who planted those dirty photos on my laptop.'

'Make sure your fed rep gets it properly analysed – when it was put on there, the provenance of the images. I don't know much about computers but I know a woman on the Surrey force who's the best forensic analyst around – I'll speak to your rep.'

'Thanks.'

'Let me have those fingerprints and I'll see what I can do,' she said as she showed him out. 'What do I do with the results while you're *persona non grata*?'

'If they're a match for Finnegan, send the results to the police at Peterborough.'

'Peterborough?'

'They've got the resources, see. Unquote.' He grinned ruefully. 'Thanks for this.'

'Don't mention it. I owe you one, Jeff. You could've told the DCS how I screwed up over Fergus, but you didn't.' She hesitated, looking a little embarrassed. 'You stayed the night once, d' you remember, when you were at Hendon with Ed? After you'd gone, I took the pillowcase you'd slept on and hid it in my knicker drawer for weeks.' A lopsided grin. 'Twelve is an impressionable age.'

# CHAPTER 100

'Graham, there's a lad across the street, keeps looking this way.'

Dilke shoved his plate aside and went to the window to see what his mother was on about.

Simon Lovelock was leaning against the wall of the house opposite, hood up, hands stuffed in his pockets. He looked furtive and damaged. Rain was on the way and he wasn't dressed for it.

'Someone from work, is it?' She turned back to the sink.

'Not exactly.' Dilke grabbed his fleece and went outside.

'Hi there,' said Simon, like they were old friends.

'You been in a fight?'

The boy put his hand up to his face as if he'd forgotten he'd got a black eye and a nose like a sweet potato. 'Slipped on something.'

'How did you know where I lived?'

'Only one Dilke in the phone book. Took a chance.'

A gust of wind, a sweep of rain. 'Better come in before we both get soaked.'

The front room was always a bit chilly but it was the best place to sit Simon down and listen to what he had to say.

'It's about Emma.' He took his glasses off and wiped them on his T-shirt. 'There were these photos—'

The door flew open and Mrs Dilke came in with two cups of tea and a saucer of Jaffa cakes.

'I'll put the fire on,' she said, squatting down and fiddling with the switches. Dilke caught Simon's eye, raised his eyebrows apologetically and offered him a Jaffa cake.

The moment the door shut again and they were alone, the atmosphere softened and warmed. And bulky Simon, with his damp T-shirt and swollen face, began to unload secrets he'd been lugging round for weeks.

# CHAPTER 101

**THURSDAY 26TH SEPTEMBER**

'I want to set the record straight.' Duncan Crane had taken the morning off work, he said, to call in at Barley Lane. Now he sat across a table from Woody and Pam in Interview Room 1.

Pam had never met him before. Tall and thin, he looked studious behind his thick-rimmed glasses, but in his dark eyes and handsome face she sensed an energy and passion that an impressionable girl like Emma might find hard to resist.

'Go ahead,' said Woody.

'A few weeks ago, I took some photos of Emma Sherman – to make a portfolio, something she could send out to agents, to help her career. All strictly professional.'

'Why are you telling us this now, Mr Crane?' Woody asked.

'Because my son might have got the wrong idea. If any of this gets back to my college...' He opened his hands. 'I want to avoid any misunderstanding.'

'We've seen the photos,' Pam said – thanks to Simon, who'd handed them over to Dilke on a memory stick. She tapped the tablet on which sixty-two images had been loaded: Emma posing in Greywood Forest one August afternoon, according to the metadata, when her mother must have thought she was at the gym.

Her poses were playful, a teenage girl seducing the camera with her lithe grace and undeniable prettiness. No nude shots, nothing especially sexy. Only once did Pam glimpse the butterfly tattoo, and then only the tops of its wings. All that pain, the tat, the Brazilian, and for what? A set of pictures that was competent but ultimately uninspiring.

One or two more provocative poses reminded Pam of the summer house photos of the little girl peeking impishly over her shoulder, a big straw hat held like a shield across her nakedness – but last month, up in Greywood Forest, the young girl peeking over her shoulder was fully clothed. And in love.

She must have sneaked a couple of photos of Duncan when he wasn't looking – a lean, dark, bespectacled man squinting irritably at a tripod he was struggling to adjust.

'How did you meet?' she asked.

'My son got me to take some photos of his drama group, the Board Treaders. I thought a portfolio would further Emma's acting career, so I offered my services.' He dipped his head. 'I should've approached her mother first, I realise that now, but at the time...'

Since he wasn't in the line-up, Pam had assumed Tom took that photo of all the players in black, Emma making eyes at the photographer.

'How would you describe your relationship with Emma?' Woody enquired. Lincoln was never that diplomatic. He'd just come out with it.

Pam found herself leaping in before Crane could answer. 'Did you have sex with her?' She brought the tablet screen to life, one of his close-ups of Emma pretending to be sad. She swiped the screen. Emma smiling coyly. Swipe. Emma blowing him a kiss.

He squeezed his eyes shut. 'No. Never. I admit it was foolish to photograph her with no one else around, but do you think I'd be here if I'd done anything I'm ashamed of? I will say this...' He pointed his bony forefinger at the tablet. 'She was a beautiful, vivacious girl, a natural in front of the camera, but she behaved in a very sexual way for a fifteen-year-old.'

'Don't you mean sensual?' Pam swiped the screen. Emma, wide-eyed, sucking her thumb.

Crane looked away. 'No, I mean *sexual*. I wouldn't have wanted to be left alone in a room with that girl.'

'So the boyfriend wasn't Crane?' Dilke looked downcast. 'Simon was so sure.'

Pam shook her head. 'I bet she had a bit of a crush on him, though. You could tell from the way she looked at the camera.'

'Had Simon seen the photos the Collins boy sent her?' asked Woody.

'He was the first person she turned to. She was in a panic because she couldn't remember them being taken, thought she must be losing her memory. That seemed to upset her more than how obscene they were.' Dilke raised his eyebrows. 'She'd already worked out who must've taken them.'

'Finnegan.'

Dilke nodded.

'How could you forget something like that?' Woody sounded sceptical.

'Kids shut things out,' Pam said, remembering how easily she'd done that herself. After her parents split up, it was years before she recalled the night her father threatened to kill himself before he'd let her go. Now it was a night she'd never forget. 'We all do. Then something triggers an old memory – a special smell, someone's perfume – and it all comes back, good stuff and bad. She was too young to know what Donal did was wrong. She loved having her picture taken and she felt safe with him. He was her best friend's father and he took advantage of that.'

Woody still looked doubtful. 'And she didn't approach Finnegan?'

'Simon was all for blackmailing him,' Dilke said, 'but she wouldn't go along with it. She'd got it into her head Finnegan was her father and she didn't want to spoil things.'

Pam thought of the summer house photos, Emma's delight in her own innocence. 'That poor kid,' she said. 'That poor silly kid.'

Woody turned back to his keyboard. 'Perhaps the DCI's right, and it was Zak Scotson she was planning to meet all along. Getting in the back of the car – like he said – could've been a game they were playing.'

Pam didn't like to admit it but he was probably right.

# CHAPTER 102

Trish shut the window of the motel room but they could still hear the drone of traffic on the nearby A303. 'God, do people ever have sex in these places?'

'I wouldn't know.' Lincoln didn't look up from the paperwork she'd brought him.

Twenty minutes ago, in the rain, she'd shown up in the motel car park with an archive folder that looked like a glorified brown paper carrier bag.

'I've got Linus Bonetti's files,' she'd said eagerly. 'I lent him a whole load of material months ago, and that's what I thought he'd given back to me when he was suspended – but when I went to re-file it this morning, I realised he'd left his own papers in here as well. Perhaps for safekeeping?'

Now, after skimming through Bonetti's papers, Lincoln knew not only the names of the women who'd been allocated flats in exchange for sexual favours but also the name of the housing officer responsible: Adam Jones, based at the Presford hub.

Trish picked up the pages as he finished reading them. 'I suppose Linus trusted me to do something with it, even if he couldn't.'

A very rough draft of Bonetti's 'secret report' – hardly more than a collection of notes – contained rumours he'd picked up from some of his clients: the families Jones placed in those flats ran the risk of being thrown out or beaten up if they didn't comply. Horror stories abounded. Certain members of Finnegan's refurbishment team were little more than violent thugs.

More than that, probably thanks to Lorren, Bonetti was able to list several of Scotson's customers by name, including Steven Short, Fergus Gee – and at least two councillors. And there, at the bottom of the list, "*Brian Marsh, a senior police officer in Presford*".

No doubt Bryn, his identity obscured by a mishearing of his name.

"*Evidence is being gathered which will implicate these ILLUSTRIOUS men without a shadow of a doubt.*"

Lincoln set Bonetti's papers aside. What a bloody mess.

Trish sat next to him on the bed, her arm pressing against his.

'Do you think someone had Linus killed?'

'The suicide verdict seemed sound enough. His life was falling apart, they wouldn't let him do his job and he felt he'd let everyone down. You've read this report – you can see how driven he was, a man on a mission. Angry young men take risks. From what you've told me about him, Linus could've seen suicide as some grand gesture to show the world what he was up against.'

'And he was about to be sacked,' she added sadly. 'They'd found out he lied when he applied for his job here – meaning instant dismissal. They were simply going to get rid of him – dismiss him, I mean.'

Lincoln stood up. The motel room felt cramped and airless. 'No wonder he felt suicidal. Look what happened to me. Someone broke into my house, sabotaged my laptop to make me look like a paedophile and got me suspended from duty. You get too near the truth, you're dangerous.'

'And you put yourself in danger.'

He scowled down at the papers spread across the bed. How could he make sure Bonetti's work hadn't been in vain? 'How much did he tell that journalist? Marston, was it?'

'I don't know – why?'

'Any way these papers could be linked back to you? If Marston found them on a park bench somewhere, say?'

'No, of course not.' She grinned. 'Did you have a particular park bench in mind?'

337

# CHAPTER 103

Pam passed Bryn in the corridor.

'I'm off to Park Street,' he said. 'Press conference about us rescuing the Burnie girl.'

'Any sign of Tyler?'

'No, and his mam's got instant-onset dementia, sounds like. Liz Gregg's talking to the girl this afternoon, now she's had time to recover. You want to join her?'

When Pam got to Park Street, paramedics were stretchering Polly Burnie into an ambulance and Lady was in the lobby looking shell-shocked.

'Everything happened all at once,' she said, close to tears. 'I was sitting here with Mum and then she hurt so much, she had to lie on the floor.'

'Come on, I'll take you to the hospital. She'll be fine, you'll see.'

Twenty minutes later, they were in the maternity waiting area.

'What about my interview?' Lady wondered. 'I was supposed to see Liz.'

'It'll have to wait,' said Pam. 'This is more important.'

The girl sighed. 'Nothing seems real. Keep thinking about where Pat was going to take me. If that policeman hadn't turned up...'

'Lady, do you—'

'Laine. I'm Laine now.'

'Laine, then... Do you remember Arlo or Pat ever talking about Emma Sherman?'

'Arlo?' She shook her head, the tears starting. 'Feel so stupid, y' know? Thinking Arlo loved me. Thinking I loved him. If I saw him now, I dunno what I'd do to him.'

'About Emma—'

'No, I don't think so.' She wiped her tears away with the heel of her hand. 'Except Pat was on the phone one time, grumbling about always having to clean up after Scoot.'

'Look, if you think of anything, call me, okay? Or text me, whatever.' She passed the girl her card.

338

Moments later, a nurse came to tell Lady she'd got a baby brother, and would she like to see him?

Pam left them to it. As she walked back to her car, she fastened the pocket of her bag where she kept her business cards. Who else had she given one to recently? Maisie, of course, in the kitchen at Marsh Pulham Hall. Clearly, Maisie hadn't felt the need to talk.

# CHAPTER 104

It was late in the day when Lincoln arrived at the offices of Finnegan Property Development, keen to share with Finnegan the information he'd gleaned from Linus Bonetti's notes. It seemed only fair to give the property developer a heads-up before Ian Marston published an exposé for *The Messenger* or splashed his findings all over social media.

'Mr Finnegan's in a meeting,' the receptionist said.

'I need to speak to him. Urgently.'

'Who shall I say?'

'Er – tell him it's Bryn Marshall. Detective Chief Inspector Bryn Marshall.' Lincoln was pleased to see this had the desired effect.

When he was shown into the office a few minutes later, he found Finnegan seated at a conference table with Steven Short, Fergus Gee, and a councillor whose name escaped him – even though he was always in the local paper. At the foot of the table sat a blonde woman in her thirties, a notebook on her lap, pen poised as if to take minutes.

Short came across to head him off. 'I'm sorry, this is a private meeting.'

Lincoln kept walking. 'At which, I take it, Bryn Marshall would've been welcome.'

Nobody answered.

A balsawood model of a starkly angular building sat in the middle of the table amid a slew of publicity material: Barbury's first dedicated arts centre.

Lincoln tapped its Perspex roof, Short still hovering. 'So this is the Paragon?'

Finnegan went for affable. 'Like the look of it?'

'Not a lot. Barbury needs affordable housing more than it needs a white elephant like this.'

'What do you want, Inspector?' Finnegan paused. 'Is it still "Inspector"? I hear you've run into some trouble.' A wide smile, cold as the moon. 'By the looks of it, face first.'

Lincoln ran a finger along his interrupted eyebrow. 'I've come to make you an offer.' He sensed a stir round the table. A whisper of nylon as the woman crossed her legs.

Finnegan glanced sidelong at Fergus, at the councillor. Salter, that was his name. Jim Salter. 'An offer?'

'My house. Free, gratis and for nothing.' Lincoln dug in his pocket, pulled his door keys out, dropped them on the table. 'You can do it up and sell it on. *Revyve* it. Or offer it as accommodation for vulnerable young people. Still plenty of those on the council's waiting list, aren't there, Fergus?'

Fergus Gee's eyes narrowed behind his wire-rimmed spectacles. To think Bella had risked her career to save this chinless wimp!

Finnegan picked the keys up and dangled them. 'No offence, Lincoln, but why would I want your house?'

'It's old and it's a wreck and I don't want it. No need for bully-boy tactics to get me out of it – I'm not going back. It's the Old Vicarage, by the way. But of course, you already know where I live – I've got the messed-up computer to prove it. I don't see Pat Tyler as a computer geek but you must have more than one fixer on your payroll.'

Jim Salter pushed his chair back. 'Donal, what's all this about?'

Lincoln answered for him. 'Your friend here is a keen photographer. Isn't that right, Donal? Buildings, rustic scenes...and images of a more salacious nature.'

Finnegan's eyes shone with anger. 'Lincoln, I'm warning you...'

'But then one of the girls in those photos decided she wasn't going to keep them a secret any longer. She threatened to go public, didn't she? To tell your wife, talk to the media? You couldn't let her do that when you were about to launch the Paragon, could you? Not to mention Revyve and everything else you've got in the pipeline. Couldn't let a silly fifteen-year-old spoil everything because she'd gone all coy about what happened when she was seven. Could you, Donal? Could you?'

Finnegan stood up. 'You've said quite enough. I don't know what you've been drinking, but—'

'Me, I'm perfectly sober.' Lincoln turned away and began to amble round the room. Behind him he heard a murmur of half-spoken questions, the woman trying to make herself heard: 'Donal. Donal, what...? Donal, can...?' Maybe not a secretary, then. Another councillor?

A display on Michaelmas House filled one wall. Revyve's first partnership project. A resounding success. Press photos of the first tenants being presented with their door keys. Among them, Jackie Walsh, not off her face for once, Lorren beside her, eyes screwed up against the sun. End of September, this time last year.

Lincoln jabbed the board and turned back to his uncomfortable audience.

'Know what Michaelmas House was, from the day it opened? A knocking shop. A public/private knocking shop. Every tenant a single mum with a child or children under fourteen. Keys exchanged for services rendered.'

Short grabbed him by the arm. 'Time to leave, Inspector.'

'I'm surprised you haven't had your marching orders, Steven, after what you got up to with little Lorren there.'

'We've been through this. You can't prove any of it.'

'We will. And we'll get you too, Donal.' Lincoln wrenched himself free in time to rescue his keys before Short marched him out the door.

Short summoned the lift. 'If you know what's good for you, you'll leave this alone.'

'You threatening me?'

'No, Lincoln, I'm warning you.' The lift arrived and he propelled Lincoln inside, keeping his hand on the door, delaying the descent. 'The case is closed.'

'Heard that from Bryn, did you? Warned him off too? You can tell your boss I've got proof of what happened to Emma. And not even Bryn will be able to bury it.'

Short let go of the door and the lift went down.

# CHAPTER 105

## FRIDAY 27TH SEPTEMBER

Pam spent a useful ten minutes the next morning on the phone to John Spooner at the traffic management centre. Before long, she was scouring CCTV images he'd sent her of Ashley Tyler's Fiesta in the minutes before Scotson drew up at the kerb beside Emma.

She wasn't sure what she was hoping to find – a shot of Scotson's face, maybe, with an expression other than a stony frown, anything to prove that he and Emma were romantically involved, that Bryn was right and Eily with her hitman scenario was wrong.

A couple of minutes before Emma got into the car, a traffic camera had caught the Fiesta turning into Spicer Street. Pam blew the image up until it scattered into pixels, then shrank it back down again. As the pixels coalesced, she saw what she'd been looking for all along.

There was someone else in the back seat.

# CHAPTER 106

Ian Marston may have been poised to break the story of a lifetime, but he was pre-empted by police from a neighbouring force barging into the offices of Finnegan Property Development and arresting Donal Walter Finnegan and Steven Short on corruption charges relating to the award of council contracts.

A few hours later, Lincoln got a phone call from DCS Youngman, who gave him an offhanded apology and mumbled something about a misunderstanding, and full reinstatement, if he'd like to collect his laptop...

# CHAPTER 107

## MONDAY 30TH SEPTEMBER

On Monday morning, Lincoln was back at his desk, feeling as if he'd returned to work after a bad bout of flu. Nothing seemed as real as it had a week ago when he'd walked out in anger, and he surveyed the whiteboard as if for the first time, doubting how much of it still meant anything to him.

'Good to have you back,' said Woody. 'You heard the DCI's gone off sick? Back trouble flared up apparently, old rugby injury.'

Lincoln admired Bryn's timing, and wondered how long the back trouble would last. 'I take it Perry French is still at large?'

'Yes, but Raj heard from a mate of his in the Met that the National Crime Agency's following up what we found on his computer at Bods.'

'And of course,' Lincoln said bitterly, 'they've got the resources, the NCA. Any sign of Patrick Tyler?'

Woody shook his head. 'Reckon he's done a disappearing act in London. We brought Ashley in again for further questioning. I thought maybe he'd turned the cameras off in the gym foyer because Pat told him to but he said no, they just forgot to do it. He did admit he knew Pat 'borrowed' his car that night, but he didn't know why.'

'Clueless idiot. If only we'd known at the start that Ashley Tyler had a brother...' Lincoln hung his jacket on the back of his chair and set his phone down on his desk, feeling as self-conscious as a newcomer. 'I take it Eily Quinn hasn't turned up.'

'Not so far. You see the local news this morning – Finnegan and Short released on bail?'

Lincoln had watched it on the motel television as he was shaving, the men's faces in close-up as they headed for their cars. They looked none the worse for being in custody. 'It'll be months before they're back in court,' he guessed. 'These corruption cases take forever. What happens in the meantime?'

'It's the talk of Knobhead's office,' said Shauna airily. 'Fergus Gee went to the chief exec and told him he'd been offered bribes of a *sexual* nature.' She chortled. 'Free rides at a brothel in Finisterre Street apparently. Can you imagine how hard it is for me to keep my mouth shut at home? Gotta hope I don't talk in my sleep!'

345

So that's how they'll play it, Lincoln thought. Fergus Gee as the victim of a scam. And Colin McTimothy? Still missing, probably dead – by his own hand or on somebody else's orders...

'So all the bids have got to be re-evaluated,' Shauna went on. 'In the words of one of Knobhead's colleagues, "It's all gone tits up."'

'And the Paragon?'

'Put on hold "pending a review of council spending priorities".' She rolled her eyes. 'We all know what *that* means.'

Pam breezed in, stopping in her tracks when she saw Lincoln was back. 'I was about to phone you,' she said. 'I've been doing a bit of detective work in your absence.'

Even before he had a chance to log on to his computer, she presented him with prints from traffic camera images: the Fiesta, Scotson at the wheel, minutes before he pulled up at the kerb. A different camera, lower angle, sharper.

'What d' you think?' She waited tensely for Lincoln's response.

'Well done,' he said, unable to believe what he was seeing. He resisted giving her a hug even though he was tempted to. 'Well done!'

# CHAPTER 108

'You were in the car with Emma the night she died.'

Lincoln dealt the photos onto the desk like giant playing cards: images from CCTV cameras in St Thomas' Lane, minutes before the Fiesta drew up in Spicer Street beside Emma. Maisie Finnegan peering out from the offside rear window.

Maisie gave the photos only a cursory glance before fixing him with a bright stare. 'So?'

Pam laid Emma's phone records on the table, highlighting the calls Emma made to her number at the end of July and the beginning of August. 'Maisie, you told us Emma called to invite you to her play,' she said, 'but she called you twice after that, when the play was over and done with. What were those calls about?'

'Just stuff.' A shrug. 'I can't remember now.'

'What happened the night you and Scoot picked her up in the car?' Lincoln tapped the photos. She couldn't deny it was her.

'Thought she'd like to have some fun.' The frightened child they'd first met at Marsh Pulham Hall had been replaced by a Maisie who was cocky and bold.

'Is that what you told Emma? "Let's go out for a night on the town? Or a night up in the woods with Arlo?"'

'Arlo? Only thing Arlo's good for is weed.' Maisie pushed her hair back dramatically with both hands. 'Thought she'd like a blind date, live dangerously for a change.'

'And she was up for it, was she, this blind date?'

'Of course.'

'And her blind date was...?'

'That was the fun part. There wasn't anybody.' She glanced sidelong at her mother, who was sitting calmly, the way she probably sat in business meetings: professional, unflustered. 'Scoot was meant to frighten her, that's all.'

Maisie felt as if she was looking down on the interview room: her and the two detectives, her mother sitting there in silence, fat old Rupert Carroll, the family solicitor. Dissociation, that's what it was

347

called. She'd read about it, when you aren't really there, when you can cast yourself off like a balloon that's been untied, part of your mind floating away...

This was all Tom's fault. If he hadn't come over to her and Joe in Starbucks that time, January, February, introduced her to "my friend Emma, from drama group, she's really good..."

'Oh, me and Em are old friends,' Maisie'd said, only she could've torn Emma's eyes out, seeing her with Tom, her hand on his arm like she was his *wife*. How long had it been since she'd seen her last? Four years, five? 'Or used to be.'

They didn't speak again for months after that, but then Emma phoned late one evening, excited. 'Guess what! You've got a sister!'

'What?'

And Emma told her, breathless, chuffed to bits, that Donal was *her* father too She'd just found out.

'Em, that's rubbish. That can't be true.'

'But it is, it is!' Pathetic, how pleased she was.

They met up a few times after that, sometimes with Joe, sometimes with Tom, sometimes just the two of them, giggling and being silly together. It felt nice, actually, having a sister.

'When should I tell him he's my dad?' They'd gone shopping together because Emma said she was doing a photo shoot with some man who'd been *so* impressed with her, he wanted to help her with her career. She'd bought fancy knickers and a bra, and she'd even had a tattoo done. Prissy Emma, with a fucking tattoo! 'Maize, when should I tell him?'

'That's entirely up to you, Em. But I'd leave it a bit. Daddy's kind of busy with stuff right now.'

Em had those tarty colours in her hair and she wanted slides or scrunchies to show them off. The two of them had stood there together looking into a mirror in Accessorize, Emma holding up first this sparkly slide and then that one, both as vulgar as each other. And Maisie had tried to see how alike she and Emma were, and couldn't.

'Are you going to tell him, Maize, or should I?'

'What? You want *me* to tell him?'

'Or d' you think he already knows?' Emma was eager as a puppy, jumping around, pawing her. Maisie was scared she'd lick her face next. 'You think he's known all along, even from when I was born? You think I look like him, Maize? Do I? Do I?'

Emma didn't look a bit like him, but then Maisie didn't look like him either, taking after her mother, nothing Irish about her except her temper. 'But Em, won't it upset your mum? She'd have told you years ago, wouldn't she, if she wanted you to know?'

Emma shrugged. 'She never tells me anything.' She slipped the slides and the scrunchies back on the display stand, taking time to slot them back *exactly* where she'd got them from.

'Oh, for fuck's sake!' Maisie'd snapped, and walked off.

And then Emma had to bring up those awful photos some boy from school had sent her, from when they were little. She'd been keeping them a secret, she said, but she wanted Maisie to see them too. 'Do you remember, Maize? Do you? Do you?' She was almost begging. 'In the summer house? You and me and him?'

'Of course I remember,' Maisie said. 'Don't you?'

And she didn't, not properly, but she wanted to tell someone – not him, not her mum, but *someone*, like she couldn't bear to keep it secret any longer. If she told Tom, if she showed Tom the photos, that'd be the end of the world because Tom would tell Joe and Maisie couldn't stand for Joe to see them.

So then, one of the times Scooter came round to Joe's, so full of himself, sex on legs, a fucking headcase, Maisie said to him, 'Will you do something for me, Scoot, if I make it right with you?'

Scooter'd looked at her like she was offering to go down on him, literally licking his lips until she told him what she'd got in mind, and even then she could tell he was up for it.

The rest was easy.

'Your idea of a joke, was it?' Lincoln asked. 'A blind date without the date?'

'She was getting above herself.' Maisie waved her hand casually. 'On and on about how she was going to drama school and having a portfolio done. She needed taking down. Last time I met her in town, I said how about going on a foursome, and she was dead keen. So we arranged it for when she was meant to be at a class so her mum wouldn't find out.'

'Did you phone her that evening?' Pam asked.

She frowned, then her face cleared as if she suddenly remembered. 'Oh yeah, I borrowed Scoot's phone to check she was still on.'

'Who did she think you'd got lined up for her?'

'Arlo, probably. She kept on and on about how he'd *loved* her voice when she sang for him, how *impressed* he'd been...' Her resentment was obvious.

'Tell us what happened after you and Scoot picked her up in the car.'

Maisie pulled her sleeves down to cover her wrists, her hands, making mittens of her cuffs. 'When we got to the campsite, I told her Arlo was up in his caravan waiting for her. So she went up and Scoot went up after her but he said...' She stared at her cuffs. 'She lost it the minute he touched her, started hitting him, fighting him off. Well, that only made him cross so...' Her fists were clenched tight inside her sleeves. 'He gave her a bit of a slap.'

The autopsy findings: friction burns on her back, the skin scraped off by something rough like coconut matting... Scotson on top of Emma on the floor of Arlo's caravan. 'Sure that's all it was?'

'I don't know. I wasn't there – I was waiting in the car. After a few minutes, she came out again, only she slipped coming down the ladder and fell in the grass. I got out of the car, helped her up. She was hysterical because she'd torn her jeans and cut her knee. She didn't know what she was going to tell her mother...'

'Wasn't having much fun, was she?'

Em had come rushing out of the caravan, screaming like a banshee, tumbling down the ladder she was in such a state. She fell headlong into the grass, bashing her knee. Maisie helped her up, watched as she brushed herself off, inspected the rip in her jeans, the blood starting to ooze as she told her what Scoot had tried to do to her.

'Take me back into town,' Emma ordered, as if Scoot was a cab driver. He didn't like that.

Maisie looked at her standing there, her jeans torn and dirty, her hair all tangled, her make-up spoiled. For a second she felt sorry for her, especially when she started to cry. But then...

This was the girl who'd been better than her for as long as she could remember. Prettier, thinner, sweeter. *Such* a graceful dancer. *Such* a tuneful voice. Maisie was the fat one who got her into mischief. Maisie was the troublemaker.

When Maisie is good, she is very, very good, but when she is bad she is horrid.

In the summer house, it was Emma her father always wanted to photograph. *Such* a natural. *Such* a perfect beauty.

If he found out he was Emma's father, he might bring her to the hall to live. Maisie would be back where she was at the beginning:

second best and overshadowed. Emma would always come first.

'I want to go back into town,' Emma said, her voice wobbly. 'Please take me back.'

'Aw, don't you want to play anymore? You want to go home to your mummy?'

'Maisie, please!' And she'd started to sob, the great crybaby. 'I want to go home!'

Scoot suddenly grabbed hold of her and dragged her into the trees. He threw her down, and as if he'd forgotten Maisie was there, he held Emma's wrists with one hand while he tore at her clothes with the other. He raped her, right there in front of Maisie, like an animal, dirty and wild.

She knew then that he could never let Em go. That *she* could never let Em go. How could she explain to her father what had happened? They'd blame her. Her father would never forgive her.

Scoot knelt over Emma, who was whimpering, snivelling. Maisie just wanted her gone. She turned away, got back in the car, curled up on the back seat. He knew what to do.

The longest nine minutes of her life. She heard him open the boot, dump something inside, slam the boot, slide behind the wheel.

'Lucky she's little. Boot's fucking small.' He caught Maisie's eye in the rear-view mirror, those strange pale eyes of his. She didn't ask him what he was going to do with the body.

He dropped her back at Joe's and Joe drove her home.

Leaving Emma near where she and Joe sometimes had sex – that was wicked, like he'd always have a hold over her, their little secret...

Lincoln stared at her. He could hardly believe he'd got it so wrong. 'Was Emma going to go to the police about what your father did to her?'

Maisie shook her head. 'Said she didn't remember any of it. And she was too shy.'

He took a deep breath. 'Did you pay Zak Scotson to murder her? Was that why you didn't stop him hurting her?'

She looked into his face: no tears, no remorse. 'When we were little,' she said, 'my father loved her more than he loved me. I couldn't let her take him away from me again.'

The instant he terminated the interview, Maisie's mother stood up and rushed out.

# CHAPTER 109

When Lincoln and Pam returned to the CID room after interviewing Maisie, neither of them spoke for several minutes.

'I never would have imagined...' Pam began, before giving up.

'I should've kept an open mind.'

'But all the evidence...'

'That's just it – there *wasn't* the evidence. Bella was right.' He sighed and went back to his desk. 'Now to see if I can write this up without losing my temper.' He could do with a drink but that would have to wait.

'News came in while you were otherwise engaged,' Woody said, waving a slip of paper. 'Nasty RTA near Andover a couple of hours ago. A van belonging to one Patrick Gerard Tyler tried to beat a heavy goods vehicle onto a roundabout and lost.' He chuckled. 'Reckon when it's between you and Norbert Dentressangle, you let Norbert go first even if the right of way is yours.'

'Casualties?'

'Tyler was declared dead at the scene. His passenger was a bit luckier: Eily Quinn was in the back. If she'd been up front next to him, she'd be dead too.'

So there was still a chance of getting a statement out of her.

News got out somehow that a fifteen-year-old girl was being held in connection with Emma Sherman's murder. Half an hour's drive from Barbury, Todd Tremlow, drunk and miserable, began to let rip after months and years of frustration. When he'd finished smashing his own house up, he got in his van and drove unsteadily but fast towards Marsh Pulham Hall.

Storming past the waiting media, and before the gates could close on him, he tailgated the van making the Finnegans' weekly grocery delivery. After executing a few handbrake turns on the lawn, he propelled his van at speed towards the front door, sending the Ocado driver running for his life.

Lindsey was already phoning the police when Tremlow barged into the house, swinging a baseball bat that gave him the reach and

352

heft his stocky build did not. By the time Donal Finnegan had come downstairs to face him, Tremlow had smashed up quite a bit of Marsh Pulham Hall.

When two patrol cars arrived to take charge of the situation, they found him in a sobbing heap at the foot of the stairs.

'No answer from his wife.' Woody put the phone down.

Lincoln frowned. 'That's worrying. If Tremlow's not at home, then Tania ought to be. Send somebody over there.'

Tremlow looked up as Lincoln entered the interview room. Crashing the van and swinging the baseball bat had resulted in a sprained wrist, a black eye and several cuts to his face. 'Is my solicitor here yet?'

'He's on his way.' Lincoln pulled a chair out. 'You've done a lot of damage, Mr Tremlow. You're lucky Mr Finnegan isn't pressing charges.'

'*He's* the lucky one. Lucky I didn't kill him for what he did to Emma.'

'You can't take the law into your own hands.'

Tremlow reared up in his seat. 'How else do you get justice these days? How else do people like him get what they deserve?'

'Smashing up their houses and frightening their families isn't the way to do it.'

'That Finnegan – everything I ever had, he ruined or stole. Derek was going into business with me before Finnegan came along. Doing up old houses – that was *my* idea. But when I found out what he'd done to my little girl, my Emma...' His bandaged wrist thudded on the table. 'I saw some of the photos my wife's been sending out. And to think she thought *I'd* taken them!' He shook his head, incredulous. 'Actually, I think my wife may be hurt. Quite seriously.'

Lincoln went out into the corridor, made sure someone was on their way to Whitpenny. Stood replaying Tremlow's words in his head: *my little girl, my Emma...*

'But you know what makes all of this worthwhile?' Tremlow demanded when he went back in. 'I'd have broken both wrists and knocked my teeth out just to see the look on Donal Finnegan's face when he found out what a piece of work his own daughter is!'

'It was weird,' Shauna declared on her return from the Tremlows' house. 'The front door was wide open and the house looked like a bomb had hit it. All you could hear was this thud, thud, thud from upstairs – Stephanie, banging her head against her bedroom wall. Her

353

mum was lying on the floor, not getting up, and the kid was having a meltdown.'

'Is Tania badly hurt?' Lincoln asked. Tremlow seemed to think he might have killed her.

'Battered and bruised,' said Shauna. 'Couple of broken ribs. Seems more upset about the house. Old Todd must've gone through it with a sledgehammer! She's taking Stephanie and moving into Crystal's until they can move back.'

'Crystal's not going to like that!' said Pam.

Shauna grinned. 'Apparently it was Crystal's idea.'

# CHAPTER 110

## TUESDAY 1ST OCTOBER

Next day, Pam went over to Folly Hill Crescent to check on the sisters.

'It was my own fault,' Tania said, wincing as she shut the front door and led Pam into her sister's kitchen. 'And at least it's out in the open now. No more secrets.'

'Tania, your husband beat you up. Don't tell yourself you deserved it!'

'He wasn't himself,' she said simply. 'If you want to see Crystal, she's down the garden. The medication's kicking in at last, so some of her wobbles have gone away. She's got a long way to go but it's a start, isn't it?'

Pam found Crystal in the summer house. The moment she stepped inside, she smelt damp fabric, pine resin, the peaty earth beneath the floorboards. No wonder Emma took fright in Arlo's caravan: childhood memories must have come surging back.

Crystal was sitting on one of the wicker chairs near the window, a thick cardigan slung round her shoulders. 'Haven't been in here for years. I'm trying to walk a bit farther every day. I can come in here and think about Em. Only it hurts, thinking about what happened with Donal.' She stood up, no sign of her usual tremor, and they sat together outside on the veranda steps.

'You never suspected anything?' Pam still found it hard to believe.

'Never. The girls were having fun, and Donal had been so kind when Derek was ill, always there if I needed anything. He made me feel safe when I had no one else.'

'You repaid that debt a long time ago. Sure it wasn't more than that?'

Crystal looked away to where Gordon Judd had lit a bonfire earlier. Wood smoke rose in a thin column. Autumn was in the air. 'Stephanie's accident, when she was little... When she fell off the swing, I panicked. She was lying there, not moving, and I didn't know what to do. Donal appeared out of nowhere, went straight over to her, called an ambulance, calmed Emma down.'

'Isn't that what anyone would've done?'

'It was more than that, though.' She took a big breath. 'Stephanie didn't actually *fall* off the swing. The girls had been squabbling all

355

afternoon, getting on my nerves. She'd been on the swing for ages and Emma wanted a go. When she tried to get on, Stephanie shoved her away.' Crystal glanced quickly at Pam, then away again. 'I'd had all I could take and… It wasn't Emma who pushed Stephanie off the swing – it was me. I smacked Stephie and she fell. She landed in the grass and the swing hit her as she was standing up again.'

'And Donal saw.'

A quick nod. 'They'd have taken Em away from me if they'd known. An unfit mother. I couldn't lose her.'

'And Donal's held that over you all these years?'

'Yes. And all these years, I've let Tania and Todd think it was Emma's fault. They never blamed her – she was too young to know what she was doing. But then the last time Em visited them, last year sometime, she said something silly about Stephanie. My sister turned on her, told her she should be ashamed of herself since it was her fault Stephie was like she was. She wouldn't go over to Tania's house after that. I should've told her, should've owned up, but I let her go on thinking it was her fault, and now it's too late.'

Crystal got to her feet, smoothed her skirt down and started slowly back up the garden. 'I've asked Gordon to get the summer house taken down. The sooner the better.'

# CHAPTER 111

Lincoln poured Trish a large glass of wine and waited till she'd sat down at her kitchen table again. 'So you're off to Essex after all.'

She nodded. 'Their first choice turned it down and I was the runner-up.' She made a face. 'Mind you, they've reduced the contract from three years to fifteen months. I think there might be a funding problem.'

'You're still going to take the job?'

'My position here's pretty untenable now. Management's convinced it was me who gave Ian Marston all Linus' papers.'

'Well, you did, didn't you?'

She smiled wickedly and sipped her wine. 'Two weeks today, I'll be heading for Essex.'

'And Kate?'

'She'll move in with Suki and Mike. I'll let the house out – unless you want to move back in?'

He shook his head. 'Thanks anyway.' His heart quickened. He was going to lose her after all. Why couldn't he tell her how much she meant to him?

'Mike said Breezy's back from his holidays. I know how much you've missed him!'

DC Dennis Breeze had indeed returned, sticking his lobster-red face round the door to see how things were going. 'Anything happen while I've been gone?' Luckily they knew he was joking. 'Hey, you'll never guess who I saw at the airport while I was waiting for my flight home. That chappie from the gym I spoke to – Gary, Gareth—'

'Gavin?'

'That's the one. Off somewhere hot by the looks of it.'

'Yes,' said Lincoln now, 'we've all missed Breezy.'

She glanced at her watch. 'Kate'll be back from Charlotte's any minute. Not that I'm trying to get rid of you...'

'No, no, that's fine. I'd better be getting back.'

'You're not still in that bloody Travelodge, are you? Promise me, if it's the last thing you do, you'll go back home!'

*

A couple of hours later, Lincoln pulled up outside the Old Vicarage, turned the engine off and sat looking across at his lunatic house for a good ten minutes before he got out and went up the path.

Broken police tape wavered across the front door. He tugged it away and stepped inside.

The house felt stuffy and smelt of dust – much as it had when he first ventured inside. He opened a window onto the dim garden and a blackbird launched itself screeching across the lawn and into the bushes. He couldn't see the stray cat anywhere. It had probably moved on to a place with richer pickings.

The police search had done less damage than he'd feared. Although his papers had been disturbed and his shelves and cupboards ransacked, none of his cardboard boxes had been broken open. Most of his worldly goods still sat unpacked in the bare afterthought the estate agent dubbed 'the breakfast room'.

'You can't do it all yourself,' Trish had said to him months ago when he'd been lamenting his lack of progress on the house. 'You always want to be self-sufficient but sometimes, you have to give in and ask for help.'

There was a lot he could get done by Christmas if he put his mind to it. *This* Christmas.

He switched some lights on, began to tidy up. Why should he let the likes of Donal Finnegan get the better of him?

This afternoon, an email had come round from DCS Youngman. "*DCI Bryn Marshall is retiring at the end of the year after 25 years' devoted service. Owing to ill health, he will not be returning to work. Colleagues wishing to make a contribution to his collection...*"

Lincoln opened the bedroom door. A dark shape in the middle of the bed took him by surprise. 'What the hell?'

Black body, white nose, four white paws. The cat opened one greengage-coloured eye and, satisfied it was only Lincoln, went back to sleep.

# ACKNOWLEDGEMENTS

I would like to thank Frome Writers' Collective for their support, and especially Alison Clink, who restored my faith in my writing.

I must also thank friends and family who've chivvied me to keep writing, even when things got tough.

# ABOUT SILVER CROW BOOKS

Frome Writers' Collective's new book brand, Silver Crow Books, is a not-for-profit brand, supporting good, local writers.

Silver Crow offers a halfway house between traditional publishing and individualised self-publishing. Our selected authors self-publish, but do so within an agreed framework of support and advice.

Book lovers can be assured that in choosing a Silver Crow title they will be buying a professionally produced book which has been quality screened by a team of trained readers.

We believe that Silver Crow provides a unique and innovative addition to the fast-changing and complex world of contemporary publishing.

Find out more about Silver Crow Books at
silvercrowbooks.co.uk

Lightning Source UK Ltd.
Milton Keynes UK
UKOW02f1359301016

286428UK00002BA/23/P